THE
Heiress
SWAP

THE Heiress SWAP

RUBY® AWARD-WINNING AUTHOR
MADDISON MICHAELS

Entangled Publishing, LLC
644 Shrewsbury Commons Ave., STE 181
Shrewsbury, PA 17361
Visit our website at www.entangledpublishing.com.

Amara is an imprint of Entangled Publishing, LLC.

Edited by Alethea Spiridon
Cover design by Bree Archer
Cover art by Teresa Colucci/Gettyimages,
VJ Dunraven/Period Images
Interior design by Toni Kerr

Print ISBN 978-1-64937-396-0
ebook ISBN 978-1-64937-420-2

Manufactured in the United States of America

First Edition August 2023

AMARA

ALSO BY MADDISON MICHAELS

For all of the beautiful dreamers out there, who, like me, believe in fairy tales and happy ever afters.

And to my wonderful husband and amazing daughter, who both insisted they be included in the dedication…lol!

At Entangled, we want our readers to be well-informed. If you would like to know if this book contains any elements that might be of concern for you, please check the back of the book for details.

CHAPTER ONE

"No. Absolutely not." Yvette Jenkins shook her head hard.

Her cousin, Aimee, regularly came up with some harebrained ideas, but this one took the cake. Never had Evie heard, let alone contemplated, such a ludicrous suggestion as the one her cousin had just proposed. "I am not swapping places and pretending to be you. Definitely not. End of story. No."

"But please, Evie, you must agree," Aimee begged, her big blue eyes pleading. "It's a most brilliant idea, for both of us. You'll get to have a holiday and visit all those museums and exhibitions you've always dreamed of, and I'll get to experience my dream of working for my father's company, and he'll have no idea I'm doing so. Just think of it, both of our hearts' wishes fulfilled in one fell swoop, if you'll only agree. It's truly an ingenious plan!"

"It's a ridiculous plan." Evie threw up her hands and marched over to the window overlooking the front of the grand residence on Fifth Avenue. She focused on staring down at the passing horses and carriages, refusing to look back at her cousin, who had the ability to talk anyone into anything, Evie most especially of all. "I will not agree to it.

Imagine if anyone found out. Imagine if your parents found out. They'd never forgive me."

In the six years since she'd arrived in America from London, after the Thornton-Joneses had taken her in following her maternal aunt's death when she was sixteen, Evie had been happy to take on the role of Aimee's companion, doing her best to impart English customs and etiquette to her extremely confident and outgoing American cousin, who was only one year Evie's junior. Thankfully, they'd become fast and firm friends, with Aimee the bolder of the two, and Evie the more sensible.

"No one is going to find out," Aimee replied, striding over to stand next to Evie and gently grabbing ahold of the sleeve of Evie's plain blue dress. "No one knows us in London."

"I'm English, Aimee, and grew up in London," Evie couldn't help but point out, turning to face her cousin with the sternest face she could muster.

The two of them were so alike in appearance and yet oh so different in temperament.

Both had porcelain complexions with heart-shaped faces, the traditional cornflower blue eyes that were a hallmark of a Thornton-Jones, and slim figures of modest stature, both standing the same five foot six inches in height. Aimee, though, had rich, sable-colored hair whereas Evie's was a pale, honey blonde. But the physical similarities were where their resemblance ended. Personality wise, they couldn't be any more different.

As was the case in point, where Aimee actually believed she could convince Evie to agree to such a plan. Though Evie had to admit in fairness to her cousin, Aimee always could get anyone to do practically anything, and not through meanness or manipulation, either. Her cousin was so joyful and enthusiastic about everything, believing anything could be accomplished if one believed it, that inevitably Aimee always achieved her desires. And Evie always went along with her cousin's plans, though none had ever included swapping places before, pretending to be the other.

"You might have grown up in London," Aimee replied, "but that was in an entirely different area of the city than where you would be staying while pretending to be me."

"You mean I grew up in a poor area."

Aimee had the grace to look somewhat abashed. "Well, yes, I do. But that's only what you've told me yourself on countless occasions. You also told me how different each of the so-called classes of people in England are and how they simply don't interact amongst one another."

"So, you do listen on occasion."

"Very funny." Aimee narrowed her eyes. "My mother has arranged for an old family friend, the Countess of Brexton, to host me at her house and be my chaperone for the six-week trip. She lives in Mayfair, which I believe is nowhere near where you grew up."

The west end of London was indeed well beyond the area Evie had lived. It was for the wealthy aristocracy, not for the penniless orphan Evie had been, along with her spinster aunt who had darned clothes for a living. "No, it isn't."

"See!" Aimee exclaimed. "You will be fine

staying with the countess in my place. She's never met me before and wouldn't have met you, so she'll have no idea that it's you taking my place instead of me."

"I am *not* switching places with you!"

Aimee grabbed both of Evie's hands and squeezed them. "This is the only chance I'll ever get to work for my father's company in your place. You know it's my absolute dream to prove to him I'll be a worthy successor to take over the family business."

"As capable as you are and as wonderfully modern as your father is when it comes to his support for women's rights, he's never going to believe a female can run his business empire." She gently squeezed Aimee's hands back and then let go of them. For a moment, her cousin appeared despondent, but then the usual glint of determination and enthusiasm was back in her gaze.

"That is only because he hasn't given me a chance to prove myself," Aimee replied with a smile. "Once I switch places with you and train as a secretary at the company's London headquarters, I'll learn so much of the inner workings of the company. And when my father discovers all I've learned, he'll change his mind and mentor me as I've always wanted him to."

"When your father discovers you've switched places with me, not that I'm agreeing to switch places, but for argument's sake if I did, and he found out, he would be beyond furious," Evie replied. "He'd probably send you to a convent, for one escapade too many." Though her uncle was a kind man, he was formidable when it came to business, and Evie doubted he'd be at all impressed that the six-week secretary traineeship he'd arranged for Evie upon her accompanying Aimee to London was in fact undertaken by his daughter instead of his niece. *Not impressed* would be a mild way to describe what Uncle Thomas's reaction would be.

"You know my father adores me." Aimee shrugged. "He wouldn't be mad for too long."

"You may have him wrapped around your pinky finger and can normally sweet-talk him out of his tempers with you, but I doubt you'd be able to do so as easily again after such a deception as the one you're suggesting. Not to mention your mother would be apoplectic you hadn't been introduced to the bachelors of London as she's arranged for you to be."

Her aunt Edith had spent months planning for the trip, only to have slipped from her carriage in the rain and broken her leg a few days ago, preventing her from traveling with Aimee to London as she'd intended. Which was why Evie was now in the predicament of having to say no to her determined cousin. Aunt Edith had been resolved Aimee should still go on her trip and had requested Evie to accompany Aimee to London on the steamer as her companion.

They'd then arranged for Evie to stay with a Mrs. Holbrook, the company's London secretary, who would not only host Evie at her residence but would take her each day to the company and train her to be a secretary, too. Her aunt and uncle thought they were helping Evie with such an arrangement, unaware that being a secretary was far from what Evie would choose to do, if she could.

But in Evie's position, she'd been unable to say no, especially not after all the kindness her uncle and aunt had shown her in the six years she'd been living with them. So, regardless of the fact she had no interest whatsoever in learning to be a secretary, she would do so as it would please her family.

That's if her cousin was going to let her, for as soon as Aimee had heard her parents had arranged such a thing for Evie, she'd come up with this grand plan of hers.

"I've argued literally day and night with my mother over her plans for me to go to London. I've begged not to go, to no avail, even though I have absolutely no intention of being a Dollar Princess and trading in my inheritance for marriage to an English gentleman with a title! Regardless of that seeming to be my mother's sole ambition at the moment."

"She just wants the best for you." As dogmatic as Aunt Edith was about the matter, she did want the best for her daughter. Evie was sure of it. "Even if what she thinks is best isn't the same as your idea on the subject."

"You know the very thought of marriage, let alone to a staid, stuffy Englishman, having to live in such a dreary, rain-drenched, smoggy place as London, is the most horrible, intolerable future I could ever imagine." Aimee's whole body shuddered. "I wouldn't survive in such an environment. The life would literally be sucked out of me."

Aimee was always a touch dramatic, but Evie had become accustomed to it over the years. Americans were, after all, a great deal more demonstrative in their emotions and reactions than the English. Her cousin most especially. "I think you would be fine, regardless of your thoughts to the contrary."

"Oh, really? I would be fine, would I? As fine as you would be living as a secretary for the rest of your life, when your passion is for history and fossils, not ledgers or notetaking?"

"I'm not in a position to have much of a choice about that. Though we may be cousins, Aimee, we come from different worlds and have different paths ahead of us."

"This is America, Evie, not England." Aimee's eyes were bright with conviction. "Your illegitimacy doesn't matter here like it does over there—providing you're not trying to seek entree into High Society. In America, you can be who you want. You can make yourself into what you want. You just have to have the courage to do so!"

"I do adore your enthusiasm." She smiled at her cousin; Aimee's unending positivity could always inspire the most unenthused of audiences. However, Evie had been brought up differently, with a great deal more limitations. "I have to be practical about matters. I'm not going to get a happily ever after as you can. I've been lucky to be your companion these past six years, but once you marry, I shall have to work and not rely on your parents' largesse."

"Being forced to marry a titled gentleman so

my mother can be accepted into New York's elite Society is *not* a happily ever after for me," Aimee replied. "I couldn't think of anything worse, to be honest."

"She's already said she won't force you to marry," Evie calmly reminded her. "As long as you play nice and are agreeable to the Countess of Brexton introducing you to appropriate gentlemen on your trip. Providing you can do that, your mother has said she will accept your decision if you do not find a suitable husband."

"I don't like to play nice, which is why we must swap places!" Aimee exclaimed. "You are the polite and calm one of the two of us. You will be perfectly placed to be charming yet turn down any offers of marriage, whereas I would make a mess of it all, and you know it. I don't have the patience or kindness that comes naturally to you. I'm bold and brash, and somewhat spoiled on occasion."

Aimee was an adored, only child. Evie would never call her cousin spoiled, but she'd grown up in luxury, never wanting for anything as the sole heiress of a shipping and railroad fortune. Confident in her position in life, Aimee often said whatever it was she was thinking; again, another trait Evie had observed was much more prevalent in Americans than the English, who often were rather tightlipped with their thoughts and opinions.

Which was certainly the case with Evie, having been raised by her English maternal aunt in a modest flat in London, after her parents had died of cholera when she was only a baby. She and her aunt had struggled at times for food and to pay the rent, and though Evie had grown up knowing she was the illegitimate daughter of a man named Peter Thornton-Jones, she'd been unaware her father was the black sheep of the Thornton-Jones family and that his brother, Thomas, had taken the family fortunes from being modestly wealthy to being one of *the* wealthiest families in America, if not the world.

In fact, Evie hadn't even known her father had any family until after her aunt's death when Uncle Thomas showed up from America offering her a home with him and his family. An offer she'd gratefully accepted given at sixteen years old she didn't have a penny to her name or any other family left alive.

So the family had taken Evie in despite the circumstances of her birth. When her aunt requested Evie act as a companion to Aimee and teach her English customs and manners, Evie had happily taken on the role, so grateful to them for having given her not only their affection, but a roof over her head as well. And what a roof it was. The hundred-room house was considered one of the grandest, most audacious residences in Manhattan, with its marble floors and walls, the gold wallpaper in the ballroom, and the crystal chandeliers imported from France that hung in every room, to name only some of the features of the grand mansion.

Evie still couldn't quite reconcile herself to the grandeur and excess of it all. She didn't feel as if she belonged, even though her aunt and uncle had done their best to make her feel like part of the family, even as the circumstances of her birth ensured she could never be fully accepted into Society and was always on the periphery of it. A fact she preferred given she was far too modest to ever feel comfortable being part of such a set of flamboyant Americans, who were confident and brash in their manners, especially compared to what Evie was used to having grown up in England.

It was books about paleontology that made Evie happy and kept her entertained, not attending balls and soirées as she'd had to do on a few occasions as Aimee's companion. Nor would working as a secretary hold any great joy, but she couldn't stay as Aimee's companion forever, given her aunt's plans for her cousin to marry a titled Englishman.

"I don't know how you'd think we could even get away with swapping places," Evie said. "I'm English and you're American. Our accents would have us caught out instantly."

"Oh, I don't know about that," Aimee said, imitating a good English accent. "I rather think I've been spending enough time with you, my dear cousin, to pick up a few things about how you speak. Which is oh so proper, I might add." Aimee finished her speech with an I-told-you-so grin.

"How long have you been concocting this idea?" Evie was astounded at how English her American cousin sounded. "And practicing speaking in an English accent?"

"I pay attention to everything," Aimee continued in an English accent. "You know that."

It was true; Aimee was always watching and observing, while simultaneously giving the impression to most she was simply a frivolous heiress, who cared naught about anything apart from her dresses and enjoyment. It was an interesting ruse as Aimee learned a lot of things by others thinking she was not smart enough to comprehend nuances.

"That might be true," Evie allowed. "But I can't put on an American accent."

"Have you ever tried?"

"Well, no. I've never anticipated having to pretend to be American before."

Aimee clapped her hands together and jumped up and down on the spot. "So that means you're considering my idea?"

"No!" Evie exclaimed, even though part of her was silly enough to be doing so. Which she had to stop doing, as such an idea was lunacy. Absolute lunacy, wasn't it?

"Haven't you always talked about going back to London and visiting the Natural History Museum? About going to the various fossil displays they regularly exhibited there? Of walking around the city again and marveling at all the history right there in London, as you'd never been able to afford to do previously? Of going to visit all of the fellow collectors you correspond with?"

"I can still do that when I'm there training as a secretary." Evie could hear the doubt in her own voice. "I've saved up some pin money."

"You'll be working at my father's London headquarters from dawn till dusk, with only Sundays off, which is the only day every museum and store is closed! You'll never get a chance to visit the museums and galleries… But if you take my place, you will. Why, your days would be filled doing whatever you wanted, going to as many exhibitions and museums as possible. Visiting all your fellow collectors! All you'd have to do in exchange is pretend to be me and go to the various balls and soirées in the evenings that the countess has organized for you to attend. You'll drink champagne and dance some dances with some dashing gentleman while there, without encouraging any of them to propose. And if they did, you'd decline."

"You make it sound ridiculously simple."

"That's because it will be!" Aimee began pacing backward and forward on the rug, as she was prone to do when plotting some scheme or another. "We're both the same size in clothing and even look the same, apart from our hair. You will put on an American accent, which I will teach you to do on the steamship across, and you can teach me how to be English, or at least how to pretend to be. Then for the six weeks we will take each other's place and both of us will enjoy this trip!"

"I hate to put a dampener on your plans, my dear cousin, but you've never worked a day in your life. How do you intend to cope working six days of the week, getting up at the crack of dawn and dressing yourself, not to mention working?" As much as Aimee was independent, she'd still led a sheltered and pampered life.

Aimee stopped pacing and swung her gaze over to Evie's. "I'm not afraid of working. You know that. Plus, you're also aware of how stubborn I am, correct?"

"Somewhat of an understatement," Evie murmured with a nod. Aimee was more stubborn than a bull when she had her mind fixed on something. She was tenacious.

"I have been begging my father to learn his business for years and years now."

"Begging or pestering?" Evie tapped her finger on her chin. "It's hard to distinguish between the two when it comes to you."

"Very funny." Aimee folded her hands over her chest. "But you know how much I want to be involved in my father's company."

"I do know that." Aimee had talked of nothing else since they'd first met. "Though you haven't managed to change his mind." Uncle Thomas was as stubborn as his daughter.

"Not yet," Aimee agreed. "But *yet* is the key in that statement. For I will change his mind. I just need to prove to him that not only can I understand his businesses but that I will be invaluable in helping him run them."

"And you really think training to be a secretary at his London headquarters for six weeks will do that?" It was not a task Evie was looking forward to at all, but as she'd told Aimee, she felt obliged to do so after all her aunt and uncle had done for her.

"It will be a good start, especially given I haven't been allowed to even get near his company, apart from meeting him at his offices for him to take me to lunch on occasion," Aimee replied, her eyes ablaze with excitement. "I am determined to involve myself in all aspects of his companies. I just need the opportunity, instead of wasting my time hunting for a husband when I have no intention of ever marrying. That's my mother's dream, not mine."

Her cousin was born to conquer the world. Watch out to all those who dared to step in her way, the English aristocracy included. "A dream your mother's been planning for years, and one she's determined about."

"Yes, well, contrary to her scheming, I have no intention of being an American Dollar Princess and invading England all in the hopes of trading in my dowry for a titled husband!" She shook her head. "I couldn't imagine anything worse, in fact."

"And yet you want me to take your place and do so? It sounds lovely."

"It's only the evenings that will be a pain for you," Aimee implored. "Like I said, your days will be your own to do with as you like. Then, in the evenings, you will be demure and proper as you normally are, making a much better impression then I ever could, and if some of the gentlemen do propose as I expect they will—my dowry is ridiculously large after all—you can politely decline."

"You make me sound so boring." Though it was true. Compared to her cousin, who men were drawn to, Evie was bland in comparison. Quiet and soft-spoken most of the time, Evie preferred to sit back and watch, rather than participate. "I doubt I would receive any proposals."

She never had thus far, not that she expected to or even wanted to. In the circles they mingled in, everyone knew of Evie's birth status, and though they tolerated her presence in their midst because she was Aimee's cousin and companion, that was as far as it went. Evie would never be considered acceptable as a Society wife, given her parents had not been married when she was born.

"Of course you will receive proposals," Aimee said, staring at Evie as if she was suggesting the sky was green. "With your looks and my dowry, which Mother will have made known to the countess for her to spread word about, many impoverished gentlemen—as they all mostly seem to be over there—will be interested in marrying an heiress. And given how kind and polite you are, I know you will turn them all down with grace and humility, ensuring my reputation is maintained. Hence, when we return, my parents will have already received a report from the countess that I conducted myself perfectly but was unfortunately unable to find a husband. It couldn't be simpler."

"It doesn't sound simple at all," Evie replied. "What if your parents find out?"

"They won't!" Aimee enthused, squeezing Evie's hands tightly. "They'll be here in New York the entire time, none the wiser."

"And what if someone recognizes me in London?"

"My dear cousin," Aimee began, "there's no way anyone would recognize you, let alone anyone discovering our masquerade."

"Masquerade or deception?" Evie grumbled. "There's a fine line between the two."

"It's not really a deception given we'll both be vastly more happy swapping places for the trip." Aimee released Evie's hands and took in a deep breath. "Besides, it's only for six weeks, Evie. What could go wrong in such a short period of time?"

Evie had a feeling a great deal could go wrong, but surprisingly, she felt like being bold. Felt that for once in her life, perhaps she should jump off a cliff and trust she would fly, even though she didn't have wings.

"You'll get to live your dreams and visit all of the museums and galleries, enjoying yourself for once, rather than having to work," Aimee continued. "And I will get to be a step closer to my dream, learning all I can of my father's business. But the both of us can only do that *if* you agree to swap places."

Could she really agree to such a thing? Could she pretend to be Aimee for six weeks?

A feeling of excitement and fear began to jostle inside Evie, because suddenly she wanted to experience something different for a change. To *be* something different, instead of good old dependable, reliable, boring Yvette Jenkins. She wanted an adventure.

"I know I'm going to regret this…" Evie began, deciding to throw caution to the wind and live boldly for once. "But very well, Aimee, I'll switch places with you."

"You will?" Aimee squealed in delight.

"I will." Evie nodded. "God help us both."

CHAPTER TWO

"I'm in love."

Alexander Trenton, the sixth Duke of Hargrave, barely managed to stop himself from rolling his eyes at his cousin's declaration. "You always think you're in love, Sam, yet in the end it's lust and nothing more." Leaning back against the armchair, Alex took another sip of his brandy and returned his gaze back to the paper in his lap.

"It's different this time," Samuel Ellingsworth, the Earl of Brexton, declared, taking a seat in the armchair across from Alex. "This lady is perfect. She's elegant, beautiful, refined, and rich, which doesn't hurt. She'll make me the perfect countess."

Alex sighed. He'd hoped to get some peace and quiet having a pre-dinner drink at his club before he and Sam were expected at Sam's mother, the Countess of Brexton's, town house for dinner. Clearly, that wasn't to be, given his cousin thought himself in love once again.

For once, Alex was glad his ex-fiancée had smashed his own heart into pieces over a decade ago. With a smashed heart, one couldn't succumb to such nonsense as thinking one was in love. Love was an illusion; Alex had learned that the hard way. If only he could convince Sam of that, too, he wouldn't have to put up with hearing his cousin constantly gush over the ladies. "Who is this paragon of a woman you think you're in love with now?"

"She's an angel," Sam enthused, his green eyes shining with unbridled enthusiasm. "Simply perfect."

As jaded as Alex was when it came to love, he never could quite berate Sam for his enthusiasm of the subject; doing so would be like kicking a puppy, which Alex could never do. So he put up with his cousin's frequent, though thankfully short-lived, infatuations. "Well, then? Who is it?"

"Miss Aimee Thornton-Jones," he declared with a sigh. "She's magnificent, Alex. Not only is she beautiful, but she's so refined for an American. She's demure and kind and so perfect. She'll make me a most excellent wife."

"The American girl your mother's playing host to for six weeks and holding a dinner party tonight for?"

"That's her."

"You think you're in love with the latest American Dollar Princess to invade London in search of a titled husband to trade her fortune for? *That* lady?"

"You're so cynical, cousin," Sam lamented, taking a glass of brandy from the tray the footman who'd just materialized to his right was holding. "You really need to let go of your own failed engagement and choose a wife already. Then you might be content for the rest of us to fall in love occasionally."

"Occasionally?" Alex laughed. "You fall in love

every other week, Sam. There's nothing occasional about it."

Sam grinned and nodded, some of his blond hair flopping lightly over his forehead with the movement. "That's true, I suppose. But I do so love falling in love. It's such a wonderful feeling."

"It's only wonderful until you do fall in love, instead of just thinking you are. Then your heart is crushed and burned into ashes," Alex grumbled, returning his gaze to the paper. "Besides, didn't you only meet the girl this afternoon? A bit soon, even for you, to be in love with her already."

"When Cupid's arrow hits, one is powerless to do anything else but accept it," Sam replied, his voice earnest. "In all truth, perhaps I am exaggerating my feelings."

Alex tsked with a shake of his head. "You're a hopeless romantic, Sam. Honestly, it's damned embarrassing."

"Women adore it." He grinned at Alex, unperturbed because not only were they cousins but also best friends, having attended Eton together when they were seven. "If only you would reconnect with that heart of yours, which I know you like to pretend is made of rock, you too would re-experience the wonder of being in love."

"No, thank you," Alex replied. "I experienced enough of that nonsense with Julia to last me three lifetimes, and I have no intention of ever succumbing to such a pathetic emotion that one calls love ever again."

"Yes, well, I suppose you're not nicknamed the Duke of Graves instead of Hargrave for nothing."

Sam shrugged. "In any event, when you meet Miss Thornton-Jones tonight, even you with your heart of stone will appreciate her beauty, her calm disposition, and the integrity shining in her stunning blue eyes. Truly, she's just lovely."

"An American Dollar Princess with integrity shining in her eyes? I doubt it," Alex scoffed. "She's here to find herself a titled husband, nothing more and nothing less. Trust me on that, and don't get caught up in the hunt, regardless of how lovely you think she is."

"You haven't even met her."

"I don't need to meet her to know that." True, his opinion of American women was particularly jaded given his ex-fiancée had been an American, and an unfaithful one at that, having been caught with another man on the eve of their wedding. But, still, in all the years since, after dozens of American heiresses and their marriage-minded mothers had traversed the Atlantic in search of a titled husband, desperately trying to entice him into the institution, Alex could say he had a good deal of experience recognizing them. "Why else would she be here?"

"She says she's here for a holiday and is keen to visit all of the museums and exhibitions that she can as apparently paleontology is her passion," Sam replied. "Made me think of you, given your interest in the subject, too. Perhaps you could give me some ideas of where to escort her, seeing as you're into all of that history nonsense as well."

"There is nothing nonsensical about history or paleontology." The subjects were close to his heart and the only things that really did bring him joy, given most of his days were taken up with the unenviable task of managing his estates and dealing with all the correspondence and accounts that accompanied such an endeavor. "And she's probably pretending to be interested in the subject. Isn't it all the rage for ladies to be taken with an academic pursuit?"

"Oh God." Sam groaned. "You're not going to quiz her tonight, are you?"

"I have no intention of quizzing her. I shall simply ask her some questions on the topic and see what she says." Alex grinned. "Twenty pounds says she can't answer a single one properly."

Sam grinned back at him. "I'll take that bet, my friend, for I believe the lady is genuine in her interest, and I expect she'll give you a run for your money, no matter the questions you ask."

They shook on it, Alex supremely confident the girl wouldn't have a clue about paleontology or any history for that matter.

· · ·

Two hours later, Alex was down twenty pounds.

Not only had Aimee Thornton-Jones answered each and every one of his questions, but she'd also gone on to extrapolate several theories relating to the ancient Egyptians that Alex himself had been discussing with several historians only earlier in the month. The woman not only knew her history but was probably as well studied as Alex was on the subject of fossils, and given it was a passion Alex had been studying since he'd been a boy and was now thirty-two, such knowledge he reluctantly found impressive.

Damn it. He hadn't expected to be impressed by the woman. Nor had he expected to find her so attractive. Not even close.

It was confounding and especially disconcerting.

The woman was as Sam had described, though she wasn't just beautiful, she was far more than that. There was something entirely alluring about her that he couldn't quite put his finger on. Whether it was her modesty and apparent lack of artifice, he wasn't certain, but he found himself drawn to her as he hadn't been drawn to another woman, not since Julia.

Clearly, the woman was a good actress given she'd been able to knock past his walls of resistance so effortlessly. Sam would be completely vulnerable to such a masterful creature, and it was no wonder he was entranced by her. Sam wouldn't stand a chance, and the woman would have him trapped in holy matrimony before he could even blink.

It was something Alex couldn't allow.

He wouldn't let his cousin suffer the agony of having his heart ripped from his chest and stomped into ash on the ground beneath all because some woman was using him to get a title. No, Sam was too kindhearted and far too good a man to have that occur; he'd never recover from such an event. It was Alex's duty as his eldest cousin and best friend to stop that from happening. He had to unmask the true woman underneath this lady's facade and do so before Sam did fall in love with her.

The only way to do that was to prove to Sam that Miss Thornton-Jones really was only after a title and nothing more. And given Alex had the highest title going around, it was obvious what he'd have to do to unmask the real purpose of the lady's visit—he was going to have to seduce her himself and prove that it was the title she wanted, not the man beneath.

CHAPTER THREE

The entire evening had been a great deal more taxing for Evie than she'd expected.

Nothing like the wonderful experience Aimee had assured her of. *It would be easy*, she'd said. *Nothing to worry about.* Well, it had been anything but easy, not even close.

At least it hadn't been after the arrival of the Duke of Hargrave.

When Evie had glanced over and first caught sight of the man standing in the doorway surveying everyone with an air of detachment, Evie's breath had hitched in her throat. He was tall, muscular, and resplendently dressed in his perfectly tailored black tuxedo. Even the dark scowl etched on his face and his dark blue eyes filled with suspicion whenever he glanced Evie's way couldn't detract from the man's undeniable attractiveness.

She'd never been so aware of a man before. Such a feeling was highly disconcerting, especially given the pressure she was already under pretending to be Aimee. Not only had she spent the whole dinner party immersed in the charade, doing her best to be charming and congenial while speaking with an American accent, too, but she'd also felt the duke's steady gaze upon her all night.

The man hadn't even made any effort to hide his perusal. And then when he'd sought out an introduction from his aunt, the countess, and he then began to interrogate her about history and paleontology, Evie had known the man was trying to test her.

Test her over what she wasn't certain, but there was a suspicion in his tone and his gaze that he wasn't bothering to conceal. Almost as if he was dubious of her motives, a fact that did not bode well for her charade.

Evie really didn't know what she'd done to warrant such close scrutiny from the handsome yet extremely taciturn duke. After she'd met the countess's son, the Earl of Braxton, earlier in the day, a meeting that had gone smashingly well as the man had been nothing but lovely, Evie had been feeling rather confident she might be able to pull off this swapping places plan with her cousin.

But since meeting the duke, she'd felt like she was being inspected by the man and found completely wanting. It wasn't a good feeling to be having. She plastered a smile on her face at something the Earl of Brexton was saying, something about hunting in the country, though she wasn't paying attention given the duke had started to stroll toward them.

"You're not boring the lady with talk of fox hunts, are you, Sam?" the duke's deep timber voice rumbled as he blithely inserted himself into their conversation.

"Of course not!" the earl declared. "I'm not, am I, Miss Thornton-Jones?"

Evie smiled graciously over at him. She liked the earl, far more than she liked his cousin who seemed to be doing everything he could to make her uncomfortable. "Not at all, my lord. Though I'm not much of a fan of fox hunts, I understand they're quite an old tradition in England, and I do love learning about history, as I'm sure you've both gathered by now. Particularly you, duke, after your interrogation of me a short while ago."

The earl spluttered on the sip of drink he'd taken while the duke merely inclined his head, staring at her far more pointedly than was proper.

"Well, you certainly do seem to have my measure, Miss Thornton-Jones," the duke said, his voice sounding unperturbed at her comment.

"If that measure is that you're a man driven by logic and suspicion, without emotion, then yes, perhaps I do have your measure." She had no idea where her boldness was coming from. Usually, when it came to men, she was as demure as could be, but ever since this man had started quizzing her earlier, she'd felt her hackles rise at his inquisition. The man hadn't believed she'd known anything about history, and that was a dangerous assumption to make when it came to Evie and her history.

It had been the only entertainment she'd had growing up, after a pile of history and paleontology books had been thrown into a street bin, and Evie had rescued them, desperate to read anything, but unable to afford to buy even a newspaper. It had been the best scavenge she'd ever done, as it had born in her a passion for learning all she could.

"My goodness, dear lady, you are fearless to say such a thing to my cousin," the earl exclaimed, appearing utterly surprised that anyone would dare to say such a thing to the duke. "Most women are far too intimidated by him to do so."

"Can you blame her? She is *American*, after all." The duke said the word as if it was dirty.

How dare he! Though she might have been brought up in England, she was still half American, even if she didn't feel American at all. "Why, thank you both for the compliments."

The duke's eyes narrowed upon her. "Was it a compliment? Forgive me, I hadn't meant it to be."

"Hargrave, stop being rude," the earl reprimanded before turning his attention back to Evie. "You'll have to forgive the duke. He doesn't interact with women much. Obviously."

"There's no need to apologize on my behalf, Sam," the duke growled.

"There's honestly nothing to forgive." Evie ignored the duke and focused her eyes back upon the earl. "His inexperience with the ladies is clear given his manner of conversation, or rather lack thereof."

The earl smothered a laugh with a hasty cough, while the duke's posture straightened, like he was readying to do battle.

"Oh, my dear Miss Thornton-Jones," the duke all but purred, his voice drawing Evie's attention back to him, like an unwanted compulsion. "I can assure you my experience with ladies is vast. In fact, my experience with *American* ladies in particular is what one could call unrivaled. I was previously engaged to an American lady, and the experience has given me an unprecedented advantage when it comes to knowing what such a lady is after."

"You can't paint all *American* ladies with the same brush, Your Grace, especially not after your experience with just one lady." She narrowed her gaze at him. "Doing so would be the same as my suggesting that *all* dukes are arrogant, pompous, *Englishmen* after having met only you."

The duke pressed his lips together, his eyes never leaving her own, while the earl smothered another laugh.

"My own experience and observations of your fellow countrywomen, who have been arriving by the droves and marrying impoverished gentlemen, tend to lend credence to my assumptions."

"And based on that, you think you know what I am after?" Evie asked, watching as his blue eyes darkened as his gaze travelled to her lips. "I highly doubt that."

"Oh, I think I have your measure," he murmured, leaning in far closer to her than what would be considered appropriate. "I'm fairly certain of it, in fact."

Evie tried to ignore the shiver of awareness that ran down her spine from being so close to him. She took a deliberate step backward, and channeling what Aimee would do in such a situation, Evie took in a deep breath and relaxed her lips, twisting them into the most glorious smile she could muster. "Perhaps I shall surprise you, Your Grace, for I am no Dollar Princess, as I believe you are trying to suggest."

"Women rarely surprise me, Miss Thornton-Jones, or at least they haven't in over a decade."

They stood there staring at each other, both

defiant in a game Evie had no idea how to play. She knew the man was challenging her on a level she'd never been challenged before. It was exhilarating and terrifying all at once. "Clearly, you haven't been mingling with interesting ladies, Your Grace."

His lips twitched up at the corners. "Perhaps not. I must say I've never met ones who like history and fossils as you do. Did you also know it was an interest of mine?"

Evie raised her chin. "I've only just met you. How would I know or even care if it was an interest of yours?"

"Perhaps because you wished to engage my interest?"

"Such a suggestion is entirely arrogant, Your Grace. But as I have mentioned, that does seem to be a characteristic of yours."

The earl began to laugh. "She's got you there, Alex."

The duke narrowed his eyes, his frown returning. "You seem to have an entirely good grasp on English titles, Miss Thornton-Jones. Not once have you faulted in using them as many of your fellow travelers from across the pond do."

Immediately, Evie felt sick to her stomach, but she kept the smile plastered to her face. If anyone was going to unmask her, she had a feeling it would be this man, with his altogether suspicious nature and dislike for American women.

"I have a cousin who is half English, and she's been my companion for the last six years, teaching me all manner of English customs." Evie smiled serenely up at him, hoping such an explanation would appease him. "So I'm rather well versed in you *English*, you see."

"You're certainly well versed with English titles," the duke replied.

The dinner bell echoed loudly in the room, and Evie glanced over to the Countess of Brexton, her new chaperone for the next six weeks. The lady was standing beside her butler, glancing at the assembled guests for the small dinner she was hosting in Evie's, or rather Aimee's, honor.

"Dinner is to be served," the countess's regal voice announced to the assembled twenty or so guests. "As Miss Thornton-Jones is the guest of honor this evening, I should like to ask my nephew, the Duke of Hargrave, to do me the honor of escorting her into the dining room." It was not a request; it was a demand. Given the duke was the highest-ranking nobleman in the room, he had the honor of leading the precession into the room for dinner, and unfortunately as the countess considered Evie the guest of honor, he would not only escort her in but sit next to her, too.

Oh, good lord. Aimee was going to owe her favor after favor for getting her immersed in this mess, a fact Evie was going to remind her of when they met for tea tomorrow at the coffee shop on Bond Street.

"Miss Thornton-Jones?"

It was the duke's voice penetrating through her thoughts as he held out a hand for her to take. She nodded and placed her gloved hand on top of his forearm that he was holding aloft. As soon as her hand touched the cloth of his jacket, embers of electricity shot down her fingers to her toes. Her breath hitched and her eyes latched onto his own as shock filled her. There was an answering awareness in his gaze and a tightening of his jaw at the contact.

Every single inch of her body felt suddenly alive and so aware of the man, with an intimate familiarity that made no sense. In a slight daze, she let him lead her into the grand salon, which had a dining table set in the middle. She struggled to pay attention to her surroundings, only barely noticing the white roses and crystal vases adorning the length of the table, as the duke led her toward the end of the table where the seats were.

"The countess shouldn't have changed the order of precedence of seating for me," Evie murmured to the duke as he escorted her to her seat next to his. Given Evie's nonexistent title, even pretending to be Aimee, she should have been last in the room, and certainly not seated next to the duke.

"You know a lot about order of precedence, Miss Thornton-Jones, for an American." His eyes were staring at her, suspicion flashing in their depths. "Been studying Debrett's, have you?"

Debrett's was the English bible of the who's who of the aristocracy. And she had been studying it, because contrary to Aimee's assumption that just because Evie was half English and grew up in London she should automatically know all about titles, she certainly didn't. Growing up in Bethnal Green wasn't particularly conducive to learning about titles and the nobility.

"Perhaps I have been. What of it?" Pushing

aside the silk skirts of her gown, Evie sat down on the seat the duke was holding out for her, ridiculously aware of every move he made as he sat beside her. She glanced around, anywhere but at the man next to her, and noticed the countess's son, the earl, was taking a seat at the head of the other end of the table as was the custom, and the rest of the guests were following suit and sitting down in their allocated positions.

"Nothing." He shrugged. "Apart from the fact that my assumption of you is correct."

"And what assumption is that?"

"That you're a title-hunting jezebel, only here to catch yourself a husband."

She blinked at his candor. "You don't think much of women, do you?"

"On the contrary, I hold ladies in high esteem. Dollar Princesses from America who study Debrett's in their hunt for a husband? Well, that's another story entirely."

The man was arrogant. She disliked him intensely. "Did it ever cross your mind that perhaps I didn't want to make a fool of myself in front of such esteemed company like yourself?" She smiled pointedly at him before turning her attention to the table, where her smile promptly turned into a frown as a wave of sickness engulfed her as she looked down at the cutlery.

The amount of silverware on the table was nearly enough to send her into a panic, and she cringed, noting some of it wasn't where it was meant to be. She might have grown up in England, but she'd only ever used one fork and one knife for her meals, not the myriad of options before her, like the aristocracy used. And an American dinner table, which she'd started to get used to, had an entirely different way of setting the cutlery, too.

Oh God, help her. She was about to make a fool of herself in front of everyone.

Her fingers began to tap nervously on the table as she focused on counting the prongs on the forks. The three-prong one was for salads, wasn't it? Or was that the dessert fork? With a sinking feeling, she knew she was about to make a mess of it all. Surely then the ruse would be up, wouldn't it? Although perhaps she could claim ignorance of their English customs?

"Is everything all right?" the duke asked, his gaze dancing down to her fingers before traveling back up to her face.

Damn, the man and his eagle eyes. She leaned slightly closer to him and whispered, "If you must know, the cutlery is not where it's supposed to be."

He appeared completely baffled for a minute, but then a grin lit up his face, transforming the man from merely handsome into devastatingly attractive. "Isn't it?"

Evie shook her head, having to focus her attention back onto her dilemma instead of the man's good looks. "No, it's not," she whispered back. "I thought the fork at the top was for salads, but being at the top, doesn't that mean it's for desserts?"

"Clearly, Debrett's needs a chapter on cutlery. Why don't you follow my lead?" He winked at her, and suddenly the tense atmosphere from earlier that had been lingering between them was broken,

CHAPTER FOUR

Alex had to admit he'd never had a more enjoyable dinner than the one he was having right now in Miss Thornton-Jones's company. She'd been so earnest in telling him of her cutlery dilemma that he'd been hard pressed to remember she was a Dollar Princess out to trap his cousin into matrimony. In fact, the more they talked, the harder it got to keep remembering that.

But remember it he must, for he wouldn't let Sam suffer the devastating heartache he had, a pain that had nearly broken him. He could still recall the physical ache he'd felt in his solar plexus when he'd walked into the greenhouse on the night before his wedding and had caught Julia in the arms of another man, her skirts pulled up to her waist, and the other man's pants pulled down to his feet.

Such was the shock that it had felt like he'd been punched. The pain of it nearly rivaled the pain of when his mother had abandoned him when he'd been a boy of six, and she'd run off with an American.

He should have heeded the first lesson of his mother's betrayal: that a woman couldn't be trusted. But he hadn't. Instead, he'd been a naive fool thinking that the bold and confident young American woman was as in love with him as much as he'd thought he'd been with her. Instead, she'd only ever been in love with his title, nothing more and nothing less. Since that night, he'd never bothered to take an interest in an unmarried female again.

Until tonight. Not that he was taking an interest in Miss Thornton-Jones for himself, but rather taking an interest in her to stop Sam from being hurt. That was the extent of his scrutiny. Though he had to admit this woman seemed about as different from his ex-fiancée as water was to wine. There was something so refreshingly genuine about Aimee Thornton-Jones that he found himself fascinated with, instead of the usual wariness he felt with other ladies. Although that could be because he found her conversations on paleontology and ancient civilizations riveting. Not many men, let alone women, knew of the topics enough to speak of them, let alone have an in-depth conversation.

"I'm sorry," she said with a small smile. "I tend to run away talking about my favorite subjects, and I imagine I'm boring you discussing some old fossils discovered in some caves in Italy."

"Not all," he replied, meaning it. "I first became entranced with natural history when I discovered fossils in the beach caves on my estate when I was a boy."

Her eyes went wide. "You have fossils buried in caves on your estate? Oh my goodness, you must tell me all about them."

Alex chuckled, her excitement palpable and contagious, especially given he hadn't felt excited about anything in quite some time. "There's an array of them. Some small, some large, and one is on display at the national museum."

Her jaw dropped open. "Are you serious?"

He grinned. "Very. You'll see my contribution in the paleontology section. It's only a small bird-like creature, but fascinating nonetheless, or at least I think so. The larger finds I've made are on display in my residences."

"Was it thrilling to discover a fossil?" she asked, excitement shining in her crystal-blue eyes. "It's always been a dream of mine to find one buried in the earth, but I've never had an opportunity."

There was something so genuine in her enthusiasm that Alex felt himself swept up in the feeling, too. "Well, if you're ever in Devon, I shall be happy to escort you down to my caves and you can excavate away to your heart's content. There are a great many fossils waiting to be unearthed."

"That would be amazing." Her whole face lit up with a smile, the likes of which Alex had never seen.

The woman went from beautiful to goddess-like in an instant, and his whole body tightened in response. He was suddenly glad for the table he was sitting down at.

For a minute, Alex couldn't look anywhere else other than her. Her creamy porcelain skin, the gentle flush of pink on her cheeks from her excitement, her rose-red lips smiling over at him...all enticing him to want to lean over and kiss her.

Good god, what was wrong with him? Wanting to kiss the lady at a dinner table, in front of a room full of his peers? He had to be losing his mind to have such a thought. But then a darkly suspicious theory crept into his mind, that perhaps Sam wasn't the woman's true target. After all, a duke would be far more prestigious to hook, rather than an earl. And what better way to try to hook Alex than by pretending to be interested in one of his favorite subjects?

The lady's attention was diverted to her left by the countess who was asking her something, and Alex got to observe her for a moment without interruption. She appeared completely genuine and interested in whatever his aunt was talking to her about, just as she'd appeared to be when discussing fossils with him. She was good, he'd give her that.

Now more than ever he was determined to prove she was the title-hungry Dollar Princess he'd first suspected. More determined than he'd been about anything in a long time.

"Well, what do you think, Hargrave?" the countess's pointed voice asked as her sharp brown eyes glared across at him.

Alex cleared his throat, unused to being caught off guard. "About what, Aunt Agatha?"

"Good gracious, Alex, pay attention, dear boy." His aunt made no attempt to hide the roll of her eyes. "Honestly, you men are all alike and cannot pay the slightest bit of attention to others when sitting next to a pretty girl, can you?"

"Clearly not," he reluctantly agreed, uncomfortable with the truth in her statement, but acknowledging it all the same. His aunt was insightful and as sharp as a tack. Much like her late brother, Alex's father.

Most in Society were wary of incurring her wrath, which Alex managed to avoid most of the time, unlike Sam, who bore the brunt of his mother's annoyance, frequently.

"What I wanted to know is if I could use your ballroom next Wednesday for Miss Thornton-Jones's introductory ball? Unfortunately, my ballroom here has gotten a leak in the roof, and the builders tell me they'll not be able to rectify it in time."

"Honestly, there's no need to host a ball for me," Miss Thornton-Jones said in a rush.

"What? You don't want all that attention rained on you?" Alex asked, his tone rather mocking.

"I'd much prefer going to balls rather than being the center of attention at one," she said through a tight smile.

"That's not very American of you, is it? Not wanting a ball to be held in your honor," he returned. "In my experience, the opposite is true of your other countrywomen."

Whatever he said had her clutching hold of her napkin to the point her knuckles were white.

"Having been previously engaged to *one* American does not make you an expert on *all* Americans, Your Grace," she replied, slowly relaxing her grip loose of the cloth. "You would do well to remember that."

"Yes, and stop being such a pain," the countess added with a sweep of her hand in the air. "Now, what do you say about the ball? Can I host it at your townhouse?"

"When have I ever said no to you, Aunt Agatha?"

The countess smiled, a slow, dignified, small

twitch of her lips upward, but a smile, nevertheless. "Good. I shall have to supervise having the new invitations printed and distributed first thing on Monday morning. Oh, but I was going to accompany you, my dear, to the museum." She turned and glanced to Miss Thornton-Jones.

"That's quite all right. I can go another day."

"Nonsense!" the countess declared, with a bang of her fist on the table. "My nephew can accompany you. Can't you, Alex? The place is practically your second home. And for propriety's sake, you two shall both accompany them as well." The countess turned her gaze on to her other nephew George, who was also Alex's cousin, and George's wife Claire, who were sitting across from him.

His cousin hadn't really been paying attention and sloshed some of his drink on the tablecloth at the countess's scrutiny. "We will, Aunt?"

George was an affable and honorable chap, the son of Alex's late uncle Arthur, which made him Alex's heir. Not that George cared at all about it, but Alex was at least glad that the dukedom would pass to a man he trusted.

Alex hadn't spent much time with George when they'd been children, as Alex's father had been far too immersed in ensuring his heir was properly educated and instructed in how best to take over the dukedom, refusing to allow Alex to do anything as childish as play with his cousins. But, thankfully, George, Sam, and Alex had all gone to boarding school together and become the best of friends.

"You will go with them," the countess affirmed with steel in her voice.

"Of course, Lady Brexton." Claire quickly placated the lady, while sending an *I'm sorry* smile toward Miss Thornton-Jones and Alex. Claire was all that an English lady should be—polite, kind, and respectful. Plus, she adored George, which made her acceptable in Alex's opinion.

"There's no need for any of you to trouble yourself," Miss Thornton-Jones said, with a shake of her head, looking aghast at the thought. "Honestly, I can wait to go. I wouldn't wish to trouble the duke with spending any more time in my *American* presence, and I'm certain Mr. and Mrs. Trenton have no desire to attend the museum."

"Nonsense," the countess declared. "They should love to attend and play chaperone, wouldn't you both?"

Both of the Trentons quickly nodded.

"It's truly not necessary," Miss Thornton-Jones once again tried to insist.

Alex found himself annoyed she didn't want to spend time with him. Not that he wanted to spend time with her, apart from trying to prove his theory as to her motivations.

"Of course, I'll accompany Miss Thornton-Jones," Alex said. "It will be my pleasure to. Perhaps you can educate me better on America and your own knowledge of fossils. We shall have quite a lot to discuss, you and I."

"There! It's settled, then." There was a smile of satisfaction on the countess's face.

"I am looking forward to it, Your Grace." She sounded anything but.

He grinned over at her. "As am I, Miss

Thornton-Jones." The more he learned of her, the more knowledge he would attain to ensure Sam stayed well away from her. He would protect his cousin from this woman. A woman who appeared demure and kind and knowledgeable, but a woman Alex knew down to his soul was hiding her true purpose for being in London.

And that purpose had to be to marry a lord, a fact he was now more determined than ever to prove. Suddenly, he was looking forward to Monday with a great deal more enthusiasm than he'd had for anything in quite a while. The thought was unsettling, especially given her nationality and his past experience. Though there was nothing to really be unsettled over.

The last American he'd given his heart to had shattered it into dust until there was nothing else left for him to give. No one could do more damage than she had, especially not Miss Thornton-Jones.

CHAPTER FIVE

"I knew my plan would work perfectly," Aimee exclaimed after hearing all about Evie's dinner last night. "And you were worried they'd suspect something. Ha! Didn't I assure you you had nothing to worry over? It was easy, like I said it would be."

"It was nothing of the sort, and I'm still worried," Evie hissed as she took a sip of the hot coffee the waiter had just delivered to their table. "Honestly, the duke suspects something, I'm certain."

She'd met her cousin at the Berkley Street coffee shop, the nearest coffee house open on a Sunday located halfway between where Aimee was staying with Mrs. Holbrook and where Evie was staying with the countess. It would have been a nice twenty-minute stroll for Evie, had the thought of the duke and her worry over his suspicions not been consuming her for the entire walk over.

She hadn't been able to get the man out of her head since last night. It was frustrating beyond anything she'd experienced before. She'd even dreamed about him, the type of dream she'd never had before that had left her all hot and bothered upon waking. Even now, recollecting the image of having his lips upon hers was making her feel slightly flushed.

"What does he suspect? That you're trying to snag a titled husband?" Aimee asked. "So what? If that's all he thinks, let him. It will mean he'll be less suspicious of your woeful accent. You must practice more, even here while we're taking to each other."

Evie exhaled harshly. "That's one of the things I hate most about this whole charade." Putting on an American accent, and yes, a bad one at that, not only took a great deal of concentration but was also starting to grate on her own ears. "I'm regretting ever agreeing to this whole thing! It was a bad idea."

"Oh, do relax, cousin," Aimee placated as she, too, took a sip of her own coffee with cream. "Aren't you going to the museum tomorrow? That will make you happy."

"No, it certainly will not, at least not now." She quickly told Aimee of the countess's intervention regarding her day trip. "I can just imagine my first visit will be ruined with *him* there. He shall be scrutinizing everything I say, watching everything I do. You have no idea how exacting his eyes can be, taking in everything. It will be exhausting."

"You said he shares your interest of history and fossils?" Aimee shrugged. "Just talk about those subjects and you'll get lost in the topics and forget all of your worries, as you usually do when talking of such *fascinating* things."

"I can hear the sarcasm in your voice."

Aimee laughed. "I'm only being sarcastic regarding the last part. You know how boring I find history. But you have nothing to worry over. I know you, Evie. You will have a lovely time, despite the duke being there. And even if he does initially think you're pretending to be interested in history, it doesn't matter, because after he sees how passionate you get on the subject, he'll know your interest is real. Everyone who talks to you about the topic quickly realizes that."

"Possibly," Evie allowed. Her cousin was making sense, and perhaps Evie was exaggerating the duke's scrutiny. Perhaps she'd even imagined most of it, given her nerves of last night? Hopefully, that was the case. "In any event, you must tell me how your adventures are going learning to be a secretary and trying to discover all you can of your father's business."

"Oh, it's absolutely horrible," Aimee groaned with an exaggerated shake of her head. "Well, I should say, *he's* absolutely horrible."

"He?"

"*He* is the head of the London office, and he's a nightmare!" Aimee replied, a shudder running through her body. "The actual job itself and learning the inside workings of my father's company is as wonderful as I'd hoped. If only that surly, grumpy, pain-in-the-ass man wasn't there making everything so horrid, I'd be thrilled indeed."

"Are you telling me there's a man you haven't been able to wrap around your finger as you normally can with most?"

"Now who's being sarcastic? But the truth of it is that no, I haven't been able to. Not even in the slightest," she bit out, crossing her arms over her chest. "I'm beginning to think perhaps being the sole heiress of my father's fortune did make men inclined to bend over backward to please me. Now that I'm pretending to be you, it seems I've lost any ability I had to influence a man—well, at least this particular one—and it's frustrating."

"Yes, I imagine being me would be horrible."

"Oh, I didn't mean it like that." Aimee gasped. "Truly, I didn't. It's just I've noticed people treat me differently now."

"Welcome to my world, dear cousin. A world where my position in life certainly has its limitations." She took another sip of the hot brew. "Though, in fairness to you, it's not just your fortune men are taken with, but I'm sure that helps. You have a way about you of making everyone feel special." She'd seen it herself on so many occasions. Her cousin was slightly indulged, but she also had a heart of gold, and people, especially men who were also attracted to the big blue eyes, thick black lashes, and rose-red lips her cousin was possessed of, were regularly entranced by the combination.

"I don't make this man feel special. Apparently, I annoy him." She shook her head, her eyes staring into space. "Nothing I've done so far has impressed him, but rather done the opposite. Darn the man!"

Evie had never seen her cousin so angry or frustrated over a person. "Who is this man?" Her curiosity was aroused. If a man could rile Aimee up like this, Evie wanted to meet him.

Aimee blew out a breath. "His name is Harrison Stone. He's a fellow American who my father put in charge of the London operations. He's completely boring, predictable, and staid for someone who grew up in Texas. Honestly, I was led to believe Texans were charming. Thus far, I can tell you that is not the case with this man. The exact opposite, in fact."

"How interesting."

"I know. It all began after I clashed fiercely with him on my first day last week after he saved me."

"He saved you? What do you mean by that?" If anything happened to Aimee because of their swap, Evie would never forgive herself.

"It was nothing." Aimee waved her hand around in an extremely nonchalant manner. "I nearly had my purse stolen is all, and Harrison Stone intervened, but then he had the nerve to tell me off after, so I gave him a piece of my mind. Neither of us knew who the other was at the time, and when I went to the office after and we were introduced, he's been annoyed with me ever since."

"You do have a temper," Evie couldn't help but point out.

"My response was warranted," Aimee replied. "Anyhow, to say we've clashed several times since is an understatement. I'm certain it's only for the fact he thinks I'm my father's niece that he hasn't dismissed me already."

"You do realize that in your role pretending to be me, you shouldn't be clashing with your boss." Evie could only imagine the chaos Aimee was causing; her cousin hadn't earned the nickname *Whirlwind Aimee* without good reason.

"I'm only clashing with him because of his ridiculous assumptions about me. Honestly, he's the most annoying man I've ever met." Aimee raised her chin pointedly, glancing beyond Evie out the shop window.

Evie felt like rolling her eyes. Her cousin always

managed to get up to some mischief or another. "What is it you're both clashing over?"

"I believe he suspects I'm stealing company secrets and selling them to the competition!" Aimee declared. "Can you believe such a ridiculous thing?" She shook her head, her eyes ablaze with indignation. "In any event, I intend to get to the bottom of the mystery. So I'd best be off and go to the office."

"But it's a Sunday and your day off."

"What better time to do some investigating while everyone isn't there, and prove that horrid man wrong."

Seeing the glint of determination in Aimee's eyes, Evie felt a moment of compassion for the man, who Aimee clearly thought of as her nemesis. Evie would have to find out more about him when they met again next Sunday, for it wasn't often a man stirred such ire in her cousin.

Leaning over the table, she gave Aimee a quick hug before her cousin said goodbye and departed the coffee shop, purposeful in her stride.

God help this Harrison Stone; he'd need it dealing with Aimee when she was on a mission.

Evie picked up her coffee and took another sip, hoping that she, too, would fare as well dealing with the Duke of Hargrave on the morrow. Perhaps, she could even turn the tables on him, given his thoughts of what she was in London to do. An assumption that couldn't be more wrong.

Yes, she'd turn the tables on the arrogant man.

CHAPTER SIX

The next morning as Evie stood on the steps staring up at the British Museum of Natural History's grand facade, all thoughts of outmaneuvering the duke disappeared in an instant. The sight of the building before her was glorious, and she was helpless to do anything but stare up at its magnificence.

She must have been standing there marveling at the design for at least five minutes since being dropped off by the countess's carriage, as she waited for the duke and the others to join her. She'd given instructions to the carriage driver to return and collect her in four hours, but given the size of the building, that had been a gross underestimation of the time she was going to need to see everything. She should have asked the driver to return for her at the end of the day.

So lost in the wonder of the building in front of her, she didn't even hear the duke stride up beside her, until his deep voice rumbled in her ear, jolting her out of her trance.

"It's stunning, isn't it?" he murmured from her left.

She glanced over to him, taking a moment to calm her suddenly racing heart. "It's breathtaking," she agreed, noting that in his expertly tailored navy-blue suit, crisp white shirt, and hat, the man was a sight to behold. Evie had never felt so drawn to anyone before.

Normally, it was her books and studies that occupied her thoughts, not an actual person, but when the duke's voice had whispered softly against her ear, a ripple of excitement had shot down her spine, quite disconcertingly.

Her eyes returned to the details of the brick work, suddenly desperate to focus on anything other than the prime specimen of a man towering beside her. "I've never seen such intricate work in the tiles and bricks before. Why, there's even sculptures of flora and fauna etched on their surface."

"There is," Alex agreed with a smile, seeming to be completely unaware of the effect his deep voice was having on her. "The Museum Trust employed a French sculptor to create molds of the species, which they used when making the bricks and tiles."

"It's ingenious." Evie's eyes couldn't help but be drawn back to the duke, who seemed more handsome now in the daytime than he had last night, if that was even possible. "You know a great deal about the building."

"It's my favorite place to visit in London." He shrugged, looking slightly awkward at the admission. "As unusual as that might be for someone in my position."

"Why? Because you're a duke?"

He nodded. "Yes. Many of my peers spend their free time at the races and their clubs, not museums."

"Then that is their misfortune," she exclaimed, her eyes once again returning to glance back over the facade. "It's already my favorite building, and I haven't even seen inside yet."

He laughed at her confession. "Well, how about

we go in, then? The inside is even more magnificent than the outside." He held out the crook of his arm for her.

She desperately wanted to do just that, but she hesitated. "Shouldn't we wait until your cousin and his wife arrive? The countess was adamant about having them as our chaperones." The woman had warned Evie numerous times over breakfast about not being seen alone with the duke for too long, as tongues would apparently wag. But, then again, Evie was yearning to start exploring inside. "The countess will be most displeased if we don't…"

"I won't say anything if you don't." He winked at her just as he had last night, and just like last night, her stomach somersaulted with the gesture.

"Very well," Evie declared with a grin, the allure of seeing all the wonders too great to deny, as was the man himself. She threaded her hand through his arm and rested her glove on his extremely muscular bicep. "Lead the way, Your Grace, for I wish to see *everything*!"

"Hargrave! Miss Thornton-Jones! Do wait up!"

They both halted on the stairs at the sound of their names, and Evie could feel the sudden tension in the duke's arm as they both glanced back toward the voice.

"Damn it," the duke muttered as the Earl of Brexton bounded up the steps toward them, an affable smile across his face.

"What the devil are you doing here, Sam?" The duke didn't sound happy about his other cousin's appearance.

"Mother mentioned you were escorting Miss

Thornton-Jones here today, along with Claire and George, so I thought I'd join you all." He looked behind them up the stairs. "Where are George and Claire?"

"They're not here yet," came the duke's gruff reply. "Need I remind you you hate this place?"

"I've never said that!" the earl declared with a grin over to Evie. "It's just your company I'm not a fan of when we're here." He inclined his head back to the duke. "My cousin tends to go on and on about the various specimens inside, which can be rather tedious to listen to."

"I must warn you I have a bad habit of doing that too," Evie replied as the earl took her hand and placed a chaste kiss on the back of it. She couldn't help but notice the duke's scowl. "I would hate to bore you."

"You could never bore me, my dear Miss Thornton-Jones," he said, sincerity ringing in his voice. "Honestly, I will adore the place, in *your* company. Hearing your thoughts on all of the exhibits will give me a completely new perspective on them all."

The duke coughed, and Evie could have sworn she heard the word *nonsense* in amongst the sound.

Evie smiled at the earl, who, with his friendly, charming nature, was the complete opposite of the duke. "It will be a pleasure to have you join our party."

"Yes. Such a pleasure," came the duke's droll reply, his expression completely negating his words.

"Excellent!" The earl enthusiastically clapped his hands together, his green eyes sparkling with good cheer, as he ignored his cousin's sarcasm.

Evie liked the earl, though she imagined anyone would as he was so affable and full of life. He was also a handsome man with his green eyes and blond hair, cut slightly longer than was fashionable, but suited the man's dashing personality to perfection. Though he wasn't as compelling as the duke.

She couldn't help but compare the two men standing in front of her. Both were extremely attractive men, one with the good looks and charm of a golden angel, radiating sunlight and happiness, and the other with the dark brooding persona of a fallen angel, who was more often than not scowling. Evie had no idea why she was so drawn to the latter when he appeared irritable all the time. But drawn to the duke she found herself, which was something she was going to have to put a stop to immediately.

"Shall we go in, then, or wait for George and Claire?" the earl asked.

"Speak of the devils," the duke said, his eyes glancing beyond Brexton to where the last of their party were striding up the steps.

"So sorry we're a bit late," George called out, waving his free hand at them, while he escorted his wife up the last few steps to the landing where they were standing.

"When are you two ever not late?" the duke grumbled as he bent over and kissed Mrs. Trenton's gloved hand.

"And when are you ever not grumpy, Alex?" Mrs. Trenton pertly replied with a smile.

Evie was surprised to hear the lady call the

duke by his first name, especially in front of Evie herself, though she supposed they were family.

"Mr. Trenton, Mrs. Trenton," Evie acknowledged them with a small curtsy. "It's lovely to see you both again."

"As it is you," Mrs. Trenton replied with a huge smile. The lady was extremely friendly and welcoming, which was not what Evie had expected of any women in Society.

"And aren't you glad to see me, too?" The earl grinned at Mrs. Trenton and leaned over and gave her a quick kiss on the cheek.

"You'll make my husband jealous, Samuel." Mrs. Trenton laughed as she swatted the earl away.

"Oh, Georgie knows I'm teasing," the earl replied, clapping Mr. Trenton on the back. "Don't you, Georgie?"

"My wife and I are well aware of the flirt you are, Samuel," Mr. Trenton replied. "Plus, my wife is possessed of far more intelligence than to be taken in by your good looks, cousin. She married me, after all."

"Cousin?" Evie couldn't help herself from saying. "I didn't realize, Mr. Trenton, you were related to the earl as well as the duke."

"Indeed, I am," he replied. "My father was the middle son, while Alex's father was the eldest, and Sam's mother the countess was their younger sister, making us all cousins."

"A shame you both didn't get the good looks that I did," the earl said, wrapping his arm around George in a half hug. "Must have come from my father's side."

"Yes, but luckily Alex and I got the brains from our fathers," George was quick to answer.

"You must forgive the men, or should I say the boys, for their teasing of each other," Mrs. Trenton said. "Not only are they family, but the three of them went to school and university together. They're more like brothers than anything, as their regular tormenting of each other would support. Although Alex rarely takes part in the activity, do you, cousin?"

The lady glanced pointedly over at the duke, who Evie couldn't help but notice was keeping himself aloof from the bantering going on between Sam and George. For a minute, she thought he seemed lonely, recognizing an expression in his eyes she often wore. Like someone looking in at the frivolity but never truly feeling a part of it.

"Why bother taking part when I can watch?" the duke replied.

It was a sentiment Evie shared. Rarely had she had an opportunity to take part in much of anything, always watching from the sidelines instead. Perhaps that was why she'd agreed to Aimee's scheme? Part of her always longed for the adventure of being involved but never had the opportunity or the courage to be.

"Now, are we going to stand out here all day chatting on the steps?" the duke said. "Or are we actually going to show Miss Trenton-Jones the museum as planned? There's a great many specimens to view, and if she is to have any chance of seeing them all, we need to get started."

It was possible Evie had imagined the

loneliness, because now his eyes were all business and his actions brusque, not even a hint of the vulnerability she'd thought she'd seen.

"You and specimens," the earl declared in a mock moan, shaking his head morosely. "Good God, man, where's your sense of fun? You will bore the lady with talk of your specimens in no time."

"Oh, I don't know about that," the duke murmured, his eyes sparkling in challenge as he eyed Evie. "Miss Thornton-Jones seems to be quite the expert on fossils, and I look forward to discussing various aspects of them with her."

"Discussing or interrogating me?" She raised an eyebrow, certain she knew his purpose.

Their three companions all guffawed in laughter.

"She's got your measure, doesn't she, Alex?" The earl clapped him on the back and winked at Evie.

"We'll see," the duke murmured, his eyes staying steady upon Evie's, a challenge radiating in them.

"Yes, Duke, we will," she replied, boldly returning his stare. If he thought to intimidate her with his knowledge of fossils, she was looking forward to the surprise he'd soon get when he learned her own knowledge either rivaled or surpassed his. "Lead the way and we shall see who knows what about the specimens inside."

He took the crook of her elbow in his hand and began to lead her up the stairs to the entrance. "Challenge accepted, Miss Thornton-Jones," he whispered in her ear. "Challenge accepted."

As a tingling awareness rushed over her skin from the feel of his breath against her earlobe, Evie got the sense that the challenge he was speaking of had nothing to do with fossils at all. Not even in the slightest.

CHAPTER SEVEN

An hour later, Evie was still marveling at the plethora of exhibits and fossils on display when Mrs. Trenton linked her arm in Evie's and declared it was time they got to know each other better, and she told the men to go ahead down the corridor.

"You seem to be enjoying yourself," Mrs. Trenton said with a smile.

In truth, Evie felt like a child in a sweet shop. "It's wonderful."

Mrs. Trenton laughed lightly. "It is impressive, I will agree with that. Though I think it's only you and Alex who are so enraptured by it."

The duke didn't seem enraptured to Evie, given the scowl often creasing his face as they had been wandering through the museum and that he was now directing back at her as he glanced over his shoulder at them.

"He cuts a dashing figure, does he not?" Mrs. Trenton commented, her gaze following Evie's over to the duke.

Evie dragged her eyes away from the sight of the man's backside, a very firm and worthy of appreciation backside, and smiled brightly at the woman beside her. "I tend to notice his frown more than his figure."

"Yes, he does like to frown," Mrs. Trenton agreed. "In the near ten years I've known him, I've rarely seen him smile. Sam and George tell me that's been the case since Alex was a child and his mother ran off with another man."

"She did?"

"Yes, creating quite the scandal in the process. But that's a tale for another time." The woman glanced over to the men. "In any event, since his broken engagement, he smiles even less. Though he was smiling a little bit at you during dinner last night."

"I think you mean *scowling* at me, Mrs. Trenton."

The woman laughed. "No, I definitely saw a few fleeting smiles. And I must insist you start calling me Claire. Mrs. Trenton is so formal, and I'm determined you and I shall be great friends."

There was such a happy smile on the woman's face that Evie found herself smiling back. "In that case, you must call me Ev—Aimee."

The woman's face crunched up slightly. "EvAimee?"

Panic clawed at her throat, but she forced the smile to stay spread over her mouth and she laughed lightly, though it sounded slightly unnatural. "Forgive me. My cousin and I have been swapping names for years as a bit of a joke, and from force of habit I was about to say to call me her name instead. So silly of me. My cousin will think it absolutely hilarious I nearly did so." If she didn't kill Evie first. "But do call me Aimee, which is my name, of course."

Could she sound any more of a complete nitwit if she tried? She doubted it. But thankfully, Claire smiled and seemed happy to accept the explanation.

"Aimee it is, then," Claire said. "I shall look forward to us becoming firm friends. I must admit, it will be so nice not to be the only lady amongst those three." She glanced over again at the three men ahead who had stopped in front of another exhibit.

George and Sam were discussing something, but the duke's attention swiveled onto Evie, almost as if he could tell she was staring at him. Her whole body tensed with the intensity of his stare.

"I see Alex has taken a particular interest in you," Claire's voice intruded, and Evie hastily broke eye contact with the duke.

"Oh goodness no, he hasn't," Evie said, a different sort of panic spreading through her with the lady's observation.

"Alex hasn't been able to stop looking at you since we arrived. His behavior is rather telling, especially as he avoids unwed ladies like the plague, yet he can't stop staring at you."

"Honestly, the way he glares at me with that scowl of his could give no one the impression he was interested in me at all," Evie pointed out.

Claire stared at Evie. "Well, as your new friend here in England, I feel it's my duty to tell you that you're completely wrong about his lack of interest. I haven't seen him so interested in anyone, not since his ex-fiancée."

"What did happen with her?" Evie knew she probably should have left well enough alone, but her curiosity was eating at her, like a puzzle that needed to be put together.

Claire sighed. "Alex was smitten with Miss

Crandell, more than he'd ever been with another before. Though he wasn't the only one, the lady was stunningly beautiful and oh so polished and poised. She held the attention of all around her effortlessly with her charm and wit, not to mention she was an heiress, too."

"She sounds like a paragon."

"She appeared to be," Claire confirmed. "And she certainly attracted not only Alex's attention, but most of the eligible bachelors that season, too. In any event, Alex was the heir to a dukedom and thus considered the pick of the lot, so Miss Crandell set her cap at him, and he was powerless to resist. Though, in his defense, he was only twenty-two and rather naive in the ways of the world, given he always had his head buried in a book."

"It's hard to imagine him as being naive," Evie replied. The man seemed far too jaded and serious by far.

"It didn't last long after his short-lived engagement." Claire glanced over to the duke, and Evie's eyes followed.

He was a head taller than most others around him, with an air of dignified masculinity clinging to him like a second skin. She felt like sighing at the fine figure he presented and had to shake her head to rid herself of the fanciful thought. There was no point in daydreaming about the man's good looks. It was a pointless endeavor, which could lead nowhere.

"Supposedly, Miss Crandell wanted a short engagement, even suggesting they elope," Claire continued on, turning back to face Evie. "Which, in retrospect, was telling. In the end, however, we convinced Alex that a short engagement with a small ceremony at his ducal estate would be a good compromise."

"What happened?"

"The night before the wedding, we were all staying at Hargrave Hall, and after dinner my mother approached me saying she'd seen Miss Crandell sneaking into the greenhouse with another man." Claire seemed uncomfortable with the memory. "I didn't want to break Alex's heart with the news, and I was hoping whatever she was doing was innocent, but I knew I had to tell Alex. He and I went to the greenhouse, and I can still recall the absolute devastation on Alex's face when he saw her with that other man. It was heartbreaking. After that night, he broke off the engagement and shut off his emotions, vehement in his declarations he would never marry."

"It sounds like he loved her a great deal."

"He was infatuated by her, that's for certain," Claire confirmed. "But I don't know if he really loved her. He barely knew her. But I think the betrayal he felt was magnified given his mother's earlier betrayal, too."

"You mentioned she ran off with another man."

"Yes, causing the scandal of the century, running off with an American financier when Alex was only six, and then divorcing her husband shortly after."

Evie could only imagine the pain he'd experienced, first abandoned by his mother as a child, and then later betrayed by his fiancée. "It does explain some of his hostility toward me."

"I don't think he means to be hostile. In fact, I think he likes you. He just doesn't know how to show it." A small smile tilted up the corner of Claire's lips. "And I think perhaps the like is reciprocated?"

"In that you're mistaken," Evie replied, rather more vehemently than she'd intended. "I am no Dollar Princess, and I have absolutely no intention of marrying anyone. Duke or otherwise."

She'd never uttered truer words in her life. Evie knew it was doubtful she'd ever marry given her illegitimacy, let alone marry a duke. The thought was laughable. Her a duchess? Never. She'd much prefer to curl up in bed with a good book rather than a husband.

The sudden image that sprang to mind of the duke climbing into her bed, with all thoughts of reading anything forgotten, was as unwelcome as it was uncomfortable. She grabbed one of the pamphlets and began to fan herself. "Has it gotten hot in here?"

Claire peered at her oddly. "Not really, though you do look flushed."

"Do I?" Evie's attention was caught by the man himself, as he began to stride back to them, George and Sam following behind.

"If you two have finished gossiping, there's a calcareous microfossil exhibit down the hall that I'm sure Miss Thornton-Jones would enjoy. That's if you know what they are?" His eyes swiveled to Evie, a challenge in their depths.

"Of course I know what calcareous microfossils are."

"Are you speaking a different language?" the earl exclaimed as he came to a halt beside them. "What on earth is a calc—something fossil?"

"Perhaps Miss Thornton-Jones can enlighten us all about what they are?" The duke smiled at her, his tone suggesting she wouldn't be able to do such a thing.

Evie shrugged. If he wanted to test her, then she was happy to oblige him on one of her favorite topics. "It would be my pleasure to educate you about them, Your Grace."

A chortle of laughter erupted from George and Samuel, which they made a halfhearted attempt to conceal with a cough.

The duke flashed his cousins a look suggesting he was unimpressed with them both before his gaze flicked back to Evie. "I can assure you, Miss Thornton-Jones, that my education on them is quite sound, though I'm interested to hear your thoughts on them."

His eyes were burning into her own, and Evie felt the hairs at the nape of her neck stand on end at his continued scrutiny. The man was dangerous to her equilibrium, there was no doubt about it.

She cleared her throat and continued on. "Calcareous microfossils are a type of fossil, however, as the name suggests, they are far smaller than normal fossils, only measuring around four millimeters in length. They are found in marine sediment, and there are three predominate varieties of them: ostracods, coccoliths, and foraminifera. The three of which I'm extremely proficient in differentiating between."

The duke's eyes narrowed upon Evie's. "Impressive, Miss Thornton-Jones, but I didn't think Americans used the metric system for measurement. Isn't the imperial system the preferred unit of measurement in the States?"

Evie pressed her lips together. Damn the man and his sharp mind. "It is. However, I'm in England, am I not? Thus I thought it best to refer to a unit that everyone is familiar with. I would hate for you to not fully understand what I was talking about given I had to explain it to you in the first place. I do hope I explained it well enough for you to understand."

Now, neither George nor Sam could hide their laughter as they openly let the sound reign in the face of the duke's scowl. Perhaps she was being a tad rude goading him so, but the man was trying to suggest she didn't know her fossils, and that was a grave sin in Evie's book.

"I think the lady's knowledge rivals, if not outshines, your own, Alex," Sam said, clapping the duke on his back. "Well done, Miss Thornton-Jones. It's not often one can best Alex when it comes to fossils."

"There was no besting done with her answer," Alex growled. "I knew perfectly well the answer before she gave it."

"Then what was the point in asking me to answer the question, Your Grace?" Evie asked. "Unless it was to try to trip me up or embarrass me in front of your friends? Or perhaps it was to reaffirm to yourself how superior you think you are?"

Evie didn't know where the fire in her belly was

coming from. Perhaps it had been born from years of people dismissing her and her knowledge because of her station in life and the fact she was a woman. Perhaps it came from this man in front of her dismissing her, too. But, suddenly, she wasn't demure, shy little Evie, and she was determined to give as good as she got.

"You shouldn't have dismissed me or my knowledge so out of turn," she continued as she eyed him in defiance, all but daring him to contradict her. "You could learn a lot from American men. They treat their wives as equals, seeking out their opinion, and they adore their daughters, ensuring they are as well educated as their sons." A fact Evie had benefited from, given all the Thornton-Joneses were more than happy for Evie to take lessons with Aimee. It had been some of the best years of her life being able to learn and read to her heart's content. "Yet here you are trying to test me, believing I don't know my history or my fossils."

She took a step over toward him and poked him in the chest. Truly, she had no idea what was possessing her, but she'd had enough of everyone treating her less than, this man most especially of all.

"Trust me, Duke, that is only a tiny drop of my knowledge when it comes to paleontology. Now, you can go on challenging me all day and come out looking the fool, or we can discuss our knowledge of the topics instead, like two rational adults."

As she glared up at him, she noticed his jaw was clamped tightly together while he stood there, staring down at her, his whole body ridiculously still.

The rest of their group all had their mouths hanging agape, their laughter long-since retired under Evie's mini tirade, and their eyes undisguisedly swinging between Alex and Evie in morbid curiosity.

Maybe she had gone too far, especially given Alex was a duke and outranked every person in the building. But he'd been trying to test her, and that was the last thing Evie wanted or needed. Slowly, she withdrew the finger she was still pointing into his chest.

"Only an American could be so forthright, Miss Thornton-Jones." The duke squared his shoulders, almost as if preparing for battle.

Well, at least he had no suspicions of her apparent heritage. A good thing, she supposed. "An educated lady, Your Grace, regardless of where she comes from, would no doubt be as forthright as you claim I am being. And considering *American* ladies are far better educated than their English counterparts in all manner of topics, wouldn't you expect me to be forthright?"

"I don't know quite what I expected of you, Miss Thornton-Jones, but you certainly haven't been it."

Evie didn't know quite how to respond to the remark, or even whether it was a compliment or criticism, so she ignored it. "I think we've wasted enough time and should return to exploring the rest of the museum, as I don't wish to waste another minute proving my education to a man."

And with that, she spun around and headed over to the calcareous microfossil exhibit. If the man thought she would be cowed by his questioning her knowledge, he really had no idea of who he was dealing with, and she was going to be happy to demonstrate that fact to him.

As many times as she needed to.

CHAPTER EIGHT

"I think I'm falling even more in love with Miss Thornton-Jones after yesterday at the museum," Sam said, dropping down into the armchair in Alex's study and leaning back against it with a sigh. "What a woman."

Alex glanced up from the papers on his desk, glad for the interruption as he'd been unable to concentrate on his work, as thoughts of that very woman kept intruding into his head. "You're not falling in love. You're in awe and lust, and that's all."

"Why must you always put a damper on my enthusiasm? You have to admit she's charming, forthright and very intelligent. Why, I've never seen you talk so much to a woman before or be so animated doing so."

"We were talking about fossils, which in itself is strange, don't you think?" Alex picked up the glass beside him and took a sip of his brandy, which was doing nothing to settle the restless energy that was plaguing him. "Her being interested in discussing fossils, of all things?"

He'd thought of little else since yesterday, remembering the delight and wonder in those crystal blue eyes of hers every time she caught sight of a new fossil, especially the microfossils she seemed so fascinated with. But it had to be all an act, to interest Alex. An act that was bloody working, too, though he assured himself that his interest stemmed more in the fact of trying to unmask her rather than becoming fascinated by her.

"You like fossils, and I don't think you're strange... Actually, maybe I do." Sam grinned at him.

Alex shook his head, his eyes staring into the flames of the hearth across the room. "I've never met a woman, let alone an American heiress, who shares my interests in fossils, at least not since Julia."

"Oh. I see now what's going on..."

He pinned Sam with his eyes. "What do you mean?"

Sam sighed and sat up in his chair, propping his hand under his chin. "It means I think you're attracted to Miss Thornton-Jones but are trying to convince yourself that you're not, so you're likening her to Julia."

"That's absolute nonsense!" Alex stood and stalked over to the window to stare out at his gardens at the back of his townhouse. The green of the trees and manicured grounds usually calmed him, but now they were only irritating him.

Of course, he knew he was attracted to her, given he'd found himself imagining dragging her up against the wall and plundering her sweet mouth with his, multiple times since he'd met her. The very thought of tasting and caressing her until she was breathless and panting for more was all but consuming him.

Why did he have to find himself so attracted to the woman? And an American woman at that, who was clearly only here to snare a husband, contrary to her suggestions otherwise.

"You seemed entranced." Sam shrugged. "Perhaps I shouldn't pursue her if you're interested in doing so yourself."

"I was entranced with her conversation, not with the woman herself." *Liar*, a voice in his head whispered.

"Then you don't mind if I pursue her?"

"Yes, I bloody mind!" Alex roared, knowing he should have stayed completely calm but being completely unable to with the suggestion. "She's just like Julia and will break your heart."

"I find it odd you would compare her with Julia when she's nothing like her."

"Please," Alex scoffed. "Julia mentioned fossils to me when I first met her. Miss Thornton-Jones did likewise."

"Miss Thornton-Jones didn't simply mention them. She's somewhat of an expert on them, maybe even more so than yourself."

"She's well researched is all. And that's the key point: she is *researched*. She's trying to hook me in and make me think she shares my interests. That is all."

"That's a load of nonsense." Sam stood and went over and poured himself a glass of brandy. "She's even more passionate about the subject than you are, and that's saying something. I find it charming. Seeing as your only objection to my pursuing her is that you think she's like Julia, I shall happily pursue her then, for I know she's nothing like your ex-fiancée."

"Pursue her at your own peril, then." Alex tried to shrug, telling himself that if his cousin wished to get his heart broken, then who was he to stop him?

"I shall," Sam replied, staring at Alex with a rather odd glance, almost as if he were testing him about something. "She fascinates me, and I do enjoy hearing what she has to say. Which is odd for me, given most women I take an interest in certainly have no love of learning like she does."

Alex could reluctantly relate, though *fascinates* was an extremely mild way of describing the feelings she aroused in Alex. Frustration and desire, perhaps even obsession, would be more accurate.

"And she's absolutely lovely," Sam continued. "Plus, my mother keeps saying it's high time I settled down."

"She's an American Dollar Princess!" Alex dragged a hand through his hair. How could he make Sam see sense? "Only here to trade her millions to marry a titled gentleman. She doesn't care about you, only that you have a title."

"All women care about a title," Sam exclaimed. "Regardless of their nationality."

"Yes, but English ladies don't pretend to love you because of a title," he grumbled. "They don't try to trade in their inheritance for it."

"No, their fathers arrange that. Americans are just more upfront about their intentions." Sam sighed. "Besides, what's so wrong with trading in their millions? It's saved a great many estates over the years and will continue to for generations to come. Who wouldn't want to marry an heiress who is as charming and lovely as her fortune is grand?"

"You don't need the blunt."

"Maybe not," Sam agreed. "But I certainly wouldn't say no to it. Besides, Miss Thornton-Jones seems kind and not brash or overly confident as most of the Dollar Princesses can be. I think she would make me a marvelous wife. Unless, of course, you are interested in her yourself."

"For the millionth bloody time, I'm not interested in her. And she would make you a terrible wife!" Didn't Sam see the truth of the situation? "She wouldn't care about you, Sam, she would only care about your title, and as soon as she secured your proposal, she would betray you."

"I know she wouldn't, and if you can get past your prejudice of her heritage and realize not every American woman is like Julia, you would realize that about her, too."

As usual, the thought of Julia's betrayal brought with it a bitter taste. It was the only time he'd let his guard down around his heart, and she'd stormed in and shattered it to pieces. He couldn't let Sam suffer the same fate. "You're wrong. Miss Thornton-Jones is here for one reason and one reason only: to marry the grandest title she can. You'd be a fool to think otherwise."

"Perhaps I am a fool," Sam retorted. "For I truly don't think that is why Miss Thornton-Jones is here."

"You're playing with fire, Sam, and it will get you burned." Couldn't his cousin see how the woman was toying with them all? Appearing so earnest and genuine, but manipulating their emotions, hiding the true purpose of her visit?

And if Sam didn't believe that purpose was to entrap a husband, he was the most gullible man in Christendom, and it was Alex's job to show him the truth of it. The truth, that underneath her beautiful, charming facade, she was exactly like Julia, and Alex would use himself to prove it to Sam.

It really was the only way to save Sam from a lifetime of unhappiness as Alex himself had to endure.

CHAPTER NINE

For the twentieth time that evening, Evie stood in front of the floor-to-ceiling mirror inside her bed-chamber, spinning around on the spot, watching the shimmering blue reflection of her glittering gown shine in brilliance with each rotation she made.

She felt like the ash girl from the Brothers Grimm story, about to go to her first ball. Had the ash girl felt as terrified as Evie did with the prospect? And terrified was an understatement for how she felt, having never danced at a ball before.

For a moment, she felt a little guilty wearing the new gowns Aunt Edith had commissioned from the House of Worth for Aimee, especially as Aimee was having to wear Evie's far plainer wool and cotton dresses when she could have been wearing these ridiculously stunning outfits. But the feeling didn't last too long when Evie remembered it had been her cousin's own plan that had gotten them into this mess in the first place.

Now here Evie was, about to head downstairs and travel to the duke's residence with the count-ess, for the ball he was hosting in her honor. Never would she have thought she'd ever attend a duke's ball after growing up in Bethnal Green. Not or-phaned Yvette Jenkins with barely a penny to her name.

Oh, good lord. How was she going to carry off

the charade tonight, when at best she'd stuck to the walls or chairs at any of the balls she'd attended with Aimee in New York? At least she looked the part of a wealthy American heiress in this glorious creation, which she couldn't stop staring at, even if she felt like an imposter.

For a moment, she thought of the duke. Would he see the truth she was trying so desperately to hide, that she didn't belong in his world and never would? Or would he see what the dress had been designed to show? An extremely wealthy, fabulously confident young lady, as Aimee certainly would have been if she'd been in Evie's place as she was meant to be.

Making her way downstairs, the blue silk slippers on her feet making nary a noise on the stairs as she did so, Evie wondered if the duke would ask her to dance. They'd had a thoroughly enjoyable day at the museum, discussing all manner of fossils, which had been as stimulating as it was surprising, especially given his earlier suspicions of her motives.

But dancing with him would be fraught with issues, she was sure of it, particularly as she'd never danced at a ball before, not to mention the man made her supremely nervous in an elemental way. When she was with him, she was so aware of his maleness that sometimes she found herself imagining touching him. Being kissed by him. Unable to concentrate on much else.

"Don't you look marvelous," the countess said from the foot of the stairs as Evie came to a halt beside her. "One can always tell a Worth gown from others. The man is a genius."

She glanced down at the dress. "It's the most stunning gown I've ever worn."

Clothing had never been a priority for Evie, as she'd never had the money for dresses, and even when Aunt Edith had offered to buy her a new wardrobe, Evie had chosen the plainest and most sensible outfits she could. After all, what need did she have for more expensive dresses when she had no interest in marriage?

But on this trip, there was no choice but to wear the boldest and most eye-catching of gowns while pretending to be her cousin. Nothing screamed excess money to the English more than an ostentatious wardrobe of clothes that cost more than some of them made from their estates in an entire year. An illusion that would only help Evie pull off the ruse.

Half an hour later, the countess's carriage pulled up at the duke's townhouse, though it took another ten minutes for it to get into a position in front of the stairs for them to alight from. They were the last carriage to arrive, as the countess had planned for them to be, given she was of the firm opinion that as Evie was the guest of honor, she needed to make a grand entrance after everyone had already arrived, and it would not do for them to arrive a moment beforehand.

Taking the footman's hand, Evie stepped from the carriage and glanced up at the facade of the duke's home. Her jaw dropped at the absolute beauty of the house before her. Unlike the countess's house and most other residences, which resided side by side, this one took up an entire block of its own. Along the front facade, there were white stone pillars that stretched from the ground upward, towering up the four stories to the roof. Candle-lit lamps had been strung along the balustrades of the stairs leading up to the elaborate entrance doors, where several footmen were standing to attention.

"It's beautiful, isn't it?" The countess's voice spoke next to her, jolting Evie out of her wonder.

All Evie could do was nod. Beautiful was too tame a word to describe the elegance of the stately mansion standing proudly before her. And she'd thought the Thornton-Joneses' residence was the most elegant home in the world. She'd been wrong. Though her aunt and uncle's house screamed wealth and new money, the duke's residence was perfectly refined and tastefully elegant, effortlessly relaying its history and centuries of wealth.

Panic gripped her. How could she do this? How could she pretend to belong in a world she had no place being part of? Suddenly, she wanted to race down the footpath and get as far away as she could. But, instead, she clamped down on her nerves and followed the countess up the stairs. It wasn't long before their names were announced and about five hundred ladies and gentlemen all glanced up from the ballroom below to stare at Evie with undisguised curiosity.

Breathe, Evie, just breathe.

Plastering on what she hoped was a supremely confident and serene smile across her face, she picked up the skirts of her gown and began to follow the countess down the stairs. Her steps faltered when her eyes latched onto the duke's below as he stood on the landing, waiting to welcome them and staring at Evie with such an intensity that her breath quickened and her heart began to race.

It seemed each time she saw him, he got even more handsome. Dressed in his expertly tailored black suit, along with the crisp white shirt underneath, the man was a sight to behold. As she got closer to him, everything else seemed to fade away. Darkly dangerous, he was a man confident of himself and who knew his own power, wielding it without effort or hesitation.

"Aunt Agatha. Miss Thornton-Jones." His deep voice rumbled as he took first the countess's hand and kissed it, then took Evie's.

His fingers brushed along the inside of her palm as he bent his head, and his lips touched her glove. A searing heat ran down her hand from his touch, and Evie was hard-pressed not to moan. What was wrong with her? No man had ever affected her so much before, though she'd never met a man like him before, either.

"You look beautiful, Miss Thornton-Jones," he murmured, his mouth lingering slightly longer over her hand than what was considered necessary. He straightened and smiled at her, a smile that made her think silly thoughts of what it would be like to see him smile at her that exact way every day.

Stupid, silly thoughts, Evie chastised herself.

"Doesn't she look stunning?" the countess agreed before Evie could reply. "You must dance the first dance with her this evening, Alex."

The smile on Alex's face fled, and he turned a rather pointed look upon the countess that seemed to convey his displeasure and annoyance at the suggestion, all in the one glance. "I don't dance at balls, Aunt Agatha. You know that."

"Oh, nonsense!" the countess declared, with a wave of her hand in the air. "As host, you must, I insist. Or perhaps I shall get Samuel to do the honors if you will not?" The countess stared at the duke with a militant expression in her eyes, almost daring him to accept the alternative.

The two of them stayed facing each other, their eyes locked in combat for a moment, until the duke reluctantly inclined his head slightly at the countess before turning to face Evie. "Will you promise to save me the first dance of the evening, Miss Thornton-Jones?"

"Actually, I can't," Evie said, managing to find her voice, slightly husky though it was. "Your son, my lady, has already asked me for the first dance."

"The devil he did." The annoyance in the duke's eyes was now directed solely at Evie.

"He asked me yesterday at the museum."

"He can un-ask you," came the duke's blunt reply.

"Yes, indeed, my son can wait his turn," the countess agreed, her eyes glancing between the two of them with interest. "It is only fitting you dance the first dance with the duke, my dear, for he has been so kind to host this ball on your behalf. Now, it is time for us all to mingle."

Without waiting for them, the countess began to

descend the stairs with infinite grace and poise, leaving Evie with the duke, who was regarding her with an entirely enigmatic expression.

Determined not to be cowed by the intensity in those deep blue eyes of his, she raised her chin and returned his stare boldly.

His lips twitched in response, and he held out his hand. "Shall we, then?"

All she could do was nod, even if the thought of touching him again was causing all manner of chaos in her body. Placing her hand in his, she drew in a swift intake of breath as a shimmer of electricity shot down her hand.

"Are you all right?" His deep voice rumbled beside her, but there was a knowing look in his gaze suggesting the cad was well aware of the physical effect he was having on her.

"Perfectly fine."

"Good." He winked at her as he began to escort her down the stairs.

Trying to focus on the steps instead of the man beside her, Evie carefully watched where she placed her feet, certain if she didn't, she would make a fool of herself by falling down them, given the close proximity of the man next to her and the ridiculous sensations of dizziness his touch evoked. The mere act of her hand resting upon his was literally making her fingers feel as if there was a fire beneath them, such was the heat scorching her skin through the material.

As they reached the bottom of the stairs, Evie saw the Earl of Brexton making his way through the crowd toward them, a determined set to his mouth. Without pause, the duke swiftly steered Evie to the left, bypassing the earl and heading straight for the dance floor.

"What are you doing?" she hissed with a smile plastered on her face while she haphazardly nodded to the strangers they were striding past. "No one is dancing yet."

Talk about being the center of attention for the evening, she could literally feel every eye on her.

"A fact we shall soon rectify, for if I have to dance, I will dance now with you," he murmured, leading her to the dance floor. "A waltz, perhaps?"

Her whole body tensed as the musicians readied their instruments. "I need to warn you I'm not very good at *English* waltzing." She'd literally had only a handful of dance lessons with Aimee over the past two years, though that was learning the Boston waltz, which she'd been hopeless at.

"I doubt that. Weren't you telling me yesterday how you American women have such a better education than your English counterparts? Surely, that would include dancing, wouldn't it?" He raised his eyebrow as he stepped onto the dance floor and held out his hand for her.

"It included American dances, not English ones," she replied through gritted teeth. Then remembering the crowd of onlookers watching her every move, Evie placed her hand in his and smiled, her lips stretching tightly across her face. *Breathe. Just breathe.* What did it matter that everyone was about to find out she was a fraud?

"Let's dance the Boston waltz, then," he said.

Evie blinked several times. "You know the Boston

waltz?" Surely, her luck couldn't be that bad…

"I was once engaged to an American," he replied with a shrug. "She taught me the dance and I'm rather proficient at it, even though it has a different tempo to the Viennese waltz."

Sickness swirled in her belly with the realization he would soon know she was an imposter.

"I might be a little rusty with it, though," he continued, "given it's been over a decade since I last danced it."

"Actually, it's changed a lot in the last few years," she blurted out.

"It has?"

"Oh yes, most certainly." She nodded her head, hoping perhaps he wouldn't want to dance if he thought it had.

"How?"

Yes, how, Evie? Once again, she reminded herself of the fool she'd been to ever agree to Aimee's idea, but she had to do something to dig herself out of the mess she'd created.

"Well…" she began, smacking her lips together as she desperately tried to grasp onto something that might convince him. "The tempo! Yes, that's it. You see, it's been influenced by the, umm…by the Southern states. Yes, that's right."

That sounded plausible, didn't it?

"And because of that," she continued, "the um…tempo is completely different to what it used to be."

"Is it slower, then?"

"No." Slower wouldn't worry him. "It's faster, actually. Much faster. And given you're used to it being slower, I'm certain to step all over your toes." That at least was true, regardless of the speed of the music. "So perhaps we shouldn't dance."

"I think we'll manage. You can even take the lead to begin with until I get a handle on the new tempo."

"Me, take the lead?" She tried to plaster a smile across her face to mask her infinite dread of doing such a thing but doubted she was doing a good job of it, given the odd look he was staring at her with. "Um, yes, I suppose that makes sense…even though a woman doesn't normally do that…"

"But aren't American women far bolder about their rights? I would think you'd relish taking the lead initially." He raised an eyebrow, almost like he knew she was telling him fibs.

"Quite so." Oh god, could this night turn into disaster any quicker? She turned to the musicians who were waiting for their music request. "The Boston waltz, please, but if you could increase the tempo by um…threefold, that would be lovely."

The head musician's jaw dropped slightly. "Threefold, my lady? Are you certain?"

"Oh yes," Evie replied, stretching her smile even tighter across her face until it hurt. "It's the latest fashion to dance it that way in the States. Everyone over there is doing it."

Oh god, what was she doing?

She couldn't even dance the Boston waltz at a normal pace, let alone faster. But hopefully making it faster would mean the duke wouldn't even notice her missteps as he tried to keep up. Him and the rest of Society.

She had to smother a groan as she realized how absurd her plan was. Surely, the ruse would be over when she made a fool of herself by dancing like a swarm of bees were chasing her across the dance floor. Because that's what it would look like.

Then before Evie could lament further over the embarrassment she was about to endure, the duke stepped over and took her in his arms in preparation for their dance.

He was heat, muscle, and strength, and Evie was shocked to feel her nipples tightening in response. Her eyes flicked up to his, which were staring down at her with intensity burning in their depths. All thoughts of dancing and embarrassing herself fled as she became acutely aware of the man in front of her.

She felt petite and delicate in his strong arms, more aware of herself as a woman than she'd ever been. She took in a deep breath, trying to clear her befuddled head, but all she did was inhale the intoxicating smell of soap and a woodsy cologne coming from him. A smell Evie couldn't get enough of and had to resist leaning in closer to his neck to drink in more of it.

But then the musicians struck up the music, and Evie gulped, her hand tightening around Alex's. "I hope you're ready for a *very* fast dance." And with that, she braced herself before leading them into a dance that all but defied description, spinning them in circles around the room so quickly the people watching on became a blur.

Her slippers stepped on his boots multiple times, but she hoped given the speed they were dancing at he'd barely even notice.

A few moments later he gave her a wink. "I think I have the hang of it now." And with that, he took over leading them, his arms like steel bands as he effortlessly continued to twirl her across the room, keeping pace with the blistering tempo of the music.

Evie hung on to him for dear life, noticing that strangely enough other couples were joining them on the dance floor also trying to replicate the speed at which they were dancing. Some were having success managing to keep up, while others kept crashing into other couples.

They raced around the room until Evie's head was spinning. Then the music came to a blinding crescendo before descending into an abrupt finale, jolting all the dancing couples into a hasty finish. The duke, though, brought them to an elegant stop at the edge of the dance floor while the guests all erupted with applause. The new American dance was a seeming hit.

For a moment, Evie had to orientate herself to her surroundings, her head still dizzy from the speed they'd been swirling around at. Belatedly, she glanced around the room and realized she wasn't the only one who was dizzy. Several other dancers were wobbling through the crowd, their legs as unsteady as strawberry jelly, with many bumping into the other guests they passed.

Quite suddenly, Evie felt like laughing. How absurd they all must look. It was hilarious and ridiculous all at the same time. Many only followed her lead, thinking such a dance was all the fashion in America. It was nonsensical, but oh so typical of Society.

"It seems you've started a new trend," the duke said as he pulled her from the dance floor, his legs as steady as a rock. "Perhaps they should call *your* new dance the Gallop waltz."

"*My* new dance?" She gulped, her mirth vanishing instantly.

He grinned at her. "You didn't really think I believed any of that, did you?"

"I'd hoped you had," she mumbled. "Why did you go along with it, then? Didn't you worry we looked ludicrous out there?"

He shrugged his left shoulder. "I don't care what any of them think, but I was curious with how far you'd take your charade."

"Charade?" Suddenly, the corset of her gown felt as if it were tightening to the point of suffocation.

Oh God, he knew.

"Yes," he replied. "Obviously, you've spent more time with your paleontology books and studies instead of your dance instructors. Why not say so, rather than making up a story about the tempo changing for the Boston waltz? It's nothing to be ashamed of."

Swiftly, she found herself able to breathe again. *Thank goodness.* If that was all he thought her charade consisted of, she was safe, at least for the moment.

"In fact, I'm jealous you were allowed to," his deep voice whispered against her ear.

A frisson of delight curled its way through her

center at the rough timbre of his voice.

"My father was not so lenient," he continued. "He believed dancing all manner of dances was a requirement of being a duke. Accordingly, he made me practice with dance instructors daily whenever I was home for the holidays, whether I wanted to or not."

Evie cleared her throat lightly. "Well, you do dance admirably. You didn't miss a step, even when I stepped on your toes."

He laughed at that. "Luckily, you're light. In any event, I thank you for the dance. It was…entertaining." His eyes glanced over at several dancers still wobbling around at the edge of the dance floor. "One thing I'm curious about, though: if you don't waste your time dancing at balls, what other pursuits do you prefer, apart from studying fossils?"

"Reading. Observing others. Learning what I can of new concepts. There's far more things I'd prefer to do than attend a ball."

"In that we are alike. I can't stand balls myself, though given my position, I must attend them."

"Why must you?" she couldn't help but ask. "To keep up appearances?"

He shrugged lightly. "I suppose so. Although in this case I was rather corralled into hosting the darn thing by my aunt."

He grinned, and Evie couldn't help the answering grin on her own face.

"Yes, you were. Though you've made the countess happy by doing so."

"I imagine I did. I saved my aunt a great deal of blunt. That always makes the old dame happy."

"It's such a waste of money, isn't it?" Evie lamented. "Imagine if all of the dollars spent on not only this ball, but every other ball for the season were instead donated to the homeless and poor. What a difference that could make for so many lives…" Evie sighed. "It would change the very fabric of Society. Instead, wealth is hoarded by the wealthy or spent on entirely frivolous things with little going to those who need it."

"I must admit," the duke's voice rumbled, "I never would have guessed an American Dollar Princess, who herself is an heiress, would be aware of the plight of the poor."

"Do you mock me?"

"Not at all," he murmured. "In fact, it's a refreshing surprise."

"Yes, I'm full of surprises." If only he knew the extent of them.

"You do make a worthy point," he continued, "though I can't help but notice you're wearing a Worth gown, which would have cost more than the combined salary of probably all of my staff for an entire year."

She glanced down at the very dress he was talking of, which was shining brightly under the elaborate candelabras suspended from the high ceilings above. A dress she had been unable to do anything but admire since putting it on. "It's beautiful, isn't it?"

"Almost as beautiful as the woman wearing it."

She peered into his eyes for a hint of sarcasm, but she could barely discern any expression in his enigmatic gaze, let alone any derision. "You're right, of course. The amount spent on this dress was ridiculous and could have been put to far better uses."

"Do you often consider the injustices regarding the distribution of wealth when you attend balls?" he asked. "It seems a heavy topic for a young lady to consider."

"I must admit I do. All the time, in fact." There wasn't a ball Evie had been to where the thought didn't cross her mind of how much money was wasted by those who had it. She knew from first-hand experience how many struggled to make ends meet, herself included before she'd been rescued by the Thornton-Joneses.

Just thinking of her family in New York had a wave of guilt swamp her. If this charade was discovered, surely her aunt and uncle would regret ever bringing her into their lives.

"I must admit I've never had such a conversation about wealth and poverty with another lady before." The duke sounded surprised with his observation. "Your thoughts and honesty are a welcome change to the conversations I normally have."

Honesty. The word sent a chill through her.

Suddenly, the guilt and weight of the deception was crushing. Spying the doors leading to the terrace outside, Evie let go of the duke's hand. "I'm sorry, but I need some fresh air, if you will excuse me."

Disregarding his expression of bafflement, Evie pushed past him and fled to the doors. She needed the cold air and space away from the man's too-perceptive stare, because she got the sense that if she stayed any longer he'd see right through her charade. And he didn't strike her as a man to forgive easily.

CHAPTER TEN

Alex watched as Miss Thornton-Jones fled out onto the terrace, feeling oddly perplexed over what he'd said or done to cause such a hasty retreat.

What a contradiction she was. Wearing a gown and tiara that cost probably more than any other lady's outfit tonight, yet with the awareness of the hypocrisy of it all. A fascinating puzzle was what she was, and he loved nothing more than the challenge of unravelling a puzzle. A puzzle that had felt so bloody good in his arms, even if he had been whisking her around the dance floor more like they were running in circles instead of dancing a waltz.

He smiled even thinking about it. Then he started thinking of how soft, smooth, and silky she'd felt in his arms, to the point he'd wanted to continue dancing the next dance with her to feel her against him. Fortunately, sanity had prevailed, knowing two dances in a row would garner undeniable gossip about his interest in her. As much as he wanted to prove to Sam that the woman was determined to marry the highest title instead of the man behind it, he had no intention of getting stuck into a forced marriage himself.

After Julia had dashed all his tender feelings for love and happily ever afters, particularly given he'd dared to open his heart to her, after he'd thought it well and truly closed following his mother's scandal and betrayal, he'd sworn that he'd damn well never marry. A vow he wasn't going to forsake for any woman.

Regardless of the fact this woman had been playing havoc with his equilibrium ever since he'd laid eyes on her. If it wasn't for Sam's interest in her, he'd damn well stay well away, knowing instinctively that how he reacted to her physically, drawn to her as he was, was dangerous.

Even with Julia, he'd never experienced such a mixture of fascination bordering on obsession. It wasn't healthy, especially not for a man sworn off marriage.

He was tempted to follow the lady out to make sure she was all right, but he could already feel everyone's eyes on him, and he didn't wish to endure any further gossip. He'd had enough already over the years to last him a lifetime, and he had no intention of adding any more fuel to the fire.

"Duke, how good to see you."

Alex turned to the matronly voice on his left, glad for the reprieve from his thoughts. Claire's mother, Mrs. Gainsborough, was approaching him with a warm smile on her face, and she was accompanied by Alex's Aunt Mildred, George's mother, who as usual was sporting a displeased expression on her pinched countenance.

"Ladies." He bowed in greeting. "I hope you're both enjoying yourselves."

"Very much so," Mrs. Gainsborough gushed. "What a lovely thing it was watching you and Miss Thornton-Jones dance together. I haven't seen you dance at a ball in a long time, though it's no wonder you did tonight with such a lovely partner."

"If one could even call that *American gallop* a dance," his aunt Mildred added, her beady eyes glaring at him. "You do seem to be drawn to American women, dear nephew. Must run in your blood, given not only your first disastrous engagement but your mother's affair, too."

His jaw clenched tightly at the dig. He should be used to the witch's poisonous words by now. As much as he loved his cousin, his aunt by marriage was the complete opposite of her son. Where George was easygoing and affable, Aunt Mildred was anything but. Many said her sour disposition had caused Alex's uncle to flee into the arms of a mistress, where he'd succumbed to what was suspected to be a heart condition in the woman's bed, causing yet another scandal for the family.

He could still remember his father's anger over the whole situation and how he believed his brother's death had reflected poorly upon the dignity of the family name. Alex had been about sixteen at the time and had thought that at least his uncle had died happy, which was an achievement given the man had been married to Aunt Mildred.

Poor George had been devastated over his father's death, getting along with him far better than he did his mother, though that wasn't hard, given not many people liked her. Alex had often caught her gazing around his residence, almost as if she owned the place given Alex's loudly voiced declarations he'd never marry and George being his direct heir.

Ignoring his aunt completely, he turned his attention to Claire's mother, who was as sweet as his

aunt was sour. "I was simply doing my hosting du-
ties and dancing the first dance with her," Alex
answered to her initial observation. "Nothing more
and nothing less."

"That is a shame," Mrs. Gainsborough replied.
"For I do think you make a wonderful-looking
couple."

He couldn't help glancing over to where Miss
Thornton-Jones had disappeared, but she was nowhere to be seen. "Come, Mrs. Gainsborough, you
know my long-held stance on marriage. I have no
intention of being a couple with anyone, let alone
Miss Thornton-Jones."

"Yes, well, one can always hope for your happiness, despite your protestations otherwise." She
smiled softly over at him. "In any event, I suppose
Lord Brexton seems rather taken with the girl, and
they too make a lovely-looking couple." Her eyes
pointedly glanced to a spot on the other side of the
room.

Alex swung his gaze over to where she was
looking, and his fists clenched by his sides. Bloody
hell. Samuel was speaking with Miss Thornton-
Jones and laughing at something she'd said.

"He appears enamored with the girl. I wonder
what Agatha will think of such a development for
her son?" Aunt Mildred posed the question aloud,
her tone matching her pursed lips. "She probably
will regret sponsoring her, even though she's old
friends with the girl's family, for I doubt she'll want
Samuel to marry a Dollar Princess." She'd said the
term as if it pained her. "One would think we could
have a rest from them, given Society has been

inundated over the past two decades with such ladies seeking marriage and a title. I daresay this girl
is looking to follow in the tradition. Goodness, just
look at her smiling at Brexton. American ladies are
so bold, are they not?"

For a moment, he was going to berate her for
her prejudice over Miss Thornton-Jones's heritage,
but then he realized that was exactly how he had
treated her, too. The realization was uncomfortable,
but then she smiled at something Sam said, and a
bitter sensation akin to jealousy rose in his throat.

The two of them seemed to be enjoying themselves thoroughly. Clearly Miss Thornton-Jones
was determined to entrap his cousin. Why else
would she smile such a radiant smile at Sam? His
poor cousin wouldn't stand a chance against such a
weapon.

Damn, Sam did appear happy speaking with
her. But what man wouldn't be happy in her presence? Alex wanted his cousin to be happy above
all else, but he knew such happiness wouldn't last.
How could it if a marriage was based on the pre-
tension of love, when love was merely an illusion?

An illusion that still had the ability to wound
deeply with its invisible barbs.

Barbs Alex still felt even after nearly ten years
since catching Julia cheating on him. He would
save Sam from such wounds that could never fully
be healed; Sam was far too kind and not strong
enough emotionally to be able to live with such
pain as Alex could.

There was no option but for Alex to speed up
his plans to unmask Miss Thornton-Jones for the

title hunter she was. He'd have to do so tonight, too, before Sam became even further entranced and really did start to believe his lofty assertions that he was in love.

Because Alex knew the harsh reality of it: love was an illusion and only a fool believed it to be anything but.

And when he saw Sam point out the far doors that led to Alex's fossil collection to Miss Thornton-Jones, before Sam turned and began to make his way through the crowd toward the refreshment table while the lady headed through the doors, Alex saw his opportunity.

CHAPTER ELEVEN

Evie really hadn't expected to enjoy the ball so much, but she couldn't deny the fun she was having as Samuel made her laugh telling the many stories of the adventures he, Alex, and George used to have as boys.

He was so different to his taciturn cousin.

Dancing with Alex had felt physical, with every single brush of his hands or fingers against hers burning with intensity. Every whisper of his breath sending shivers of delight through her body. Whereas she felt none of that with Samuel, merely that it felt pleasant to be talking to such an entertaining gentleman, rather than being interrogated as it felt like the duke did with her.

Glancing out of the corner of her eye, she spotted the man himself talking with two women, one who was staring at her with a particularly frosty glare and an even haughtier expression on her sour face. She was dressed finely, in a gown of deep burgundy with black lace woven through the bodice and skirts that complemented the pale complexion of her skin and regal bearing.

"Who are those women talking to the duke?" she asked Sam.

Sam looked over to Alex and frowned. Probably the first frown Evie had seen the man wear.

"The one with the smile on her face is Claire's mother, Mrs. Gainsborough. The other, with the pinched mouth, is George's mother, and my aunt Mildred."

Evie raised her brow. "You don't like her?"

Sam's expression softened. "It's that obvious, is it?"

"Completely. From this distance, she certainly doesn't appear as congenial as George is and seems to be glaring at me with daggers."

"That's because she's a rather mean-spirited woman, I'm afraid, and you were dancing with Alex before," Sam said.

"Why would she care if I danced with the duke?"

Sam screwed up his face, seemingly weighing up what to tell her. "I daresay it might have concerned her, given she believes the dukedom will eventually be inherited by her son. She worries over anything that might threaten that."

"How does my dancing with Alex affect George's inheritance?"

"It doesn't, except for the fact that Alex *doesn't* dance at balls, period. Given he's made an exception with you tonight, I daresay that's invited a lot of speculation from everyone."

"He was simply being polite dancing with me because your mother asked him to. If one could even call what we were doing a dance," she mumbled the last part under her breath.

"Alex doesn't care if he's polite or not." Sam was peering at her with an odd expression, and Evie started to feel slightly unsettled with the look. "You know he hasn't danced at a ball since he was engaged to Julia."

"He hasn't?" Ten years was a long time. "He must have loved her to be so devastated by her betrayal."

"He was hurt, there's no denying that, but I don't think he truly loved her. In any event, I'm glad he may be opening his heart up again."

Panic welled up in her throat. "He's doing no such thing. At least not with me."

"I didn't mean to alarm you," Sam placated. "I suppose I'm hopeful he can find happiness."

"Is that why you're feigning an interest in me?"

Now it was Sam who appeared panicked. "What do you mean?"

Evie smiled at him. "I've noticed you paying me particular attention when the duke is close by, in a far more pronounced way to the attention you're paying me now, which is more like that of a friend."

He cringed, and a sheepish expression grew on his face. "You're insightful."

"Just observant," she replied. "But if you're trying to make him jealous, it won't work. He's made it plain what he thinks of me, and of my American heritage, and it's not complimentary."

"He is stubborn," Sam admitted. "He had to be, to achieve all of his father's exacting standards, or he'd be punished."

"Claire did mention a little of that. Was he really that hard on Alex?"

"My uncle was merciless to the point of cruelty. Alex actually enjoyed when school started each term, because it meant he didn't have to live with his father and be subjected to the man's punishments with a whip when Alex didn't perform as he should."

Evie gasped. "His father sounds like he was a monster."

"I hate to say it, but he was. My mother tells me he got worse after Alex's mother ran off with an American man. Poor Alex already had to deal with his mother abandoning him, to then have to contend with a father he could never please. He didn't have an easy run of it."

Her heart broke for the young boy that Alex had been.

"He's kept himself closed off from everyone, even George and I to a certain extent." Sam sighed. "Instead, burying his head in books and collecting fossils, at least when his father wasn't looking. I think it's been far easier for Alex to love fossils and history rather than an actual person."

Books had been Evie's salvation, too. It was far safer to immerse oneself in them, instead of the cruel and harsh realities of the world. "That I can understand."

"Shall I fetch you a drink? Perhaps a lemonade or champagne?" he asked, his eyes glancing beyond her for a moment.

"A lemonade would be lovely," Evie said, making certain to elongate the vowels in the word lemonade in her continued attempt at an American accent. An attempt that she was getting better at the more she spoke, though would no doubt be completely ruined if she combined having to put on an accent with drinking alcohol.

Sam nodded. "I shall be back shortly. If you'd like to see Alex's collection of fossils while you wait, they're housed in his gallery, which is a large room through that doorway and down the end of the corridor." He pointed to a doorway behind her. "Alex won't mind, trust me."

"I can wait for you, if you prefer."

"No, go ahead. I've seen them many times, unfortunately," he mumbled. "And it will take me a while to navigate through the throng of the crowd to get to the refreshment table. I shall bring your drink into the gallery."

"All right, then," Evie said with a smile. She'd much prefer seeing a collection of fossils, than having to wait at the side of a cloying and stuffy ballroom. She'd get into far less trouble looking at fossils than pretending to be an heiress in front of this crowd.

CHAPTER TWELVE

Alex began weaving his way through to the same hallway Miss Thornton-Jones had disappeared down, suddenly eager to implement his plan to save his cousin. Because that's all this was, a way of saving Sam from heartache.

Coming to a halt at an intersecting corridor, he glanced down toward the end of the hall where his collection was housed, and as expected, he saw Miss Thornton-Jones disappearing inside its doorway.

Just perfect, particularly as no one at the ball would ever bother to venture down this way to view his collection, which most considered extremely boring and unworthy of their interest. Most people didn't have any taste, in Alex's opinion. Though that obviously didn't include Miss Thornton-Jones, whose interest in fossils rivaled his own and was now going to present him with the ideal opportunity to show Sam exactly how interested the lady also was in Alex's title, too.

He had to suppress the surge of guilt he suddenly felt at the thought of hurting his cousin, particularly given he'd seemed to take a marked interest in the lady, a bit more than he usually did. However, the short-term pain of realizing the woman was only after a title would be nothing compared to the pain Sam would suffer if Alex did nothing.

Pausing at the threshold of the open doors to his gallery, Alex breathed in the smell of wood and eucalyptus that permeated the room. The space had originally been used by his mother as her salon and sitting area, until Alex had had some builders knock out the walls to make one giant space, which he'd then happily transformed into his own mini museum to house all the fossils he'd collected and found over the years.

It was a room that now brought with it contentment instead of the bitter memories of having spent time visiting his mother here when he was a boy. Visits he'd adored as a child, when she'd lavish him with hugs and praise, telling him how she loved him and he was her little man, but in retrospect were just fanciful memories, given her actions of running off with another man, leaving him alone with his father, never to return.

No mother could have loved her son as much as his mother claimed to have loved him, only to leave him in the hands of such a cruel taskmaster, whom Alex could never please, no matter how hard he tried to. If his mother had loved him like she'd said she did, she would have kept her fervent promise she'd made to him on that day she left, and she would have returned for him. But she never did. And never would, not after a pneumonia had taken her life when Alex had been eighteen.

Though he hadn't found out about her death until the following year when he'd returned from college for the summer break and his father had offhandedly told him of her passing, not even bothering to send word of it when he'd received notification of her death himself, six months prior. Not that that fact had surprised Alex. His father had been a cruel bastard, relishing in his faithless wife's death, as he'd called her repeatedly over the years.

Shaking his head free from the memories, Alex's eyes sought out Miss Thornton-Jones and immediately spotted her on the far-left side of the room, her blue ballgown standing out like a brilliant star. She was staring in fascination at the specimen in front of her that was hanging on a wall, framed in a large glass casing. There was such wonder on her face that not for the first time Alex was himself fascinated by the specimen she presented.

He wanted to study her, to observe her, to know all there was to know about what was going on inside that beautiful head of hers. The depth of his curiosity surprised him. Most women were open books in his opinion, but not this lady. No. There were layers and secrets she was keeping that Alex knew he had to unearth.

Unable to resist the pull she had on him, he walked across the room to where she was standing, and he couldn't help but smile when he heard the little sounds of wonder she was making upon seeing the fossil, even going so far as to murmur aloud to the specimen, telling it how marvelous it was. The fact made his smile deepen. He often spoke to them himself, thinking he was odd for doing so, but given they were such amazing specimens, he usually couldn't help himself. And here she was doing the same, completely oblivious to the fact she wasn't alone.

"I see you found my gallery."

She spun round, her hands going up to her chest in surprise. "Oh my goodness, you scared me!"

"I didn't mean to." He glanced past her to the exhibit she'd been marveling over. "It's wonderful, isn't it?" Housed inside the large glass casing was the fossilized foot of some ancient creature. "I believe it to be some form of primitive lizard."

She spun back around to face the specimen, and her eyes shone in reverence. "It's amazing! I see going off the description of the card you found this one yourself on your estate. How incredible of you to have discovered and excavated such a specimen."

For some reason, her praise had him eager to hear more of what she thought about the find. "It was remarkable. I can still remember the excitement I felt when I first uncovered a hint of the remnant, and the more I carefully excavated the rock from around it, the more I realized just how remarkable it truly was. When I traveled to Washington the other year, I took a photograph of it and showed it to the head of paleontology at the Smithsonian Institute, Mr. Tibs, who had never seen another like it before. Indeed, he believes it is one of a kind, undiscovered anywhere else, at least to his knowledge."

Her mouth dropped open. "You've been to the Smithsonian Institute? Oh my! Was it as marvelous visiting there as I imagine it would've been? Did you know it is the largest museum in the world, with the largest collection of fossils, too?" She sighed heartily. "It's always been a dream of mine to go there one day."

Alex furrowed his brows. "You haven't been?"

"Not yet." She smiled softly over at him.

He found her admission odd. He'd never met a lady in her position that wouldn't have insisted on a trip, especially given her parents' wealth. "I would have thought a lady with your interest in such things would visit there regularly, considering New York is not far from Washington."

Her mouth clamped shut, and she spun back around to face the fossil. "Yes, well, I haven't been yet, um, because my parents don't believe such pursuits are at all appropriate."

"That I can understand," he murmured, thinking back to the many times his own father had belittled him for his interest in the subject. To a man like his father, a future duke should be interested in horses, the management of his estates, and improving upon the farming practices of his tenants to increase the wealth of the family, and all in that order, too, without any room for deviation. "Let's just say my father wasn't amenable to my interest in studying such topics, either."

She bit her lip, and a jolt of pure lust shot through him as the image of him taking those cherry-red lips of hers in between his own lips ran rampant in his head. Would she murmur in delight from his kiss, as she had simply from seeing the fossil? Would her breath quicken and her pulse race as he touched her like he longed to?

Even the thought of pulling her into his arms, his hands cupping around her buttocks and pressing her close against him, had his cock stirring to attention. Damn, he'd be in trouble if he didn't control his unruly imaginings.

He cleared his throat roughly and twisted to the side, stalking over to one of the other specimens he'd collected after the lizard foot. "I found this fragment of spine, not long after the foot. It belongs to the same creature."

Her soft footfalls were light on the rug, but he heard her approach nonetheless. Hell, she could have floated in the air over to him, and he'd still know she was close. Whether that was from her fragrant rose scent or because his whole body seemed to be aware of her physical presence on a level that he'd never thought possible, he didn't know. But what he did know without a doubt was that he'd be able to pick her out of a crowd blindfolded, such was the reaction he felt in her presence, almost as if his skin could sense she was near and burned in proximity to her.

"It's amazing," she murmured in wonder as she came up next to him and stared at the ancient, fossilized remains of a creature long since dead.

No woman had ever shown such an interest before in his discoveries, or at least had done such a convincing job of feigning to, which had to be what she was doing. Otherwise, she seemed damned near perfect, and no woman was ever that. No, most women had an ulterior motive, which was exactly the thought he needed to remember as to what he was doing in here in the first place.

"Why do you frown so much?" she asked, and the question floored him.

"Do I?"

She nodded earnestly. "Yes. You smile and then you suddenly frown, and regularly, too, in my presence. I find myself often confused by your expressions."

She wasn't the only one. "I both smile and frown when I'm with you because you perplex me greatly. It is I who am confused in your presence."

"Why should you be confused when you're with me?"

"Because all I can think about is kissing you."

For the second time her mouth dropped open and her lips formed a little *O*. "I thought you wanted to throttle me, not kiss me."

He couldn't help the chuckle that left his mouth. "That, too, but I mostly want to kiss you."

"That's entirely inappropriate." She gulped and opened her mouth to say something further but then closed it again and pressed her lips together tightly.

"It might be inappropriate, but it's the truth," he replied. "Can you honestly say you haven't thought about what it would feel like to kiss me? To have me hold you in my arms and press you against me?"

She gasped. "Again, that's an inappropriate conversation to be having, Your Grace!"

"Don't you want me to kiss you? To feel my lips upon yours?" Alex knew he was pushing the edges of decency and that of being a gentleman, but this woman did something to him that had all good sense fleeing and he couldn't help himself. He wanted to see her reaction, needed to see it, almost as much as he was beginning to need to feel the sweet softness of her skin beneath his hands. "Haven't you at all imagined me kissing you?"

Crossing her hands over her chest, she shot him the crankiest expression he'd seen on her face. "No, I have not."

The wild pulse just below her jawline suggested otherwise.

He leaned down, close to her ear, and satisfaction surged through him when he saw her light shiver in response. "Liar," he whispered.

CHAPTER THIRTEEN

Of course, she was lying, but what else could she do when her body was begging her to close the distance between her lips and his, while her head was telling her to run as fast as she could for the wide-open door?

Instead, she stood her ground and boldly raised her chin up to stare at the man creating absolute havoc upon her senses. "What is it you want from me, Duke? You're an extremely attractive man, one can't deny that, but if you expect me to compromise my morals to see what it feels like to kiss you, and thus prove true your silly assumption that all American women are alike, then you've severely underestimated me."

"Alex."

"Excuse me?"

"I want you to call me Alex, not Duke or Your Grace, but Alex." His eyes never left hers, hot and intense as they almost seemed to be cataloging her soul. "I want to hear my name on your lips, especially when I see the satisfaction in your eyes after I kiss you."

The burning heat in his gaze was more intense than Evie had ever experienced, and her breath caught in her throat. She'd never been kissed by a man before, not even one little peck, and suddenly she wondered if this would be her only chance to ever feel what it was like when a man pressed his lips against hers. And not just any man, but this infuriatingly annoying yet ridiculously handsome man in front of her. A duke who wanted to kiss her.

Licking her suddenly dry lips, she watched in fascination as Alex's own eyes were drawn to the movement, and a small groan left his lips at the action.

Power, unlike anything she'd felt before, surged through her. He might be playing some sort of game with her, but he couldn't disguise the true desire she could see flaring from his eyes. The yearning all but radiating from him as he stared mesmerized at her mouth.

Could she be so bold as to let him kiss her? They were alone, with little chance of anyone coming upon them. Perhaps just this once she could be brave, instead of worrying about the consequences? Live in the moment, as it were.

"Can you feel this passion between us?" His voice was gruff as he dragged his eyes back to hers. "This energy that won't go away but instead gets stronger the more I see you, the more time I spend in your company. My head might be telling me you're trouble, but my body doesn't care, and it's burning for you regardless of how unsuitable you are."

His voice was hypnotic, and her body swayed toward his, but then his actual words penetrated the haze of passion he was stirring inside her. "You think I'm trouble and unsuitable?" Her voice raised noticeably on the last word, her anger starting to grow, with her only just managing to continue speaking with an American accent. "But you want to kiss me anyhow? How dare you insult me so, you rotten swine! How's that for a name instead of Alex?"

She swiveled around to stalk from the room, but his hand reached out and grabbed her upper arm.

"Don't go. Please."

The very touch of his bare fingers on the skin of her arm was enough to stop her in her tracks, let alone his forlorn plea. "Why?" Twisting her head back to his, she glared at him, noting the blue of his eyes was tinged with flecks of gray. "So you can insult me more, all the while pretending you want to kiss me?"

"I'm not pretending about wanting to kiss you." His voice was a gravelly whisper. "Do you think I like feeling like this when I'm with you? Feeling as if I can barely control myself? Feeling so totally comfortable with you and yet so totally at your mercy, so completely vulnerable and almost obsessed by your very presence?" He dropped his hand and took in a deep breath. "Well, I don't, but I can't seem to help myself." He suddenly seemed so despondent at his own confession of weakness.

Evie didn't know what came over her, but there was such a depth of vulnerability in his eyes, an anguish she knew he'd buried deep inside himself after being constantly betrayed by the women he'd loved, that for a moment, all she wanted to do was soothe away his hurt, rid him of his distress, promise him that she'd never hurt him like the other women had.

She took a step over to him and picked up his hand, bringing it to her chest near to where she imagined her heart was. His eyes latched onto hers, almost desperately, and Evie felt lost in the blue depths of them.

They stood there, staring at each other for what felt an eternity, but most likely had only been seconds. Never had she felt so drawn to a man before. Never had she wanted to be kissed as desperately as she suddenly wanted this man to kiss her.

As if sensing her thoughts, he drew his mouth inexorably closer to her own, until it was but a breath away. Everything faded into the distance, except this man in front of her and the feelings he conjured inside her.

Desire, anticipation, a thrilling wantonness she'd never thought to feel.

Not her, not sensible Yvette Jenkins who always did as she was told. Always followed directions. Never spoke out of turn. But in this moment, she didn't want to be sensible. She wanted one moment where she could be wild, and just be. Feel what it was to be kissed by a man that drew her to him like a flame drew in the oxygen and then consumed it.

Not knowing where the courage came from, Evie leaned over and pressed her lips against his. She was hit with such a blinding force of pleasure. His lips were so soft, yet hard and delicious, and oh, how she wanted more.

He groaned and wrapped his arms around her, his mouth slanting over hers, gently parting her lips with his, nibbling and teasing at the edges, until Evie moaned and wound her arms around his neck. She had to have more of him. She pressed her chest to his own, and her hands smoothed down behind the muscles of his shoulders, marveling at the sheer strength and breadth of him.

Then he touched his tongue to hers, and a white-hot desire swept through her.

"Oh God, you taste delicious," he mumbled against her mouth as his hands travelled lower and cupped her buttocks.

She gasped as the hot, hard length of him pressed against her belly, sending a shaft of wanton pleasure down her body to the center of her womanhood, which began to throb in reply.

His lips began to feast on hers again, soft yet so exquisitely thorough in their exploration of her mouth that Evie felt like melting into a puddle on the floor. If this was what it felt like to be kissed, no wonder so many women dreamed of it. She tried to protest when his lips left hers, but then he began trailing them down her neck, and shivers of delight cascaded down her entire spine.

"Does that feel good?" he asked between kisses.

"Oh god yes, Alex, it does." She could barely pant out the words as her body continued to be wracked with pleasure.

"Say my name again," he roughly whispered, pulling back to stare at her, his eyes heavy with passion.

"Alex…" she replied, and his eyes darkened at the sound, his lips finding her own again with a groan of contentment.

Time lost all meaning for Evie as he kissed her more thoroughly and expertly than she'd ever dreamed possible. Her own tongue mimicked his, flicking and stroking, in a frenzy of heat and desire.

Alex groaned, his shaft hardening against her even more.

It was so wicked and wanton, and oh how she wanted more from him, so much more.

Gradually, almost as if from a great distance, she heard some gasps and the echo of people talking. Before she could even comprehend what was happening, Alex wrenched his lips from hers and took a hasty step backward. Her body reeled at the loss of heat, and belatedly she blinked, her gaze slowly focusing back on her surroundings instead of the man in front of her. Her heart dropped down to her toes at the tableau in front of her.

Standing there was not only Sam, but his mother the countess, along with Claire, her mother Mrs. Gainsborough, and George's mother, Mildred. A group of five, all staring at Evie and Alex with varying degrees of shock and surprise on their faces at having walked in on her and Alex in a completely compromising position of being plastered all over each other. Mortification flooded her with the knowledge.

"God damn it," Alex muttered under his breath as he dragged a hand through his hair, his gaze swinging wildly between the others, then back over to Evie. "Did you plan this?"

"Plan this?" she asked, confusion swamping her with his accusation. "What are you talking about?"

"Come now, both of you, it seems the jig is up, as they say," the countess said, taking charge as she stepped forward between them and shot both Alex and Evie a pointed glare. "Obviously, you shall have to announce your engagement now, instead of waiting until later tonight as you'd originally planned to."

Engagement? What was the countess talking about? Had the kiss completely rattled Evie to the point of her losing her mind? "I don't understand…"

"Of course you do, my dear," the countess said brusquely. "You and my nephew had been planning to surprise everyone with news of your engagement later tonight, but given young love and the fact you both clearly couldn't keep your hands off each other, the duke can announce your engagement now. Can't you, Alex?"

The lady turned the full force of her glare onto her nephew, her eyes all but daring him to contradict her.

As the haze of passion well and truly subsided, Evie started to slowly comprehend what was going on. The countess was trying to save her reputation from having been caught in a truly compromising position, but she needed Alex and Evie to go along with the ruse, to convince the others. But that ruse itself meant she would be engaged to the Duke of Hargrave. The knowledge was like a blow to her solar plexus, and a bitter and vile nausea rose in her throat, threatening to spill out.

Oh no. What had she done?

CHAPTER FOURTEEN

It was his worst nightmare come true.

For the second time in his life, for all intents and purposes, Alex found himself engaged to another Dollar Princess. Fuck. What had he been thinking when embarking on such a reckless idea as to kiss her? He hadn't been thinking, and that was the crux of the problem when it came to how Miss Thornton-Jones affected him to the point of lunacy.

How could he have been so stupid to get swept up in the moment of kissing and tasting her? So swept up he hadn't even heard five people walking into the gallery and stumbling upon them.

Stupid. Stupid. Stupid.

There was no other way to describe his actions that had led down this path of finding himself un-avoidably engaged after vowing never to be again. And to another American heiress surely only here to hunt for a title, contrary to her protestations.

Then again, what the hell had Sam been doing, bringing others with him to join Miss Thornton-Jones? The very action of him doing so inadvertently ensured Alex's forced engagement to the woman. The truth stood glaringly obvious. Sam had been bringing chaperones with him, as he was a bloody gentleman and had wanted to maintain the proprieties and ensure he wasn't caught alone with Miss Thornton-Jones. Alex should have con-sidered that in his assessment of the situation.

Instead, he'd been like a bull in a china shop, full steam ahead, trying to show Sam that Miss Thornton-Jones was here in England for one thing and one thing only: to marry a title. Now, through Alex's own stupidity and loss of control, she was damn well going to be a duchess. His duchess. Damn it all to hell and back.

As much as he wanted to rage at them all that he wouldn't marry her, how could he not when he had most definitely compromised her? Fuck, he was still semi-aroused after touching her and caressing the softness of her lips and inner mouth. She'd felt more delicious than any other delicacy he'd ever tasted, and he hadn't been able to get enough of her. Hadn't wanted to stop, and still wanted more.

Something had to be wrong with him to feel like this even after the woman had successfully trapped him into an engagement. Not that he could blame her for what had transpired, as much as he wanted to. It had been his fault and his alone. He was the one who'd followed her into the gallery, determined to unmask her purpose. He was the one who'd suggested a kiss, hoping Sam would catch them. And he was the one who'd been so damn intoxicated by the taste of her that he'd been completely oblivious to their surroundings, directly leading to their being caught in such a position. The truth of it was he could blame nobody for his terrible judgment except himself, and now he was going to have to deal with the direct consequences of such a lapse.

"Alex?" his aunt prompted, her gaze swinging

between him and his supposed new fiancée. "You were going to announce your engagement to Miss Thornton-Jones, were you not?"

He cleared his throat and nodded. "Yes, indeed, Aunt Agatha."

Perhaps one day he'd be able to look back and laugh at himself. Laugh at God's cruel joke of finding himself once again engaged, and to another American heiress, of all things. Laugh at how his noble plan to save Sam from a loveless marriage had spectacularly backfired and instead turned into his own macabre future.

Glancing over to Miss Thornton-Jones, or rather Aimee, as he probably should start calling her in his head, given they were engaged, he noticed she seemed even more shocked with the unfolding events than he was. Her already porcelain skin had gone deathly pale, and her crystal-blue eyes, normally bright with curiosity, were stark with nothing short of terror shining in their depths.

Nice to know he had such an effect on her.

Though her appearance was odd given Alex would have thought she'd be over the moon with such a turn of events, considering she couldn't have made a better match than to marry a duke. Her reaction was puzzling. Although if it was as she'd told him many times, that she really didn't have any intention to marry, then it was the sort of reaction to be expected.

But he hadn't believed her protestations, and still didn't, not really. What American Dollar Princess sent to England by her parents wasn't here hunting a titled husband? None so far, in Alex's experience.

"That is wonderful news," the countess continued, a smile stretching across her face. "I expect you will be announcing your engagement shortly to the gathered assembly."

"Of course." Alex could only agree, the thought of being engaged causing his whole body to tighten in discomfort. He imagined his aunt would be pleased with herself for engineering the match while saving her charge from disgrace. The darn woman had always pestered him to marry, regardless of his denials of wishing to do so. But Alex really only had himself to blame. It was he who had lost control.

"Yes, congratulations," Sam said, sounding surprisingly happy for someone who had only recently professed to be in love with the woman Alex was now engaged to.

Alex turned to his cousin, his eyes narrowing. "Did you know I followed Miss Thornton-Jones in here?"

"I had no idea, cousin." Sam shook his head, the champagne from the two glasses in his hands spilling slightly onto the floor with the action. "How could I have predicted you would do that?"

Suddenly, Alex had a sneaking suspicion that this accidental interruption wasn't so accidental at all.

"There'll be time enough to discuss this later," his aunt Agatha said. "But first you must announce this most joyous news of your engagement to everyone! Come along, the two of you." She grabbed first his arm and then Aimee's, much like she would schoolchildren, before starting to march them out of the room toward the ballroom.

And Alex let her. He'd screwed up, regardless of possibly Sam's involvement in the matter, and now it was time to face the consequences. Consequences he couldn't escape.

He was engaged to another Dollar Princess, and there wasn't a thing he could do to stop it.

CHAPTER FIFTEEN

Pulling her cloak in tighter against her chest, trying to ward off the chill of the night air, Evie rapped her knuckles once again on one of the windows of Alex's study. It was a long shot that he was still up, but she'd thought it best to try speaking to him this way rather than seek an audience through his butler, especially given it was five in the morning and she was alone.

Not the usual way to visit one's fiancé, but when one was desperate to sort out the mess of a completely unwanted engagement, drastic measures were warranted.

The ball had wrapped up earlier than anticipated, given their shock announcement, with Evie feigning a headache shortly after as she'd been unable to stand the thought of smiling and pretending to be happy with the turn of events when she was anything but. However, after she'd returned back to the countess's residence and had started truly understanding the ramifications of the night, she knew she had to do something to avert the disaster.

Given that before she'd departed with the countess, she'd heard Alex grumble about drowning his sorrows with a good bottle of whiskey in his study for the remainder of the evening, she'd made her way back to the duke's residence, hoping he was still in his study. Even if he was asleep in there, surely her knocks on the window would wake him.

If not, then she'd have to march around to the front of his residence and bang on the door.

Not an ideal scenario, but it was imperative she speak with Alex, especially now that the shock of the surprise engagement had finally worn off and she'd come up with a sound plan to fix things. And fix things she absolutely had to; there was no other option.

Which meant she had to convince him of her plan. That shouldn't be too difficult given he hadn't seemed at all thrilled with finding himself engaged to her, a mild description of his reaction. Goodness, when they'd all returned to the ballroom and he'd announced their engagement to the assembled guests, it was like he'd been reciting a eulogy at a funeral, such was his level of enthusiasm.

Everyone had clapped, of course, and the congratulations flowed in fast and thick after, though Evie had seen the greedy speculation in all their eyes, almost like they could smell a whiff of a scandal and were eager to pounce upon it. A scandal was the last thing she needed.

Raising her fist back up to the window, she pounded on the glass again, louder this time. Still nothing. Well, she'd just have to go and wake his butler. As she spun around in the shrubbery, she heard the window open, and a deep voice swear.

Good, he was awake.

"What the devil are you doing out here?" Alex poked his head out the window, glancing around into the still darkness of the early morning. "And you're on your own? Have you completely lost all good sense, woman?"

Evie glared back at him. "I had to speak with you. Now, will you help me through the window so I can?"

He swore again, though she couldn't make out the gabble of expletives he was muttering as he reached his hands down and assisted to lift her through the opening and into his study. She grabbed his shoulders and steadied herself on her feet. Instantly, the memories from last night slammed into her, and she was reminded with infinite clarity of just how she'd come to be in such a predicament in the first place: being in his arms while he kissed her senseless.

His sharp intake of breath suggested he, too, was remembering exactly what they'd been up to only a few hours ago. Taking in a shaky gulp of air, Evie walked around him and into the center of his study. It was a deeply masculine space, with two oversize, dark brown leather lounges in the center, with a green-and-blue Persian rug between them. Dominating the left side of the room was an overly large, walnut-colored wood desk, and opposite that was a large fireplace, the embers inside glowing a dull orange and casting bits of light and shadow across the mostly dark room.

Striding over to the hearth, she grabbed the poker and nudged the coals back to life, then took some wood from the small pile against the brick and tossed a few logs onto the flames. Growing up, the hearth had been the only thing to save her and her aunt on many a freezing winter's night, the sort of night that chilled one to the bone, as only the frigid English weather could. Letting such a fire die down to nothing was a fool's choice. She spread her hands in front of the gradually growing flames and warmed her cold hands.

"Very industrious of you," Alex said from somewhere behind her. "Though the servants usually stoke the hearth when they wake."

She shrugged. "I'm cold, and one shouldn't let a fire die down, not when so many don't have the luxury of one."

"You are quite the reformer, aren't you?" He quirked his brow. "However, I feel it only pertinent to point out that you probably wouldn't be cold if you hadn't traipsed back here at such an hour, now would you?" He walked over and stood next to her. "How did you get here, anyhow?"

"I walked. I couldn't very well wake the countess and ask to borrow her carriage to come and see you."

He swore loudly, stalking over to the side table and pouring himself a drink.

"Isn't it a bit early to be drinking?" she couldn't help but observe.

"When it comes to you, no." He took a lengthy gulp of the liquid. "But if you must know, it's water."

"Oh."

"Yes, indeed." He shook his head and sighed. "How did you even find the place, let alone not get lost walking through London on your own? I'm surprised you weren't set upon by ruffians."

"In Mayfair, Your Grace? Please," she scoffed. "This is one of the safest areas of London. There was no risk in me dashing down a few blocks from the countess's residence to your own." If only he knew how she'd walked around far worse streets and areas of London when she'd been younger, he'd be even more shocked. This short walk, with her cloak covering her so she could blend into the shadows as her aunt Beth had taught her, along with a kitchen knife in her pocket, had been akin to an afternoon stroll in the park.

Thinking of her aunt Beth brought back with it the heartache she always felt. Her aunt had been more of a mother to Evie than anyone, given she'd looked after her since her parents' deaths when she was only a baby. Being back in London was a blatant reminder of where Evie had come from and of what she wanted to forget.

Shaking her head free from the memories, she focused her attention back onto the man in front of her, whose eyes were narrowed upon her own, questions rife in their depths.

"What was so important you had to see me at this hour? Are you wanting to rush an early marriage by being caught alone with me again?"

"Goodness no," she exclaimed. "That's the last thing I want."

"In that at least we are agreed," he grumbled, taking another sip of his water before striding over to the oversize lounge and sinking his frame down onto the cushions of it. "So? What was so urgent you risked life and limb to speak with me?"

She couldn't help but roll her eyes. "Whoever thought women were more dramatic than men clearly needs to meet you." She walked over and stood at the back of the other lounge facing across from him. She wasn't quite ready to sit in his presence. Not with the restless energy swarming through her. Taking in a deep breath, she stared at him for a moment, as much to gather her courage as to assess his reaction to what she was about to propose. "Contrary to what you might believe, I really *cannot* marry you."

"Are you already married, then?"

The question nearly rendered her speechless. "No, of course not. I wouldn't have kissed you if I had been."

He laughed at that, though there was little humor in the sound. "Forgive me, my dear Aimee, but many married women do."

"Well, then, shame on you for kissing them back." She raised her chin and eyed him with censure, even though it was she who was feeling shame at hearing him call her by her cousin's name. This masquerade was getting beyond uncomfortable; it was starting to become unbearable. How was she meant to do it for another five weeks? Especially if he was going to start calling her Aimee. "You really shouldn't use my first name, either. It's not proper."

This time, the laughter that burst from his mouth seemed entirely genuine. "I think we're well beyond the proprieties now, my dear, given how our engagement came about."

"Perhaps," she grumbled, supposing she'd just have to get used to it, as much as she might hate her cousin's name coming from his lips. It reminded her too much of the charade she was partaking in. "In any event, let's return to our main topic of conversation."

"Ah, yes," he said, leaning back against the lounge, stretching one of his arms out along its length. "Why you can't marry me."

It was then she noticed how he was dressed, without a jacket or tie, or even a waistcoat for that matter. He'd unbuttoned several of the top buttons of his white shirt, exposing some of the dark chest hair beneath, and had rolled up his sleeves, revealing the rippling strength of his forearms that the material had hidden.

Good lord, the man was a living Adonis. So finely chiseled and cut to perfection that Evie had to wonder if God was playing a joke on her, showing her the perfection of a male, but one she could never truly touch or possess. If he realized who she was, an orphaned and illegitimate cousin to Aimee, and one who was lying to his face about her identity, he'd throw her out on her backside as quick as he could, and he wouldn't look back.

Perhaps that was being slightly unfair to the man, but when had life ever really been fair to her? The only time it had was when the Thornton-Jones family had taken her in, but that was about the extent of it. She doubted someone who was born and raised a duke would at all take kindly to being deceived about who she really was. None of them would. Not that Evie could blame them when she herself regretted ever saying yes to her cousin in the first place. Damn Aimee for being so convincing.

"Well then, are you going to tell me why you can't marry me?" the duke asked, his deep voice sending a jolt of awareness through her.

Oh God, not again. She couldn't let her attraction to him distract her from her purpose. "We just can't."

"A bold assertion given we were found in a completely compromising situation together not even six hours past."

Evie pressed her lips together, firming her resolve against his rather dismissive attitude and her body's ridiculous response to him. "I'm not a fool nor am I naive enough not to realize the difficult position we find ourselves in, one that generally only a marriage would save. However, I have a compromise, one I think you'll find agreeable given you have no wish to marry me, either."

"I'm so eager to hear it." The sarcasm was all but dripping from his voice as he leaned forward in the chair, bracing his elbows on his knees as his fingers rested under his chin. "What is this compromise you are proposing?"

"That we pretend to be engaged," she rushed out the words. There, she'd said it. Now all she had to do was convince him. "I'm due to return to America in about five weeks. Obviously, after last night, if we don't play the part of being engaged, my trip will be ruined as I would be shunned by English Society."

"True."

"Which means I won't be able to go anywhere, and your aunt would be placed in an extremely awkward position as my host and chaperone. But if we pretend to be engaged, then Society will be happy, and I won't be bothered by any fortune hunters. Then when it comes time for me to leave, I shall cry off and return to America, with the whole episode in your gallery forgotten, as I won't be here. You'll be free to stay a bachelor and return to your life, and I will return to America with none the wiser. That's if you don't post notice of our engagement in the paper and convince the countess not to, either."

He stood and walked over to glance out the window he'd pulled her through, but he stayed annoyingly silent.

"It will be a win for both of us," Evie continued, speaking to his back. His very broad, very masculine back that looked so much bigger under the white shirt than it did in a tailored jacket. For one mad moment, Evie wondered what it would look like without the shirt. She really did have to get a hold of these wayward thoughts. "Your honor will be satisfied, and you won't have to sacrifice yourself in marriage. It's a perfect plan, really." Perhaps Aimee and her shenanigans were rubbing off on her?

He turned back to face her, perching his backside on the window ledge. "Do you really expect me to believe you don't want to be a duchess? That your trip to England was just for a holiday and not to find a husband?"

"I honestly don't care what you believe. The truth is I don't want you for a husband, which is why I've come to reason with you and get you to agree to this plan of mine."

He stayed silent, skepticism still rife in his gaze. Goodness, the man was as stubborn as a bull. She crossed the floor to him and stood about a foot away. A dangerous position possibly, given what had taken place between them earlier, but she had to make him see the truth of her statement in her eyes. "I absolutely promise you I have no intention whatsoever of marrying you. None. Is that really so hard for you to believe?"

"Honestly? Yes. For a woman, marriage is usually the only way to better her position, and American women seem to want that more than their English counterparts. I've been hounded by mamas and their debutant daughters since I hit eighteen years old. It's a long time to have been chased to believe there is even one woman who doesn't want what I could offer her."

His reluctance to believe her was starting to truly anger her. "Well, contrary to your belief that all women, especially American ones, must want a titled husband, I can assure you that is the furthest thing from my mind. I do not want to be your duchess, period! Why, just the thought of being married to you terrifies me."

"Why would being a duchess terrify you?"

"Being a duchess wouldn't terrify me." She raised her chin. "Being married to you would. There's a distinct difference."

"I would never hurt you." He sounded incensed, yet there was a hint of hurt, too, in his expression.

"I'm not terrified of you in that manner."

"Then what…" A slow grin grew across his mouth. "You're scared of your physical reaction to me, aren't you? Scared you can't control yourself when you're with me."

"That is not it at all!" she lied.

His grin only grew with her denial. "Your eyes flash fire at me when you get upset, did you know that? They absolutely glitter in frustration. It's fascinating to observe."

Crossing her hands over her chest, Evie flashed him the most annoyed expression she could muster. "Similar to this expression?"

He laughed. "Exactly like that. Though you also wear the same expression when you're excited and breathlessly aroused." He straightened from his perch and stepped toward her until she was staring at the open buttons of his shirt and his dark chest hair curled underneath the fabric. "At least that was what I observed last night," he murmured low, against her ear. "Perhaps we should try it again so I can see if the same expression flashes in your eyes."

For a minute, all she could think about was what it would feel like to have him do just that. For her to run her fingers through the hair of his chest. To slowly unbutton more of his shirt, until all of his naked chest was exposed to her view. Good gracious, she was a wanton. At least she was around him. *Get a control of yourself, Evie!* "That's a highly inappropriate comment to make."

"We are engaged," he murmured. "Certain things are allowed when one is engaged, are they not? Kissing and touching being some of those things…"

He was purposefully trying to rattle her to say such provocative words. There could be no other reason for his remarks. She took in a deep breath but only managed to breathe in the rugged male scent of him, which washed through her, befuddling her senses and making her lose her train of thought. God, he smelled good.

"What do you think of my proposal?" she managed to ask, her voice husky as thoughts of him touching and kissing her kept swirling in her head.

"It has merit," he said. "An engagement without the hassle of a marriage at the end. I can't really complain about such a proposal, if that's what you intend to do."

She desperately wanted to step away from him to clear her head, but she knew if she did, he would know how he was affecting her and would certainly use that knowledge to his advantage. So, instead, she stayed rooted to the spot, flicking her eyes up to his, to at least not be staring at his partially naked chest.

Clearing her throat, she wrestled her thoughts back to their deal. She had to, or she'd collapse into a puddle at his feet, all but begging him to kiss her again. "I don't know how I can get you to believe me. You seem determined against doing so, even though I'm telling you the truth."

He stood there, not moving a muscle, instead simply watching her, much like a hawk would its prey. "Are you?"

"Yes. And what do you have to lose if I'm not?" Perhaps if she appealed to his logic that might sway him. "At the moment, as things stand, you will have me as your wife regardless, but if I do honor the deal we make, then you'll only have a fiancée for a few short weeks. There's nothing for you to lose by agreeing, is there?"

"Perhaps," he murmured.

"There's no perhaps about it," she snapped, her temper getting the best of her. "It's a perfectly good plan. Surely, you can see the merits of my suggestion."

"Oh, I see the merits, but perhaps I've changed my mind about not wanting a wife."

His suggestion had her stopping short. "Excuse me?"

He shrugged a shoulder, looking rather cavalier all of a sudden. "I don't know, perhaps a wife is just the thing. Someone to look after my households, manage the servants, warm my bed each night... Now *that* idea certainly has merit, don't you think?"

"No, I don't!" Was he teasing her on purpose? He had to be. "Are you broke and need my inheritance to rescue you?"

"Of course not! I have no damn need of your American money, lady."

Evie raised her brow, projecting the most imperious expression she could muster. "What else am I to think given your sudden change of stance on marriage? You accused me initially of setting up the situation so we were found in such a compromising position, but perhaps it was you who arranged for that to occur?"

She could have sworn a fleeting look of guilt flashed in his eyes, but it was gone before she could even be certain. After all, why would he do such a thing? If he was after her money and thought she was after a title, he would have just proposed and gotten her agreement, surely. Though she had told him she wasn't here for that purpose... Could he really be after her money? Or Aimee's money as was the case.

"I'm not after your money," he replied in a clipped sentence. "And trust me, I certainly didn't arrange for everyone to find us in such a position. I'm damned surprised one of them didn't faint at our feet or worse when they saw what we were up to."

"Your aunt Mildred did look murderous." It was an understatement to say the woman hadn't been happy to hear of their engagement. If looks could kill, Evie would have been dead on the spot last night. "In any event, I know this talk of marriage is only you trying to rattle me, and it won't work. I've heard how your last fiancée hurt you and how you have no intention of repeating such an event, so don't try to pretend you've changed your stance on marriage."

"She was cheating on me the night before our wedding, so she betrayed me, *not* hurt me." His jaw was clenched as he said the words, and Evie got the sense that hurt was far too mild a word to describe the effect the woman's betrayal had had on him. "But you're right. I didn't want to ever marry after that."

"Then there you go, you can agree to my plan, and we'll both get what we want."

"You really don't want to marry me?" This time it was a genuine question he was asking, almost as if he couldn't quite let himself believe it.

Evie sighed. "I don't." She couldn't marry him; there were no ifs, buts, or maybes about it. Though, hopefully, given she'd be returning to America with

Aimee in five weeks, he'd never find out that truth and they could go on with their lives returning to normal, this pretend engagement a distant memory.

"Very well, then," he said after a moment. "I'll agree to this pretend engagement you're proposing."

"Excellent!" She already felt lighter with his acquiescence. "And you won't publish a notice of it in the papers?"

"No, I won't. Though I don't know if that will have the intention you are hoping it will."

"What do you mean?"

"Well, I'm assuming you don't want someone back in the States to find out, which is why you don't want word of it printed."

He was a clever man. "Something like that." If he did post notice of their engagement in the paper, it would eventually end up in the hands of her aunt and uncle as they often read English papers to stay abreast of what was happening abroad. And they couldn't find out. They just couldn't. They'd never forgive her if they did, and then she'd truly be alone with no family at all.

"Is there a man you have feelings for back in New York?" His eyes narrowed in suspicion as he glared pointedly at her. "Is that why you're so adamant you don't want to marry? You believe yourself in love with someone else."

"That's none of your business." Perhaps if he thought she was, it would keep him less suspicious of her motives for not wanting to marry him. Though she wasn't going to lie to him about it, but if he inferred she was, well, that was his choice to make, wasn't it?

"I beg to differ. If I am to be your fiancé, either real or pretend, then it most certainly is my concern."

"Oh, for goodness' sake, you're impossible!" Evie threw her hands up in the air. "There is no other man! Satisfied?"

"I am. Because when I kiss you again, I don't want you to be thinking of anyone else but me."

"What makes you think I'll kiss you again?"

He leaned in closer to her, his nose tracing around her earlobe, and Evie couldn't help but gulp in a shuddering breath. "You tremble when I get close to you," he whispered. "Your breath quickens, as does the pulse at your neck. You want to kiss me again. Just as I want to kiss you."

He wanted to kiss her again? The thought sent a shaft of heat across her cheeks all the way down to her toes. "A kiss got us into this mess in the first place…"

"A kiss we didn't get to properly finish." He stepped closer to her, but Evie remained rooted to the spot, her eyes not daring to leave his. Slowly, he reached his hand down to hers and picked up her gloved hand, the pads of his fingers slowly brushing against her palm.

She couldn't control the tingle of awareness that spread up her arm from his touch.

"And, really, shouldn't we seal our new deal with a kiss?" he whispered against her cheek, his other hand slowly circling around her waist. "Kissing you again is all I've been able to think about since my lips touched yours."

In that moment, she did want him to kiss her. Wanted him to kiss her more than she'd wanted anything before, even knowing it would be a mistake doing so. But at least it would be a mistake she'd never forget. "Kiss me, then," she whispered back to him, unable to do anything but watch in wonder as his lips slowly descended to hers. Then, before she could summon another thought, his lips pressed against hers and she was lost. Lost in the desire that he stirred inside her.

Lost completely in his touch.

CHAPTER SIXTEEN

Alex hadn't intended to kiss her again. Had tried to avoid pulling her into his arms since he'd pulled her through his window and felt the soft silkiness of her against him. But as she'd stood there boldly proposing a pretend engagement, he hadn't been able to think of anything else except kissing those sweet, juicy lips of hers.

Which was how he found himself doing just that, marveling at how bloody luscious she tasted.

The smoothest brandy could never compare to the deliciousness of this woman, the sweet scent of her driving him crazy with longing all evening. When she'd initially shown up, he'd thought he'd conjured her from his wildly erotic dreams, dreams where he'd been kissing her everywhere, tasting her and pleasuring her until she was writhing in his arms in passionate abandon.

And now here she was, in his arms, gasping in pleasure as he gently pried apart her lips with his mouth. His tongue deftly flicked against her own, tasting and stroking until she was whimpering in delight. Damn, he could get used to this.

"God, you taste good," he murmured, pulling away from her and staring at the passion and wonder burning hotly in her eyes that she was making no effort to disguise. Eyes he could lose himself in if he allowed it. But he couldn't allow it. If he did, he didn't know what would happen, which was completely unacceptable.

Abruptly, he stepped backward and away from the temptation that the woman in front of him was presenting and cleared his throat. "I think that should seal our deal well enough."

She stumbled slightly, her eyes dazed in passion, and Alex had to clench his fists together to stop himself from pulling her back into his arms. What was it with this woman and how he could barely control himself around her? She was bewitching him without even trying.

Perhaps he was just lonely for female companionship? That had to be it. He hadn't had a mistress in as long as he could remember, so it was most likely his male needs that were causing such a reaction with her. Well, that was easily fixed. Although the idea of seeking solace in someone else's arms didn't sit at all well with him, not while she was standing in front of him with a bemused expression on her stunningly innocent face and her lips appearing thoroughly kissed.

Not that he believed she was completely innocent, no one was in his experience, and he still got the sense she was hiding something. Perhaps she did have a man she was enamored with back in America? Though, surely, she wouldn't be as consumed by their kisses if she did, her lips opening so innocently against his own.

He sighed, knowing it probably wouldn't even matter to him if she did, such was his obsession with her, that he was confident he could make her forget about any other man, especially given the way she responded to him.

"I suppose I should be getting back," she replied, her hand briefly coming up to touch her lips.

Alex's eyes were drawn to the daintiness of her fingers, to the fullness of her mouth, to the pulse still thrumming wildly at her neck. Again, the urge to cart her over his shoulder and take her to his bed nearly floored him, but he gritted his jaw and resisted. Only just. "Yes, I will have my carriage brought around."

"At five o'clock in the morning?" She smiled. "Your poor servants. No, I'm more than capable of walking myself back. It's no more than a few blocks."

"That won't be happening." The woman was living in a dream if she thought he would allow her to purposefully place herself in potential peril. "Pretend fiancée or not, I'll accompany you."

She shrugged. "If you wish, though I will be quite safe on my own."

"Really?" He raised a brow. "This may be Mayfair, but that very fact can attract cutthroats willing to rob you for your shoes."

"I'm well aware, though it's nearly dawn, and most would-be cutthroats have already retired for the evening, plus I'm armed." She pulled out a knife and appeared surprisingly adept at holding it in a defensive grip. "And, as you see, perfectly capable of defending myself if need be."

An odd observation for an American heiress to make, who from all accounts was a slightly pampered and spoiled only child. "A Dollar Princess aware of the routines of cutthroats and armed with a knife? You are an unusual heiress, aren't you?"

For a moment, Alex could have sworn he saw an expression akin to panic flash in her eyes, but it was gone before he could even be certain, and instead the cool glance of a woman completely unfazed by his comments was staring back at him.

"Not at all. Haven't you heard about Americans and their love of weapons?" she remarked as she returned the knife to the pocket sewn into her blue dress. "I would have thought you'd be more surprised I was armed with a knife instead of a derringer."

He couldn't help but smile at her comment. "Yes, I suppose I should have been. In any event, come along. I'll get you home safely without the need to spill any blood, so we can continue this charade of ours."

She was oddly silent for a moment. "I've come to truly hate charades, though this one is necessary."

He walked over to her and held out his arm. "We can use the front door this time, rather than going on a safari through my garden beds."

"How droll of you, Duke," she said, threading her hand through the crook of his elbow.

Instantly, Alex's gut tightened at her touch, and he couldn't help but breathe in her rose scent, his whole body hardening in response. "Perhaps you should start calling me Alex given the circumstances."

She pressed her lips together but nodded. "If I must."

"My, how enthusiastic you sound."

She made no effort to hide her eye roll as she

stared up at him. "The more I call you Alex, the more you will call me Aimee, and the simple fact is I hate being called that."

"Yes, we don't have much choice over the names our parents give us, do we? My full first name is Alexander, which is what my father would always call me by, despite my preference for Alex. He thought Alex wasn't appropriate for a future duke and had always felt Alexander was dignified for his heir. I suppose your parents called you your name as it had some special meaning to them, too?"

"I'm not sure. I didn't know my parents." She sighed but then coughed loudly, her eyes going wide. "What I meant to say was that I *don't* really know them… They're so busy, you see, that I don't really feel as if I spend enough time with them to know them, and really, who truly knows anyone?"

She sometimes did say the oddest things, but rather than comment on it, he nodded. After all, in his experience, most women often said odd things, or at least they seemed odd to Alex, so it was generally far safer to observe instead of comment. And, suddenly, he wanted to hear more of her odd comments. "I intend to go to the College of Natural History tomorrow," he found himself blurting out. "They have some new specimens I want to look at. Did you wish to come with me?"

Her face lit up. "That sounds marvelous."

He grinned back at her. "I'll pick you up in the morning then, but come along, it's time to get you safely back to my aunt's with hopefully her none the wiser. I don't really fancy a wedding this week, do you?"

He couldn't help but laugh at the expression of horror that instantly gripped her face with his comment. Perhaps she was telling the truth when she said she didn't want to marry him.

Why the thought of that was suddenly so disappointing, he didn't want to consider. It was only to his benefit if she didn't want to get married. He didn't, after all, so it would save him from doing so, along with a lifetime of unhappiness at that.

But then the thought of visiting museums, discussing their shared love of paleontology and history, as well as sharing discoveries with her, suddenly didn't seem to present such an unhappy future at all.

Quite the opposite.

CHAPTER SEVENTEEN

"How could you get engaged?" Aimee's voice was somewhat shrill in the countess's sitting room as she paced across the floor, while Evie sat on the settee watching her cousin's mad march backward and forward on the rug.

"And to a duke of all people?" Aimee abruptly stopped her pacing and spun around to stare at Evie. "You're meant to be the sensible one out of the two of us. Yet here you are engaged. Oh, good lord, our ruse will be exposed. What are we going to do? When Mother and Father read about your engagement, they'll think I'm engaged! Oh my god, we're going to be in such trouble!"

"They're not going to find out. At least, I hope not," Evie said, trying to appear calm and composed, which was particularly important when Aimee was slightly agitated as her cousin certainly was now. Quickly, she explained the pretend engagement deal she'd struck with the duke. "He's assured me he won't post any notices in the papers, so all should be fine."

"What if he is in dire need of my inheritance?" Aimee lamented, flouncing down on the seat next to Evie in a particularly inelegant manner. "That could be why he kissed you and had prearranged to have those people attend at just that moment to catch you both. Why, he could be posting news of your engagement right now as we speak."

"Aimee, you must calm down." Evie shook her head. She should be used to her cousin's rather emotional lamentations after several years of living with her, but sometimes Aimee was far too passionate about things to think rationally, let alone calm down. "Honestly, I don't believe he's after your inheritance. I truly think he was as shocked as I was to be caught in such a position in the first place."

Aimee shook her head. "I can't even believe you were kissing him... What happened, Evie? You are always so sensible and proper, so very English, in fact. Honestly, I doubted you would ever do anything risqué, apart from agreeing to my plan to switch places, and even then, I didn't think I'd get you to agree to it. Yet here you are, accidentally engaged because you were found *kissing* a duke? I would never have believed such a thing possible."

Certainly, neither had Evie, but she found herself annoyed her cousin would think that. "Why wouldn't I kiss him? He's a handsome man, and it's not like I get many offers to embrace such an opportunity."

"Well, you *embraced* this one, didn't you?" Her cousin shot her a pointed look.

"Yes, I did," Evie conceded, with a slight clearing of her throat. "In any event, I fixed the disaster that it potentially could have been, so there will be no need to worry from your end about any ramifications from it."

Sighing, Aimee took one of Evie's hands in her own. "I hope you're right, cousin, for the both of us." She paused and turned very inquisitive eyes toward Evie. "Was he a good kisser?"

A hot flush swept across her cheeks at the question. "He was." A far too tame way to describe the skills of a man who'd sent Evie into an ecstatic state of near delirium simply from touching his mouth to hers. Though she wasn't about to outline the man's expert touch to her cousin; she'd never hear the end of it if she did.

"I take it he was a marvelous kisser going from the red spreading across your face." A grin stretched over Aimee's lips that she didn't bother to hide. "Well, I'm glad for you, cousin, for I think one should always have an amazing first kiss."

"Have you had a first kiss?" As close as they'd become in the few years Evie had been Aimee's companion, she'd never delved into such a subject with her far more vivacious cousin.

"I don't know if one could really call a sloppy press of wet, scaly lips against mine a first kiss." Her whole body shuddered at the recollection. "More a warning against the whole thing. In any event, I'm saving my true first kiss for a man that is so romantic that he weeps over his love of me. He will be so besotted with me that he will only be able to speak in poems and sonnets, regaling me with his chivalry and earnest attention." She sighed. "That is the sort of man I am waiting for to have a true first kiss with. I want a noble prince who will adore me and fawn all over me."

"You want a man from a fairy tale, my dear cousin." It was a tale Evie had often heard. Even though Aimee was usually pragmatic about most things, when it came to her knight in shining armor, she was most definitely living in a delusion, for no such man existed, or if he did it was an illusion meant to entrap a woman instead of liberating her. "A sop of a man who doesn't exist."

"You're right. He doesn't exist. Which is why I shall dedicate myself to convincing my father that there is no man I will ever wish to marry and that instead I am more than capable of taking over the family business when he eventually retires."

"How is your secretary training going with Mrs. Holbrook?" The one good thing to come from their swap was Evie not having to do it herself.

"Oh, that part of it is fine." Aimee waved her hand breezily in the air. "The lady adores me as I'm so diligent in applying myself. It's just that ogre of a boss I cannot stand. The man is insufferable. Once I'm in charge of the company, I will happily fire his ass."

"Aimee!" Evie chastised. "Not only have you dropped your English accent, but that's not how you're meant to talk while pretending to be English. We would never say such a word as ass."

"Oh, fiddlesticks," Aimee replied. "We're alone. No one can hear us. And you are half American, too, remember?"

"That's beside the point." She certainly didn't feel half American, though sometimes she wished she did. To be confident and bold like her cousin would be liberating. "Just the other day, you were reminding me to always stay in character."

"That's true, I did, though clearly you didn't listen to me having been caught kissing a duke. That's not the sort of behavior even I would have engaged in, no matter how dashingly handsome the man."

"How would you know how handsome he is?"

Aimee grinned. "He'd have to be to entice you away from your books into taking part in an illicit liaison."

Evie couldn't help it; she grabbed a cushion and threw it at her. "It wasn't an illicit liaison, merely a simple kiss we had the unfortunate luck of being discovered in the process of."

Though, in truth, there had been nothing simple about the feel of his lips against hers the first time, and most especially not the second time, either, which had been even more shattering to her equilibrium. A second kiss she was definitely not going to tell her cousin about, otherwise she really would think Evie was enamored with the duke, which certainly was not the case. *Liar*. Again, that darned annoying voice in her head! She really needed to have a good talking to herself.

She wondered if there'd be more kisses. They were engaged now, even if it was a sham, so being caught kissing again wouldn't be at all considered beyond the pale. Not that she should be thinking of kissing him again, let alone being caught doing so. That would lead down the path of really having to get married, but surely once he found out the truth about who she really was, he would loathe her and most likely refuse to marry her despite the scandal, ensuring she was completely and utterly ruined and homeless.

"So what's the plan?" Aimee asked.

"Excuse me?" Had Aimee been able to tell her wicked thoughts? Goodness, she hoped not.

"The plan, with your pretend fiancé. He's really going to go along with it?" Aimee strummed her fingers on the tabletop, as she was prone to do when thinking things through, which usually meant she was up to something and generally never boded well for Evie's peace of mind.

"He says he will," Evie replied. "He doesn't want to marry, not after the catastrophe with his previous fiancée."

"I vaguely remember Mother talking about it," Aimee said. "Though I was only ten at the time, so I didn't really understand the significance of it. They say she was found in a highly compromising position with another man, a fellow American who had followed her out here as they were in love apparently, but she was still going to marry the duke for his title. It was her mother, Cornelia Crandell, that had pushed for the match and was devastated by the broken engagement. But Miss Crandell wasn't too devastated, though she probably was when she lost her inheritance after her parents cut her off when she eloped with the man. But still she ended up marrying the man she truly loved."

"Probably why the duke asked if I was in love with another man. He thought I was perhaps in the same situation."

"He did?"

Evie nodded. "He doesn't believe me when I say I don't want to marry him. He's entirely arrogant."

"Well, he is a duke, so I suppose that's only to be expected. Annoying as it clearly is for you," Aimee hurried to placate after obviously catching sight of Evie's narrowing eyes.

"His arrogance would give your boss a run for his money, I'd wager," Evie replied.

"That is a bet I would win. Your duke wouldn't touch the arrogance of Harrison Stone, I guarantee it."

Now it was Evie who doubted that. The duke was unlike any man Evie had ever met or observed, and she'd observed a great many of them from the ballrooms and drawing rooms of the wealthy gatherings she'd had to attend as Aimee's companion. "He's not my duke, either, by the way." He'd never be hers. Such a thing was simply impossible.

"He's your fiancé, or at least pretend fiancé, so for the moment, yes, he's yours."

There was something so very right and so very wrong with her cousin's statement. Evie had to shake her head as she glanced over at the wall clock. "In any event, he's due to collect me in about an hour, as he's taking me to visit one of the largest paleontology collections at a college in London. At least one good thing to come from my sham engagement."

"Only you would consider that a good thing, and only you would manage to find yourself engaged to the only gentleman in London who shares your passion for those old *things*."

"They're called fossils, Aimee, and they inform us of our past—"

"And our future," Aimee interrupted. "Yes, yes, you've told me their purpose many, many times before."

Evie narrowed her eyes. "Don't you need to be back at work by now?"

"Not really," Aimee pertly replied. "I told Mrs. Holbrook I had a family emergency that might take slightly longer to resolve than the break I normally have for lunch. Hence, I don't need to rush back."

"Well, you didn't have to *rush* over here in the first place after getting my note." She'd sent a small note this morning outlining her engagement, knowing it would be best to tell Aimee the news sooner rather than later.

"Of course I had to!" she insisted. "What else did you really expect me to do after reading your ridiculously brief note that said, 'Dear cousin, I've accidentally become engaged to a duke, but don't worry, I have everything under control, and all will be fine'? I mean, really, Evie. What did you think I'd do? Think to myself, *Oh that's just wonderful, Evie's just happened to get herself accidentally engaged, but there's no need to worry at all*? Really, cousin? Of course I had to come and find out what was going on, straight away."

"Yes, I suppose I was deluding myself to think you'd be content with a note," Evie said with a sigh.

"Deluding yourself to think it was all fine, too," Aimee muttered. "At least it does seem as if you have the matter in hand, as long as you can resist kissing the man again."

Evie gasped. "Of course I shall be able to." At least she hoped so. He'd arranged to pick her up later this morning and take her to the College of Natural History with him, but without any chaperones, something she'd have to convince the countess was perfectly fine, even if part of her was doubting her own self-control around the man.

"Please, whenever you talk of the duke, you get this faraway expression on your face along with a blush that suggests you're thinking all sorts of wicked things about him."

For a moment, Evie didn't quite know what to say, her mouth hanging rather agape at her cousin's description of her own behavior. Did she really blush each time she thought about Alex? Maybe she did. Darn traitorous body.

"If you are going to kiss him again, then at least don't get caught."

"Aimee!"

"What?" Her cousin shrugged. "It's true. And here I thought I would be the one that jeopardized our swap being discovered, when instead it's sensible Evie that could jeopardize the entire endeavor."

"An endeavor I'm severely regretting agreeing to in the first place."

Rather than being upset, though, Aimee laughed. "Oh please, you were caught kissing a duke. You can't be all that upset at such an event. Even if you are, it's something you won't soon forget."

That was true. How could she ever forget the touch of his lips and the press of his tongue as it swept along hers? Such an encounter would stay with her until she was an old, lonely spinster.

"At least promise me this, cousin," Aimee said as she stood and strolled over to where Evie sat. "If you are going to let him kiss you again, don't get caught. You'll enjoy yourself far more without risking discovery." She gave her a quick kiss on the cheek. "Now I will be off. We'll catch up again on Sunday at the coffee shop, and you'll be able to tell me then of what new scandal you've been embroiled in."

"Very funny." Evie watched as Aimee collected her small clutch and waved from the door before strolling out of the room, presumably to return to her office. Now, alone in the sitting room, Evie had a moment to gather her thoughts before her pretend fiancé came to collect her.

"Good morning, my dear," the countess's voice sang out a few moments later as she glided into the room, her lavender perfume following in her wake as she walked over to the bell pull and yanked down on the blue rope. "Who was that young lady I saw leaving down the corridor?"

Evie stood as the countess strolled over and sat across from her before she sat back down, too. This morning, the lady was dressed in a burgundy day dress trimmed with cream lace that was buttoned up her neck with creamy pearl beads. As usual, the lady took refinement and elegance to another level. "That was my English cousin, Evie. She heard about my engagement and wished to congratulate me."

It sounded odd to speak of herself in the third person, but she didn't have many options.

"Ah, I see," the countess tittered. "I daresay a lot of people will be wishing to pay you a visit and congratulate you. Though I didn't realize you had family in England, my dear." There was a pointed *please explain* expression on the lady's face as she stared at Evie. "And I have been friends with your family for decades, so how did I not know this fact?"

"She's a distant cousin," Evie improvised, not wanting to go into the specifics of her own progeny with the lady, because clearly Evie having been born on the wrong side of the sheets meant that her birth hadn't really been announced to anyone. "Do you think a lot of people will wish to visit with me?" Best to try to turn the woman's attention back on to a more neutral subject.

"Of course, they will," the countess replied. "They shall be wanting to try to get the gossip about what happened between you and the duke."

"Well, that's annoying." Evie sunk back against the lounge, imagining the horrid hours ahead spent having to make small talk with strangers, all of whom were only trying to see if the rumors that she imagined were already swirling about regarding the circumstances of her engagement were true. "Oh, but I can't stay." She bolted back upright, remembering her prior engagement with Alex. "The duke has promised to take me to look at a collection of fossils at the College of Natural History."

"When did you and he organize that?" The countess's eyes narrowed upon her. "After the incident of catching you both in each other's arms last night, I made certain to stay plastered to your side for the rest of the evening."

"We arranged to do so before the incident," Evie again improvised. Goodness, she was getting uncomfortably good at the skills of improvisation and lying of late. Skills she was not enjoying at all.

"Hhm," the countess harrumphed. "I don't know if that's wise to do so without a chaperone."

The woman was probably correct, but not many people wanted to attend an exhibition of fossils. In any event, Evie could resist the duke, even if they were alone. Yes, he was ridiculously handsome and had the unfortunate ability of making her whole body feel as if it were on fire and melting from his touch, but she was strong enough to resist him. Surely?

"Is it not the case that as we are engaged now, we are allowed small trips together in public during the day?"

"I suppose so," the countess reluctantly acknowledged. "I don't know how it's done in America, but don't get caught kissing him again, all right?"

"That's what my cousin said, too…"

"A sensible girl," the countess replied, just as the butler arrived at the door with a tea tray.

"The Duke of Hargrave is here waiting to collect Miss Thornton-Jones," the butler said as he deposited the tray of tea in front of the countess.

"Do show him in, then," the countess replied.

"No, that's fine!" Evie stood and rushed over to the door. The last thing she wanted was for the countess to start questioning the duke. What if he accidentally mentioned something about her late-night visit to him? Not that she thought he would, but she'd rather not risk it. "I don't wish to keep him waiting as there's so much to see in the collections he'll be showing me. I will be back in a few hours, my lady."

She quickly curtsied to the countess, noting the woman's slightly confounded expression over Evie's haste as she turned and rushed out of the door before the countess could even stop her. While she hurried down the hallway to the entrance, exhilaration filled her. Not that that had anything to do with the man waiting for her only a few rooms away. No, clearly, she was excited to be going to see more fossils.

Yes, that was it. It was the fossils and not the duke that was causing such anticipation for the outing. An outing that should be an uncomplicated affair, providing she could do what her cousin and the countess had both warned against and not get caught kissing the duke.

Odd that they'd warned about getting caught but hadn't warned about kissing him? Perhaps it was a usual thing to kiss one's fiancé? Hm, she wondered if that extended to a pretend fiancé.

CHAPTER EIGHTEEN

The carriage ride had been torture for Alex. Pure bloody torture while he sat across from Aimee and had to resist pulling her into his arms every damned second.

Now they were walking around in the basement of the College of Natural History, and he was watching her face light up with delight every time she caught sight of a fossil she hadn't seen before, and all he wanted to do was unbutton the tiny red buttons along the back of her dress and expose her creamy skin underneath to his touch.

Watching her and not being able to touch her was pure agony. And try as he might to convince himself to pay attention to the displays of fossils in their dusty glass cabinets, which normally kept him entertained for hours, he was failing miserably. All he could think about was pulling her in close and kissing her senseless. Kissing her until she was breathless and panting for more. Kissing her until she was staring at him with the same rapture and delight that she was staring at the fossils with.

He'd never thought he'd be jealous of a fossil, but the way she was cooing over the East Essex display of an ancient sea creature was making him ridiculously so. Not for the first time, he glanced around the space, which, apart from row after row of towering bookshelves that divided the massive room up into corridors of books with display cases

of fossils in the middle, was empty, except for the
two of them. And it wasn't likely they would come
upon anyone else for hours. The College of Natural
History was for scholars who were rarely up at this
hour.

For all intents and purposes, apart from the
young man that let them inside, Alex assumed they
were the only people in the entire building, which
rose some three stories and was jam packed with
floor-to-ceiling fossils and books on all sorts of
things relating to natural history.

Normally, he would be as entranced with the
displays as his pretend fiancée was, his attention
solely on them, but when she was around, everything else paled into the background, all his
attention instead focused on her and her alone. It
was damned inconvenient.

"Oh my goodness, look at this one, Alex," the
very subject of his obsession enthused ahead of
him as she brushed aside the dust on the glass display case with her glove, caring little that her white
gloves were now gray with dirt. She bent down and
pressed her nose nearly against the glass as she
peered into the display. "It has to be thousands, if
not millions of years old." She twisted back over to
smile at him. "Isn't it magnificent?"

Her smile felt like a kick in his stomach, so brilliant and so damned tempting.

For a minute, as he stared at her, all he wanted
to do was stride over and kiss the hell out of her
and then take her on the bloody floor. Fuck, he had
to control himself. Never had he reacted this way
with another woman before, to the point where

nearly all good sense and reason was abandoning him.

Alex cleared his throat. "Yes, magnificent."

"Is everything all right?" Her brow furrowed as she stared over at him and straightened. "You seem out of sorts."

He felt like laughing. "That's one way of describing it." She'd be running for the hills if she knew just how out of sorts he was right then, with the thought of pressing himself into her tight passage nearly consuming him. With a shake of his head, he walked over to the bookshelf on the other side of the cabinet from where she was standing. "Here, this book discusses that particular find."

Pulling out the voluminous tome, he handed it to her as she strolled over and paused beside him. Again, the scent of roses wafted over his nose, and he couldn't help but greedily inhale the smell, his head bending down a touch closer to her hair than was proper.

She smiled up at him and her gloved fingers brushed his as she took the book from him. Soft and delicate, and so silky smooth that he wondered what they would feel like sans material and dancing over his rock-hard shaft. Bliss. Pure, damn bliss.

Alex had to fight the urge to groan as an instant jolt of desire surged through him with the thought.

"It's fascinating, isn't it, to think that for centuries, these ancient creatures have remained buried in the earth, preserved for us to discover and learn from?" she enthused as she flicked through the pages of the book, completely unaware of the erotic turn of his thoughts. "Simply wonderful, really."

Abruptly, Alex turned on his heel and strode over to the opposite bookcase. Space away from her and her intoxicating scent was what he needed. But even being several feet from her wasn't working. He could still sense her across from him, each gentle brush of her fingers against the parchment of the book, akin to him imagining what it would feel like to have the pads of her fingers brushing over his cock. Softly at first and then harder, until she wrapped her whole hand around him and began to slide her palm up and down his shaft, until he could barely stand it and was pulsing with the need to release his seed.

"Are you certain you're all right?" she asked again, concern etched across her brow.

There probably was cause for her concern, given where his randy thoughts were taking him.

A slight rustle above her, at the top of the high bookshelf, diverted his attention for a moment and his heart nearly froze when he saw a large rock perched precariously on the edge of the bookcase, wobbling directly above where she was standing.

Without even thinking, he bolted over and dove toward her, pushing her sideways onto the ground, just as the rock gave way and crashed down heavily, landing right on the spot where she'd been standing.

• • •

Evie's breath left her in an almighty whoosh as Alex dove on top of her and pushed her to the floor, his body covering hers as a loud bang echoed ominously throughout the room. For a minute, she lay there dazed, trying to take in a deep breath but not quite managing it, slightly winded from the fall.

Belatedly, she became aware of Alex hefting himself up onto his forearms, so his full weight wasn't pressing her into the hard floor, and gradually her lungs were able to take a full breath in. Slowly, she blinked, her gaze staring at the dust swirling in the air above them before finally latching onto Alex's eyes, which were staring intently at her own.

"Are you hurt?" he asked, concern filling his voice as he looked over her for injuries.

She shook her head. "I don't think so." Apart from feeling somewhat dazed, the rest of her felt normal, though it was a bit hard to tell with his lower body pressing against hers. "What happened?"

He pushed himself to the side and glanced back to where a huge rock was now sitting on the floor, exactly on the spot where Evie had been standing only a moment ago. "I don't know exactly, but I damn well intend to find out." His gaze flicked to the top of the bookshelves, and then around the room, until they returned to her. "Are you certain you're not hurt?"

Sitting up, she briefly patted her hands over her body. "I'm fine, just a bit rattled."

She couldn't help but notice his eyes following her hands in their exploration, unbanked hunger in their depths. Or was Evie imagining it? Because when he glanced back to her, there was no expression in his eyes except for perhaps annoyance.

Abruptly, he stood up and held his hand out to her. "Come on, we need to find out what happened."

Evie took his hand until she was standing next to him and then quickly brushed off the dust that had settled on her skirts. "Surely, it was an accident and the rock overbalanced."

"Do you see any other rocks perched precariously on the top edge of any of the other bookcases?" he asked, his whole body braced in alert.

Glancing around the rest of the room, she realized there weren't any others. "No, there's no loose rocks, anywhere."

"Exactly," he replied, hurrying around to the other side of the bookshelf from the one the rock fell from.

"What are you suggesting? That someone pushed a rock down on me? I thought we were alone down here." Evie followed him around to the other side of the wooden bookshelf to see a replica bookshelf standing on the other side, stuffed full of old books.

"The dust on the shelving has been disturbed," Alex said, his frown turning downright fierce.

"That could have been done yesterday for all we know," Evie replied, though the marks would be consistent with someone possibly climbing up the shelving to peer over the top. But such a thought was ludicrous. After all, who would want to hurt her? She didn't have enemies in England, or anywhere for that matter. She was just plain Yvette Jenkins with neither fortune nor foes. Although she

wasn't just Evie here in England. She was masquer-
ading as Aimee, but Aimee didn't have any
enemies, either.

"It could have been, but I thought I had heard
footsteps running off after." He took ahold of her
hand and led them over to the door. "Let's find out
who else is in the building."

A few minutes later, they were back at the entrance of the building, standing in front of the desk
where the young clerk who'd admitted them was
sitting.

"Is anyone else in the building?" Alex demanded without explanation as he marched over to the
clerk.

The young man, who couldn't have been more
than twenty years old, stood to attention in front of
Alex, his spectacles slightly askew as he pushed a
hand through his already disheveled hair. "No,
Your Grace." He gulped at the savage gleam in
Alex's eyes. "Not apart from the three of us."

"It must have been an accident," Evie remarked.

"So no one else has been in the building this
morning apart from us?" Alex asked the clerk.

"Well, there was that other chap that got here
just after you, and he left only a few minutes
ago…" the young man murmured, his eyes squint-
ing as Alex's brow furrowed. "But he's not in the
building at the moment …"

Alex strode over to the entrance table and
grabbed the visitor book they'd both signed their
names into when they'd arrived. "Bloody hell," he
growled as he read over the page. "John Smith." He

turned back to the young man. "You didn't think to question his rather generic name?"

"Um… no?" The young man's shoulders hunched over as he glanced up at the duke. "I didn't…"

"And why would he?" Evie stepped forward and placed a hand on Alex's arm. "There's no need to blame him for anything. Just because a man came here after we arrived and left before us does not mean he tried to push a rock on top of my head."

The young man gasped. "A rock was pushed on top of you, my lady?"

There was genuine distress in the young man's face as his gaze swiveled between Evie and Alex, fear and confusion clouding his eyes.

"We don't know that for certain," Evie tried to placate him. There was no point in jumping to conclusions just yet. "I'm sure the rock was already on the edge of the top shelf of the bookshelf, and when we pulled out a book, it lost its balance."

"It would have fallen on me then and there, if that were the case," Alex interjected with a growl. "Not waited for me to walk away from you."

"We don't keep rocks on the bookshelves," the clerk said, looking confused.

"See?" Alex raised a brow at her before turning back to the attendant. "What did the man look like?"

The clerk blew out a breath and spent a moment contemplating the question. "I'm not good with paying attention to things, well, except for fossils."

"Obviously," Alex grumbled. "But you must have noticed something about him. How tall was he compared to me?"

"Um…probably up to your chin, maybe?" The young man didn't seem too confident in his own observation. "And he had brown hair, though not as dark as yours, and he was dressed in a rather ill-fitting suit that was somewhat dirty with grease, but I thought he must have been so consumed with his studies that he forgot to bother changing, as many who visit here do."

"Anything else?" Alex asked.

Pressing his lips together, the young man thought over the question. "I think he might have had a tattoo on his neck." He pointed up to his own collar, between where the starched fabric ended and his jaw line. "At least, I think it was a tattoo as it looked like ink, but I wasn't close enough to tell for certain."

"Did he speak to you at all?" Alex asked.

"Apart from a grunt when he entered, no, not really," the young man replied. "You don't think he tried to harm the lady here, do you?"

Alex shrugged. "I don't know, but if he returns, don't mention any of this to him but send word to me immediately."

"Of course, Your Grace." The young man bobbed his head earnestly.

Turning toward her, Alex nodded over to the entrance. "Come on." He gently gripped a hold of her elbow and began to escort her outside and down the road to where his carriage was waiting.

"Do you really think someone tried to push a

rock onto my head?" The idea was ridiculous, although there had been recently disturbed dust marks on the bookshelf behind where she'd been standing, which would correlate with someone standing on the shelf to get high and see above it.

"I think that's exactly what happened."

"But such a thing doesn't make sense." Evie couldn't fathom it. "I have no enemies here." Which was true, regardless of if it was Aimee or herself who had been targeted.

"Honestly? I'm not certain what's going on. But I do know the way the rock was wobbling before it fell wasn't natural; someone was pushing it from behind." He stopped in front of his carriage, and his footman opened the door for Evie. She stepped inside, with Alex following behind and settling himself on the opposite seat from her.

"But it doesn't make any sense," she said, settling her skirts out in front of her. "Unless someone was aiming for you instead of me?" That theory was far more logical.

"You think I have enemies?"

"I know it sounds odd, given you have such a friendly and welcoming personality, which has people gravitating toward you," Evie said, with slight sarcasm.

"Very funny." His lips twitched briefly at the corners.

"Perhaps, just maybe," she continued, "you've annoyed someone with your highhandedness? As hard to believe as that is."

He raised his brow. "I'm a duke. I'm meant to be highhanded."

"Exactly, which gives my theory credence. Or perhaps it has nothing to do with you being a duke but instead relates to your interests in paleontology," Evie said. "You know how passionate scholars and other collectors can get."

"Passionate? They can be damn vicious if they feel another is threatening their work. Or they're trying to steal someone else's work."

"That's my point. Have any of your recent fossil studies or discoveries earned the ire of any fellow collectors or scholars?"

"I've unearthed several new and rather impressive specimens in my caves over the past few years," he answered. "One I'm certain is an extraordinarily large ancient lizard."

Evie gasped, and her mouth dropped open. "Oh my goodness, a large ancient lizard? Truly?"

"Yes, truly. Though I haven't had time to fully excavate it yet. So not only does no one know about it but no one else has seen it, either."

It had always been a dream of hers to be one of the first to see a newly unearthed fossil. "Would you be able to show it to me? I've always longed to discover a fossil for myself, but obviously I've never had a chance. It would be simply amazing to be the second person in the whole world to see a new discovery."

"I imagine New York ballrooms and assemblies wouldn't present much of an opportunity for a young lady to unearth a fossil." He stretched his legs out, and his thighs brushed against hers.

"Something like that," she murmured, trying to ignore the frisson of heat that filled her from his accidental touch.

He smiled, and Evie had the distinct impression that the man was well aware of the effect he had on her. The cad.

"How did you come to be so interested in fossils and history?" he asked, the intensity in his expression as he stared at her suggesting he truly wanted to know the answer. "It's not something most people even know about, let alone are fascinated by, especially not an American heiress who should be more interested in balls and parties."

"You do like to paint people with the same brush, don't you?" Not that she could blame him, as most everyone didn't think a woman would be interested in such intellectual pursuits, even if that wasn't the case. "Tell me, do many dukes or other gentlemen in Society take an interest in the subject, too?"

His lips twisted into a grin. "Point taken. Tell me then, what makes *you* so fascinated by dusty old fossils?"

She'd never been asked that before, not even by her family, who all knew of her odd interest in the subject. "When I was a young girl, I found some books on natural history and paleontology, and the drawings inside of the fossils fascinated me, completely and utterly to the point where I became obsessed by the subject and wanted to learn all I could about it. In truth, I think learning about them took me away from my surroundings and into a world of possibilities."

The memory of turning page after page of the drawings of shells, fish bones, and giant lizard skeletons from the past still sent a wave of awe through her. It had been her first taste of history and the world eons before civilization, and it had captivated her.

"The fact that our past was filled with ancient creatures and civilizations," she continued, remembering sitting on her bed and poring over the pages, literally losing herself for hours on end as she devoured the pictures and text of the book, imagining herself exploring such a lost world. "The fact that nature itself was able to preserve such creatures in a fossilized form, for us to study centuries later… well, it was inspiring, and I've been entranced by the subject ever since."

It also helped she'd made a friend along the way who happened to be a professor of paleontology. A friend she wouldn't be able to visit on this return trip, given the masquerade she was taking part in. Although perhaps she should go and see him? Especially if someone was behind the bookcase and trying to harm Alex because of his collection, there was no greater expert on paleontology than Professor Burton.

"How did *you* become interested in fossils?" she asked.

"You might have already gathered that my childhood wasn't filled with rainbows and sunshine."

"I'd gathered that."

"Well, let me say that when my father was in one of his moods and I was able to sneak out of the house, I fled down to the beach at our estate in the country. That's where I discovered the caves, and within the walls and floors of them I discovered an array of fossils. More than any one person could excavate in a lifetime."

"That sounds amazing," she replied. "I've always dreamed of what it would be like to discover a fossil. Your collection at your house, is most of that your own discoveries?"

"Mostly," he said. "My main ones I keep at my country estate, Hargrave Hall, as they're generally too large to transport here without organizing special transportation. However, I do have a few in my townhouse I brought with me that I haven't yet had a chance to put on display in my gallery."

"I'm already eager to see them," she enthused, trying her best to think of fossils instead of his thickly muscled thigh, still resting against hers. It wasn't working. She was more aware of him in the small space of the carriage than she'd ever been.

"Then I shall have to show you them."

"I would like that." She smiled at him. "Though I'll have to bring the countess with me as a chaperone."

"You didn't seem to worry about that last night." He winked at her, and Evie felt her tummy roll again. "But I'm glad you've come to your senses and don't intend to repeat such a foolish and dangerous midnight escapade again."

"It was dawn, Your Grace, with the sun happily rising when you walked me home, and not once were we accosted, need I remind you." Evie raised her chin. "And I'd appreciate if you don't mention my visit to anyone, especially not your aunt, who was rather reluctant to let me attend the college with you today without a chaperone."

"Yet you convinced her to."

"I did," Evie agreed. "It's not like we can get into a compromising situation in a college or a carriage, now, can we?"

His eyes suddenly flared as he leaned forward. "Oh, I don't know about that, my dear lady. True, it would be unlikely in a public place like the college; however, my carriage is certainly not a public place now, is it? It is a small, confined, and private space, with just the two of us in it. I could ravish you in here until you screamed in ecstasy, and none would be the wiser."

He paused and looked at her for a good minute. "Shall I do that? Shall I make you scream in pleasure?"

CHAPTER NINETEEN

Her whole body braced in shock and anticipation. What he spoke of was wicked and wanton, and it was creating havoc with every single part of her body as an unquenchable need to experience what he said ran through her like wildfire. "You are being entirely inappropriate asking that."

"Perhaps," he said, his mouth twitching up at the corners. "But our whole engagement isn't appropriate, is it? So does it matter if we're slightly more inappropriate with each other as long as we don't go too far beyond the bounds of propriety?"

"Of course it matters," she insisted, trying to sound breathless with outrage rather than anticipation. "As you said yourself last night, we don't want to be forced into an actual marriage, as would happen if we were caught in a compromising situation again."

"But that's the key, is it not?" He raised a brow. "We just have to ensure we don't get caught. Unless you're scared of kissing me again. Scared of a simple kiss."

There was nothing simple about it when he kissed her. "I'm not scared of your kisses." If anything, she was thrilled when he kissed her. Thrilled to the point of oblivion, which was what she was scared of—losing control and getting carried away by passion. Because she had a sneaking suspicion he was correct; she would want him to do more than just kiss her.

"In that case," he said, leaning forward, "why don't we make our pretend engagement more interesting for us both?"

There was a gleam of anticipation in his eyes that made Evie as equally wary as she felt exhilarated. "And how would we do that?"

He shrugged lightly, but there was an intensity in his eyes as he stared at her, almost as if he wanted to devour her. "Pleasure each other. Nothing that would truly compromise you. However, we're adults and can control ourselves when enjoying each other's kisses, can't we? And they were enjoyable, I think we can both agree upon that."

All Evie could do was nod. Enjoyable was another mild description for what she'd felt when his lips were pressed against hers. Wild, forbidden, and beyond delectable were more apt descriptions, in her opinion. Not that she'd tell him that. He was far too confident in his skills as it was for him to know how susceptible she was to his touch. If he didn't already know.

"If we ensure no one sees us kissing, then we will be in exactly the same position as we are now, except we will have gotten to enjoy kissing each other over our time together." He leaned further forward, his breath softly caressing against her ear. "That's surely a desired outcome for both of us."

Ripples of delight ran through her neck from the whisper of his mouth so close to the nape of her neck. It was all Evie could do to stop herself from shivering in pleasure. The man and his wicked words were tempting her as nothing else ever had. He was right, though: what harm was there in a few kisses? A few kisses she could lose herself in and that she'd be able to relive in her mind when she returned to New York? A few kisses that she found herself desperate to receive, more desperate than she'd ever been before?

"Very well, then," she mumbled before she could change her mind. "Kiss me."

He pulled back for a moment, slight surprise on his face. "Really?"

"Were you teasing me, then, or simply trying to torment me?"

"No, I was serious. I just didn't think you would agree…"

His words trailed off as Evie licked her bottom lip and her hands pressed up against his chest. He was so strong and warm, and she had an urge to feel what his skin felt like in the flesh, without the barrier of his white shirt between them. "I have agreed. Clearly, I shall have to take matters into my own hands."

Then without thought or reason, she pressed her own lips to his, teasing and nibbling against him as he'd done to her last night. He tasted so good.

Evie gasped as he lifted her from her seat and settled her on his lap, then his lips claimed hers once again. Boldly, he nudged her mouth open, and his tongue began dancing along the edge of hers. She was in bliss, pure, unadulterated bliss. Wrapping her arms around his neck, she brought herself in closer against him, her breasts straining against the material of her gown, begging for him to touch them.

But he was keeping his hands on her waist, so Evie grabbed one of his hands and dragged it up to cup her breast.

Alex groaned in reply, his fingers gently squeezing against the flesh of her bosom. "You're so damn delicious," he murmured, his lips leaving hers for a moment as he stared down at her. "I can't get enough of you."

"Then keep going," she whispered, pulling him back against her and devouring his mouth with her own.

She'd never realized kissing was so delicious. Or, at least, kissing Alex was. The man was playing her mouth like an expert musician would a violin. Nibbling, sucking, stroking, until Evie was panting with desire. Unable to help herself, she began to undo the buttons of his shirt.

"What are you doing?" he managed to mumble between kisses.

"I want to explore you," she replied, for once in her life not caring about the consequences as a desperate longing filled her to touch him, to feel him, to taste him.

She pushed open his shirt to reveal the broad expanse of his chest underneath. The man was all muscle and steel, his chest a sight to behold with the sprinkling of dark hair across it. Evie's hands began to stroke across his skin, lightly at first, and then her fingers grew bolder, tracing over toward his nipples.

He groaned heartily in response. Encouraged, she lowered her mouth to his nipple, flicking her tongue against it and marveling as it hardened under her touch. While her mouth began to lick and suck upon it, she reached up and began to tweak his other nipple between her fingers, rubbing it until it, too, was a hard peak.

"Oh fuck, that's good," Alex groaned, his eyes closed tightly as she continued to play with his nipples.

His words emboldened her, and her hand slowly reached down between their bodies, rubbing tentatively against the hard length of him jutting up and tenting the material of his pants. He felt so strong, almost like a rock, and then before she could change her mind, she slipped from his lap to sit next to him, then reached her hand under the waistband of his pants and felt his manhood, flesh against flesh.

His shaft throbbed against her palm, and she didn't know why but she slowly started to stroke her fingers across the hard length of him, her curiosity aroused. The skin of his cock felt like smooth, warm marble, straining to be free of the constraining material of his pants. She'd never felt anything like it. Never imagined anything like it.

Alex groaned, and Evie stopped her strokes. "Am I doing it wrong?"

He let out a half moan, half chuckle. "You're doing it just right. But if you keep going, I'm going to ejaculate everywhere."

"I don't know what that means."

He swallowed heavily. "Perhaps we'll leave that for another day."

"No. I want to know."

"It's when someone experiences the most intense burst of pleasure, little ripples cascading through their body, as they orgasm and experience the most exquisite bliss. A man shoots his seed when he orgasms, and a woman's passage becomes wet with her own pleasure."

Evie could feel the heat from his words infuse her whole body. "And can one experience this *pleasure* without being completely compromised?"

He was silent for a second. "It's a fine line, but yes."

She bit on her bottom lip, her head warring with her body. Her body won. If it wouldn't compromise her, she wanted to experience such a feeling, with him. "Then show me. Please." Embarrassment flooded her, but she lifted her chin. She knew she'd never have such a chance ever again, and she was sick and tired of always being sensible. For once she wanted to experience passion, and she wanted to experience passion with Alex.

Slowly, he nodded. Gently, he leaned over and kissed her, and Evie forgot all about being embarrassed, once again lost in the thrill of his touch. He reached down between them, his hands going lower until he reached the edges of her skirts, then he slipped his fingers under the material, dragging them up until his hand was at the top of her thigh.

Evie nearly jumped as his fingers found the opening of her pantaloons and pushed through until they were touching her curls. Then he started to caress her with his fingers, pressing against the little nub of her womanhood until she was squirming in her seat.

"Oh God," she moaned as her hips began to rub against his hand, urging her closer to him, building toward a peak of such pleasure. Pleasure she'd never felt before. And then he inserted a finger in her passage and pushed it in and out, the pad of his thumb still caressing the nub at her core. Another finger of his joined the first, and Evie ground down harder on him.

"That's it, my darling," he murmured against her hair. "You like that, don't you?"

She could only nod as a sense of urgency built inside her. She rubbed against his hand, his fingers thrusting in and out of her wetness, and then suddenly time stood still as she came to a cliff and everything exploded around her. Her passage clenched tightly against his fingers as wave after wave of rapture ran through her, until she collapsed against him, totally spent. He gently removed his fingers and hand from her and resettled her skirts around her.

"So that's what it feels like to be pleasured?" she was eventually able to ask once her heartbeat had settled and she could breathe properly again.

He grinned at her. "It is."

"It was…amazing." She sighed, knowing such a description didn't adequately convey what she'd come even close to feeling. "Did you feel such pleasure, too?"

"Not this time," he replied. "But perhaps next time, as we're nearly back at Aunt Agatha's."

It took a second for Evie to process his words, and then panic filled her. "You're serious?"

He winked at her and nodded. "Probably another minute or so until we arrive."

She launched herself onto the carriage seat across from him and began to hastily smooth down her dress and push back some wayward strands of hair. "Oh my goodness, will your aunt be able to tell what we've been up to?"

"No." He chuckled. "You look fine. Though perhaps your lips are a bit swollen, and she might think I snuck another kiss, but that's only to be expected now she thinks we're engaged."

"Only to be expected?" She blinked at him. Was he serious? "She'll never let me go anywhere alone with you again."

"Already planning a trip alone together?"

"Oh, you're incorrigible!" She took in a deep breath and focused on calming herself. It wouldn't help to seem flustered when she returned to the countess's. A minute later, she gave up on the endeavor when she couldn't think of anything but having another carriage ride with Alex and hoping it was soon.

She was turning into a wanton who craved the man's touch. But try as she might to berate herself over that fact, she couldn't. All she could think of was having his hand rub against her once again until she felt the sweet bliss of release.

Just wonderful! His mere touch had turned her into a woman obsessed.

God help her, she really was in trouble now.

CHAPTER TWENTY

What had he been thinking to suggest another kiss? A simple kiss, at that. Well, he hadn't been thinking, at least not with his head. That was obvious.

A simple kiss with *that* woman could never be just a simple kiss for Alex. She was far too intoxicating to him for a kiss to be anything as mundane as simple. Volatile, brilliant, and explosive were more apt descriptions when it came to kissing her.

And, God, when she'd opened his shirt and kissed his nipples, it had felt like he was in pure, blissful agony, her touch so darn electric he'd barely been able to control himself. Then when her hand had reached down between them to stroke his cock, which had been straining against the cloth of his trousers, he'd nearly forgotten where he was, such was the pleasure she'd aroused in him. He could still feel the exquisite ecstasy of her hand stroking his shaft. He started getting hard again just thinking of it.

And then when he'd rubbed his hand against her mound of curls, and she'd orgasmed around his fingers... He'd nearly spurted his seed in his pants, right then and there, like some randy bloody schoolboy. Thankfully, though, he'd managed to control himself, but only just.

Lately, he'd been doing a lot of foolish things when it came to her. Everything about her was clouding his normally sound mind and astute senses. Now that he'd dropped her back to his aunt's and told her to stay there, he'd hopefully have some respite from thoughts of her. He had to work out what the hell had happened at the college, and the only way he could do that was with a clear head, which he didn't seem to be able to achieve with her around. Instead, his mind would be imagining peeling off every single inch of clothing from that delectable frame of hers, revealing inch by inch of her silky skin underneath.

Damn, he needed a drink. He flung his gloves off and dumped them on the side table in the entrance of his residence, followed shortly thereafter by his hat.

His butler, Carrington, as usual didn't say a word, instead tidying up after him in his quiet, efficient manner.

"I hope you don't mind, Your Grace," Carrington said, his smooth voice conveying an equal measure of deference and familiarity as he hung Alex's hat on the hat stand. "But your cousin, Mr. Trenton, arrived not ten minutes ago seeking an audience with you, and he wouldn't be deterred from waiting. I took the liberty of showing him into your study."

Of course George was here, probably wondering what in the hell Alex was up to getting engaged to a woman Samuel had been infatuated with. "That's fine, Carrington. Thank you."

Then before Carrington could nod, Alex strode down the corridor to his study. Though George was more than amiable in most situations, when he wanted answers, he was also like a dog with a bone. And he'd want answers about the situation Alex now found himself in, even if Alex didn't have that many answers to give.

"George," he said a moment later as he crossed through the door of his study and strode over to his cousin, who was sitting in the chair across from Alex's desk but stood as Alex entered.

"What were you thinking?" was George's greeting. "Not only were you caught in a compromising position, but you were secretly engaged to Miss Thornton-Jones all along? Were you going to tell us? And why wouldn't you say anything? Sam and I are your best friends, or at least I thought we were."

There was hurt in his cousin's deep brown eyes.

"I didn't say anything, because we weren't engaged at the time."

"What were you doing kissing her, then?"

"Not thinking."

"You? Not thinking?" George appeared shocked. "You must be enamored of her for that to happen."

"It's nothing like that," Alex insisted, walking over to his chair and collapsing down on the soft leather of its cushion. "Yes, I might have gotten somewhat physically carried away with the woman." Who could blame him, though? She was bloody beautiful. "But I was only doing that because I wanted to prove a point to Sam that she was only here to marry a title, as all American Dollar Princesses are here to do."

George shook his head and sat down, too. "Well, that spectacularly backfired on you, didn't it?

You're now marrying her instead."

"That's one way of putting it." A rather nice way to describe the mess Alex found himself in, because if he wasn't careful and kept pushing the boundaries of propriety when he was alone with the lady, he would indeed find himself irrevocably wed to her. It was one thing to kiss the lady, but quite another to take advantage of her more than that. Not that he'd intended to let things get so out of hand in his carriage, but when he was with her and touched her, all rational thought flew out of his head.

Damn, even the thought of her sweet pleas of desire from earlier was enough to give him a semi erection. Luckily, the desk was hiding his lap from George. Even that loss of control, showed how much of an impact this woman was having on his normally iron-willed control. It wasn't good.

"Although, in a way, I'm glad for it," George said.

"Glad I'm being forced into marriage?" That didn't sound like his cousin, and though Alex wasn't technically being forced into anything after he'd agreed to his fiancée's plan to only pretend they were engaged, George didn't know that.

"Yes. It's about time you marry and stop all of this nonsense about staying a bachelor for the rest of your life." George nodded his head, appearing unusually firm. "You deserve happiness."

"And you think being forced to marry an American Dollar Princess will make me happy?"

"You were the one plastered all over her," George scoffed. "And, besides, what other woman have you met that genuinely shares your interests in stones and history?"

"They're fossils, not stones," Alex grumbled. "But simply sharing such an interest doesn't necessarily make for a happy marriage."

"True," George agreed. "However, you couldn't keep your hands or lips off her, either, so I imagine that will help make you happy. Isn't it time you settled down?"

Alex leaned back and stared at his cousin. George was normally never one to give his opinion unless specifically asked. The fact that he was doing so now, with confidence, was somewhat surprising, especially as Sam and Alex were usually the ones to dominate the conversations, with George happily sitting back and listening instead of proclaiming his opinions.

The fact that George was mentioning marriage brought with it a dark suspicion about the events of earlier in the day at the college. "If I do marry her and have children, that will mean you won't be my heir anymore."

"Good," George proclaimed. "I've never liked being your heir anyhow."

"I went to the College of Natural History with my fiancée earlier today." Alex watched his cousin for any hint of a reaction.

"Given your interest in such things and your fiancée's, I imagine you both had a wonderful time."

"We would have done, if not for someone trying to drop a rock on her head."

George blinked, shock clear in his face. "What happened?"

"I think someone climbed up on the bookshelf behind the one Aimee was standing in front of and deliberately pushed off a rock from the top."

George rubbed at his chin. "But who would wish her harm? Unless someone is jealous of her for snaring you."

"What do you mean?"

"Well, you've made it abundantly clear to all of Society you have no intention of marrying, but then you go off and get engaged to an American, much to everyone's surprise. Perhaps someone doesn't like that?"

"It's a possibility," Alex allowed, wondering if George could have had anything to do with it. After all, if Alex married the lady as everyone rightly assumed he would, then it would be unlikely George would ever inherit anything. "Maybe someone doesn't want me to marry and have children?" His eyes stayed steadfast on his cousin. George had never cared about money or a title, or at least he'd always said he hadn't, but men had done a lot less for those things before. However, this was George. Not only his cousin, but one of his best friends. He was as honorable as they came, to the point where Alex would trust his life to him.

Suddenly, George's expression changed, filling with a large measure of wariness as he, too, stared back at Alex. "Surely, you don't think I had anything to do with trying to hurt her."

"Don't you want to be the duke?"

"You know I never have. That the idea of running all of this"—he waved his hand around the room—"terrifies me. You can't think I would try to harm her."

"And what about Claire? You've said many times that you'd do anything for her. Does that include making her a duchess if that's what she wants?"

"Damn it, if I didn't love you like a brother, and it wasn't illegal, I'd call you out for even suggesting my wife would mean you harm just for a title!" George stood and banged his hands on the desk. "We've only ever wanted the best for you, Alex. We don't want your damn title. In all honesty, it would be a curse."

"It certainly can be."

George sighed and sank back down in his chair. "Though I can't blame you for thinking it. It is only logical, but truly, cousin, your attitude about what a woman wants has been greatly colored by your ex-fiancée. Not every woman is out to nab a title."

"Most are."

"Some, not most," George replied. "And certainly not my wife. Claire knew perfectly well when she married me that it was doubtful she'd ever be a duchess, contrary to your protestations otherwise. Trust me, we've spoken about it over the years, and neither of us wants the responsibilities currently hanging upon your shoulders. That's why we've always encouraged you to seek a wife, even though we haven't at all been effective. Well, until now. Lucky for us Sam was right about your interest in Miss Thornton-Jones and his plan worked."

Alex sat up straight, his whole attention narrowed in on his cousin. "So he did plan for me to get caught with her?"

George's mouth went wide and opened to say something, but nothing came out. He cleared his throat, shifting in his seat as if he couldn't quite get comfortable. "Er, I didn't say that."

"You didn't have to." Alex felt anger simmering through him. "He set me up. He knew I was determined to do something to show him that Aimee was seeking a title. So he made sure to come to the gallery with witnesses, to force me to marry her."

"I think it better if you talk to Sam about that. I don't know the ins and outs of it…"

"What nonsense!" He banged his hand on his desk, and George jumped in response.

"Good God, man, calm down." George tried to inject a note of authority in his voice but failed. He held up his hands in a placating manner. "All right. All right. He thought you were rather taken by Aimee, and well, I think when he saw you leave the ballroom, he assumed you'd be following after her…so he might have suggested to his mother along with Claire, her mother and my mother that they accompany him to the gallery."

"I can't believe he set me up like that." Betrayal, hard and sharp, stung him with the confession. "That he wanted to force my hand into marriage?"

"I don't think he thought he was setting you up," George rushed out to explain. "After you first met the lady and most especially after our visit to the museum, it became clear to all of us, except perhaps you, that you and Aimee are perfectly matched. You both have an odd love, or perhaps obsession is a better choice of word, for those ston—fossils. Why, the two of you couldn't stop talking with each other about them, leaving the three of us to watch on in an odd sort of fascination. We've never seen you so entranced with a lady before. We all commented to each other about it after."

"Oh, you did, did you?" Alex felt like raging. How could his friends, the few people he trusted in the world, betray him?

"We're your family, Alex. We know you better than anyone, so yes, we did speak about it with each other, given how noteworthy it was seeing as you've all but shut yourself off from any romantic attachment for the last ten years."

"A great lot of family you all are, with Sam trying to set me up, which doesn't even make sense. He was the one waxing on and on about how in love he was with her. Was that bullshit, too?"

"At first he probably was besotted. You know how he gets with the ladies. Always infatuated with them for short periods," George said. "However, I think after it became apparent how fascinated you were with her, his attention turned toward seeing how interested you were in her instead."

"By what? Pretending he himself was interested?"

"Yes, that's exactly it," George said. "I think Sam thought he was doing you a favor."

"Doing me a favor? Sam led me to believe he was in love, which was why I thought I was doing him a favor by pointing out she wasn't interested in him." Alex pushed back his chair and stood, feeling anger and outrage at what was becoming clear to him. He'd been manipulated by his cousins.

Stalking over to the very window he'd pulled the lady through only hours ago, Alex dragged a hand through his hair.

"Well, she's not interested in him, is she?" George said from his chair. "She's interested in you, having been caught kissing you, not Sam."

"She's interested in me because I'm a duke," Alex growled. "Nothing more and nothing less. Just like Julia. Which is what I was trying to prove to Sam before everything blew up in my face."

"Aimee doesn't strike me as a lady determined to marry a title like Julia was. And I think you know it, too, given how smitten you are with her."

"I am not smitten with her!" Alex roared, turning back to face his cousin, rage coursing through him like wild electricity. "I'm attracted to her, but what man wouldn't be? Fuck Sam. And fuck you, too, for taking part in any of this. Forcing me into a marriage I do not want or need. All because the two of you think I'm *smitten*? When nothing could be further from the truth."

George stood and stared at Alex, his chest puffing out as he straightened to his full five foot eleven inches. "We didn't force you into anything, Alex. You were the one caught kissing her, not us. It was your actions that created this. Sam knows you too well, probably better than yourself, if you won't admit you've never felt this way about another lady before. Not even Julia."

"Who the hell are you to comment on my feelings?"

"I'm your best friend and cousin. I know you better than anyone, or at least I thought I did."

There was a tinge of sadness to George's voice. "And Sam and I have only ever wanted the best for you. It broke our hearts, too, when Julia crushed yours. Seeing you look at Aimee like you have been gave us both hope that perhaps your heart wasn't completely shattered and that perhaps, just maybe, you might find happiness with the lady. A happiness you deserve but won't allow yourself to believe is possible."

"You and Samuel need to stop meddling in my life!"

"You're upset at not being in control of the situation, as you have to be for every aspect of your life. Always regimented and doing what is expected of you, just as Uncle Charles trained you to be."

"My father instilled in me a sense of duty." Alex took in a deep breath and tried to calm down. "I didn't have the luxury of having fun as a child like you and Sam did."

"I know that," George replied. "But your father's long gone now. You don't have to keep pleasing him by living with his rigid dictates for proper behavior befitting a duke. Not at the expense of experiencing happiness and love."

"How did this conversation turn into a discussion about my father and his influence on my life?" Alex couldn't stand thinking about his father at the best of times, a man so rigid in his beliefs, so determined that Alex would be a proper and dutiful heir, that he set about the task as he would a military campaign. No fun, laughter, or enjoyment permitted for his son, for that would be a foolish waste of time.

"I think you need to learn to enjoy yourself more."

"That's all well and good for you to say, George, while enjoying the largess of the ducal estates and the monthly income it pays you but having none of the responsibility of managing those funds or worrying over ensuring they continue."

"That's not fair, Alex, and you know it." George's brown eyes shone in upset. "I have made a good enough income with my investments, without the monthly allowance the estate provides me as your heir. If it wasn't for having to support Claire and her mother, I wouldn't take a cent of the family money."

The indignation Alex was feeling suddenly gave way to weariness. George had never been involved in the ducal estate as it was never really his place to have been, and even though he was Alex's heir, he'd never cared about that for as long as Alex had grown up with him. In fact, his cousin had always shied away from being Alex's heir, hating the possibility of one day having that weight of responsibility on his shoulders.

"Look, I'm sorry." Alex dragged a hand through his hair. "The events over the last few days have been unexpected, to say the least. I just didn't think Sam would try to trap me into a marriage when he knows how much I don't want that very thing, and most especially not to another American heiress."

George took in a deep breath. "Sam wasn't setting you up, Alex, at least not really. It was more a case that even he could see how attracted you are to Aimee, and I think he was trying to help you acknowledge that attraction, for we all know you're entirely too stubborn to do so without some help."

"A great help he's been." Alex walked over to the side table to pour himself a brandy. "So helpful that I find myself engaged." Even if the lady in question had made him agree to a pretend engagement. A fact he couldn't disclose to anyone unless he wished to ruin Aimee. And he certainly didn't want to ruin her, not as it was his fault in the first place they were both in such a predicament.

Though damn Sam for bringing an entourage with him.

"You find yourself engaged based solely on your own actions, Alex. After all, if not Sam and the ladies that had caught you, it could well have been anyone else," George said. "Surely, you knew the risk involved if you were caught. Or were you merely wishing to be caught by Sam to prove a point?"

Guilt, hot and hard, swamped him. George always did have an uncanny knack of being able to see under the surface of matters. It had been rather frustrating at times, as it was now, too. "I was trying to help him. Trying to get him to see the lady was more interested in whomever had the largest title."

"Aimee doesn't strike me as the sort who cares about that."

"She's an American. Of course she cares, contrary to her protestations otherwise."

"You're prejudiced when it comes to Americans, Alex. You do Aimee no credit when you liken her to your ex-fiancée." He stood. "Now, I best make my way back to my wife, who will be eagerly waiting for an account of what has just occurred."

"She's your wife. You don't have to tell her everything."

George smiled. "You are the smartest of us all, I will admit that, but you certainly are not smart when it comes to women, and wives in particular. You will soon learn when you become a husband that a wife wishes to know everything, and when you love her as much as I love Claire, you will do everything to make her happy."

"I will never be such a sap," Alex declared. What nonsense, trying to make a wife happy was the opposite of what Alex had been taught. One kept one's emotions to oneself, especially when it came to a wife.

It was the only way to protect one's heart, after all.

Look what had happened with his own mother and father: a scandalous divorce that his father had never forgiven his mother for, and not that Alex could blame him, as she'd run off with another man. Then again, his father had been a harsh man to live with, and Alex had only had to do so in between school breaks. He imagined it would have been even harder to live with his father every day as his mother had had to. His father had been neither kind nor affectionate, believing such emotions were weaknesses for a man and far more so for a duke.

"Never say never, dear cousin." George nodded to him. "I'm guessing we'll see you tonight at the Jamisons' ball."

Alex sighed. He'd forgotten he'd said to the

countess he would escort her and Aimee there.
"You will."

"Good." George turned and strode to the door
but then paused on the threshold. "Oh, and don't
be too hard on Sam when you do eventually speak
with him. Just like you thought you were doing him
a favor, he thought the same thing."

Narrowing his eyes, Alex stared back at his
friend. "His favor resulted in my unwanted engagement."

"A fact you'll thank him for eventually."

"Like hell I will!" Alex roared to his cousin's
retreating back as he disappeared down the hallway. If George thought he would ever thank Sam
for his involvement in Alex's forced engagement,
or pretend engagement, or whatever the bloody
hell it was, the man was dreaming.

Alex would be thankful once this pretend engagement ended, and the quicker the better. Yes,
the sooner Aimee sailed back to America and Alex
could put this whole episode from his mind and
forget the woman, the better.

The fact that he felt uncomfortable with the
thought of never seeing her again was irrelevant.
Though it did suggest he'd formed a slight attachment to her, which was something he had to put a
stop to immediately.

CHAPTER TWENTY-ONE

An hour after George left, Alex heard knocking at the window of his study, and he thought he had to be dreaming. Surely, Aimee wouldn't dare visit him here again, not after he'd specifically told her not to go anywhere after he dropped her off at his aunt's earlier in the day.

But another tapping at the window suggested he wasn't dreaming, so he got up from his chair and strode over to the window where, sure enough, his fiancée's face was visible through the glass, the afternoon sunlight making a halo around her head.

He swore heartily as he opened the window and pulled her through once again. "What the devil are you doing here? Does the countess even know you're here?"

"Unlike you, she doesn't believe she's my keeper," the darn woman said, raising a brow at him and crossing her hands over her chest.

"Do you Americans not use front doors? And let me guess, you walked here again, too?" The woman was going to be the death of him, he thought, blowing out a breath. "I don't remember my previous fiancée being so damn difficult. No woman, in fact."

"That's because she wanted to marry you, whereas I do not," came the woman's pert retort. "And, yes, I walked here. I have legs, Your Grace." Her hands fisted on her hips, and she looked as if she were ready to go a round boxing him. "I'm perfectly capable of using them on such a fine day. There was no need to bother the countess's carriage driver or waste a penny on a hansom cab for such a short distance."

For a second, he debated throwing her over his shoulder and marching her to his carriage to return her to his aunt's, then he thought he'd rather march her to his bed. "Are you going to tell me why you're here, then?"

"After you left, I sent a note to an old friend, Professor Burton, asking him if he knew anything about any murmurs in the world of paleontology about trying to scare or harm someone. And he replied straight back with some useful information."

She smiled up at him, and it was all Alex could do to stop himself from pushing her against the wall and kissing her until she was moaning his name. Instead, he pressed his lips together and counted to five. "An old friend? How do you even know this professor?"

The man was a lecturer at Cambridge University and one of the foremost experts on paleontology in the world. Alex knew him, but not well enough to send the man a note.

"I've been corresponding with him for years, discussing various hypotheses regarding calcareous microfossils." She shrugged, and Alex got the distinct impression she wasn't telling him the entire truth.

"In any event," she continued, "after what happened earlier and the possibility it could be a fellow collector behind the attack, I thought of the

professor and decided I'd ask him if he knew anything, which he does. Well, sort of."

"What does *sort of* mean?"

"I'll explain in your carriage," she said, striding
past him to the doorway, leaving Alex standing
there staring at her retreating back.

She stopped at the door and pivoted slowly
back to face him. "Well, are you coming or not?"

This time, he raised his own brow in reply and
crossed his arms over his chest. "If you think I'm
taking you anywhere except back to my aunt's
house, you're fooling yourself."

"It is you who is fooling yourself if you think
you're taking me back to your aunt's." She smiled
sweetly at him while squaring her shoulders as one
would when preparing to do battle.

He didn't know why, but he felt like grinning as
he stared at the blunt determination on her face. It
wasn't often anyone dared to stand up to him as
this five-foot-six-inch bundle of woman was doing,
and he liked it. There was something so animated
and vital about her, a spark of goodness and honor,
that he was drawn to. He sighed, knowing some
battles weren't worth fighting. "So where is it we're
going, then?"

She grinned at him and relaxed her shoulders.
"To Mr. Anderson's antiquities."

"That was who the professor said to see?"

"He did. He believes if anyone will know something about it all, it's Mr. Anderson."

Taking in another deep breath, he counted to
ten this time. "*The* Michael Anderson who dabbles
in selling stolen antiquities to collectors on the

black market? That Michael Anderson?"

Surprise flashed in her eyes for a moment. "I don't know about that aspect of his business, but yes, I'd say that would be him as I doubt there are many other Michael Andersons in the antiquities business."

She didn't seem fazed at all. He pinched the bridge of his nose. This woman was going to drive him to Bedlam. "I suppose you at least had the good sense to come and get me before you went traipsing off to visit him on your own."

"It was thoughtful of me to do so, wasn't it?" She winked at him.

A sharp pang of desire hit him in his solar plexus, and, in that moment, he was more attracted to her than he'd ever been. It wasn't just her looks, either; it was her bold spirit that was drawing him to her. She was a woman who stood up for what she wanted and wasn't cowed by his title or position. She treated him like a man and not a duke. It was beyond invigorating; it was intoxicating.

"Come on, then." She reached out and took his hand in her own. "Let's go see what he has to say for himself."

Alex let her drag him down the hallway, relishing the feel of her hand on his and marveling at how he didn't mind her taking charge of this little adventure.

His old fiancée would never have gotten herself involved in anything to do with such matters, let alone actively wanting to visit a black-market antiquities dealer. Aimee was as different to Julia as night was from day, causing his normally regimented routine to be thrown into chaos over the last few days. But rather than frustration over that fact, he found himself glad of it.

She was slowly starting to turn his world upside down, and he liked it, just as he liked her. Liked her so much that for a moment he'd forgotten their engagement was pretend, merely an illusion that would only last for another few weeks until she returned to the States. And when she left, he'd go back to living his life, every minute of every hour carefully planned and executed, his days running like clockwork. The very thought, which once brought him so much satisfaction, now left a bad taste in his mouth. A taste it seemed only Aimee Thornton-Jones had the cure to.

As he summoned his carriage, he knew down to his toes he really was in trouble now. He was starting to care for her, which he couldn't continue to allow. He just couldn't. But with a sinking suspicion, he thought it might already be too late.

CHAPTER TWENTY-TWO

Thankfully, the carriage ride to Mr. Anderson's antiquities store was short, and Evie managed to keep her hands firmly entwined together tightly in her lap for the duration of the trip. A feat, given she'd been able to think of little else except what Alex had been doing to her in here only hours ago and that her body was begging for a repeat of the experience.

Darn, traitorous body.

At least Alex had seemed as uncomfortable as she'd felt, his jaw rigid as he stared out the window for the ten-minute trip. Though he was probably only cranky she hadn't stayed at his aunt's. She couldn't imagine what they'd shared had been as earth-shattering to him as it had been to her, given his experience with other women.

"Have you had much to do with Mr. Anderson before?" she asked him as the carriage came to a stop in front of Mr. Anderson's store.

Alex turned to face her, his brows drawn together in a frown as the footman opened the carriage door. "I try not to," he replied as she stepped out of the carriage and he followed. "Although Anderson does deal in legitimate items, there are many times where he dabbles in the black market. As I prefer to avoid any hint of scandal or untrustworthiness in my transactions with fellow collectors and dealers, I try to limit my contact with the man. Though he often seeks me at various exhibits and the like, trying to sell me his services and convince me to sell some of my fossils to him. But I never will, for I don't take kindly to liars."

Evie swallowed the sudden lump in her throat from Alex's vehement declaration. She could only imagine what his reaction would be if he ever found out about her deception. He couldn't find out. There was no other option.

Returning her attention back to her surroundings, Evie stared up at the brownstone building, which was nondescript for an antiquities store, with its two modest windows, one on each side of the small wooden door, with some dust-covered statues standing vigilant behind the glass panes of each.

She followed Alex inside, the bell above the door tinkling loudly to herald their entrance. He began to walk down a crate-strewn path toward the far end of the room just as a man hurried through the back alcove with a flourish of arms.

"Welcome, good people, to Mr. Anderson's Antiquities Emporium," the man said with an elaborate bow. He was dressed in a brown gingham suit, with a green pinstriped waistcoat, followed by a bright blue bow tie knotted around his neck, and matching blue shoes. "I am Mr. Anderson himself! How can I assist you both today? Perhaps you are in the mood to buy some Egyptian statutes, or given the beauty of the lady before me, perhaps some of Queen Cleopatra's jewels to adorn your lovely neck with? Jewels with red rubies that would perfectly match the rich red of the lady's gown."

Anderson's eyes scanned Evie up and down,

and she could see the quick calculation in his gaze
as to the cost of her outfit. The man was a swindler;
she didn't need her experience of growing up in
London to tell her that.

"Put on your glasses, Anderson," Alex growled,
clearly not impressed with the man's perusal of
Evie. "And maybe you'll recognize me and stop the
sales pitch."

"Your Grace? Is that you?" The man sounded
surprised as he fumbled in his pocket and pulled
out a pair of spectacles. "It is you!" he exclaimed as
he hooked his glasses over his ears and peered
across at the duke. "What an honor to have you
here! Have you finally decided to sell me some of
your collection?"

The man rubbed his hands together, a gleeful
smile stretching across his wide mouth as he eyed
Alex, much like he'd been eyeing Evie, as if he
were a bank.

Evie had known many men like him from her
past. Men who thought money was the most precious of creatures, a creature that many would do
anything to obtain. Not that she could blame him.
The streets of London could be harsh for anyone
not born into privilege and prestige, which was
most of the population.

After her aunt had died, she'd been dreading
having to navigate them on her own, but thankfully,
she hadn't had to, given the generosity of the
Thornton-Joneses and their offer for her to live
with them. Even the thought of her family and of
them finding out about her swap with Aimee sent a
wave of guilt rippling through her. But she didn't

have time at the moment to feel guilty, so she pushed the feeling down as far as she could.

"Do you know anything about the incident that occurred earlier today at the College of Natural History?" Alex asked Mr. Anderson, not bothering to answer the man's own question.

Anderson rubbed his jaw. "Relating to an American lady? Yes, I might have heard something."

Evie gasped. "What have you heard?"

"Why, you're American," he exclaimed, turning to face her and regarding her with interest. "You wouldn't happen to be the lady in question, now, would you?"

"That's none of your concern," Alex answered. "Now, do you know anything else about it or am I wasting my time here?"

"That depends. My memory is not what it used to be. But perhaps some money will jog it slightly?" Anderson shrugged, trying to muster a look of innocence across his face, but not doing a very good job of it.

"Of course it will," Alex said before pulling out his billfold and retrieving a five-pound note from inside.

Anderson's eyes went wide at the offering. "I feel my memory getting much better already."

"Remember fast or this will return to my wallet." Alex held the note out to Anderson, but as quick as Anderson went to reach for it, Alex had already returned his hand to his chest, the note still gripped in his fingers. "The information first."

Anderson's face pinched in much the same

manner of a child being denied dessert. "I honestly don't know much."

"Then we shall leave," Alex said, turning on his heel and nodding to Evie.

"No, wait." Anderson held up his hands. "I know a little bit. Only whispers, though."

"Let's hope you know at least five pounds' worth, if that's what you wish to receive in recompense," Alex replied.

"Well, for the full details, you'll need to have a chat with Ned Garlick. From what I hear, he and his crew were approached by someone with a job to scare an American heiress who has a hankering for natural history. Sounds like the information you need, does it not?"

"Does Ned still hang about at the Lion's Den?"

"Yes, indeed, he can always be found there after midnight."

"You always have an ear to the ground, or gutter, don't you, Anderson?" Alex's voice was a deep rumble, his eyes pinning the man with an unwavering intensity.

"I do," Anderson agreed. "Information is power and is also extremely profitable. It pays to listen out for it."

"Didn't you think to try to warn anyone?" Evie asked, her outrage at realizing she had in fact been targeted starting to surface.

"My dear lady." Anderson turned to her. "I can't warn people about what I hear. If I did, I'd never get an informant willing to tell me anything."

"A charming attitude you have," she replied, shaking her head at the man's dishonorable stance.

"It's practical." Anderson shrugged before glancing back to Alex. "Honestly, that's all I know. I basically dismissed the information as it held little interest to me."

"It didn't involve an artifact or fossil you could steal for one of your clients, so why would it interest you?" Alex said.

Anderson scoffed. "I never steal, Your Grace. I *acquire* things, hard-to-attain things."

"Of course you do," Alex said, sarcasm dripping in his voice. "Now, if you so happen to become aware of any more information about this or future events involving an American lady, you *will* let me know. And I do hope I'm being clear, for you'll not like my reaction if you don't."

Hastily, Anderson bobbed his head up and down. "I will, Your Grace. That you can count on."

Alex stared directly at him for a good minute while Mr. Anderson squirmed under the scrutiny. Eventually, Alex extended his hand, holding the note out to the man. "Good."

Anderson snatched the money and pocketed it before Evie could even blink.

"Perhaps we can do business again, more in line with both of our interests," Mr. Anderson said, his smile slowly returning now he'd been paid. "I do have several clients who are actively seeking a large lizard fossil, which I've heard rumors you may have found?"

There was such a hint of undisguised questioning in the man's tone that Evie knew he was fishing to see if the rumors were true.

"Good day, Anderson." Alex nodded to the man

without any hint of an expression in reply.

"Remind me not to play poker with you," Evie whispered in Alex's ear as they made their way back through the store to the entrance.

"Isn't that an American card game?" he asked as they exited the building and walked along the footpath to where his carriage was waiting.

"That's one way of describing it." Evie smiled, taking his hand as he assisted her into the carriage. "I think with your ability to remain expressionless, you'd be remarkable at playing it."

"Sounds interesting," he murmured, sitting next to her instead of across from her as the carriage lurched forward down the street on its way to return her to the countess's. "Though I must admit I find it difficult to hide my thoughts when I'm alone with you. Can you tell what I'm thinking now?"

Evie turned her eyes to his, and her breath hitched in her throat. Gone was the neutral expression he'd stared at Mr. Anderson with, and in its place was raw, unfettered desire, directed solely at her.

Already, she could feel her heart starting to thrum wildly against her chest as the now-familiar sensation of arousal he caused in her began to consume her. It seemed every time they were alone together in his carriage, the passion between them couldn't be contained.

"You're thinking about kissing me again," she whispered, their mouths now only inches away as they leaned forward toward each other.

He laughed lightly. "I'm thinking about far more than just kissing you."

"You are?" Evie didn't know whether to be scared or thrilled with his words. The idea that they could do more was like a burning need filling her whole body with wicked promises of what could be.

"I am. I shouldn't be, but I can't seem to help myself when it comes to you," he murmured against her cheek, while he breathed in the perfume she'd dabbed at the pulse point of her neck. "You always smell so darn good. Like sweet flowers in spring. It's as intoxicating as it is compelling."

She likewise breathed in his scent, and as usual her tummy did a flip. "The feeling is entirely mutual," she felt compelled to also confess, taking in another heady breath of his scent, sending another thrill of delight cascading through her. "You smell of soap and sandalwood. 'Tis a combination I could breathe in all day."

He chuckled at her confession. "You are delightfully honest, my dear pretend fiancée. I like it. It's entirely refreshing in my world."

Everything in Evie froze with his words. Honest was the last thing she was at the moment. At least she hadn't been since arriving back in England and carrying on this deceptive charade. When she'd agreed to Aimee's plan, never even for a moment had she anticipated meeting Alex, let alone starting to like him. Because, with a heavy heart, she realized she did like him, a lot, and doing so would only lead to heartache.

For a desperate moment, she wanted to tell him the truth, to confess all, but if she did, everything would be ruined. He'd never want anything to do with her again, and she'd destroy Aimee's reputation in the process. So she refrained and instead pulled away from him, steeling her resolve to stop any more of these moments, regardless of how her body craved him. A cool head was what she needed, and distance was the only way she could get that when he was near.

"Whatever this is between us is a bad idea, and I think we both know it." The words were torture, as her body wanted nothing more than to experience his touch over and over again, but she was starting to care about him, which she couldn't allow herself to do. And it would only get stronger if she continued to let him kiss her, as much as she hungered for that very thing.

"We're adults," his voice rumbled as his eyes creased in confusion. "Surely, we can enjoy kissing each other without letting it get too far. I know I went a bit far earlier, but you enjoyed it, didn't you?"

Enjoyed it? She still craved it. "I did, but we're nearly at the countess's in any event…"

He regarded her for a moment but then nodded. "That we are."

She bit her bottom lip and had to clench her hands into fists to stop them from reaching out and grabbing his shirt to twist him toward her and kiss him senseless for the few minutes they had left until they arrived.

Just barely, she managed to stay completely still. She had to change the topic of their discussion; her willpower when it came to him wouldn't be strong enough if he kept looking at her like that. "What did you think of the information Mr. Anderson shared?"

He stared at her for a good minute, and she got the sensation he was trying to see into her soul, knowing she was changing the topic deliberately to avoid discussing the matter of anything further occurring between them. "I think I shall have to speak to Ned Garlick and see what he knows."

"When shall we go to the Lion's Den, then?" The topic was working to distract her inappropriate thoughts of wanting to plant herself on his lap. Only barely. "Tonight, after the Jamison ball perhaps?"

His eyes darkened considerably, and his usual frown returned. "You are going nowhere near the place."

Thoughts of jumping on his lap swiftly fled and were replaced with thoughts of throttling him. "You have no say over what I do or don't do!"

"I'm your fiancé—"

"*Pretend* fiancé."

"Pretend or not, I'm still not letting you go to the damn docks with me!"

"Would you rather I go alone?" she asked, raising her brow at him.

"You wouldn't dare to." Fury was now rife in his expression.

"Wouldn't I?" She crossed her arms over her chest, her expression militant.

"A dockside tavern is no place for a lady," he ground out through gritted teeth. "Your gown alone is worth more than what most of the patrons in the Lion's Den earn in a year. They'd want to cut the damn dress from your body simply to sell it, given the price it would fetch."

He was being overly dramatic, Evie knew from her own experiences, but she couldn't very well say that to him without igniting any further suspicions. "Then you agree it will be safer if I go with you."

"I said no such thing!"

"Then I shall have to go myself and wear a plain dress to blend in."

"You couldn't blend in if you tried," he replied, jerking a hand through his hair. "You're too damn attractive, even if you were wearing a sack for a dress."

"Then I shall have to dress as a man, won't I?" Evie smiled at him.

"I beg your pardon?"

He seemed shocked, and Evie imagined the Duke of Hargrave rarely got shocked about anything, though she doubted many of his female acquaintances would talk about dressing as a man, let alone do so. But it was the perfect solution, and one she'd done successfully in the past living with her aunt, to ensure no one paid her any attention.

"I'm certain you heard me," she replied. "I shall borrow some men's clothes from somewhere in the countess's house and dress the part of a young man. No one will think twice about me accompanying you."

"Absolutely not." His jaw was set in a firm line, and the look he was sending her would surely cow most, but Evie wasn't one to be cowed by any look.

"I either come with you, or I sneak out on my own later tonight and make my own enquiries."

She shrugged. "Either way doesn't bother me."

He swore vehemently into the small cabin space. "Goddamn it, woman, you can't be serious."

"I think you know me enough by now to know I am." She raised her chin and stared steadily at him. His ferocious glare might intimidate others but not her. If she or her cousin was in danger, she intended to find out, and no duke, as handsome and attractive as this one was, would stop her.

"Bloody stubborn American," he muttered, shaking his head not in defeat but reluctant acceptance. "Fine! I'll let you come with me, but you'll stay in my carriage, and that is non-negotiable."

"But—"

"No, and I mean it," he interrupted, his voice like a whip. "You'll stay in the carriage, and if you darn well try to disobey me, or attend the tavern on your own, I'll put you over my shoulder and return you to my aunt's with instructions for her to place you under lock and key!"

As much as she hated the idea of sitting idly by in the carriage while he was in the tavern, she could understand his concerns. Perhaps, though, she could change his mind on the carriage ride there later this evening. "Fine, I will stay in the carriage, but I could be an asset to you in the tavern."

"You'd be a liability, because when I'm with you I can barely think about anything else except pulling you into my arms and kissing you thoroughly. I can't concentrate properly with you around."

"You can't?" They were probably the most romantic words she'd heard from him, and she felt like hugging him.

He crossed his arms over his chest. "No, and I really don't understand my reaction, given you're the most obstinate, foolhardy, opinionated, and darn difficult woman I've ever met."

Now she wanted to throttle him. "Sounds like how I would describe you, except the woman part."

He smiled briefly at her response. "Are you going to stay in the carriage tonight if I take you with me?"

She sighed. "Yes, I will. Unless I can convince you to change your mind."

"You won't be able to."

"Never say won't, Alex." She would stay in the carriage if she had to. At least it was better than being either at the ball or the countess's and worrying about him.

"I say it with confidence, sweetheart. There's nothing you can say or do that will change my mind."

"Challenge accepted."

For a moment, he appeared confounded, but then he laughed, a loud bark of laughter that filled the carriage. "You really are the most determined person I think I've ever met. Do you ever give up?"

"Not if I want something."

And suddenly she realized that what she wanted above all was Alex. She wanted him in her life, even knowing such a thing would never be possible, no matter how determined she was. She'd really gone and made a mess of things for herself now, hadn't she? She'd done what she'd vowed not to and had started to care for a man. And not just any man, but the most inappropriate, unattainable man she could have ever chosen. A duke who she had no future with, ever.

The thought was entirely depressing, especially as she was starting to realize what a future with him could look like, even if it was just a fairy tale in her mind.

Only a fairy tale, Evie. Remember that.

CHAPTER TWENTY-THREE

Alex still couldn't believe he'd agreed to let Aimee accompany him to the Lion's Den tonight, though she hadn't given him much of a choice. Knowing her as he was coming to, he knew without a doubt she would have followed through on her threat and visited the darn place on her own. At least this way she'd agreed to stay in the safety of his carriage.

She damn well better stay in there, especially as he knew how determined she seemed to find out why she was being targeted. The fact confounded him but also reluctantly impressed him, too, and the more he got to know her, the more he realized how different she was to Julia. And just how much he was starting to crave spending time in her company.

He glanced at his pocket watch again, noting she was already five minutes late. They'd arranged for him to pick her up in his carriage at the back of his aunt's townhouse, thirty minutes after she and the countess had left the Jamison ball.

And here he was, standing outside as arranged, leaning against the side of his carriage waiting for the darn woman to exit the back gate. Just as he straightened to find her, the gate hinge groaned in protest as it opened, and out she came.

The very breath left Alex's lungs as he caught sight of her.

A groan filled the night air, but this time it

wasn't the gate. It was Alex himself. "What are you wearing?" he asked her as she came to a halt in front of him, a grin on her face in stark contrast to his frown.

She glanced down at her black trousers and matching jacket, then looked back at him. "Men's clothing, of course, as I said I would."

"You agreed to stay in my carriage. You didn't need men's clothing to do that."

She shrugged. "It's always best to be prepared in case you change your mind."

"I won't." The woman really would drive him to Bedlam, but for the life of him, he couldn't resist a quick glance down at her legs again, the tightness of her trousers leaving little to the imagination, as her hips hugged the fabric, boldly showing off her curves, far more than what a skirt ever could. At least the white shirt and black jacket were covering up her bosom. "Couldn't you at least have found an overcoat to wear to cover the top part of your legs?"

She frowned. "It was rather difficult finding this outfit in the first place. As it was, I had to sneak downstairs to the laundry room and rifle through some of the male servants' clothes to find some I thought would fit, all without getting caught." She pulled up the jacket to reveal the pants were slightly bunched up underneath at the waist. "They were a bit big, but I used a belt to tighten them, so they don't fall down."

He closed his eyes briefly as the image of her bare-naked legs flashed in his mind. It was going to be a long night. "Here, put this on." He shrugged off his overcoat and handed it to her.

"Won't you get cold?"

Cold was what he needed right then, though an ice bath would be better. That would at least cure this rampant desire he experienced whenever he was in her presence. "I'll be fine. And make sure you damn well stay in the carriage like you've said you will. Just because you're wearing men's clothing, doesn't mean you'll be mistaken for a man."

She pulled on his coat. "People rarely look beyond the surface of things, and in these clothes, I doubt they'll do more than give me a mere glance if I had to get out for some reason."

"I'm serious." Alex tried to impart the gravity of the situation into his voice. "It's a dangerous part of London we're going to."

"It's not that dangerous," she scoffed. "The east docks are far worse."

He peered at her, wondering how a Dollar Princess would know anything about the docks in London. "How do you know that?"

She blinked rapidly up at him, almost looking like a fox caught in his sights, before she glanced away and nervously tugged at the hem of his jacket she now wore. "Well, obviously I don't know that for certain… But I've heard my English cousin Evie comment on the docks. Yes, that's exactly why I know such a fact."

"Hm," he replied, wondering why she seemed so uneasy. "Regardless of whatever danger level your cousin thinks of the docks, you will stay in the carriage. My footmen have strict instructions to keep you safe while I'm in the tavern, so I hope you won't risk their livelihoods by doing something as silly as trying to follow me inside."

"You can't be serious," she declared, her unease forgotten as she fisted her hands on her hips, which thankfully weren't as exposed now that she was wearing his jacket. "You would fire them if I left the carriage?"

"I will do whatever it takes to keep you safe. So don't test me over it." He wouldn't, of course, fire them over her actions. That would be unfair, but she didn't need to know that.

They stood there staring at each other for a moment, and she must have believed him because she nodded reluctantly.

"In any event, it's you who will garner the attention." Pointedly, she glanced over at him, still wearing his tuxedo from earlier in the night.

"Trust me, the sooner they all know I'm there, the better."

"You have that much of a fearsome reputation, do you?" There was a sparkle of amusement in the woman's eyes, and Alex got the distinct impression that she thought the exact opposite to be true.

"The Lion's Den is known as a place to congregate for those more nefarious members of the antiquities and paleontology world. And, yes, in that world, I do have a reputation." He pulled out his pocket watch and glanced down at the dials. It was nearly two in the morning and the perfect time for those at the tavern to be slightly inebriated to make their tongues loose, but not so drunk that they had already passed out. "Now, come on, the sooner we can get this done and I can bring you back, the better."

Thirty minutes later, Alex walked through the entryway of the Lion's Den, having left Aimee in the carriage outside, with strict instructions for her to stay there. He damn well hoped she listened, and with the threat of firing his footmen she might; even though most heiresses wouldn't care about a threat to a servant's employment, Aimee would. She was different from the other heiresses he knew.

Returning his attention to the room, Alex's gaze swept over the bustling room. The place was a rabbit den of activity, consisting of a mix of gentlemen from Society and workers from the slums, who were all doing deals with each other to bypass having to secure collectibles and items of interest through more reputable establishments and auctions. Which meant everyone was on edge, with suspicion and greed rife in their eyes.

Making his way to the back of the establishment where he knew Ned Garlick would be, he ignored several gentlemen he recognized, instead heading straight for the back wall. In the far corner, sitting at a table with two other men, was his quarry, with a half a pint of ale in front of him.

Ned appeared as canny as ever, his weedy five-foot-eight-inch frame garbed in head-to-toe black, his thin mustache trimmed to the point of fastidiousness, and his beady brown eyes darting about the room looking for another mark. They landed on Alex and flinched. But before the man could flee, Alex strode over to the foot of the table where Ned sat with one of his men sitting next to him and the other sitting on the seat opposite.

"Fancy seeing you here, Ned," Alex said, smiling at the man, with little humor. "You two," he pinned Ned's companions with a stare, "leave now."

The two men hastily nodded, and without even looking at Ned, they scuttled out of their seats and dashed away.

"Yer Grace," Ned replied, with a nervous tug at his collar now that he was essentially alone with Alex. "What brings ya to these parts of the woods?" His eyes flicked over the room, like he was looking for someone to come to his rescue but coming up empty handed.

"I hear you've been busy, Ned," Alex drawled.

Ned's eyes widened in alarm. "I ain't had nothing to do with trying to knick any of yer stuff or find yer caves," he rushed out. "I know what ya said would happen if I tried to again, and I ain't, I promise." He nodded his head vigorously as if that somehow would convince Alex of the truth.

Garlick was a cunning swindler at the best of times, but he was also scared of prison after a short stint there last year, and that fear was usually what held him in check. Usually, except when it came to a large deal of money. That would entice the man to not worry so much about prison, as his greed often outweighed his fear.

Alex held up a hand. "What I'm here about has nothing to do with our last conversation."

"Well, that's good, then." Ned sighed in relief. "So, what can I help ya with, then?"

"I'm hearing whispers you've been hired by someone who has a keen interest in a particular American item."

The man gulped, and Alex could see the flash of knowledge in his eyes. "I don't know what yer talkin' about."

"Oh, I think you do," Alex growled softly. "I've heard from reliable sources you're involved up to your neck in a little incident that occurred yesterday at the College of Natural History."

"Well, ya heard wrong," Ned declared with a decisive shake of his head. "I don't know nothing about no American lady, and I had nothin' to do with any of them events of yesterday."

A long sigh left Alex's lips. "I never said it had anything to do with an American *lady*, now did I?"

Panic shone in Ned's eyes, bright and as clear as day. "Didn't ya say so? I'm sure ya mentioned a lady."

"All I mentioned was an American item. You were the one to mention a lady." Alex placed his hands on top of the table and leaned toward Ned, who cowered backward under his glare. "Though it doesn't surprise me you would take on such a job, but what does surprise me is you would be happy to incur my wrath by doing so."

Ned licked his dry lips. "Yer wrath? Why would ya care about an American lady? Thought ya wanted nothing to do wif 'em?"

It shouldn't have surprised him that Ned knew that tidbit. The man traded not only in physical items but information as well. "I care as I find myself engaged to that very same American lady."

"Oh fuck," Ned swore, the color leaching from his already sallow complexion. "Yer don't say?"

"I do," Alex confirmed, this time with a grin that

held the promise of retribution. "Now, you will tell me all you know about your employer, and then you will forget you ever took on board this job and will leave my fiancée alone. Am I making myself clear?"

"Crystal," Ned squeaked out. "But, honestly, I didn't take on the job. I might deal with stolen— umm, borrowed goods, that is—but trying to scare some wealthy Society heiress? No thank you very much. Dabbling in stolen goods might get you a stint in prison, but dabbling in people will get you a death sentence sure as all hell. So, no, I didn't have nothing to do with it, and if I'd known she was yer fiancée, I would have sent ya a warning about it all."

Alex stared at him for a good minute and got the sense the man was telling the truth. "If you're not being honest with me and I find out you were involved, I will see you on a transport to Van Diemen's land quicker than you can blink. Do you understand me?"

His head nodded up and down. "I do. And I swear ta ya I didn't have nothing ta do with it. But I know who did."

"Tell me."

Ned drummed his fingers across the table in a nervous staccato. "A chap came in here the other night looking for some men to do a quick-and-easy job, so of course the barman sent him my way. The chap seemed real nervous, he did. Said his employer wanted an American lady scared so she'd leave England and go back home."

"Sounds like a simple job," Alex said. "Are you

sure one of your boys didn't decide to take it on behind your back?"

"One can never know what another will do," Ned replied with a half shrug. "But my boys get a healthy enough cut in all me other dealings to know if they skim a job on the side after I've turned it down, then they won't be working for me for too long after. Besides, I heard someone else ended up taking the job."

"Who?"

He pressed his lips together and whistled lightly. "Don't think it right if I tell you. Honor among thieves, and all that."

"We both know your honor is for sale, if the price is right."

"True that is, I suppose," Ned replied, leaning his elbows onto the table and resting his chin in his hand. "So, tell me, Yer Grace, is the price right?"

Alex was surprised it had taken Ned that long to ask about money. Normally, he was a lot quicker trying to extort a quick quid from anyone. "If your information pans out, then I'll give you five pounds."

"Five pounds?" Ned scoffed. "You can afford ten at least. From what I hear, yer fiancée is loaded, a blooming heiress with a million pounds to her name. I'm surprised no one has tried to kidnap her for that sort of money."

The suggestion sent a white-hot rage through him, and without even thinking, Alex leaned over and hauled Ned to his feet, dragging him out from behind the table and hefting him up until his legs were dangling in the air and his eyes were level with Alex's. "What did you just say?"

"I meant no offense," Ned rushed out, his eyes wide with fear, though no one around them even blinked or stopped their conversation. Such occurrences were commonplace in the pub. "And I didn't mean *I'd* do anything like that."

"Have you heard whispers of anyone wanting to kidnap her?" Alex's voice was a deathly whisper as dread filled him with the thought.

"No, I ain't," Ned whimpered. "I swear I ain't, and I'd let you know if I do, I swear."

"You better had. And trust me, Ned, I'll blame you if anything happens to her."

Alex dropped him to his feet, and Ned scooted back against the back of the table. "What do you know about what happened at the college?" Alex had to force his jaw to unclench. "And my patience is wearing thin."

"All right, all right." Ned held up his hands and sighed. "I really don't know much. The man who came in looking for someone to do the job, well, I ain't seen 'im in here before and don't even know his name."

"You'll need to do better than that," Alex warned.

Ned grunted. "Honestly, I don't know much, though what I can tell ya is that he seemed to be a servant, cause he was dressed in similar clothes to what they all wear and was nervous and slightly deferential, unlike most of you toffs who think you rule the world."

"A servant. Was he wearing livery?"

Ned shook his head. "Nope. Just a black suit

with nothing distinguishing on it. I got the impression his master 'ad sent him."

That meant it could be anyone as mostly all junior servants dressed in the same black suits. "And who did you suggest for the job instead of yourself?"

Ned's mouth dropped open. "I don't know what yer talking 'bout."

"Drop the bullshit." To Ned, money was king, and he would have made certain to arrange a cut in what was on offer. Altruism was not part of his modus operandi. "Who did you suggest in place of your services?"

"There's a man on Bristow Lane. He runs a small gang of men who will do anything for a price. I might have told this chap about how to contact them."

"And to make sure he mentions your name, no doubt, when doing so," Alex said.

"Aye. How else am I meant to get a commission for me referral service?" Ned grinned. "You know the game I play, Yer Grace."

Unfortunately, he did. "I'm going to need his name."

"Aye, I do," Ned agreed. "But when ya speak to him, I definitely don't want you to be mentioning my name. It's one referral I'm happy to not lay claim to."

CHAPTER TWENTY-FOUR

Evie must have been waiting in the carriage for close to ten minutes, and there was still no sign of Alex re-emerging from the tavern doors. Surely, it couldn't be taking him this long to seek out this Ned Garlick and speak with him?

Maybe Alex was in trouble? Perhaps she should take a peek through the tavern windows to check? But then she remembered his semi threat of firing his footmen if she did, and her hand stilled on the carriage door handle.

Damn the man. How dare he make a threat like that? A threat she couldn't very well call his bluff on, even if she was certain it was merely that, a bluff. But she wasn't going to risk someone else's livelihood on being fairly certain about anything.

So, stay in the carriage she would. At least for the moment.

A few minutes later, she heard some noises outside. Good, that must mean Alex was done, and sure enough, a second later the door to the carriage opened. But instead of Alex's head, a strange man peeked into the carriage, his brown eyes latching onto Evie's.

"I think you have the wrong carriage," she said, noting his work-worn clothing of brown pants and a jacket, which had a month of grime and sweat caked onto his sleeves and collar.

"Don't think so," the man's rough voice crowed

as his lips twisted up into a grin that sent a shudder of fear down her spine. "Yer the American that we're after."

"I'm no such thing," she replied, dropping her American accent and replacing it with her English voice. "You need to leave here now before the duke returns and sees you."

"Hold up, what happened to your voice?" Absolute confusion crossed the man's face as her words and accent reverberated around the small space. "We was told you were an American."

Evie raised her chin high and looked down her nose at the fellow from her vantage point. "It seems you've been misinformed, doesn't it? For I'm as English as you. Now, I once again suggest you leave before the duke returns and is supremely annoyed that you would dare to accost his guest."

"Nah." The man shook his head. "You gotta be her, no matter what sort of accent you have. Come on then, love, yer coming with me."

Think, Evie, think. How to convince an oaf she wasn't Aimee? "Firstly, I am not your love, and secondly I most certainly am not going with you." Her eyes flicked past him to the street, and with a sinking heart she saw one of the footmen's legs on the pavement. "What did you do to the footmen?"

"Clipped 'em on the head." The oaf in front of her shrugged. "They'll be fine in a bit, just have a bit of a bump and a sore noggin, I reckon. If you don't wanna end up like them, I suggest you get out of this ruddy carriage now. Don't you make me come in after you."

There was a determination on his face, and Evie

knew he meant business.

Her options were getting limited. Reluctantly, she nodded. She needed to stay in control as much as she could in such an uncontrollable situation. "Fine. If you'll remove yourself from the door, I will remove myself from the carriage."

The man pulled back his bulky frame, leaving the space free. Quickly, her eyes darted around the interior of the carriage, searching for anything she could use as a weapon. The only items were a couple of velvet cushions leaning back against the seats. Darn it.

She pushed herself to her feet and exited the carriage to find not only the one man there, but a companion of his, too. Glancing down to the two footmen who were lying on the ground, she was relieved to see no blood on either of them. Hopefully, they'd just been knocked out as the man said they'd been.

If someone wanted her scared, they were doing a remarkable job. "What is it you both want?" She returned her attention back to the two assailants, straightening to her full height and staring at them with as much aloof confidence as she could muster. A hard ask, given the two were close to six foot apiece, with the bulk to suggest they'd perhaps done some boxing in their youth, though had let themselves go rather than stay fit. Still, they were intimidating men, particularly as they would have each weighed more than twice, perhaps three times, Evie's own weight.

"Me boss has a message for you, love," the first man said. "But wants to give it to you in person."

She tried her best not to let them see how that bit of information rattled her. There was no way she could allow them to take her anywhere. Glancing up the street, Evie saw a few patrons from the tavern going in and out of the place, but no one was paying any attention to them. And there was still no sign of Alex.

For a mad moment, she wondered if these men had hurt him, and perhaps that was the reason he was taking so long. "Have you hurt the duke?"

The man screwed up his face. "Do you think we're daft? Hurting a blooming duke would invite a death sentence from the courts. Ain't no job worth risking that for."

She exhaled the breath she hadn't even realized she'd been holding. He was safe, thank goodness. "So you're getting paid to do this, are you?"

The man scoffed. "We ain't doing it for the love of it, that much is true."

"I'll pay you more not to take me anywhere." If the pin money Aimee had given her for the trip wasn't enough, she was certain Alex would cover the rest, if she could get these men to agree. "Just tell your boss you couldn't find me."

There was a gleam of interest in the man's eyes. "How much?"

A good question, and one Evie didn't have a clue about. How much was kidnapping worth? She really had no idea. "How much will it take?"

The man scratched at his chin, and his eyes wandered over to his companion. "What do you reckon, Murph?"

"I reckon we need to gag this woman," Murph

replied. "We can't get no reputation for double crossing."

"Aye, you're right," the first agreed.

"I doubt your boss will appreciate you showing up with the wrong woman," Evie was quick to point out.

"You ain't the wrong woman," Murph replied. "You match the description we were given, exactly, well, except for your accent and your outfit." His eyes scanned down her clothing. "We was told you'd be in some fancy gown, not no men's clothes."

"Perhaps she ain't the right lady?" the first man said, rubbing at his temple as he eyed Evie's outfit much like he would a foreign object.

"Oh, she is. She's got the blond hair, the blue eyes, and the pert little nose we were told she'd have," Murph replied.

"Who is this boss of yours?" Evie asked.

The first man grinned and spat onto the ground next to where he stood. "That you'll find out shortly when ya come with us, now won't ya?"

He went to take her arm, but Evie ducked out of his reach and weaved between the two of them. "Help!" she yelled at the top of her voice.

One of the men grabbed ahold of her overcoat and yanked her backward. She stumbled against him and rammed her elbow into his stomach. He grunted in pain, and his hands lost their grip.

She pulled away from him, but the other man grabbed her and twisted her around. The momentum pulled her off balance and she began to fall backward. She latched on to his shirt, but the man overbalanced, too, falling forward with her onto the ground. As Evie's body hit the pavement, the man landed on top of her, and her breath left her lungs in a great whoosh. For a moment, all she could do was lie there, completely winded as her lungs struggled to get air back into them while the man floundered to pull himself off her.

From a distance, Evie heard a bellow and a few seconds later she watched in a daze as the man was lifted off her and flung onto the pavement a few feet away. Reflexively, she took in a big gulp of air and then another as the crushing weight eased from her chest and she could finally breathe.

She twisted onto her front and placed her palms on the ground before pushing up onto her hands. It took her a minute to get enough breath in to finally feel as if the pressure that had been squeezing against her lungs was gone, and then another moment to reorientate herself back to the situation at hand.

From the corner of her eyes, she saw Alex ducking the punch of the man named Murph before he threw one of his own, landing squarely on the man's jaw and knocking him off his feet and onto his backside to land in the gutter. The man moaned but stayed still, lying on the spot he'd fallen.

"Behind you, Alex," she yelled out as the first man got back to his feet and charged at Alex.

Alex spun around and stepped to the side just as the man was about to crash into him. Instead, the man went headfirst into the carriage door, collapsing into a heap on the ground.

"Are you all right?" Alex rushed over to Evie

and helped her to her feet, his eyes glancing back quickly to check neither of the men were moving. "Did they hurt you?"

Evie winced slightly as the muscles in her back protested and her head began to throb. Her fingers felt along the back of her head and brushed over a small lump from where she'd hit the pavement. Thankfully, though, there was no blood. "I'm fine," she tried to reassure him, but Alex was already gently twisting her around, his hands brushing over the back of her head until his fingers felt the bump in the center.

"Did you black out at all?" His voice was an urgent growl as he gently turned her back to face him.

"No, I didn't," she replied, noting a few patrons from the tavern had spilled out into the street, watching them from a distance with undisguised curiosity. "But I think your footmen did." She nodded over to the two men who were only now blinking their eyes open, nursing their heads in their hands, small moans of pain coming from their lips.

Alex swore under his breath as he strode over to his men and bent down to check on them. "Are you both all right?"

The two men nodded, both with lumps the size of an egg on their foreheads that made Evie's one on the back of her head seem tiny in comparison.

"Good," Alex said as he straightened and turned to stare at the onlookers who'd wandered closer to take a more in-depth look. "A pound to whoever fetches the bobbies first." Several of the gathered crowd all nodded and quickly rushed off, pushing at each other as they did so, to presumably be the first to fetch the police and receive the reward.

A low moan diverted Evie's attention over to the man who had initially accosted her, and though he was still crumpled in a pile on the ground beside Alex's carriage, he was slowly starting to stir as he began to whimper aloud.

From the corner of her eye, she saw Alex finish speaking with another onlooker in the crowd before striding over to the man. He bent down and grabbed ahold of the man's shirt and hauled him to his feet, pushing him up against the side of the carriage, as if the man were a featherweight instead of the heavyweight he surely was.

It was hard not to be impressed by Alex's strength. Strength she'd certainly felt when she'd run her hands over the thick band of muscles of his arms and chest, but a strength that still surprised her, given the other man outweighed him greatly, even though Alex was several inches taller.

"Wake up!" he growled to the assailant, giving him a slight shake, but to no avail. The man grunted and a loud snore broke free from his nose as his body slumped slightly in Alex's hands. Alex shook his head in disgust and lowered the man back onto the ground.

While he did that, a small noise sounded to her right, and Evie glanced over to where the second assailant had been, but now there was only an empty gutter where he'd fallen. "Alex, the other one's gone."

"Damn it!" Alex swore, dusting his hands off as his gaze flicked over to the vacant spot before returning with a vengeance onto the man lying asleep by his feet. "What did they say to you?" He looked back at Evie.

"That they were being paid to take me to their boss." She wandered over to where Alex was, her body slowly starting to shake, whether from the chill of the night or the aftermath of what occurred, she wasn't sure, but suddenly her teeth were shaking, too. "I don't know what's wrong with me," she managed to say, her teeth chattering heavily between words.

"It's a surge everyone gets after a violent or stressful encounter," Alex replied. "It means you're in a bit of shock." He reached over and pulled her in against the side of his body, his arm draping around her shoulders, while his hand vigorously rubbed up and down her arm.

"Th…that's probably true," she chattered again, grateful for the warmth that was penetrating through her jacket from his hand and body being close to hers.

"What's going on here?" a voice yelled out from the depths of the ever-increasing crowd, which slowly parted in the middle to reveal two policemen weaving through the throng as they made their way over to Alex and Evie.

Both policemen's eyes flicked down to the man lying on the ground, then back up to Alex and Evie.

Alex introduced himself and briefly explained the situation, inferring that the men had tried to rob them rather than tell the full story of what occurred.

As soon as the police heard who Alex was, their behavior turned deferential, though Evie wasn't surprised. Clearly, being a duke had many advantages. Money and position meant everything in England, and America, too, to a certain extent. Hence why Aunt Edith was hoping Aimee would marry a titled Englishman, then the Thornton-Joneses would not only conquer English Society but New York Society, too. After all, even Mrs. Astor herself wouldn't be able to deny entree to the mother-in-law of a peer of the realm.

In a way, Evie was glad she was on the periphery of that world rather than being in the middle of it. Well, she was when she was being her true self. Pretending to be Aimee had put her dead center of it, with someone clearly wanting her removed from the sphere. Who, though, was the question.

And as Alex finished talking with the police and bundled her into the carriage to take her back to the countess's, she wondered if whoever that was would be content with the failed events of the evening. Somehow, she doubted it, which meant she would have to be on her guard for the remainder of her stay in England. With her senses already on edge, given her attraction and physical reaction to Alex himself, Evie didn't really know if she was up for continuing the charade any longer.

But what choice did she have?

She'd survived far greater difficulties in life than all of this, though she'd never faced the challenge of battling herself before. Because battle herself she would have to do to resist the pull she felt toward Alex. It was going to be a bloody battle, of that she had no doubt. A battle she feared she may have already lost.

CHAPTER TWENTY-FIVE

"I'm getting you out of London and taking you to my country estate, Hargrave Hall."

The words were out of Alex's mouth before the idea had even fully formed, but the more he thought about it, the more it made sense.

Aimee, who was sitting across from him in the carriage and staring silently out the window into the dark streets as they made their way back to the countess's, turned to stare at him like he'd lost his mind. "Excuse me?"

He adjusted his frame on the carriage seat, a restless energy from the events of the night starting to ignite in him like kindling. It was usually what happened in the aftermath of a physical encounter. "It's becoming too dangerous here in London. Those men were far too bold and clearly prepared to hurt anyone who got in their way. It's likely they will try again, and I won't risk your safety or that of anyone else in the process."

His footmen both had rotten headaches from being knocked on their heads, and Alex would send for his physician to examine them and ensure they were all right. Not for the first time that night, since exiting the tavern and hearing Amiee's scream for help, did he berate himself for even agreeing to bring her with him in the first place.

He should never have done so. But, damn it, that's what happened when he let a woman convince him to go against his better judgment. Well, he wouldn't allow such a thing to occur again.

"You can't take me to your country estate all alone," she replied smoothly, her teeth chattering having finally subsided. "Everyone would find out and we would literally be forced to marry if you did."

"You didn't seem to worry about that possibility when insisting on sneaking out tonight to accompany me."

"That's because no one will find out about tonight," she hissed. "However, they would if we jaunted off to the country together."

"I'm not suggesting a jaunt," he replied, trying to keep his tone moderate to convey some logic to the woman. "I want to get you out of London for your safety. It's eminently sensible."

"No, it's eminently not. We can't go to your country estate. How will we find out who is behind all this if we do?"

"I've hired some men to make enquiries. They can do so while you are safely tucked away in the countryside."

"Has it ever occurred to you I don't want to be safely tucked away?"

Even in the dim light inside the carriage he could still see the gleam of annoyance in her eyes.

"Yes, why on earth would you wish to be safe? How silly of me to suggest that."

She folded her hands in her lap and pressed her lips together for a moment. "It is the tucked-away part I have issue with. I'm not used to being cosseted."

"Why are you American women always so independent and stubborn?" Couldn't she see he was trying to protect her? Instead, she acted as if he was behaving like an ogre, wanting to lock her in a castle.

"It has nothing to do with being American or not," she countered. "It has to do with the fact that I find it difficult to be idle, especially when trying to find out who is attempting to scare me and why. I want to take an active role in finding out those answers."

"And I am trying to protect you." He dragged a hand through his hair. "In all honesty, I don't want to go. I try to avoid Hargrave Hall as much as possible, and if it wasn't for my responsibility to manage the estate, and that my caves are there, I damn well wouldn't go at all."

"Why do you hate it so much? Your aunt says it's beautiful."

"It's the damned prettiest estate in the country." He sighed. "But to me, the bad memories it holds of both my parents far outweigh any of its beauty. In any event, it's safe, which is what you need at the moment and why we will be going."

She was silent for a minute, and Alex thought she might try to find out more about his parents, but instead she raised a brow. "You intend to whisk me there right now?"

"I don't intend to whisk you anywhere." He let out a harsh breath, glad that she wasn't asking more questions of his parents but annoyed she wasn't agreeing with his eminently sensible suggestion. "What I intend to do is arrange for us to leave tomorrow morning with Aunt Agatha accompanying us as your chaperone. With her presence, no one would dare to suggest anything untoward about our trip. Trust me, the proprieties will be kept and not only your reputation but you yourself will remain safe."

"You expect the countess to hare off to the countryside with us, dropping all of her plans and social engagements without even checking with her first?"

"She's my aunt, so yes when she hears you're in danger, I do expect her to accompany us."

Aimee narrowed her eyes. "You're so presumptuous, it's infuriating."

"I've been called worse." A small smile twisted the corner of his lips upward. As frustrating as this woman was, he did enjoy talking with her, even when she was berating him or being completely contrary, which was often.

"Yes, I bet you have." She crossed her hands over her chest and exhaled sharply, her eyes pointedly turning to stare back out the window.

"Once I tell Aunt Agatha of the danger you are in, she will agree with me completely about relocating you to a safer location for the interim, until the police can apprehend the culprits and ensure it's safe for you to return." He pressed his lips together, wondering why she seemed so reluctant to leave London. "I don't anticipate it taking any longer than a week or two at most. Besides, I thought you didn't enjoy attending all of the balls and being the center of attention?"

"I don't," she emphatically agreed, but then her

eyes clouded over slightly. "But given what's been occurring between us," her hand waved back and forth between them both, "I don't think it wise to be sequestered at your country estate alone with you, even with the countess playing chaperone."

He raised a brow. "Are you worried you won't be able to keep your hands off me? I suppose that's a legitimate concern for you to have."

She gave him the filthiest of looks, and he couldn't help but laugh again. He so enjoyed teasing this woman.

"If it eases your mind, I have at least thirty staff there," he said. "So we won't be alone at all. And just think, being at my country estate means you'll be able to explore my caves and hunt for fossils to your heart's content."

A gasp left her lips, and her eyes literally went wide with excitement. "Are you serious? You would allow me to explore and dig for fossils in your caves?"

He nodded. "Completely. There's so many caverns down there yet to be explored. You can take your pick, providing you choose the appropriate times to do so, given the dangers the changing tides can present to those in the caves."

"Oh my goodness...how wonderful!" She clapped her hands together in glee. "Doing that will be a dream come true for me! I've always wanted to dig for fossils."

"Yes, you've mentioned that before." He grinned at the palpable excitement shining on her face and being demonstrated through her enthusiastic actions. "I'm assuming, then, that the idea of going to my estate for your safety is more acceptable to you now?"

"It was an edict, not an idea," she replied. "But, yes, I'm happy now. You should have led by mentioning that aspect of it in the first place and I wouldn't have argued at all."

He couldn't help but laugh once again. "You're right, I should have. Though in my defense, it's not often a lady will be swayed with the argument of spending her time digging in the dirt, all in an effort to discover a fossil she can put her name to."

"I suppose that's true," she murmured before turning to look back through the window.

For a moment, he could have sworn he saw a glimpse of something in her eyes before she turned to the window. But it was probably a flash of light in her eyes from the gaslit streetlamps they were passing, which were intermittently flickering light into the carriage from outside. Although her enthusiasm had departed as swiftly as it had arrived, and he knew she was upset.

He didn't know what he'd said to cause such an abrupt change in her, but something had rattled her. The fact he was starting to know her moods after such a short acquaintance should have surprised him, or given him reason for concern, but instead he felt neither. Rather, he felt an odd sense of comfort to be so attuned to someone else and not quite as alone as he'd imagined he was. Perhaps this sense of companionship was what it felt like to have a wife, as George incessantly insisted it did.

Not that Alex wanted a wife. God no. Though he imagined at times there were benefits to the whole institution. Limited ones, but benefits, none-theless. Disadvantages, too, given the speed at which a woman's mood seemed to vary.

Perhaps Aimee's sudden change in tempera-ment was more the case of the events from the evening starting to sink in. That would make sense. He could still feel the fear, outrage, and anger that had surged through him when he'd heard her scream for help and seen her falling to the ground with a thug on top of her. Everything inside him had rebelled at the thought of someone hurting her, and he'd reacted on instinct, racing over to de-stroy the men who had dared touch her.

He'd managed to barely satisfy his need for vengeance by knocking the two assailants out. He was still annoyed one had gotten away. Hopefully, though, the police would interrogate the first one successfully and find out the identity of the second one, and who had employed them both.

"We haven't talked about what happened to-night," he said softly, knowing that as much as she might not want to think about it, let alone talk about it, sometimes it helped doing so. At least it sometimes helped keep the nightmares at bay.

She shrugged. "What's there to say? Those men tried to kidnap me to take me to their boss, a man whose identity we have no idea of, though he seems to know me well enough to describe my ap-pearance so that the men were confident it was me, even though I tried to convince them otherwise. Thankfully, though, you returned in time to thwart their plans. Not much else to it, is there?"

He rubbed his cheek, finding it difficult to deny

the logic in her words. "You say he described your appearance well enough. What was said to give you that impression?"

"He described my hair and eye color and said I fit the description he'd been given." She pushed back a stray lock of hair that was caressing her cheek.

Instantly, Alex's attention was diverted to her delicate finger as it gently brushed over the silky skin of her cheek, trailing a path to behind her ear, as she tucked away the errant strand. For a moment, all he wanted was to feel her finger brushing over his skin, caressing it with the same softness and exquisite attention. He could almost feel the feather lightness of her touch and he nearly groaned.

Clearly, being in such a small confine as the carriage was playing havoc with his mounting desire for the woman, which was only getting worse each time he was in here with her. He wanted her beyond all reason, and it was a dangerous need that was starting to consume him.

"In any event," she continued, none the wiser of how much his thoughts had veered off course and onto a far more treacherous path, "did you find out anything when talking to that man inside the tavern?"

"Not a great deal." He shrugged lightly, glancing out the window and noting they were only a few minutes away from the countess's. "He said a man came in wishing to employ his services to scare an American, but he turned down the job and instead referred him to someone else. Garlick thought the man seeking his services was a servant doing so on behalf of his employer."

"I suppose that would make sense if someone wanted to keep their identity a secret." She tapped her finger on her chin for a few seconds. "It doesn't help us narrow it down as many middle and upper-class Londoners have servants. Though it does seem more likely his employer will be from your world. Otherwise how else would I have become a target?"

"My world?" He raised a brow. She did say some odd things sometimes. "You're part of that world, too."

"I'm not really part of any world," she said, a slightly sad smile flittering over her face. "But the kidnapping must have something to do with our engagement."

"Yes, I'm starting to think that, too."

"Is there any particular debutant or mother who was set on changing your mind about marriage before I came along?" There was a keen light of speculation in her eyes.

"There's many of those, but none would be foolish enough to think scaring you off would change my mind."

"I don't know about that." She drummed her fingers on her lap, her eyes never leaving his. "It might have been the case before our engagement was announced, but now that it has been, it would have changed everyone's perceptions."

"It would, would it?" he murmured, finding himself entranced, watching her train of thought play out across her expressive face.

"Undoubtedly," she said emphatically. "They would all believe you've changed your mind about marriage, so if I was out of the picture, you would be available and back on the marriage mart."

"You make me sound like a piece of meat."

"You are. You're a duke, and a handsome one at that, so yes, in the eyes of marriage-minded females, you are akin to a filet mignon."

"You think I'm handsome?" He leaned across the short distance between them, until his face was only inches from hers.

She didn't retreat even so much as an inch as she eyed him coolly. "You know you are. I'm stating the obvious, not giving an actual opinion."

"But it is an opinion, my dear lady," he murmured against her ear. "How can it be not?"

Alex heard her swift intake of breath and knew that she was as affected by their closeness as he was. Electricity all but crackled between them.

"Fine, I think you're handsome—"

This time he did grin as he pulled slightly back from her to see how she would react. And just as he'd hoped, her eyes narrowed and a flush of annoyance spread over her cheeks. "God, you're beautiful when you're riled."

"Which is often when I'm around you."

She sounded adorably disgruntled, and it took all his willpower to resist pulling her over and onto his lap. Instead, he sat back and kept his hands firmly by his side. He couldn't keep kissing her every time they got into a carriage together; he had to show at least some measure of self-control, hard as it was in her presence.

"But, back to the matter at hand," she continued. "It's quite possible someone in Society is trying to scare me to go back to America to leave you open to a new engagement."

"It's feasible," he agreed as the carriage came to a halt in front of the countess's residence.

Aimee glanced out the window, and her hands clutched the seat as she swung back to face him. "What are you doing having your carriage drop me off at the front instead of the back? The countess will find out I've snuck out with you!"

The woman did try his patience at times as he'd never had his decisions questioned by anyone so much before. "I'm coming in with you to speak to my aunt." The carriage door was opened by his footman, and Alex gestured for her to go ahead of him.

"She'll be sound asleep by now." Disregarding the hand he was holding out for her, Aimee made her own way down the two steps of the carriage onto the footpath outside. "It's got to be after three in the morning by now."

"She's awake." He spotted the lady herself peering out from behind the curtain of the sitting room window. "I had someone in the crowd come and relay a message that I needed to speak with her urgently and was on my way to do so."

The door to the townhouse flew open, but rather than the butler, it was his aunt standing there in her dressing gown and slippers, an expression of outrage on her proud face.

"Alexander William Edward Hargrave!" She managed to convey her anger and upset all in a harsh whisper as he and Aimee made their way up the stairs to the entrance landing. "What were you thinking accompanying Aimee alone at this hour? Good gracious, you really are determined to push the boundaries of an engagement, aren't you? And you, dear girl." Her gaze spun over to Aimee and a fleeting look of apoplexy graced her complexion. "Oh good lord, what are you wearing?"

His aunt's eyes scanned down over the jacket and men's trousers before sweeping back up to Aimee's face. "Men's clothing?" She threw up her arms, and then before either of them could answer, she turned on her heel and strode back inside the foyer.

Agatha paused and looked back over her shoulder. "Well, hurry up, the both of you! You need to get inside before anyone sees you. Then you can explain why I shouldn't have the priest fetched to come and marry you both immediately!"

CHAPTER TWENTY-SIX

It hadn't taken Alex long to quickly explain the pressing situation to his aunt for her to agree with him that yes, they should remove themselves to the country immediately, though she'd also garnered a promise from him that she could throw a ball while they were there to celebrate Aimee's and his engagement.

Though a ball was the last thing he wanted, it would give his aunt something to occupy herself with, other than focusing on him. And given his lack of control around his *pretend* fiancée of late, it was probably best his aunt was well occupied.

He'd given them until ten in the morning to prepare for the journey while he went home and instructed his staff, too, before returning to collect them, along with their mounds of trunks and baggage. He hadn't realized two women could have so much luggage. Then again, he hadn't had much to do with women since his mother had left, but in the last week it seemed all he'd been was surrounded by women. Especially by the woman he was sitting across from, who he'd barely been able to drag his eyes away from since they'd gotten in the carriage nearly two hours ago.

She'd been sleeping for the better part of the entire trip, her head resting against the side of the carriage with a cushion between her cheek and the wood. There was such an innocence to her, a goodness that made him want to be more than he was. Made him want to be better. Made him want to do whatever he could to see her smile.

It was an odd feeling to have for someone who prided himself on being quite content to be on his own without the need for a companion.

"She's exhausted, the poor dear," his aunt whispered next to him, obviously having seen where he was looking. "Which I imagine you've observed in great detail thus far, unable as you seem to be to look anywhere else."

Alex cleared his throat and straightened his back against the carriage seat. His aunt missed nothing. "She's sitting directly in front of me. Where else would I look?"

"Where else indeed." She snorted lightly, but then her expression turned serious. "Do you think those men mean to harm her?"

"Honestly, I don't know," he answered, trying not to let the fear he felt over her safety consume him.

"I suppose we probably should have expected something like this."

Alex's attention swung sharply to his aunt. "Why do you say that?"

Agatha shrugged. "She's an heiress, and worth a great deal of money. Not to mention she's snagged you, the most eligible yet unattainable bachelor for the tenth season in a row. That's bound to ruffle some feathers."

"Seems a leap to jump from ruffled feathers to kidnapping." He still couldn't quite understand the motivation behind it all, or who would gain from having Aimee flee back to America.

"One would think so, but when it comes to either a fortune or a title, who knows what some will do?"

"Do you think George might have anything to do with it?"

"George?" She tapped her finger to her chin and contemplated the question. "Though he does have a lot to lose if you marry and have children, he loves you too much to hurt you. Honestly, I would think it more likely someone's mother is hoping to scare her off to leave you in the pool of bachelors, now you've shown an interest in marrying, contrary to your years of vehement protestations to the contrary. But if that's the case, there is one thing they are not considering."

"And what is that?"

"That for you all of the debutants will pale in comparison to her." She glanced at Aimee still asleep and sighed. "I've never seen you more fascinated by anyone, not even that other American girl you got yourself engaged to."

Alex merely grunted at her observation. "She irritates me, not fascinates me." *Liar*, the voice in his head whispered.

"Hm," his aunt murmured, raising an imperious eyebrow as she pulled out her fan and flicked it open with a practiced snap of her wrist. "Have you and Samuel spoken yet after what occurred at your ball?"

He should have known his aunt was going to mention that subject. "No, not yet."

"Things can indeed get complicated when a

woman comes between two cousins and best friends, especially if things are left too long."

"I was only trying to protect him," Alex replied. "Though it's doubtful I even needed to, given Sam most likely set me up to be discovered."

"If he did so, I'm sure it's only because of how you look at her." She clucked her tongue.

"I don't look at her differently." He glanced over to Aimee, her thick eyelashes resting softly on her porcelain cheeks, her full pink lips slightly parted while she slept, a wholesomeness within her so different to the other ladies out there. "Even if I did, it's only because *she* is different. I knew if I didn't pay attention to her and the situation, Sam would have fallen headfirst in love and stayed there until she broke his heart, which eventually she would have. You know that no Dollar Princesses and their husbands have stayed happily married."

"Well, it depends on your definition of happiness, dear boy." She shrugged. "True, most of the marriages the Dollar Princesses have secured over the years are certainly not love matches, but nor did they ever pretend to be. Or if they were in the beginning, their love was soon redirected toward others by both parties in the marriage. Yet most are happy with their arrangements. The wife is a peer of the realm belonging to the upper echelons of English Society, while her husband can enjoy all of his wife's money. For most, that is a match made in heaven."

"That wouldn't have worked for Sam, and you know it."

"No, it wouldn't have. He's far too like his father to settle for anything less than love," Agatha agreed, her sharp eyes keenly assessing him. "And yet you now find yourself in the position of having to marry a Dollar Princess. A steep price to pay in your efforts to protect my son."

"I consider Sam my brother more than a cousin. I will always protect him."

"I know you will. But surely you don't still think she is chasing a title?" She nodded over to Aimee. "Her mother wrote to me warning me she was completely against the idea of a husband but hoped that perhaps she'd find one anyway. And, yes, she's engaged to you, a duke at that, but somehow I think that was more because of your machinations than hers."

"I damn well didn't have any intention of becoming engaged to her," Alex whispered harshly to his aunt.

"And yet you are." His aunt didn't smile, but Alex got the sense she was amused by the whole situation. "Undeniably through your own actions, too."

The truth was always an uncomfortable thing to hear, even when he knew it was the case.

"Though I imagine you and Miss Thornton-Jones have come to some understanding that she will cry off just before she's due to return to America, leaving you unencumbered as you profess to prefer."

Alex had to clamp his jaw shut to prevent it dropping open. "What gives you that impression?"

Agatha shrugged, appearing supremely

unperturbed at the fierce expression he was now shooting her. "Not only didn't you post notice of your engagement in the papers but you were both shellshocked upon being caught in an embrace and then having to announce your engagement after. Obviously, at the time, I knew you weren't engaged, but to save her reputation I said you were, and gentleman that you are, you went along with it to protect her."

"Yes, I think everyone in the room guessed that, Aunt." But now he wasn't so sure a pretend engagement would ensure Aimee's reputation remained safe, even across the Atlantic. But did that mean convincing her to stay and marry him? When he'd vowed to never marry? If it was a marriage built on mutual respect instead of the illusion of love, then perhaps it could work...

For a moment, he imagined being married to Aimee. Searching for fossils together in his caves, discussing their finds and the latest scientific discoveries and theories of evolution over their meals. He had to admit, such a picture was enticing. They could build a marriage on friendship and shared interests instead of any nonsense to do with love.

"In any event," his aunt continued, oblivious to the direction of his thoughts, "the day after when you both suddenly seemed content to be engaged, I reasoned such a change must have meant you'd come to a mutually suitable arrangement for a temporary engagement while she was here in England. Is that not the case?"

His aunt had always been a canny lady, and one

who liked to meddle in her family's affairs, too. "That's not really your concern, now is it?"

Her eyes stayed steadily upon his, but Alex didn't blink.

"I suppose not, though if my guess is correct, you will need to be careful of yourself, Alexander."

"I'm always careful."

"You have been in the past," she agreed. "But lately? Your actions don't suggest so, especially not when it comes to her. Just make sure you don't compromise her further, or if you do, you will do the right thing."

"When do I not do the right thing?" It was the story of his life really. Obligation, duty, responsibility...all were at the forefront of every decision he made, except when it came to *her*.

"The right thing is not always doing what you think your father would have expected of you." She paused for a moment, her expression softening. "You don't have to be just like him, Alex. Yes, he elevated the dukedom to a viable and thriving estate, but it was at great personal cost. His callous disregard of your mother pushed her into the arms of another, and then his rigid dictates and expectations of you had you striving for his praise that could never be earned and then suffering his temper."

He could still remember the angst he felt having to return to Hargrave Hall each and every school holiday, and it left a bitter taste in his mouth.

"Nothing was ever good enough for my brother, unfortunately," his aunt continued, "and he only got worse over the years. Don't end up like him,

Alex, pushing everyone away, pushing love itself away, until you're all alone."

Compassion shone in his aunt's green gaze. Compassion that was as unwarranted as it was unwelcome, and Alex bristled under it. There was nothing that annoyed him more than being compared with his father.

"I'm a duke, Aunt Agatha. The position demands high expectations, and I will not compromise those for the illusion of any nonsense such as love!"

His voice rose on the last word, and Aimee began stirring from her slumber, putting a halt to his conversation with his aunt.

It took her a moment to fully awaken as she yawned and her eyes slowly blinked open, a dreamy smile spreading across her mouth as she caught sight of Alex. Then her gaze wandered over to his aunt, and she hastily straightened upright in her seat. "I'm so sorry, I must have fallen asleep."

There was a huskiness to her voice that sent a hot stab of desire through him, as he imagined her waking naked in his bed each morning and whispering hello to him in just such a manner. Quickly, he crossed his right leg over his left. Damn, how the hell could something as simple as her speaking make his cock leap to attention?

"It's fine, my dear," his aunt assured her. "You had a trying early morning. But the good news is we are nearly arrived at Hargrave Hall, the home I grew up in, as did my nephew." She pointed out the window, into the distant field of green trees that were surrounding a white jewel in their center. Hargrave Hall.

As usual, the mixed feelings that the estate always caused rose in Alex. The undeniable beauty of the place was so at odds to the harsh regime his father had rigidly implemented throughout Alex's childhood. A strictly controlled routine that had no time for play, no time for mistakes, and had to be exactly adhered to, and if any of those edicts weren't met, it would result in a whipping, and an even larger lashing if Alex made the slightest of mistakes with his schoolwork.

Then there were the memories of when his father travelled to London and left Alex and his mother at the estate. He and his mother would revel on such occasions, and she'd take him outside and chase him around the gardens while he laughed in glee. He could still see her laughing with him as she would catch him and pick him up, then swing him around when he'd been little.

But then she left him here and never returned, even though she'd promised she would. She'd left him, knowing how cruel and emotionless his father was. Left him here to fend for himself against a tyrant who demanded perfection from his six-year-old.

Reflexively, his hands clenched into fists as the carriage crossed through the entrance gate and began the long ride up the drive to the house itself. Try as he might, whenever he visited, he could never control the mix of memories from surfacing, both the good and bad. Memories that always left him feeling empty.

If Hargrave Hall wasn't his responsibility to

maintain and didn't have the caves he could nearly lose himself in when searching for fossils, he'd never return to the place. As it was, he couldn't do more than four trips a year there without the memories swamping him. This visit would be his third for the year, and already he was starting to feel the need to escape to his caves to get away from his horrid recollections.

He glanced up in shock as Aimee took his hands in her own, leaning forward in her seat toward him, caring little that his aunt was watching on in fascination.

"It will be all right." She smiled and gently brushed her thumbs across his knuckles, back and forth, the soft little movement calming him as nothing else ever had. "Just think, we shall be exploring your caves soon and discovering the most amazing fossils together."

And for the first time since he could remember, Alex smiled as the carriage stopped in front of the entrance to Hargrave Hall. It was only a small smile, but a smile nonetheless, as he gripped her hands in his and returned the squeeze. "Thank you."

They stared at each other for a moment, their eyes locked, caring little for the now-open carriage door the footman was holding open or the fact that his aunt had alighted from the carriage. In that moment, all Alex cared about was Aimee. Sweet, wonderful Aimee.

He realized with a sinking heart that when she eventually left and returned to America, she would take the last little piece of his heart with her. A

CHAPTER TWENTY-SEVEN

For the sixth day in a row since they'd arrived, Evie found herself wandering around the halls of the estate, staring at portraits of Alex's ancestors, after having visited his fossil collection in the house for probably the tenth time, with the man himself nowhere to be found, yet again.

Apart from mealtimes, she'd seen neither hide nor hair of Alex. It was almost as if he was avoiding her, which didn't make any sense. He hadn't even shown her his caves yet, which he'd promised to, but kept muttering about the estate needing his attention for the moment, and he'd show her when he was done. Whenever that would be.

Though given there was still no word from the police in London, they probably would be here for another week or two. Another week or two of absolute boredom if things continued the way they were.

The first few days after her arrival had been wonderful, as she'd spent nearly all day, every day examining every single piece of his fossil collection, multiple times. She'd literally been lost in the wonder of it all, amazed to be able to examine his finds in person, but after poring over his collection multiple times already, she'd found herself itching to explore the caves themselves.

The countess, having seen her burgeoning boredom, had offered for Evie to assist her with the ball preparations, which were well underway given the ball was scheduled for tonight. Knowing how prepared the lady was for the event, and how bored Evie herself would be helping to finalize floral arrangements and the menu to accommodate over a hundred guests, she'd declined the offer. Such an activity would only have added to her ennui, not relieved it.

Instead, she'd meandered around the house and gardens of the estate, which had provided her with some amusement, but now she'd essentially seen everything and found herself floating around aimlessly, her mind occupied with wanting to explore Alex's caves and filled with frustration over not being able to do so.

And if she were being honest with herself, she missed talking to Alex. Even at dinner, he barely said much, letting the countess fill the conversation with updates on who was coming to the ball and how the preparations were going.

Evie really didn't understand what had happened for him to essentially sequester himself in his study and have little to do with her. Had she done something wrong? He'd seemed to appreciate her words of comfort as they'd arrived, but then after that, it was as if he'd seen a ghost and had run for the hills. Perhaps it was the house itself? He'd mentioned something about memories and only coming here when he had to, and for his fossils. Fossils he should be showing her but hadn't yet.

Shaking her head, she saw the groundskeeper, Mr. Montague, in the distance and changed her direction to head over to him. She'd shared some interesting chats with the old man in the past few days, learning a great deal about the estate itself as the man had been employed for the ducal family since he'd been a teenager, spending over fifty years tending the grounds and keeping them immaculate.

Apparently, the late duke had been fastidious about how everything on the estate had to be maintained. Nothing less than perfection had been accepted, and Mr. Montague and his team of gardeners had delivered.

Even when Evie had accompanied Aimee and stayed at some of the grand estates in the Hamptons, none could compare to the magnificence of Hargrave Hall. There was a maze in its grounds that one could get lost in, a tree-lined drive that stretched for miles from the main road all the way up to the house, and the flowers that proliferated through the gardens were a sight to behold. Mr. Montague had been a fount of knowledge about the estate, and its surroundings, even mentioning a few interesting tidbits about the caverns and Alex's love of them.

Hhm...perhaps Mr. Montague would know about the tides and could educate her on their pattern? Then she'd be able to go and explore them without Alex's assistance. She'd already seen where he kept his tools to excavate fossils, having stumbled on a small nook at the back of the house that housed them. Surely, he wouldn't mind if she borrowed them for a bit? Not that it was even likely he'd realize she had, given his self-imposed isolation from her, but even if he did, she doubted he'd have an issue with it.

Who was she fooling? He'd be furious, but did he really expect her to be content with twiddling her thumbs and whiling her time away when she could instead be excavating some fossils? Especially when she'd dreamed of doing exactly that since she was a young girl. His annoyance would serve him right, because by ignoring her he was not living up to his word. Really, the man could have shown her the caves at any time during the past six days—no one was that busy that they couldn't take a few hours' break to honor their word.

With her mind set, she marched across the rolling green lawns, heading straight for Mr. Montague, closing the distance in a few minutes. "Good morning, Mr. Montague," she said with a smile as she came to halt in front of him.

"Good morning, Miss." He tipped his cap at her as he straightened from where he'd been bending over pruning a hedge. "How can I help you this fine day?"

"I was walking around the grounds and thought that as it *is* such a wonderful day, I should use it to finally head down to the cliffs and explore the beach and see where the caves are."

"Aye, today would be good for that, but I don't think His Grace would want you to go into his caves alone." The man scratched at his beard for a moment.

"The duke has already assured me I can explore his caves." It wasn't exactly a lie, as Alex had done so, obviously with the stipulation he went with her, but when the man was purposefully ignoring her, clearly, she had to take matters into her own hands. "Not that I intend to explore them today. I don't have a lantern with me." But tomorrow she'd be sure to bring one.

"The master keeps a lantern and some matches inside a box at the top of the stairs of the beach," Mr. Montague said.

"He does?" Her excitement grew. Perhaps she would indeed take a quick peek inside.

"Aye, and he keeps a few inside some of the caverns, too. He's always prepared, he is. But are you sure you want to go exploring them caves by yourself? They can be dangerous, with the changing tides and all."

"Yes, the duke did warn me of the tides, though I'm afraid I've forgotten when low and high tide are. Could you remind me?"

"Hm…at this time of year, low tide usually is around seven in the morning, and then high tide comes in just before about midday," he murmured, dropping the pruning shears to the ground and dusting his hands off on his pants before he pulled out a rather dented pocket watch from his pocket and glanced at the dial. "Which means you've probably got about forty minutes or so before the late morning tide starts coming in around eleven thirty-ish."

"And how far is the beach from here?"

"About a twenty-minute walk or so. So you'll have a bit of time to look at them. But don't go in the caves too far, or you'll be trapped there for a good eight hours or so, and trust me, a dark, dusty cave ain't no fun to be in. Well, unless you're the master who sometimes sleeps in them."

The offhanded comment was surprising. "He sleeps in them?" What gentleman, let alone a duke, would choose to sleep in a cave? He really was an avid collector of fossils.

"Aye, the master gets so caught up in his excavating of them ancient bones that he often loses track of time and misses the evening window between the low and high tide, then he has to stay the night in the caverns until the morning."

She didn't know if the shiver that shot up her spine was from finding the idea of having to stay overnight in a cave thrilling or terrifying. Thrilling because she'd get to search for fossils without interruption, and terrifying as the idea of sleeping the night in a cold, damp cave was not something she imagined being enjoyable. "He must get uncomfortable doing that."

Montague shrugged. "Don't know about that. He tends to forget about things like comfort when he digs. Though he must have realized he was uncomfortable at some stage 'cause he made sure to take down a makeshift tent bed and some supplies in case he did it again, which he's done, many times."

"He has?" She'd never imagined Alex roughing it anywhere. He was always so precisely dressed in his tailored clothes, everything as it should be. Well, except perhaps his hair, which did on occasion get slightly ruffled from him dragging his hand through it frequently in her presence.

"Aye, he has." He shrugged. "Enough that we all

know if the master says he's going into his caves, then we don't need to worry none if he don't come back until the next day."

Fascinating. It was an aspect of Alex she hadn't known existed. She wondered what else there was to know about him. A lot, she imagined. "You've known Alex since he was a boy, haven't you, Mr. Montague?"

"Aye." The man was peering at her with a long, steady stare.

"What was he like when he was younger?"

Mr. Montague was silent for a moment. "Always a curious lad, though reserved. Probably cause that's how the late duke expected him to be."

"Yes, I've heard the late duke was…demanding in his expectations?"

The man scoffed. "He was a downright taskmaster he was. Everyone was on tenterhooks when he was in residence. It wasn't as bad after he married Lady Hargrave, but he was always a cold and distant fellow, probably why the lady left." He sighed heartily. "Unfortunately for the young master, after she did go and the scandal she caused by doing so, the duke only got harder and far more demanding of him, to the point of cruelness when the young lad made a mistake."

"I've heard he beat him." The thought that someone could do that to their child was abhorrent.

"Aye, on occasion," Mr. Montague confirmed. "Nothing that could be seen, but from what I hear, a whip to his back and legs is what the young master had to endure if his father was displeased with him."

Her heart ached for the pain Alex must have endured as a boy. "Did it happen often?"

"Often enough in the first few years after his mother left, before he was sent away to boarding school. Best thing the duke ever did for the lad." The man shook his head and blew out a heavy breath. "The poor boy paid for his mother's actions, that's for sure. He used to smile and carry on like a young boy should before she left, but afterward, well, it changed him. He rarely smiled after and never got to run around laughing anymore. His father saw to that."

As difficult as Evie's own life had been when she and her aunt had struggled to pay the rent and get food on the table, she'd always known her aunt loved her. Never had she had to worry about being whipped.

"The caves, at least, make him forget all the bad memories, I reckon."

"I'm sure they would," Evie agreed. "I find myself entranced when I read about fossils being unearthed. I can only imagine how it would captivate one's attention and make one forget about everything else when excavating for them in person."

The man peered at her like she had two heads. "I see you share the same excitement the master has for rocks. Probably a good thing to go into a marriage with."

It would have been, she supposed, if she was actually marrying Alex. "Speaking of caves, where along the beach is the entrance to them?"

He seemed to accept the change in topic with a

nod. "When you get down the bottom of the stairs and you're facing the water, it's maybe five hundred yards or so to your right. Doesn't take more than a few minutes to find them after you hit the beach."

After thanking him for his help and promising him she wouldn't stay long on the beach, Evie soon found her way across the grounds of Alex's estate to where the cliffs bordered the ocean, her trek there filled with thoughts of Alex and what he'd had to endure as a child. No wonder he was always so proper and dignified; at least he was outside of his carriage. The thought of what his fingers and mouth did to her in the confines of the vehicle still sent a blush across her face.

She didn't know if having those memories to relive as she got older was a good thing or a terrible thing. Would she grow to regret kissing him or regret not experiencing more of what it was to be his lover? She rather suspected the latter.

Stopping a few feet from the cliff's edge, she breathed in the crisp salt air of the sea, drinking it in until she couldn't take any more air into her lungs. It was magnificent. Her eyes scanned across the vista, delighting in the crystal blue of the ocean as it sparkled across the vast expanse of the horizon until it met the sandy shoreline below.

She glanced to her right and saw the box of supplies and the steps down to the ocean just as Mr. Montague said were there. Without wasting another moment, Evie hurried over to them and took a lantern and then pocketed a tin of matches. Gripping the wooden railing that followed the stairs down to the beach, she began her descent onto the rock-scattered sand below.

The minute she stepped off the last wooden step and her shoes hit the sand, Evie stopped and stood there, marveling at the sight and gentle sound of the waves rolling onto the sandy beach. The soft rhythm of their movement was calming and yet invigorating all at once.

She closed her eyes and breathed in the sea air once again.

If she lived at Hargrave Hall, she'd come down to this beach every day, breathing in its tranquility and vitality, never wanting to leave. Not that she ever would live here. Such a thought was pure fantasy, a dream that never could be. So she'd enjoy staying here in the interim and keep the memories from the experience close to her heart, to be remembered when she needed some magic in her life. But rather than images of the beach and the beauty of the estate filling her mind, instead it was Alex's face that swam into view.

His strong, handsome, and chiseled face that caused all sorts of quivers of excitement to run through her. He was unlike any man she'd ever known. A man she was drawn to but who was so far removed from her own true station in life that he never would have even looked at her twice if not for this darned charade. A man she was slowly starting to fall in love with.

Her whole body froze in denial. Love? No. She wasn't in love with Alex. She couldn't be. What she felt was simply infatuation, and a curious fascination to know more about him, that was all.

Panic began to claw at her throat with the realization that perhaps it was more. Perhaps she'd done what she'd vowed not to. Perhaps she'd fallen for Alex. But that couldn't be the case. Her feelings for him could easily be rationalized. After all, he was the first man she'd ever met who wasn't only handsome but also shared her love of fossils. She could talk to him about subjects that barely anyone else understood, let alone enjoyed discussing. Not to mention, he was the first man she'd shared a kiss with, and the first man to touch her in places no one ever had.

Even the mere thought of his fingers caressing her breasts and rubbing between her thighs sent a wave of pure need through her body. No wonder she was infatuated with him. What woman in her position wouldn't be? And that's all it was, an infatuation, pure and simple. An infatuation that would end as quickly as it had begun, and one she had to stop thinking about.

With that thought firmly in mind, she turned her gaze from staring out at the ocean and back onto the cliffs along the shoreline. She'd come here to look at the caves, not obsess over Alex. So find the caves she would.

Following the shoreline, she strode down the beach, scanning along the face of the cliff. She'd never been good at calculating distances, but after a few minutes of walking, she spotted an opening in the rock face ahead. It had to be the entrance to the caves.

Excitement filled her with the thought that she was finally going to get to see some fossils in situ, instead of merely reading about them or seeing fossils someone else had excavated.

She came to a stop outside the mouth of the cave. The opening was about twenty feet wide by about ten feet high, and the rock and sand floor was wet from the previous tide, but clear of water now. Walking up to the entrance, Evie peered inside and could see about thirty feet into the cave, but then the sun's light was obliterated by the inky blackness within.

Given what Alex said about there being multiple caverns inside, the cave must stretch underneath the cliffs for miles and miles. She wandered inside, her free hand tracing over patches of surprisingly smooth rock walls. The ocean must fill the bottom part of the cave when the tide was in, to have smoothed the rock walls like this. Veins of quartz were running haphazardly through the rock, sparkling in the afternoon sun.

Venturing into the cave, she decided she still had a bit of time to take a quick peek further inside the caves before the tide was anywhere near coming in, and given Mr. Montague's estimate, she probably had another fifteen to twenty minutes to take a quick look.

The decision made, she put down the lantern and took out the tin of matches, striking a match several times against the tin's edge until the end of it flared to life with a brightly burning flame. She bent over and picked up the lantern, using the match against the wick until it ignited and filled the cave with light.

Holding it aloft toward the back of the cave, she

saw the sandy path trailed down into the depths of a wider opening at the back of it. A slight amount of trepidation rattled her normally calm demeanor at the thought of being alone in a cave, something she'd never done before, but then she shook off the feeling and raised her chin.

She was not going to let a little fear stop her from at least seeing the first main cavern. Taking a bold step forward, she walked further down the path, the sound of ocean waves receding with each footstep she took, until it was a mere hum in the background as the eerie silence of the cave engulfed her.

Up ahead, an opening in the rock wall loomed large, and when she came level with it, she swung the lantern into the gap and her jaw dropped open. Shining on the walls to her left were fossils partially buried in the walls. Shells, fish bones, and some other crustacean remains were scattered through the rock of the walls like wallpaper. She rushed over to the nearest specimen, her free hand gently tracing over what looked to be a fish skeleton.

She didn't know how many minutes she stood there marveling at the feel of the fossil under her hand, but it had to have been about five, as entranced as she was. Then she began to walk along the cave wall, her eyes drinking in the sight of so many fossils still in their resting places. To think all these creatures had lain entombed in the cave for centuries, possibly longer, preserved and just waiting to be discovered. It was awe inspiring.

"Damn it, I told you I'd bring you here eventually. I should have known you wouldn't listen."

CHAPTER TWENTY-EIGHT

Evie nearly dropped the lantern, barely managing to grip her fingers around its handle at the last minute as she spun around to see Alex standing there, an extremely vexed scowl on his face. "You scared me half to death!"

"You should be scared," he growled, striding over to her, stopping mere inches in front of her. "These caves can be dangerous if you don't know what you're doing. Which you don't, having decided to show yourself them when the high tide is near approaching."

"I'm only taking a quick look," she replied. "And if you'd kept your word and showed me them soon after we'd arrived, instead of pretending I didn't exist and avoiding me, I would know exactly what I was doing down here."

"I haven't not kept my word." He sounded incensed that she would suggest such a thing. "I've been busy sorting out the estate. I told you I'd eventually bring you here."

"Eventually sounds a lot like never to me." She fisted her free hand on her hip and glared at him.

As they stood there staring at each other, the lantern hanging down from Evie's hand by her side, Alex's features were brought into stark relief against the shadows of the cave, and all she could think about was kissing him again. With a start, she realized she'd missed being alone with him. Missed being with him. Missed speaking with him. Missed the touch of his lips upon hers.

"How did you know I'd be down here anyhow?" she asked, trying to return her mind back to far more safe and mundane thoughts. "Were you spying on me?"

He let out a harsh breath. "Of course not. I happened to glance out my window and saw you speaking with Montague. Then with the way you were hurrying off in the direction of the beach, I knew this was where you'd be heading. And I was right, because here you are."

Evie had to suppress a gulp as a thrill of awareness skimmed over her skin at his nearness. She could all but feel the heat radiating from him, and she had to clench the fingers of her free hand tighter to stop herself from grabbing his shirt and pulling him to her.

"The tides can be unpredictable, and you aren't familiar with them," he continued, his head leaning closer to her own, his breath a whisper near her lips as his anger seemed to drain away.

"Well, as you can see, there's not a scratch on me." She gestured down her body, and his eyes followed her movement. "Miraculous, isn't it?"

"Sarcasm doesn't become you," he replied, having difficulty dragging his eyes back up to her face.

"Just as overbearing brutishness doesn't become you," she said, noting the huskiness of her own voice. "Though it seems to be your preferred method of communicating with me."

His lips twisted up at the corners. "Overbearing, perhaps. But brutish? I don't know about that." His right hand brushed over the top of her hand where she was holding the lantern handle, and his fingers closed around hers. It was all Evie could do to stay upright from his touch, his fingers so strong against hers. The longing for him to caress her again grew and began to overwhelm her.

Before she could even blink, he'd deftly switched the lantern into his own hand, then reaching behind her, his chest pressing against hers, he hooked the lantern on a nail high up on the rock wall.

"See how helpful it is to have me here?" He pulled back, but only slightly, and winked at her. "Makes it much easier to see the fossils and feel for them if both of your hands are free."

Then he wandered over to the near side of the cave and pulled out a match tin from his pocket and quickly lit a lantern already hanging on the far wall that Evie hadn't even seen.

"It would have been far more helpful if you'd shown me all of this at the start of the week," she replied as the second lantern flared to life, sending more light across the walls of the cave. Her eyes wandered over the space, desperate to latch onto anything but him as he walked back over to her.

Glimpses of partially uncovered fossils in the rock walls glimmered all around her, and that's where she firmly directed her attention. "I would have been down here every day if you had."

"Yes, I've no doubt about that."

"Is this the main cavern, then?" There, that was good, talk of the caves and fossils, not think about how damn handsome the man in front of her was.

"Not even close. There's another tunnel over to your left that leads to many more caverns, much larger than this one." He pointed over to another opening in the rock wall on the far side of where they'd come through that was now visible with the second lantern lit. "Many that have even larger fossil specimens in them than this one."

Evie's heart quickened at the thought. "Can you show me?" The anticipation of seeing such things in situ was thrilling, especially if Alex was the one showing her. With him sharing her fascination for the subject, it made it all the more exciting when looking at a fossil and discussing the features of it.

"I'll have to show you another day, or we'll be trapped alone together in these caves for the next eight hours, and I doubt the countess would appreciate us being late for the ball tonight."

"I nearly forgot about that," Evie replied. "I think I'd much rather spend the time in here excavating for fossils and suffer the countess's wrath with being late to the ball."

He laughed. "If she found out we spent the entire high tide in here alone, then we really would have to marry."

As if such a thing would ever be possible. Someone like Evie could never marry someone like Alex. Although part of Evie didn't mind the idea of spending the night in the caves alone with him...

But who was she fooling? She could barely handle being in this little cave with him for a few minutes without feeling the breathless anticipation of desire. How could she handle being in the caves with him for hours more? Already his very nearness was affecting her to the point of breath-lessness, which was ridiculous in and of itself as she wasn't some woman who would wither be-cause a handsome man was in the room.

Or at least she hadn't been before she'd met him.

Taking in a breath, she tried to calm her emo-tions and not let him see how he was starting to affect her equilibrium. Evie was determined to overcome this ridiculous lust she had for him. A difficult task, as she felt hot and bothered all over with the closeness of his body only a few feet away. *Focus on the fossils*, she tried to remind herself, but despite the self-direction, all she could do was stare at his full lips, his aquiline nose, and the shadow of stubble across his jaw.

She had missed him, and she didn't know quite what to make of that realization.

"Why have you been avoiding me?" she blurted out before she could stop herself.

His jaw tightened, and the laughter in his eyes was replaced by an enigmatic stare. "I've had many things requiring my attention. Besides, I thought you and the countess would be busy planning the ball."

Evie raised her brow at the statement. "I think you know me well enough by now to know that would never be the case."

"I do know that." He exhaled and rubbed his chin, almost appearing somewhat lost for words, which was odd for him. "The truth is…it's hard enough already coming to Hargrave Hall with all the memories it holds of my parents. I didn't know if I was ready to add you to the list of memories here, too."

"I don't understand."

He took a step back and strode away from her, dragging his hand through his hair as he did so. "If I spent more time with you here, then every time I returned without you, I'd see you everywhere. It's bad enough already as I can't stop thinking about you."

"You've done a good job of not thinking about me for the past week."

He gave a mirthless laugh. "Not think about you? You've filled my thoughts and dreams every single day we've been here. I thought avoiding you would help stop that, but it hasn't. It would only be worse if those memories included being down here with you"—his hands swung wildly about the cave—"sharing this space with you. After you return to the States, every time I come down here again, it wouldn't be my sanctuary anymore, it would be my prison. A prison of memories of you, and it would be torture. Pure. Damn. Torture."

His eyes latched onto hers from across the room, and she saw the pain and angst in them. Licking her suddenly dry lips, Evie didn't know what to say. Didn't even really know how to process what he was saying, what he even meant. "What are you saying, Alex?"

"I don't know." He blew out a sharp breath and walked back over to her. "I don't even know myself at the moment. I've never felt the way I do with anyone as I do with you, and it's confusing the hell out of me."

Her heart leaped at his words, but then an agonizing trepidation filled her. If he knew of her charade, of how she'd been lying to him the entire time, he'd feel nothing but loathing toward her, and any attraction, if that's what one could call these feelings growing between them, would be gone as quickly as it had come. "I don't know what to say."

"Neither do I," he replied. "I just know that try as I might to avoid you and to push you from my thoughts, it hasn't worked. All I can think of is kissing you. Of being with you, always."

His words sent a sharp pang of need through her. Suddenly, Evie felt like throwing caution to the wind. Why shouldn't they kiss? Why shouldn't they at least experience the bliss of doing so before she returned to the reality of her life in New York?

Boldly, she stepped over to him. "I've been thinking of your lips against mine, too."

"You have?" he asked, much like a man drowning and begging for a boat.

"I have, so very much."

He groaned and closed the distance between them, his lips crashing down onto hers in a frenzy of hunger and need. Evie moaned and wrapped her hands around his neck, pulling him closer to her, pressing her breasts against him and marveling at the feel of his hard chest, as his tongue plundered her mouth. This man made her forget everything but him. His heat, his strength, his very maleness that left her breathless.

"God, I've missed kissing you," he mumbled

between kisses. "I've missed tasting and touching you."

"So have I," Evie replied, her hands sliding down his back until she grabbed his buttocks and pulled him to her center. She gasped at the hard length of him pressing into her. Her eyes found his, and she saw the fierce desire reflecting in his gaze.

"See what you do to me," he murmured. "I only have to touch you. Hell, I only have to be in your presence and I'm as hard as all the bloody rocks in this cave."

Then his lips found hers again, and she couldn't think of anything but the thrill of his mouth against hers. She couldn't get enough of him, her body craving him to the very center of her being.

"Well, well, well. Looks like we got here in the nick of time," a deep cockney accent spoke from the entrance of the cavern.

Alex's mouth wrenched away from hers as he reached behind her and grabbed the lantern from the wall, before spinning around to face the intruder, his body deftly blocking her from the threat.

Evie peered around him to see two men standing next to each other, filling the small space of the cavern entry. With a sinking heart, she recognized one of the men as one who'd accosted her the other week in front of the tavern, and the man was holding a pistol in his hand.

A pistol aimed straight for Alex and her.

CHAPTER TWENTY-NINE

With Aimee safely behind him, Alex assessed the situation, holding the lantern aloft with his left hand as he glanced at the intruders.

Two men stood side by side, blocking the main exit out of the cavern, with one holding a pistol and the other a lantern and knife. He recognized the one with the pistol as one of the men who'd attacked Aimee in the carriage the other week. Clearly, the men had followed them to the estate or else discovered that's where Alex had taken Aimee.

Both men looked like cheap hired thugs, with perhaps some boxing experience, given how each of them were balancing forward on the balls of their feet. If it hadn't been for the weapons in their hands, Alex would have charged them and yelled for Aimee to flee while he did so.

As it was, he needed to gain control of the situation first, and quickly, too. Men with weapons tended to be overconfident, especially if they weren't trained in handling them, as neither of these two appeared to be.

"I'm not sure if you're aware, but you're both trespassing on my land," Alex warned them, his tone firm and sure. "I suggest you leave now before I take issue with that fact." Perhaps he could talk them into leaving.

"You might be a duke," the one with the pistol said, a swagger in his voice. "But you ain't holding the cards in this here situation. I am. As I'm sure you can see." The man nodded down to the pistol he was waving about in his hand. "So I'll be the one to make the suggestions, not you."

"What do you want?" Alex asked, slowly positioning the weight of his body onto the balls of his feet, ready to spring forward and attack.

"Nothing you'll like, I'm afraid," the man replied, a sly grin spreading over his face.

Alex calculated how long it would take Aimee to run to the other opening on the far wall of the cavern if he created some sort of distraction. She'd have enough time to get into the other tunnel and run, he was sure of it. "Do you intend on keeping us in suspense? Or are you going to tell us what this is about?"

The man jutted out the pistol, pointing it sharply at Alex. "You're an arrogant prick, ain't you? I can see why we've been hired to get rid of you."

He raised a brow. "Get rid of me?"

"Yeah. Originally, we were hired to scare that there lady behind you into leaving." The man waved the pistol and shrugged, paying no attention to where the muzzle of his weapon was pointed. The man obviously had no experience with wielding a gun, or else he was completely blasé about doing so. "But things have changed and now we're being paid even more blunt to get rid of you both. And it's too good an offer to pass up. Sorry about that."

Aimee gasped from behind him, but it wasn't in fear. Alex could hear the outrage in the sound of her voice. Funny how he'd gotten to know her so well in such a short time, which was why he knew she wasn't going to be able to stay silent.

"Who on earth is paying you to do such a thing?" she demanded, proving Alex's thoughts correct as she took a step out from behind him to his right, a fierce frown on her face as she positioned herself next to him.

Alex's scowl swung down onto her. "Now is not the time. You need to stay behind me."

"They're threatening both of us, so now is the perfect time." She narrowed her eyes upon him before her attention returned to the two men. "Who is behind all this?"

"Don't know," the man answered. "We're being paid by a middleman, me lady."

"You're risking your lives to the hangman's noose by hurting either of us. You do know that, don't you?" she replied. "Killing a duke and an heiress? The authorities won't take kindly to that."

"There ain't no witnesses here, love," the man replied with a chuckle, while the second man joined him, though his laugh sounded nervous. "By the time they realize you're both missing, the tide will have come in and carried your bodies out to sea. They won't even find you, or if they do, you'll both be too rotten from being in the ocean to even identify, let alone for them to work out what happened to you."

He shrugged. "Everyone'll assume you both got carried away in these here caves together and forgot about the tides. A tragic accident is what everyone will say, which is what we're being paid extra to ensure."

"No one would believe I would ever forget

about the tides." Alex paused for a moment as the sound of the waves started getting louder from behind where the men were standing. "And from the sounds of it, the water will soon be upon us, which means you won't have time to kill us without getting trapped yourselves."

The second man stepped backward into the passageway and peered back down toward the main cave. "He's right, Pete. Sounds like water might be coming up the tunnel."

A flash of panic flared in both men's eyes, and Alex knew their fear could be used against them. "In another five minutes, this cave will be up to our heads in water. You probably only have another two or three minutes to get back to the beach before the lower cave fills." The cave filling with water was true, but Alex didn't mention they had to simply go further into the deeper, higher caverns to avoid it.

"Then we'll have to work quicker, won't we?" The first man's eyes narrowed at Alex, and his finger inched closer to the trigger of the pistol. "Now come closer over here to us." He used the gun to wave toward him and his companion.

Alex could see the anxiety in the man's eyes as they darted back to his companion, who was glancing nervously down the pathway.

"We need to get out of here," his companion whined, his eyes pinned down toward where the sound of the ocean was getting louder. "We'll be trapped if we leave it any longer. The water's already starting to brush at my boots. I don't want to be trapped and die in here."

"We've been offered too damn much to get rid of them, not to see it through!" the first man berated his companion, and the two began to bicker between themselves.

Alex's eyes briefly flicked to Aimee. "When I yell out, run to the other opening on your left, and then turn left and keep running. Don't wait for me," he whispered.

"I'm not leaving you," she replied in a hushed tone, her eyes wide in alarm but filled with determination.

"You have to for us to have any chance of surviving this. Please." He tried to convey the gravity of his request in his tone, which must have worked as she reluctantly gave him a quick nod.

He turned his attention back to the threat in front as the men stopped their bickering and quickly glanced back to Alex and Aimee.

"Stop talking!" the first man roared as he stepped a bit further into the room and raised his pistol, aiming for Alex's chest. "Your turn first."

"You're too late. The water's already coming in." Alex pointed with the lantern over to the men's feet where a trickle of water was indeed starting to lap past their boots and into the cavern.

The second man glanced down and swore aloud, while the first flicked his eyes down but didn't move a muscle. Instead, he clenched his jaw, and his finger began to pull back on the trigger.

"Now!" Alex yelled, throwing the lantern directly at the man's chest and twisting to his right as Aimee sprinted over to the other cave opening, while the man in front simultaneously depressed the trigger.

A blast of gunfire filled the small chamber, the bullet whizzing past Alex's head and lodging into the rock wall behind him, sending up a plume of dust just as the lantern smashed into the man's chest and rebounded to the ground, shattering into pieces and plunging the area of the cave they were standing in into near darkness, with the other lantern on the far side of the room only just shedding enough light to make out the men's bodies.

Alex heard the pistol clatter onto the rock floor, and without wasting a second, he launched himself straight at the first man, determined to give Aimee enough of a head start to get away from the danger and into one of the upper caverns where she'd be safe from the incoming tide and these men. He crashed into the man, his body pushing the man backward with Alex falling on top of him.

They landed on the floor with a thud, the air expelling from both of their lungs with the force. Alex pulled his right arm back and launched his fist at the other man. His knuckles struck the bone and flesh of the man's jaw, and an accompanying groan of pain from the man echoed in the cave.

The man tried to punch him back, but Alex twisted his head and the man's fist glanced across his shoulder as the echo of the second man's footsteps pounded away into the distance. Thankfully, it was in the other direction to where Aimee headed, leaving Alex and the first man wrestling each other on the floor.

Alex grunted as the man's other fist connected with his stomach. Immediately, Alex used his elbow to ram it into the man's solar plexus and was rewarded with a grunt as his elbow struck its mark. But the man was as strong as an ox and grabbed ahold of Alex's arms, trying to struggle up into a sitting position and dislodge Alex from on top of him as the water quickly started to fill the floor of the cavern.

"What the hell?" the man spluttered as some water splashed in his face.

Alex heard the panic in the man's voice from being surrounded with water, which was at least a couple of inches deep now and building in depth quickly as the tide began to roar in hard and fast. In another few minutes, the lower cave would be full of sea water with this one not far behind.

Pulling back his fist again, Alex rammed it into the man's chest, who exhaled sharply from the contact. Twisting off him, Alex rolled into the few inches of water and came up into a crouch. He could barely see in the near darkness, but the small bit of light from the other lantern was like a beacon. Without hesitation, he sprang to his feet and raced toward the second opening, his feet splashing in the rising water. He grabbed the lantern on the wall as he dashed past into the second tunnel, then fled to the left.

He sprinted down the passage until it intersected with another tunnel, then he pulled left into the other intersecting tunnel and stopped, pressing his back against the rock, listening for signs of the man following.

"Thank god you're all right," a voice to his left said.

Alex spun around, nearly launching his fist at

the sound before it registered in his head just in time that it was Aimee's voice. "Damn it, I told you to run and keep running," he whispered harshly as a sense of profound relief filled him, knowing that she was all right.

"It's a bit hard to run in the dark. Besides, I couldn't leave you alone," she whispered back. "I thought I'd hide in this tunnel to see if you came past, then I was going to go back if you didn't in another minute."

He could hear both fear and defiance in her voice, which was to be expected given she'd fled into a pitch-black tunnel she'd never been in before, on her own. Most people were terrified of caves, even when they had a lantern, let alone being in the dark in them. He couldn't resist quickly pulling her to him and kissing her, such was the overwhelming relief he felt.

"Of course that's what you'd do," he muttered as he pulled away and hushed her, holding up a finger before turning back to listen for further sounds of the man following behind. It was difficult to hear much of anything over the noise of the waves crashing in and out of the cave opening further back down the tunnel, but thankfully, he couldn't hear any footsteps following. The man must have decided to get out of the cave before the water rose further, but just to make certain, Alex waited another minute until he was satisfied the man wasn't following them.

But the water was. In another five minutes, this whole tunnel would be filled.

"They don't seem to be following us," he said,

turning back to face Aimee. "But we need to move quickly before the water floods into this lower section of the tunnel."

She nodded in understanding, and Alex grabbed her hand with his free one, and then holding the lantern in front of him, he swiftly guided them further up into the tunnel, toward the upper areas of the caves where the ocean couldn't reach. After walking for a few minutes, the tunnel opened up into a large circular space, with several openings in all directions, leading down into further tunnels and caverns.

"Are you certain they aren't following us?" she asked, stepping over a rock on the ground as Alex drew them over to the far-right opening, where a new tunnel led them to Alex's favorite cavern where all his main supplies were.

"If they are, they'll get lost without a light or without knowing which tunnel to go down."

Men had died in these caves over the years, lost forever in the labyrinth of twisting tunnels and caves that all seemed alike. Alex had spent the better part of his life exploring them, making them more of a home than his estate ever had been, especially after his mother had left him. After that day, the house had never felt like home ever again, more like a prison, where his father had told Alex over and over again that it was because of Alex himself that she had deserted them both.

And for a long time, Alex had believed him. At least he had until he was old enough to understand it had been his father's cruel and callous inattention and coldness toward his wife that had driven her into the arms of another. Though, even now, a small part of Alex thought if Alex himself had been more worthy, then perhaps she would have stayed or at least taken him with her like she said she would come back and do. Though she never did.

"And you definitely know where you're going, don't you?" There was a slight edge of worry in her voice, which was understandable. These tunnels were tight and dark, and she'd just been running blindly in them a few moments before, all because Alex had told her to.

He squeezed her hand. "I do. Only a few minutes more and we'll be safe."

At least safe from the rising tide.

He didn't know how he was going to resist kissing her or touching her, having to now spend about seven hours all alone in her company, waiting for the tide to recede. He'd spent the better part of nearly a week avoiding her to stop himself from giving in to any further temptation. Yet, here they now were, alone and trapped together, with this thrum of desire thick between them.

As he stood staring at her, he could already feel the threads of his tenuous control starting to slip. And if he gave into what his body was begging for, such a transgression would demand a wedding, his honor would allow nothing less.

With a sinking feeling, he suspected he was going to end up marrying a Dollar Princess after all.

CHAPTER THIRTY

Evie watched as Alex walked around the large cavern he'd taken her to, lighting some lanterns left hanging from hooks on the rock wall, presumably to assist in his excavating of fossils when he was down here.

She couldn't help but admire his lithe and athletic form. Tall and strong, she had to literally stop herself from grabbing him and pulling him as close against her as possible. To avert her wayward thoughts, she glanced around the now-lit space and could see the entire cavern, which was about three times larger than the other cavern they'd been in. Over at one end of the space was a mattress on a makeshift bed stand, which must be the tent bed Mr. Montague had mentioned, and several feet from that was a rickety wooden table. Leaning on the wall next to the table were several tools, including a couple of pickaxes, along with a backpack and some large tin canisters sitting on the floor beside them.

"You're well set up down here," she said, turning back to face Alex, who was standing near the third lantern he'd lit, a rather enigmatic expression on his face as he simply stood there watching her.

"It pays to be prepared," he said, and for a minute it appeared as if he was about to say something else, but instead he walked over to the canisters and bent down next to them, retrieving some tin cups from the backpack. "Would you like some water?"

Of course, Alex would make sure he had a supply of water here, especially if he did often sleep down here. "Yes, thank you," she replied, realizing just how parched her throat was. But then she also saw that his hair was wet, and for that matter, too, so were his clothes. "You're all wet."

Alex paused for a moment before placing the two cups on the makeshift table and picking up one of the canisters. "I wrestled one of the men to the floor and the water was already flowing into the cavern by then."

"You'll catch a cold if you stay in those clothes."

"Are you suggesting I take them off?" He glanced back over at her, appearing completely serious in contemplating doing so.

She pressed her suddenly dry lips together and felt her heart start to race at the suggestion. "No." But then he could catch a chill. "Actually, yes." But then he'd be naked. "Oh goodness, I don't know, maybe?" Glancing wildly around the room, she looked for anything that might stop that from needing to be done. She really didn't think she would be in any coherent state if he got naked in front of her. Even the thought of him doing so was enough to warm up her insides. "Can't you make some sort of small fire in here to dry you?"

"There's no wood in here."

"You'll catch a chill if you stay in those wet clothes." There really was no other choice.

"Then it seems I will have to undress... Are you offering your body heat to keep me warm?"

Her eyes latched onto his, and she saw the twinkle of amusement in them. The cad was enjoying teasing her. She narrowed her eyes, and from her peripheral, she caught sight of a blanket lying on the makeshift bed. Almost like a woman possessed, she rushed over and grabbed it. "You can use this for warmth, not me."

She balled up the blanket and threw it at him, which he caught deftly with one hand and chuckled.

"You would have been so much softer than this rough blanket." He laughed at her expression of outrage. "Here, come and have some water." He dropped the blanket on the table and unscrewed the lid on the canister, then poured a little bit of water from it into the two cups. "I'll sort myself out in a minute."

Walking over to where he stood, Evie took the cup from his hands, the tips of her fingers brushing briefly against his own. They both exhaled harshly at the fleeting contact, and Alex took a hasty step back from her, picking up his own cup and downing his water in one go before replacing the cup onto the table with more force than was required.

As he dragged a hand through his damp hair, Evie got the impression he was upset with her. Did he blame her for coming down here in the first place and putting them in danger?

"I'm sorry about what happened," she began as the dire situation they'd faced really started to ram home. "I didn't realize those men had followed us from London."

"That's not your fault."

"No, I suppose not. What did happen in the cavern after I fled? Did you manage to disable them?"

"The one with the dagger fled, but I wrestled with the first before he then fled, too," Alex replied, refilling his own cup. "The water scared them, and I'm hoping they'll give up and flee, but I think that's doubtful. However, we won't have to worry about them for the moment as no one can access these caves when the tide is in."

She took a healthy swallow and finally allowed herself to start to relax. "I'm glad of that. Though do you think they'll try to harm us again? Surely, they'll be discouraged after what happened."

"Money is a powerful motivator." Alex glanced over to the entrance of the cavern, and Evie could tell he was still on alert, despite his assurances they were safe. "It makes people do terrible things sometimes."

"Who do you think is paying them?"

"I'm not sure. Whoever it is, they've changed their mind from simply trying to scare you into returning to America to actively trying to have both of us killed. Whoever is behind that is powerfully motivated. Going from threats to murder is not a light step to take."

"And who would be motivated enough for that?" she asked.

"Money or love are generally the two most powerful motivators that make people do the most reprehensible things," he replied grimly. "As I mentioned earlier, it's either a man on your side who is jealous of our engagement, or from my side it would have to be someone who has the most to gain from my death."

There was such a bleak sadness to Alex's statement that Evie had to resist the impulse to rush over and comfort him. "Surely, your cousin wouldn't be behind this." It had to be what Alex was referring to, and as much as she couldn't imagine George being behind such a plot, it did make a sick sort of sense. The attack on Evie had only occurred after they'd gotten engaged, and prior to that everyone had assumed Alex would never marry or have children, given his assertions to do just that. Which their engagement, pretend though it was, had quickly changed.

"I really don't know. I truly hope not. George has been like a brother to me, but it is the logical assumption." There was a heaviness in his words, and Evie could hear the note of despair behind them. "In any event, when we return to the estate tonight, I will gather some of my men and we'll try to apprehend the assailants and get some answers from them."

"Tonight?" she exclaimed. "We really have to stay in here all day? Alone together?"

A strange look came over his face, and Evie belatedly realized that her American accent had slipped on the last sentence. Darn it! She cleared her throat and focused on the American twang that she'd gotten somewhat used to imitating over the last few weeks. "It's just I've never spent time in a cave before, let alone hours and hours."

"Well, the tide won't recede fully until about seven this evening, so we're essentially stuck here until it does." The expression of questioning was replaced by a look of acceptance. "I know it's not ideal, but it is what it is, and if anyone finds out, we can face the consequences then."

"The consequences?"

He raised a brow. "If it were discovered we'd been alone together down here for seven hours, people would presume I'd compromised you and we'd have to marry."

"Why would we have to do that?" What on earth was he talking about? "They already know you've compromised me. Yet I still intend to cry off, so why would this be any different to being caught kissing?"

"Kissing can be overlooked. The assumption that I've taken your virginity cannot." He shrugged. "That sort of gossip would follow you across the Atlantic and absolutely ruin you."

Evie felt sick with the thought. That couldn't happen because it would mean Aimee's reputation would be ruined.

"In any event, I doubt anyone will find out." He took her cup from her and returned it back to the table with his own. "We'll just have to find something to entertain us for the next seven hours. If you're hungry, there's a preserved jar of fruit in the bag."

Food was the last thing her stomach needed. "I'll be fine."

His very words of having to be alone down here together for so long made Evie nervous as nothing else had in a long time. Though why it did, she wasn't sure. Perhaps it was the cave itself rather than the man standing in front of her, and the thought of spending hours alone with him, in complete privacy, with a makeshift bed…

She shook her head, desperately trying to push aside the thoughts that had sprung into her mind of him kissing and touching her again. A hard ask, when night after night, all she'd dreamed of was what it would feel like to have him kiss her *everywhere*.

"You probably should get out of those wet clothes." The thought was enough for a blush to start to sweep over her cheeks. Quickly, she swiveled away from the scrutiny of his gaze and her eyes landed on a pile of rocks and dirt dumped into small mounds on the other side of the cavern. Next to them was a large tarp covering a space in the middle that had to be around twenty feet long by twelve feet wide.

She walked over to the spot, desperate to get some distance between her and Alex.

The lanterns Alex had lit around the room were providing enough light for her to see most of the space around the cavern, but they didn't obliterate all the dark shadows and crevices in between. Evie's imagination started running wild with thoughts of what might pounce out of the darkness. Then she glanced up at the dark rock that made up the roof of the cave, and thoughts of it crumbling down upon them while they slept started to intrude, and a slow sliver of claustrophobia crawled up her spine.

Taking in a deep breath, she focused on the tarp in front of her and tried her best to suppress her fears. Slowly, as her gaze flicked over the outline of the fossil under the tarp, her dread was replaced with a frenzied sort of excitement. "Oh my goodness, Alex, is this your lizard under here?"

The tarp was draped over something extremely big, with the rough shape under the material suggesting it could very well be the extremely giant lizard he'd mentioned he was in the process of excavating.

"It is," his deep voice murmured beside her.

Evie jumped at his nearness, so absorbed in the fossil before her that she hadn't even heard him approach. And now he was standing next to her again, his shirt and jacket removed, his bare shoulder brushing her own and sending a searing heat through the material of her dress, right to her very core. Try as she might to deny her attraction to the man, she couldn't. Her body craved him as it craved the very air around her. It was a hunger that couldn't be denied.

And she didn't want to keep denying it anymore. Didn't want to deny the enthralling physical pull she felt toward him. Didn't want to deny herself from experiencing the pleasure of being with him. Why should she?

She was returning to America in a few weeks, back to the mundane world of being Aimee's companion, a part of the family, but still relegated to the shadows, more of her own choice than her family's, but given her birth, Evie could never really feel as if she fit into their world. A world where most in Society ignored her as they would a servant. A world where she would never get another chance to experience what it was to fully feel like a woman, to feel what it was to be Alex's woman, at least for a short time.

There was desire and passion flaring in Alex's eyes, and Evie knew that this moment, here in this cave, would be the one defining moment in her life, to either embrace passion or deny herself forever. Because she knew with a deep certainty she would never meet anyone like Alex again. A man that filled her with excitement and passion. A man she belatedly realized she'd fallen in love with.

The realization was as terrifying as it was emboldening.

Terrifying, because she knew her heart would be broken very soon, as she wasn't stupid enough to think she could have a happily ever after with him. Such a thing was impossible as much as she might desperately wish that wasn't the case.

But she could at least enjoy this moment, knowing without a doubt that if she didn't embrace this chance to experience what it felt like to be with Alex, she would spend the rest of her life forever regretting not having had the courage to do so.

She bit down on her lower lip and stared at his own lips. "Alex?"

"Yes?" he murmured, his eyes flicking down to her mouth.

"Kiss me."

"Kiss you?" he groaned. "If I do, I don't think I'll want to stop…"

Slowly, she placed her hands on his bare chest and slid them up and over his shoulders, pulling him toward her until they were mere inches apart.

"And what if I don't want you to stop?"

"Excuse me?" His voice was suddenly hoarse.

"I want you to kiss me. I want you to touch me. I want you to be inside of me."

He was silent for a moment, the pulse at the base of his neck beating wildly. "Do you know what you're asking of me?"

Taking in a deep breath, she nodded. "I do. I want you, Alex. I want you more than I've wanted anything in my life." And she realized how true that was. How this would be the only chance for her to experience such pleasure with him.

And she was going to take that chance and damn well enjoy it.

CHAPTER THIRTY-ONE

With a hoarse moan, Alex pulled her fully against him, his lips pressing down upon hers, hot and demanding a response as they teased open her mouth and his tongue swept inside its depths. Plundering, tasting, and tormenting with exquisite ecstasy.

Evie groaned in response, her hands winding tighter around his neck, her breasts pushing against his chest, while he kissed her with a devastating and delicious thoroughness.

He lifted his head, and she whimpered at the loss of his lips against hers, but then in one fell swoop he scooped her up into his arms and carried her over to the makeshift bed. Gently, he put her down on the straw-filled canvas before lying next to her, his mouth finding hers as his hands began to unbutton the pearl buttons at back of her dress. Inch by inch, the bodice of her dress was loosened, and she shrugged it off, glad she hadn't bothered with a corset, and then she pulled her chemise over her head, exposing her naked breasts to Alex's hungry gaze.

"You're so beautiful," he murmured, his hands reaching out to softly cup her breasts. "So damn perfect, I can't get enough of you."

She arched her back as the pads of his fingers drifted across her nipple. "Oh my," she moaned.

"Does that feel good?" he asked before starting to trail kisses down the column of her throat while his fingers began to gently stroke her nipples.

All Evie could do was nod. Then when his mouth latched onto her nipple, she groaned and grabbed ahold of his hair, urging even more of her breast into his feasting mouth. "Oh yes, Alex. Yes."

She'd never thought such a thing could have felt so ridiculously good.

Pushing him back onto the bed, Evie pressed her hands against his chest and marveled at his muscles. The man's chest was like hard steel with a sprinkling of dark hair across it; Evie couldn't help but run her hands through it, gazing at the smooth planes.

And then she did something she never imagined she would: she pressed her naked breasts against his chest and kissed him with a furious passion she couldn't contain. She had to get more of him; her body was demanding it. Tingles of delight were radiating through her entire body, and then when she felt the hardness of his cock pressing against her legs, the center of her core began to thrum, begging for him to be inside her.

He flipped her onto her back and quickly finished the job of undressing her, tossing her skirt and petticoats onto the ground and slowly pulling down her drawers before tossing them to the floor, too.

She was completely naked in front of him, and suddenly she felt slightly shy. But before she could think further on her embarrassment, he quickly stood and unbuttoned his pants before pulling them from his legs and discarding them.

Evie's eyes widened and her jaw dropped as she

stared as his manhood stood to attention, jutting proudly out, thick, long, and surprisingly silky looking. She had to stop her hands from reaching out to touch the smoothness of it.

Then she found herself worrying about whether this would work. Though she was a virgin, she'd read enough ancient texts to understand the mechanics of what they were about to do. But she wasn't so sure he was going to fit inside her. His manhood was far thicker and longer than any she'd imagined, and she was filled with doubt for a minute.

Alex lay down beside her, beads of sweat on his brow and an expression of concern on his face. "We can stop if you want."

"No, I don't want that!" she hurried to assure him. "It's just you seem too big. I don't know if this will work."

He laughed lightly. "Trust me, it will work, but it will work better if you're relaxed. Would you like me to relax you?"

She could only nod and then stare at his head as he slowly started trailing kisses down her body, over her chest, then down onto her stomach, and she nearly bolted from the makeshift bed when his mouth settled in between the center of her legs. "Oh God," she moaned, her hands clutching his hair as his mouth started to kiss and taste her. Then his tongue flicked against her little nub down there, and Evie arched her back as a feeling of desire consumed her.

She was powerless to do anything except experience the sweet bliss of surrender as he sucked on her, feasting on her essence, sending a cascading pleasure through every cell in her body as she slowly started to build to a peak.

"That's it, my darling," he whispered against her thighs as his fingers replaced his mouth for a moment, and he began to rub them against her. "You're so wet. So damn delectable, I could feast on you for hours."

Evie couldn't help herself; she began to rock against his hand, feeling like she was about to launch off a cliff and there was nothing she could do to stop the momentum. Nothing she wanted to do to stop it. Then it felt as if almost everything in her whole body clenched for a moment in agony before a burst of ecstasy exploded inside her and wave after wave of pleasure rippled through her.

Swiftly, Alex's cock replaced his hand and he pushed himself gently inside her passage with a groan of delight. A sharp pain pierced through her haze of pleasure, and Evie gasped, her hands latching behind his shoulders and her nails digging into his skin.

"I'm sorry, my darling," he whispered, holding himself still above her, his manhood now fully inside her passage. "It shouldn't hurt for long."

She didn't know what to think. Her body was still riding on the waves of elation now mixed with a sense of slight discomfort of having him filling her. "I thought you'd be too big."

He half moaned and half laughed, but then he reached his hand down between them and rubbed at her little bud again, and suddenly those feelings of joy began to ripple through her once more. "It's fine, I promise."

She nodded as her body started to become used to the feel of him inside her, and her hips started to grind against his, bringing his manhood deeper inside her.

"That's it," he urged her, as he, too, started to slowly push in and then out of her.

"Oh, that feels better," Evie said as the pain quickly began to be replaced by the same buildup of pleasure from a moment ago. "Oh yes," she moaned, forgetting everything else except for the feeling of having Alex inside her.

She began to meet him thrust for thrust, her hips knowing what to do instinctively, as her body kept urging him more deeply into her passage as he pumped his cock in and out of her.

"Oh god, you're so wet," he murmured against her cheek. "So fucking delicious."

The pressure in her very center was starting to build to a point of no return, and suddenly Evie's whole body tightened, before pleasure once again exploded inside her, and she was lost in the sensation.

Alex pulled out of her with a groan and pressed his cock onto her stomach as his own release rippled through him and he spilled his seed onto her belly.

Evie's ears felt like they were ringing from a distance as she floated high on a blissful sea of contentment. Bliss unlike anything she'd ever experienced before, wrapping around her like a cocoon.

She was only just aware of Alex standing and walking over to the backpack and pulling out a cloth before returning to her and gently wiping his seed from her belly, then wiping himself, too. She smiled as he lay down beside her, then pulled the blanket over them and wrapped his arms around her.

"That was wonderful." She sounded inebriated, so relaxed and content was she as she snuggled in his arms after experiencing the most joy she ever had.

He grinned and kissed her forehead. "It truly was, my love."

"Can we do it again?"

This time he chuckled. "We can, but I will need a little bit of time to recover. Although perhaps not as long as I thought I would. I'm already starting to stir for you again."

"You are?"

"Feel me," he whispered. "I haven't gotten this hard so soon after orgasming since I was a young man. Can you feel what you do to me? How much I desire you? How much I need you?"

Evie reached down and her fingers closed around the smooth hardness of him, which was definitely starting to grow harder and longer the more she tentatively stroked him. "You feel so smooth and strong, like hot marble."

He grinned at her. "Why don't you climb aboard and see what it feels like to ride me this time?"

"Ride you?" What did he mean by that? But he rolled her on top of him and guided his manhood inside her passage, and she quickly learned what he meant.

"I think I do like this position," she said after a

moment of feeling him inside her.

"I rather thought you would." He laughed and then groaned as she tweaked his nipples between her fingers, while she began to ride him as he'd said, until they were both panting in pleasure.

As she crested the peak of another orgasm, Evie knew she could get used to this activity.

Get used to it a lot.

CHAPTER THIRTY-TWO

Lying there in the makeshift bed, with Aimee sound asleep and snuggled in his arms, Alex felt the most overwhelming sense of contentment settle over him, a feeling he hadn't felt in as long as he could remember, if ever in his entire life.

He glanced down at her sleeping face and marveled at her. She really was perfect, even when she was scowling at him, her brow twisted in displeasure, or when she was taking him to task for being too autocratic as she called him, or when she was biting her lip in nervousness. He'd never met a more authentic and kinder woman than her.

To have been brought up with such privilege being Thomas Thornton-Jones's daughter, Alex was amazed by how down to earth she was. Where most other women he knew were vain and so very conscious of Society's opinions of them, Aimee didn't care about that. She was more aware of the social plight of those less fortunate than her than she was of what the latest fashions were, a subject that her contemporaries all seemed to obsess over.

She was compassionate, intelligent, and honest, and she knew her own mind, a quality Alex appreciated greatly. The fact that she also wasn't afraid of standing up to him, too, was as intriguing to him as it was fascinating. Probably what garnered his interest in the first place. As a duke, Alex was used to being treated with the utmost formality, people often forgetting there was an actual man behind the facade of his title. But not Aimee. Never once had she stood on ceremony with him. Whether that was because she was American or just who she was as a person, it was a trait in her he admired, and one that would make for an excellent duchess, even though she did like to disobey his directions on occasion—in fact, most of the time. But even that filled him with a strange happiness, instead of frustration, or at least it did at the moment.

She stirred lightly in his arms, her face tranquil, her bare skin soft and warm against his own. His cock stirred in response, already pulsing to be inside her again. But it was fast approaching low tide, and as much as Alex wished they could stay in such a cocoon of comfort and safety for hours more with the rest of the world all but forgotten, once the tide retreated, the threat could return.

Even just thinking about the threat the men presented, Alex's thoughts turned dark. As much as he didn't think his cousin could be behind it, he had the most motive if something were to happen to Alex. George was the main one that would be impacted if Alex married and had children. His heart rebelled at the thought. Not George, who was more like a brother to him than a cousin. George who had been his best friend since they'd attended school together as young boys... But if not George, then who?

The only other person that would benefit would be Claire, but she'd never cared about being a duchess, even going so far as to actively encourage him over the years to marry. He doubted it would be her.

There was one other who'd always wanted George to be a duke: George's mother, Aunt Mildred. Could she be the one behind everything? She'd always despised Alex, but even then, it was a stretch to think she'd know who to contact to hire some men to try to kill him. The woman was rather vindictive, and she certainly liked the idea of her son as the future duke, but to take things further and hire men to kill him and Aimee? As much as they disliked each other, Alex couldn't quite reconcile to Aunt Mildred being involved in trying to have him murdered. She was cruel but not evil. At least he didn't think so.

Perhaps it could be another collector who was trying to steal Alex's latest find, though that seemed farfetched, too. But men had killed for less, and those in the world of paleontology were known to be a bit eccentric when it came to finds.

Still, Alex's intuition was telling him it had started after his engagement, so it had to be linked to that. He had to find the two men and get answers from them; it would be the only way to find out who was behind the whole mess, and the sooner the better.

Reluctantly, he dislodged Aimee's hand from resting on his chest, then pushed back the blanket and rolled off the mattress. Finding his hastily discarded and damp clothes scattered on the dirt floor, Alex shook them free of dust and quickly dressed. The cave was cold, and the one lantern he hadn't extinguished before sleep had taken him was nearly down to the end of its wick. He pulled out a match and lit another lantern, pulling it from off the wall and walking back over to where Aimee was happily sleeping. He grabbed her discarded clothes with his free hand while he did so.

He dropped the clothes on the end of the bed and then reached down and gently shook her arm. "Aimee, it's time to wake up."

"No, Aimee," she mumbled rather incoherently, her hand batting his away, while her eyes remained closed and a slight frown drifted over her forehead. "Leave me be."

He smiled. Who would have thought she would nap so soundly? Though they had been rather busy exploring each other's naked bodies over the course of the day. "Aimee. Wake up." He raised his voice slightly, returning his hand to her shoulder and shaking her a little bit more this time.

Her glorious blue eyes blinked open, and instantly her frown was replaced by a brilliant smile as her gaze latched onto his. Then her smile quickly turned into a grimace as she glanced down at her naked body, covered only by the blanket, then back to him. Her mouth widened as her hands gripped ahold of the blanket and pulled it up to her neck.

Alex couldn't help but grin at her sudden modesty, given his mouth and hands had explored every single inch of her. "It's time to go."

"It is?" she replied, her voice husky, her eyes darting anywhere but at him as a blush spread across her cheeks.

She really was embarrassed, it seemed, and for some reason Alex thought it adorable. "I'll head out into the tunnel to give you a few minutes to dress." He nodded down to the foot of the mattress where he'd put her clothes. "There's an empty bucket in the corner if you wish to use it."

Her blush seemed to get brighter, and Alex winked at her before turning and striding from the room. If he stayed any longer, he wouldn't be able to help himself and he'd undress himself and join her back under the blanket before she could even blink.

When it came to Aimee, he had no control over his desire for her, and he had a sneaking suspicion he'd give her the world if she asked it of him.

About five minutes later, and after he'd relieved his bladder, Alex headed back into the cavern to find her mostly dressed, except for the buttons at the back of her dress, exposing her creamy upper shoulders and neck, with her chemise underneath covering her mid to lower back. Alex had to pause and clench his fingers into fists to stop himself from striding over and pushing her gown right off her shoulders, an action that would delay their departure and ensure they missed the start of the ball, drawing far more notice to their absence than needed.

"Here, I'll help you," he said, walking over to her as she tried to button the back of her dress herself.

She startled around, not having heard him reenter. "Thank you. I don't know why anyone would order a dress with so many buttons at the back of it."

Another odd comment, given she or her mother would have ordered it and normally she'd have a maid to help her. "You don't talk of your parents much."

Her whole back stiffened slightly as he began to button up her gown, his fingers only lightly brushing across her skin as he did so. He was proud of his restraint given the temptation she presented.

"Like I said, they're so busy that I often don't feel as if I know them all that well…"

Her words trailed off, and Alex was curious as he could hear the reluctance in her voice to talk about the subject.

"You don't often talk of your parents, either." She swiveled around to face him now that he'd finished buttoning the last button.

"They're dead," he bluntly replied. "Not much to talk about, really. My father was a harsh, distant man who demanded perfection in everyone and everything. I guess my mother grew tired of that, and lonely too perhaps, so she ran off with another man, leaving me alone with him. End of story, really."

"You said she promised to return for you but never did?"

"She did." He shrugged, trying to brush off the small pang of hurt her actions still caused. "It was a difficult but valuable lesson in understanding that most women lie and don't keep their word."

"Perhaps she didn't mean to lie," Aimee replied, but then her face grew distant. "And even if she did, perhaps she didn't know how to tell you the truth."

"It doesn't matter anyway," Alex said, trying not to let the bitter disappointment he always felt when he thought of his mother rise up. "She did what she did, and I am who I am because of it. At least you've never lied to me."

She blinked, and a rather panicked expression filled her gaze. "Alex, there's something I should tell you."

"Given you were a virgin last night, it can't be that you've cheated on me with another man. Can it?"

"No, of course not." She shook her head wildly.

"Well, then, whatever it is, consider it water under the bridge just as long as you promise never to lie to me once we're married."

"Married?" She stared at him for a moment, confusion filling the blue depths of her eyes. "But we're not getting married."

"I took your virginity, so, yes, we most certainly are."

CHAPTER THIRTY-THREE

Panic clawed at her chest from his words. Married? No, that simply wasn't possible.

Not only had she lied to him about who she was, which he'd never forgive her for, but she was illegitimate. A duke could never marry someone of her social status. He just didn't know it yet.

"There's no need for us to marry because you took my virginity." She tried to project as much authority in her voice as possible, but the wobble in her tone didn't really give it the effect she'd wanted.

"There's every need," he replied. "However, we can discuss it later as we need to leave now."

Evie stood rooted to the spot, wanting to argue the point, but knowing what he said was true. Those men could be waiting for them on the beach, and they needed to focus on that before discussing his wild assertions of marriage. There'd be time enough later to talk about marriage, or rather how she wouldn't be marrying him. She'd have to tell him the truth about her swap with Aimee, of course. She had to. It was the right thing to do when he was seriously talking of marriage, and once she told him it would put an end to such a discussion.

Yes, it was the only way, though the thought of doing so, and the look of betrayal she was certain to see on his face, made her feel sick to her stomach. He would never want anything to do with her ever again. Would never want to see her again. The thought was like a dagger to her heart, especially now that she had been foolish enough to fall in love with him.

Not for the first time, she berated herself for her choices. She never should have allowed herself to get into such a position, but she'd been hard pressed to ignore the feelings he stirred inside her, almost effortlessly. Feelings she was starting to suspect he might share, but that would vanish once he learned the truth. But it was the only way he wouldn't want to marry her, as much as part of her wished it could be otherwise.

She took in a deep breath to calm herself, watching while he went back to his backpack and dug inside it until he pulled out a pistol and what looked to be a box of bullets.

"You keep a gun in your backpack?"

He shrugged as he loaded the weapon with some of the bullets, then tucked the thing into the waistband of his pants. "It pays to be prepared for all contingencies." He grabbed a lantern from the wall and then quickly extinguished the few remaining lit lanterns. "Come on."

Motioning to the opening of the cavern, he led the way out into the passage, and Evie followed closely behind him. It was good to be moving after spending hours on a rather uncomfortable straw mattress, even if that had been in the blissful cocoon of Alex's arms.

Shaking her head free from such thoughts, Evie knew she had to stop remembering the heat and feel of him against her and instead concentrate on any threats that lay ahead.

About ten minutes later, Alex paused at the junction of the main entrance cavern and motioned with his fingers against his lips for quiet, then extinguished the lantern. Tentatively, he peered around into the space, then nodded for Evie to follow him. There was still some water spilling into the cave, but with each small wave that pushed inside and then retreated to the ocean, it lessened, signaling that the tide was indeed going out to sea.

Without the lantern lit, though, the darkness of the cave looked ominous, but as they made their way closer to the exit and the beach beyond, a small sliver of moonlight beckoned.

Carefully, Alex led them out onto the beach where thankfully no one was waiting in the shadows to pounce on them. Swiftly, they made their way across the beach and up the stairs onto the cliffs above, the moon lighting their way.

"Stay close to me," Alex said, squeezing her hand. "We'll stick to the path, but I don't want to light the lantern and give away our position in case the men are lying in wait somewhere, so be careful of your steps."

Evie nodded, and they began the trek back to the estate. Fifteen minutes later, the lights from Alex's house blazed brightly in the distance, a beacon of safety. As they crossed through the woods, she could hear the strains of the orchestra echoing into the night.

"The ball's already started." She cringed, knowing their absence would most definitely be remarked upon.

"Only just," Alex assured her as they crested a rise and saw the lights from the ballroom glowing.

He stopped abruptly, and Evie came to a halt beside him as she spotted what he'd seen, some people with lanterns ahead. She braced automatically, but then she recognized the familiar faces of George, Claire, and Samuel.

It was George who caught sight of them first. "Alex? Aimee? Is that you both?"

"Yes," Alex answered, nodding to Evie to continue on over to the group who were already hurrying across the lawn to meet them.

"Oh, thank goodness you're both all right," Claire said, rushing to keep up with her husband and Samuel. "We were so worried when we arrived a short time ago and you both were missing."

"Has everyone noticed that fact?" Evie asked, with a sinking heart as all three of them surrounded Alex and Evie, relief shining on their faces.

"Oh no, not at all." Claire shook her head. "We came slightly early. All the other guests are only just starting to arrive, and in any event the countess is deftly deflecting their questions about your whereabouts, with hints that you both wish to make a grand entrance. What happened, though? We thought perhaps you'd both gotten trapped in the caves with the tide."

"We did, though it wasn't by accident," Alex replied, quickly filling them in about what had happened down in the caves.

"Those men could still be on the estate," Sam said, his eyes darting over to the woods.

"I'm sure they are, though I imagine they'll lie low while the ball is in full swing," Alex replied. "But still, we need to make certain they aren't in the immediate vicinity. Then I'll post some of my men to keep a watch." He glanced back to Evie. "You need to change and get to the ballroom as quickly as you can. The longer both of us are absent, the more people will talk."

She didn't like his plan. Not one bit. "I don't think it's wise for you to be looking for them, considering you're their target."

"Worried about me?" He had the audacity to smile.

"Yes, in truth, I am." She crossed her arms over her chest.

"I'll be fine." Then, in front of all his friends, he leaned down and kissed her, and Evie's heart melted. "Now get going. Claire, would you ensure my fiancée gets to the ball?"

Claire tried to hide her grin but couldn't. "Of course."

"Very well," Evie grumbled in concession. "Just be safe, all right?" She knew he'd be fine with George and Sam, and with the pistol in his waistband, but it worried her that those men were probably out there somewhere hoping to get another chance to hurt Alex.

"I will." He winked at her. "Stay inside and stay safe."

"It's a ball. Nothing will happen to me."

"I'm serious. I need to know you're safe or I won't be able to concentrate on anything else while I'm out here."

Her heart thumped in her chest with his words. "You won't?"

"Not for an instant." There was such an intensity in his gaze that Evie felt her knees weaken. "You're going to be my wife, Aimee, and I will protect you with everything I have and everything I am."

My wife, Aimee. The words filled her with such longing and devastation knowing she never could be that to him. Knowing she couldn't keep lying to him, especially not now that she realized she truly did love him. He deserved the truth. "Alex, there's something I have to tell you…"

"You can tell me when I get back." He smiled. "When we dance a waltz together. A proper waltz this time, and not your special gallop waltz. All right?"

A proper waltz. One final dance before she told him the truth and he never wanted to see her again. Yes, that would be fitting. She nodded her head. "Very well."

Delaying telling him was being a coward and she knew it. But she *would* tell him at the ball, or maybe just after. He deserved to know the truth, and the longer she delayed doing so, the worse it would be, for them both.

"Good," he rumbled before he leaned down and pressed his lips to hers a second time.

The touch was over before it had even begun, and Evie's lips felt the loss keenly as he pulled away and stared down at her for a moment. Each and every kiss they shared until she told him the truth was precious, and she'd savor them while they lasted.

"Now get back to the house with Claire and change," he said. "The boys and I won't be long, my love." Then he turned on his heel and stalked off toward the side of the house, Sam and George following him.

"I knew you two would be perfect for each other," Claire gushed as she linked her arm in Evie's and they headed back to the house.

"I don't believe in perfect," Evie replied, spending the short walk to the back door convincing herself that Alex's throwaway endearment of calling her his love was exactly that and did not mean anything more. It couldn't.

But even if it did, there was naught that could come of it. Sometimes, there was just too much of a divide for even love to conquer, especially after she told him the truth and he found out who she was. Then any affection he may have felt for her would vanish.

Tonight, she had to tell him the truth, no matter the cost.

CHAPTER THIRTY-FOUR

"Oh, dear girl! Thank goodness you're all right," the countess whispered as Evie made her way into the ballroom, having spent a furious thirty minutes with Claire and three maids dressing and getting her hair done in a third of the time it usually took.

The finished effect was Evie wearing a gorgeous sapphire blue creation, her hair upswept into a chignon with some blue crystals scattered through the up style, looking for all the world as if she'd spent all afternoon getting ready.

"Were you and the duke stuck in the caves as his staff said you must be?" the countess asked through the smile plastered on her face as she nodded to some ladies who were watching them from across the room.

"We were, but all is fine now," she assured her as Claire began to wander around the room, mentioning Evie's supposed dress mishap that they'd come up with to explain her delay in attending the ball on time, which hopefully would work to allay any suspicions of the gathered crowd.

"Good." The countess patted Evie's hand, relief washing over her expression. "And where is my nephew? The guests have been asking. Though it's probably best you didn't show up together. People would suspect something if you did."

"I think he might still be changing." Evie cringed at the lie, but she didn't want to worry the countess with the truth. Although perhaps Alex was already back by now and changing.

From the corner of her eye, she saw Claire's mother, Mrs. Gainsborough, hurry into the room, concern etched on her brow as she rushed straight toward Evie. Oh god, had something happened to Alex?

"What's wrong?" Evie asked as the woman stopped in front of her and the countess.

"Oh, nothing is wrong," Mrs. Gainsborough replied, though the worry in her eyes belied her words. "But can I have a quick chat with you in private, my dear? Out in the hallway?"

Evie nodded and followed Mrs. Gainsborough through the large doors of the room and out onto the upstairs landing.

"What is it?" Evie asked her as soon as they were well away from the prying ears of others.

"It's the duke," she rushed out. "He's been shot."

Everything inside Evie froze as an unbearable anguish filled her. "Oh my god, is he alive?" *Please let him be*, she fervently prayed.

"I don't know." The lady wrung her hands together. "Apparently, he's in the old barn, and George told me to come get you. I don't know anything else, but he said we must hurry."

"Has a doctor been sent for?"

"Yes," Mrs. Gainsborough said with a hasty nod of her head. "George hurried off to see to that after he found me. But come, we must go."

All Evie could do was nod as Mrs. Gainsborough took her hand and led her down the corridor to the west wing of the residence, then down the back stairs to the ground floor.

The few short minutes it took them to rush down the long hallway that led outside felt as if it were an hour, with Evie barely being able to concentrate on anything except for her fear over Alex. *Oh please, God, let him be all right. Let him live.* She continued the litany over and over in her head as they hurried toward the French doors to the outside of the estate.

Pushing through the doors, Evie began to race down the path, heading straight through the back gardens to the side of the estate where the old barn was. The crunch of gravel under her feet sounded ridiculously loud in the night as she and Mrs. Gainsborough hurried toward the abandoned building. A few minutes later, the barn doors loomed large ahead, with one door slightly open and a small light shining from inside. Her footsteps slowed, and everything around her seemed to fade away as she came to a halt at the door. Slowly, her heart thumping in her chest from the fear of what she might find, she pulled the door wide open and stepped inside the barn.

She took a few steps into the middle of the room and stopped short, blinking in confusion as she glanced around the empty space. "Alex? Alex, where are you?" The barn looked completely deserted, except for a lone carriage and horse attached to it. Where was Alex?

Mrs. Gainsborough rushed in behind her and abruptly stopped in her tracks, too, while Evie strode over to the carriage and opened the door. It was empty.

"Alex isn't here." Evie swiveled around to face her. "Are you sure George said the barn?"

"In truth, I haven't seen George for several hours," the woman replied with a soft smile. It was then Evie noticed the black pistol she was holding in her hand, pointing right at Evie.

"What's going on?" Fury began to burn through her. "Was Alex shot or not?"

The woman shrugged. "Not that I know of. At least not yet. But I hope to rectify that soon now that I have you."

Relief all but swamped Evie upon hearing that Alex was all right. Thank God. Then a horrid understanding gripped her as the pieces of the puzzle slowly began to fit together. "You're the one who paid those men to scare me. The one who wants Alex dead…"

"I am. My daughter can't very well be a duchess while he's alive, now, can she?" she said, staring at Evie as if she were simple. "Originally, I'd planned to wait a bit longer to have him killed, given everyone knew he had no intention of ever marrying, but then you showed up and all that changed."

"Are Claire and George involved in this plan of yours?" She desperately hoped not. Alex had already had enough betrayal in his life and would soon have more when he found out the truth about Evie. He didn't deserve any more.

"Goodness, no," the woman scoffed. "They're both far too good-natured to have the foresight to do what is necessary to secure their future. Luckily for them, I am not so burdened and will do what I must to ensure my daughter's security."

"And that is your justification for hiring men to murder Alex? To murder me?"

"I tried to have you scared off in the beginning, so you'd go back to America, but it didn't work." The woman's smile tightened, and her eyes glittered in malice. "So, you see, this is all your fault, not mine! If you hadn't come along and spoiled my plans, I wouldn't have had to do any of this yet. I would have waited as I'd intended to, with the duke suffering an unfortunate accident in another five years or so. But as soon as I saw the way he looked at you, I knew there would be a problem and that I couldn't keep waiting."

"My, how *patient* you were going to be," Evie said, not even trying to hide the sarcasm in her voice.

"It was pragmatic, my dear, not patient," the woman replied, her knuckles whitening around the grip of the pistol. "The duke is excellent at ensuring the estate is kept profitable, as the old duke trained him to be."

"Beat him to be, don't you mean?"

"Regardless of how it was achieved, it worked," Mrs. Gainsborough said. "Unfortunately, my son-in-law doesn't have the same discipline or knowledge when it comes to running such a vast estate and making it profitable. Hence, I was content to let the duke continue to build up the estate's fortunes for a bit longer to ensure my family's ongoing prosperity when he is no longer with us. But, unfortunately, *you* derailed my plans."

The woman truly was mad. Evie glanced around

the space, looking for anything she could use as a weapon. There were a few pitchforks over in the far corner, but she'd have to get to them first, and there was no way she could outrun a bullet. "So, what now? You plan to kill me here? You'll never get away with it."

"I don't plan to kill you, at least not yet." She raised her shoulders in a dainty shrug. "But I do plan to use you as bait."

"Alex won't fall for that. He knows there are men out here trying to kill him. He's not going to blindly rush to my rescue."

"A man in love will do anything to protect that love, including risking his own life."

"You're wrong," she replied, her body clenching in anguish. "He's not in love with me."

"You're the one who's wrong, my dear. Perhaps he hasn't said the words, but anyone with eyes can see how he looks at you. How he can't *stop* looking at you. And for someone like the duke, who never shows his emotions or gives anything away, such behavior is telling." The woman raised her pistol and motioned over to the carriage. "He loves you and will come for you, that I know. Now, enough talk. Get in the carriage. My men will be here soon to convey us to a more secluded location away from the duke's estate."

Glancing back to the vehicle, Evie knew if she got in, she'd be trapped and completely at the woman's mercy, which she couldn't allow to happen, but what could she do to stop it? The woman had a pistol, though that didn't necessarily mean she knew how to use the thing. After all, how many women had practice firing a gun, let alone being an accurate shot with one? Few if any, Evie would bet on it.

It was a bet she was willing to risk her life on if it stopped Alex from being lured into a trap. Though he might not be in love with her, she knew him well enough to know he was so honorable, he would willingly sacrifice himself for her. And she would not let that happen. "People saw me leaving with you. If something happens to me, you'll be a prime suspect."

The woman sighed as she strolled up to Evie, pointing the gun inches from her stomach. "Oh, my dear, do you not think I've already planned for that? I shall simply tell everyone that two men accosted us at gunpoint and kidnapped us, but thankfully I managed to escape, though you weren't so fortunate."

"If you mean the two men that tried to kill us in the caves," Alex's deep voice rumbled from behind Mrs. Gainsborough, "we've already apprehended them."

CHAPTER THIRTY-FIVE

Evie's eyes darted over to the door, latching on to Alex who was standing there with Samuel and George next to him, and thankfully without a scratch on any of them.

"She has a gun!" she yelled in warning as Mrs. Gainsborough spun around to face the men, too, before she quickly grabbed Evie and dragged her next to her, pressing the gun into Evie's side.

"Don't come any closer," the woman said, jabbing the pistol harder against Evie.

Evie couldn't help but wince, and she saw Alex's jaw clench in response.

"Damn it, don't hurt her," Alex yelled.

"What are you doing, Mother?" George stepped forward, utter bafflement on his face as he stared at his mother-in-law.

"Making you a duke," she replied, her eyes wildly flicking between the three men.

"Don't be silly."

"I am not being silly!" the woman roared. "And don't come any closer, George. None of you come closer, or I will shoot her."

George raised his hands and took a step backward. "We won't. But why don't you put down the pistol? There's no need for any of this."

"There's every need!" Mrs. Gainsborough grimaced, swinging the gun out toward the men. "I didn't spend years raising my daughter and using the last of my husband's money to see her marry a *nobody*! You *will* be the duke and she *will* be your duchess. I will not accept anything else."

"How will Claire feel about that? She wouldn't condone you hurting us," Alex said, his voice calm in the face of the woman's rising ire. "In fact, I think she'd look upon you with horror if you did."

"My daughter will not find out about any of this." She grinned madly at them all.

"A bit hard for you to keep quiet, I think," Sam said, and Evie saw him exchange a subtle look with Alex.

They were going to do something. Evie was certain of it.

"Not if I make it look like a lover's tiff," she crowed. "It will be too easy to suggest the duke caught you and his fiancée cavorting together here in this barn, and after having discovered his last fiancée in a similar position, the duke lost his mind and shot you both before killing himself. A rather ingenious spur-of-the-moment plan, don't you all think?"

"I won't let you get away with murder," George said, thrusting out his chest.

"You won't say anything, dear boy, because if anyone else knew what I intend to do here tonight, Claire would be ruined. Utterly and completely ruined." She glanced over to George, her pistol returning to press against Evie's side. "You wouldn't want that, would you, George? Not if you love my daughter, as I know you do."

"Of course, I love Claire, but she would never forgive me if stood by and did nothing," George replied. "Which is why you will have to kill me, too, if you want to get away with all this. Then your plans will all be for naught."

"You're a damn fool, which is why I have had to do this for both of you!" Mrs. Gainsborough yelled. "You do not have the nerve to do what needs to be done, but I do…" The woman's chest was rising and falling sharply, and for a moment, she struggled to calm herself. "Prison shall be a small price to pay to ensure my daughter's future and that of any eventual grandchildren of mine."

"It will be the hangman's noose you face, not prison," Alex said, drawing the woman's attention back over to him, along with the barrel of her gun.

"They won't hang the mother-in-law of a duke," Mrs. Gainsborough scoffed. "But I'd do it regardless, if it means my daughter will be a duchess."

"Then just kill me, and only me. There's no need to hurt anyone else. Let Aimee and the others go and I will gladly stand here and let you shoot me. Then George will be the duke and you will have what you want for Claire."

"No, Alex!" Evie yelled, seeing the intent in his eyes as he raised his hands and took a step toward the woman. "Don't you dare sacrifice yourself!"

His eyes latched onto hers, and a sad smile twisted his lips up. "If it means you're safe, I would sacrifice myself a thousand times for you. I love you, and I'm sorry I didn't tell you sooner."

A great sob bawled up in her chest as she saw the love and the determination in his eyes. "I love you, too, Alex, and I won't let you do this."

"Let her go, Mrs. Gainsborough." Alex returned

his attention to the woman, his hands held up in surrender. "I give you my word I will not run nor try to stop you from shooting me."

"No, Alex, you can't," Sam said, stepping forward and grabbing the back of Alex's arm and stepping in front of him, as George did likewise.

"Stop! All of you!" Mrs. Gainsborough screamed. "I will kill her if anyone comes any closer." She swung the gun back onto Evie. "I mean it, not another step."

The three men held up their hands and stopped in their tracks.

"Mother?" It was Claire's voice. "What's going on here?"

"Claire? You shouldn't be here," Mrs. Gainsborough cried as Claire stepped around from behind the men, her eyes widening in alarm as she caught sight of the gun in her mother's hand. "Go back to the ball, my dear."

"Why do you have a pistol pointed at Aimee?" Claire asked, her eyes swinging between her mother to Evie, then back to her mother.

"My darling, I'm trying to make you a duchess. Now go back to the ball!"

"A duchess?" Claire looked taken aback. "You're the one who hired those men to try to hurt Alex and Aimee?"

"Darling, this doesn't concern you." Mrs. Gainsborough plastered a desperate smile on her face as she looked at her daughter. "Go back to the ball."

"Doesn't concern me?" Claire exclaimed. "Mother, I don't want to be a duchess. I never have and I never will. Now, stop this madness and put down the gun." She took a step toward her mother.

"Stop right there!" Mrs. Gainsborough screamed. "I'm doing this for you! So don't tell me to stop anything."

"Mother, please, I don't want this. Alex is like a brother to George and me. I won't see you hurt him and the woman he loves."

"I will do what is necessary!" Mrs. Gainsborough's voice was shrill in the dark night. "I am doing what is best for you, even if you don't realize that."

"Murder, Mother?" Claire replied. "That is not best for anyone. Please, just let Aimee go. It's not too late."

"I can't," Mrs. Gainsborough beseeched, her tone getting desperate. "Don't you understand? I will not have you without money or position as I had to endure being, as I still must. A part of Society, but never truly belonging. Almost forgotten as soon as I step foot in a ballroom. You deserve more than that. You deserve to be a duchess, to have everyone look up at you and admire you."

The pistol shook in her hand, and Evie glanced down and saw the woman's finger twitching over the trigger.

"Once I kill her," Mrs. Gainsborough continued, "the duke will be happy to die and follow her to the grave. It will be the best solution for everyone. Surely, I'm not the only one who sees that?"

The woman truly was unstable, and Evie felt her hands go clammy as she heard the certainty in the woman's tone. She was about to do something, and

Evie had to stop her, no matter the consequences.

"You don't need to kill either of us!" Evie yelled at her. "The truth is, Alex and I will never marry. We can't, you see."

"Do you take me for a fool?" the woman screamed, the pistol trembling in her hand. "He declared his love for you. He'll marry you."

"He won't," Evie replied, knowing just how true her words were. "Not after he knows the truth about me."

For a moment, there was confusion in the woman's eyes as she glanced wildly between Evie and Alex. "What truth?"

"The truth that I'm not actually Aimee Thornton-Jones." Evie took a deep breath and her eyes found Alex's. "I'm her illegitimate cousin, Yvette Jenkins." She hoped he could see just how sorry she was for the lie, but his face remained surprisingly expressionless. Evie turned her attention back to Mrs. Gainsborough. "So, you see, he can never marry me as I'd never be a suitable duchess for him."

"What?" the woman gasped. "But it can't be. No, you're obviously lying to me to try to save him!"

"I'm not," Evie replied. "I promise I'm not. My cousin and I swapped places, which is why I'll never be able to marry the duke. There's no need to do any of this, as Alex will never marry me."

"Do you really think I'm stupid enough to believe such nonsense?" the woman scoffed. "Well, I'm not! And you will soon see just how serious I am." She raised the pistol more pointedly at Evie.

"Damn it! Don't hurt her," Alex roared, stepping forward, his hands clenching into fists by his side as he tried to draw the woman's attention back onto him. "Just let her go and shoot me instead."

It worked as Mrs. Gainsborough swung the pistol over to Alex.

Almost in slow motion, Evie saw her finger start to flick down to pull the trigger. With a roar she didn't even realize came from her own lungs, Evie lunged forward and grabbed the woman's shooting arm, knocking them both off balance and toppling them to the ground.

"Damn it, no," Alex shouted as Evie began to wrestle with Mrs. Gainsborough for the gun.

Everything seemed to draw out in an excruciating slowness, and Evie felt like she was floating above, watching herself grappling with the lady as the woman depressed the trigger and the sound of an explosion from the bullet bursting from its chamber ricocheted around the room.

With her ears ringing, Evie saw the woman cocking back the gun to pull the trigger again, but before she could, from the corner of Evie's eye, she saw Claire wrench the gun free from her mother's hand. Her mother screeched wildly and launched herself at her daughter, but Claire swung the butt of the gun down onto her mother's forehead and the woman crumpled into a pile at their feet.

The men quickly surrounded them, and Sam and George dragged a now-still Mrs. Gainsborough away from Evie.

"Are you shot?" It was Alex's desperate face that swam into her vision, as gradually Evie became aware of her surroundings as she sat up on the dirt floor of the barn. Belatedly she looked down at her body. She didn't feel shot. "I don't think so?" she murmured as Alex's hands quickly patted over her body, his eyes shining in relief after he did so.

"You're not, thank god," he groaned, pulling her into his arms and holding her tightly against him. "For a minute, I thought she'd shot you. I've never been so terrified in my life." He pulled her back from him to stare at her sternly. "Damn it, don't ever scare me like that again!"

"Don't go suggesting someone shoot you, then!" His ire was restoring her equilibrium as nothing else could, and she gave him her crankiest frown.

He suddenly grinned before his lips pressed against hers, and he kissed her with such a fierce passion that Evie could only just manage to stop herself from moaning in delight. It was then she realized he didn't seem to care about her confession. Was that even possible? "Alex, about what I said—"

He winked at her as he stood and held out a hand to help her to her feet. "It was clever of you to try to distract her, even if it wasn't a very believable lie."

"Not believable…" Did he also think she'd been lying when she'd told the truth? "But it wasn't—"

"Oh my goodness, Aimee!" Claire interrupted as she rushed over and embraced her in a hug. "Are you all right? My mother didn't hurt you, did she?"

Evie shook her head as Claire pulled back, and her gaze travelled the length of Evie from top to toe, almost as if she were satisfying herself that Evie was indeed fine. "I'm fine. I'm so sorry, though." There would be time enough shortly to talk to Alex and convince him of the truth.

Claire smiled sadly at first to Evie, then back to her mother, who seemed to be staring into space, lying on the floor with blood dripping from her head as Sam and George tied her hands behind her back. "I should be the one to apologize to you both. I had no idea she'd gotten so...so..."

"Lost," Evie replied.

Claire nodded. "That's a nice way of saying it. And that was such a brave thing to do, trying to pretend you were your cousin."

Did no one believe her? "I wasn't being brave, I was—"

"Of course you were brave," Sam interrupted, coming to stand next to them. "Now, what are we to do with her?" He glanced down at Mrs. Gainsborough.

"The police have already been summoned for the two men we caught earlier," George replied. "She will have to go with them."

"I think she needs a doctor and a good, secure institution for her to get help in, rather than a prison," Alex said. "I know of a place in the city that would be suitable, if you agree to it, Claire."

"I had no idea she was as unwell as she is," Claire said, taking in a deep breath. "But, yes, she's obviously not mentally sound and needs assistance. You're talking of an asylum, though, aren't you?"

"I am," Alex replied. "However, this one caters to those with money, and as such they treat their patients with more dignity than the state-funded ones. I will cover the costs."

"I can't ask you to do that." Claire shook her head.

"Absolutely not," George seconded.

"You're family," Alex replied. "You were both prepared to risk your lives for me and Aimee, so please, let me do this for you."

"Only if Aimee is certain, too," Claire said, her eyes finding Evie's. "My mother tried to hurt you, and I understand if you would prefer to see her punished in a prison."

Evie reached over and gave her hand a brief squeeze. "She needs help as Alex said, not a prison." She'd tell them all the truth again later, and perhaps then they might believe her.

"That's settled, then," Alex said. "We shall take her back to the house where she can be secured in a room, and I shall have some of my men guard her until arrangements can be made for her tomorrow. When the police come for the men, there will be no need to mention any of this part of the night to them."

"I'm glad you caught the men," Evie said to Alex.

"I suspected they'd be close, and they were," he confirmed. "They were waiting in some bushes by the stables, presumably to try again after the ball. But you're safe now, Aimee. I will do all in my power to never let anything happen to you again. Now, let's get back to the house."

They all nodded, with Sam lifting Mrs. Gainsborough to her feet, and then holding on to the back of her wrists, which were tied behind her back, he began to lead her down the path toward the house, with George and Claire following behind.

Alex took hold of Evie's hand and squeezed it before guiding her down the path, too.

As they walked beside each other, the house edging closer into view, Evie suddenly remembered his declaration of love. "There's no need to pretend you love me anymore. I know you were probably only saying that to convince Mrs. Gainsborough to try to protect me."

He was silent for a moment as they continued walking. "I said I love you because it's the truth."

Her heart skipped a beat at his words. "It is?"

He stopped walking and gently tugged Evie to a standstill beside him as the others continued on to the house. Picking up her hand, he placed it against his heart and smiled. "I love you, Aimee Thornton-Jones. I've loved you from the first moment I saw you, even though I tried desperately to deny it. I will always love you, and I will always keep you safe."

She closed her eyes and felt her heart lurch. Happiness and sadness clashed in her chest. Hearing him say those words was like a dream come true, but it was a nightmare, too, because she wasn't Aimee Thornton-Jones and never would be, and he deserved to know that was the truth.

Opening her eyes, she saw the huge smile on his face, and guilt nearly floored her.

"What's wrong?" he asked, concern suddenly replacing his happiness. "You do love me still, too, don't you?"

"Of course I love you, Alex," she replied, feeling her eyes start to well with tears. "I love you more than I thought it possible to love another. But there's something I have to tell you. Something I should have told you from the start, but I didn't have the courage to, and I fear you won't love me after I do."

"That's not possible," he vowed, taking both of her hands in his. "I will always love you, and you can tell me anything."

She nodded and took in a deep breath. She could do this. She had to. "I was telling the truth back in the barn. You see, I—"

"Evie!" Her uncle Thomas's deep voice hollered from behind her. "What on earth is going on? Where is Aimee?"

CHAPTER THIRTY-SIX

With a sinking heart, Evie turned to the sound and saw her uncle Thomas striding up the path toward them, the countess hurrying to keep pace beside him.

"What are you talking about, Thomas?" the countess spluttered as they came to a halt in front of them. "Aimee is right here." She pointed at Evie.

"This is my niece, Evie, not my daughter," Thomas exclaimed.

"Not your daughter?" the countess exclaimed, her hands coming up to her throat, her eyes wide in confusion. "But...I don't understand?"

"Evie?" Alex let go of her hand, his whole posture stiffening as he pulled away from her. "You were telling the truth back there? Your name is Evie, not Aimee?"

"I can explain," Evie rushed out, already seeing the cold distance seep into his expression as the betrayal crept into his eyes. "Truly I can. Please." She reached out to touch his hand, but he recoiled from her, and Evie shuddered at the look of loathing on his face.

"And you're English?" He shook his head, hearing her true accent for the first time.

"I'm half English, half American," she said. "Though I grew up in England." She watched as an expression of utter betrayal flashed on his face.

"You've been lying to me ever since we met."

There was such a lack of emotion in his voice that Evie felt empty, and all she could do was nod.

"Could someone please explain to me what on earth is going on?" Uncle Thomas said, a stern frown on his normally smiling mouth. "Why do they all think you're Aimee?" he asked Evie before swiveling his gaze to Alex. "And why were you holding my niece's hand?"

"This is my nephew, the Duke of Hargrave, Thomas," the countess hurried to explain. "He's engaged to Aimee...or rather to your niece, who we all thought was Aimee..."

"Evie, you need to start explaining things right now," her uncle demanded, crossing his hands over his chest.

She took in a deep breath, resignation mixing with her devastation. Of course, it was bound to be discovered; she just wished she'd had time to explain it properly to Alex first. "Aimee convinced me to swap places with her before we left New York. When we arrived in England, I took her place with the countess, and she took my place as a trainee secretary."

"My daughter is pretending to be a secretary?" Thomas swore heartily. "Goddamn it! I should have known she'd do something like this, and you're too kindhearted to say no to her! I should have accompanied her myself. None of this would have happened, then."

"I'm so sorry, Uncle Thomas." Evie hoped he could see how sorry she was. "She was desperate to learn what she could of your company, and well, I was happy to have the time to visit the museums and to"—she glanced over to Alex—"enjoy being free for once."

"Free to trap a duke into marriage, don't you mean?" Alex said bluntly.

"I never wanted to trap you into marriage, and you know it!"

"I know nothing of the sort! This was all a game to you, wasn't it?"

"No, it wasn't."

"Of course it was," Alex continued, as if he couldn't even hear her. "And then you decided you'd use the situation to your advantage and trap me into marriage, despite having lied to me ever since we met."

"I hated lying to you!" she yelled, the emotion and weight of having had to do so for the past few weeks building up like a furnace inside her. "I didn't want to keep doing it, but how could I tell you the truth?"

"Quite easily. You could have told me a thousand times."

"You're right, and I'm sorry I didn't. But I never meant to hurt you."

"What a load of nonsense, but I was the fool who fell for it all." There was a bitter accusation in his gaze.

"I wasn't lying to you about my feelings. Please, you have to believe me."

"Believe you?" he scoffed. "I will never believe you again. All you've done is lie to me. Lied when you said you didn't want to marry me. Lied when you said you loved me. Lie after lie after lie."

"No, that's not true. What I told you about my

feelings was true. I do love you, Alex."

"And to think you nearly had me convinced you weren't after a title," he continued, not even listening to her pleas. "I should have known better."

"That was never it at all." Evie stood her ground, refusing to shrink back from the look of absolute contempt on his face. "I was the one that convinced you we could make it a pretend engagement, that I didn't want to marry you."

"Yes, well, we've already established how much of a liar you are." Alex pressed his lips together into a tight smile. "And quite the schemer, too. Talking of a pretend engagement to allay my suspicions. I have to hand it to you, you did an excellent job of fooling me."

"Please don't be like this."

"Like what? Finally realizing the truth that you slept with me and spoke of love all just to make certain I'd marry you?" Alex gave a mirthless laugh. "And you would have gotten away with it, too, if your uncle hadn't shown up."

There were looks of shock on the countess and her uncle's faces, and Evie felt the burning mortification sting her toes. But she refused to let him see how his words were hurting her. "You might not believe me, but I never had any intention of marrying you, not even after today."

"Stop lying to me!" he growled, dragging a hand through his hair. "You wanted to marry me and become a duchess. That was clearly your end goal all along."

"Oh, you think so, do you?" she nearly yelled at him, her anger starting to burn through her sorrow.

"I know so!"

"Well, you're wrong! I can't marry you, Your Grace, because what I also said about being *illegitimate* was true."

He was silent for a good minute. "Well, no wonder you tried to fool me, then, and hats off to you. You did a damn fine job. I fell for it hook, line, and sinker. Luckily, I learned the truth before it was too late."

"Alex, please. Don't be like this."

His expression hardened. "How do you expect me to be after discovering the woman I thought I was in love with was merely a figment of my imagination? That whoever you are, standing in front of me, is nothing more than a deceptive illusion? An illegitimate liar who hoped to lie her way into becoming a duchess?"

"It wasn't like that at all."

"Bullshit it wasn't! You used me. You lied to my face. And you pretended you loved me. Whatever this was between us was all a lie. A lie I'm glad to have discovered before I made the worst mistake of my life. And don't call me Alex. You've lost any right to do that."

His words cut her like a knife, and she saw the absolute conviction on his face. In that very moment, her heart shattered as she realized with a sense of finality he would never forgive her. He would never believe her. He would never let himself love her.

"I did lie to you about my name," she said, pulling her spine straight and trying to not crumple at his feet. "That much is true. But what we shared was not a lie. Fool that *I* am, I did fall in love with you. And though you might be angry with me and lashing out cruelly because of that, underneath it all, I think what you are is scared, and you're using this as an excuse to push me away. To push away any chance of happiness we both might have found together."

"Now who is fooling who?" He narrowed his eyes upon her. "You said it yourself, you're illegitimate, whereas I am a duke. We never could have married if I'd known that, and yet you knew it all along, but it didn't stop you from pursuing me. You were chasing a title all along like I first thought you were. I should have listened to myself from the start."

She drew up her chest and took in a deep breath. She would get through this pain. She had to. "I'm sorry I hurt you, *Your Grace*. That was never my intention, no matter what you might believe. But you lied to me, too."

"The hell I did!"

"Just a few minutes ago you told me you loved me and that you always would, no matter what." She could still hear the ring of his words in her ears. A bittersweet memory she would replay in her mind. "That was a lie."

"Oh no, you don't. Everything about you has been a lie, so don't you dare turn this back on me. I love a woman who doesn't exist!"

"That's not true, and I think part of you knows it."

"What I know is that you lied to me repeatedly, trying to manipulate me into a marriage knowing we could never be together if the truth was revealed."

"Now you're lying to yourself," she countered. "I never intended to marry you, despite what you think. What I did was try to enjoy the moments we had together so I could remember them in the years ahead, because you're right, I knew we could never be together, even if a tiny part deep inside me was desperately hoping for a fairy tale."

"I stopped believing in fairy tales when I was six. You'd do well to do the same."

"I've never believed in them," she replied. "I was born a bastard, and my mother was a maid. That combination doesn't produce a princess, I'm afraid."

"Your mother was a maid?" the countess, who had been pretending to not listen to Evie and Alex's heated words alongside Evie's uncle, exclaimed. "Was she my lady's maid, Odette? Who ran off with your brother, Thomas?" she turned and asked Evie's uncle.

"Yes, that was her," Evie answered for him. "Which is why I knew I would never get a happily ever after." She glanced back to Alex. "I am sorry you were hurt. Like I said, that was never my intention. Perhaps, though, it will comfort you to know my heart is completely and irreparably shattered." She took in a deep breath and smiled sadly at him. "Goodbye, *Alex*. I hope one day you can forgive me and that you find happiness in your life. You deserve to be loved and to love."

Raising her chin and holding her head high, she turned to her uncle and the countess. "Can we please go now? I'm ready to go home."

Uncle Thomas nodded, and Evie turned on her heel and marched down the path to the house, keeping her back ramrod straight and her face locked straight ahead onto the house in the distance. She wouldn't look back at him. She couldn't, or she'd crumple into a ball on the ground.

As tears started to fall unbidden down her cheeks, Evie realized this was what a broken heart felt like. It was nothing like she'd imagined and everything she'd dreaded. And the pain would be with her for the rest of her life, a weight on her chest that would never fully heal.

CHAPTER THIRTY-SEVEN

"You're being a fool, you know."

Alex glanced up from his desk and saw his aunt Agatha standing at the threshold, a determined tilt to her chin as she stood staring at him. "You'll have to be a bit more specific, Aunt, for I'm not in the mood for guessing games."

"You let her get away."

He pressed his lips together and leaned back in his chair. "She lied to me. She lied to us all."

"So what?" Agatha waved her hand in the air as she strode into his study and wandered over to the window and perched on the sill. "Yes, she lied about who she was, but what else could she do after swapping places with her cousin? She was in an awkward position, really."

"She could have told me the truth at any time." Alex returned his attention to the ledger in front of him, trying to focus on the numbers but failing miserably.

"You love her, Alex. Don't let her go."

"I loved someone who wasn't real. End of story, Aunt."

"She was real, Alex, and she loved you, too. And you're throwing that all away."

"She wanted to be a duchess, Aunt. That is all any woman wants from me. I should have bloody let Claire's mother kill me, then I wouldn't have to deal with it ever again."

His aunt sighed heartily. "They're all returning to New York today. There's still time to rush down to the docks and stop them."

It had been a week since that fateful night when Alex's whole world had felt like it was crumbling around him. A whole week he'd kept thinking over and over about his time with *Evie*, not Aimee as he'd thought of her for so long.

All of those little slip-ups she'd made that he'd thought odd but hadn't connected together. A week trying to see the manipulation in her actions but coming up woefully empty. Try as he might, every time he replayed their time together, instead of manipulation he saw honesty, which made no sense when she'd been lying to him the entire time.

He really was a fool if he could only see honesty in her actions.

Well, a man is often a fool when he is in love, isn't he? the voice in his head whispered to him. Firmly, he pushed the traitorous voice to the bottom recesses of this mind. He wasn't still in love with her. She'd lied to him. His love had died the moment he'd discovered the truth.

Liar, the voice whispered again.

He pushed back from his desk and stalked over to the side table and poured himself a whisky. "I'm not rushing anywhere, most especially not to the docks to stop them. Good riddance back to the States, I say."

"Then you're a fool like I said." Agatha sighed. "A fool who will end up alone and miserable."

"I'm already that, dear Aunt Agatha."

"Only because you don't think you deserve love."

"Maybe I don't." He downed the shot of amber fluid in one sip and poured himself another. "Perhaps I'm too like my father and simply not lovable."

"My brother was a hard man to love, that is true. But you're nothing like him, Alex."

"He made me to be exactly like him!"

"Perhaps in running the dukedom, yes, but not when it comes to who you are inside. You have so much love to give, if only you'd let yourself." She stood and walked over to him, then took his glass of whisky and poured it into the potted plant beside her.

"What are you doing?" Alex grumbled. "That's expensive whisky."

"It's far too early in the day for you to get drunk as I've noticed you've gotten into a habit of doing this past week."

After they'd returned from the country, his aunt had visited him the next day and noticed he was inebriated. Stinking, rotten drunk, to be exact. She'd then made up some story about a water leak in her residence and said she would have to stay with Alex for the time being. Alex hadn't believed a word of it but knew she was concerned after what had happened, so he'd agreed to let her stay with him temporarily, part of him grateful for the company.

Though not now she was trying to talk him into going after Evie, which he wouldn't do.

"Don't let love slip through your hands, Alex,"

the countess murmured, reaching up and patting him on his stubble-covered cheek. "Don't end up alone like your father did."

"Perhaps I want to be alone," he grumbled. "In fact, I prefer to be alone."

"Don't you want children?"

"No. I don't." Desperately, he tried to push aside the image that had suddenly sprung to mind of Evie holding his child in her arms. A little girl with blue eyes exactly like her mother's and with Alex's dark hair. Fuck. He was in trouble imagining things like that.

And then for a moment he panicked. What if she was pregnant? He hadn't even considered that when he'd essentially spurned her after he found out about her deception. "She's not pregnant, is she?"

His aunt pressed her lips together for a moment. "Well, I suppose that depends on how long ago you dishonored her."

"A week ago." There wasn't much he could say in response to dishonoring her because he had. No matter her lies, she'd been a virgin when he'd slept with her. Even the searing memories of that were enough to make him want to groan.

His aunt sighed and shook her head. "It is far too soon to tell, in that case."

He knew that, but she could still be pregnant even if it was too early to know for certain.

"But what does it matter to you if she is or not? You've decided to have nothing to do with her again, haven't you?"

"Well, I can't just leave her pregnant."

"Perhaps you should have thought of that before sleeping with her, my dear boy." She raised her brow. "But what can you do in any event?"

"She was the one who lied to me." Alex couldn't understand why he was the one having to defend himself. His aunt was carrying on like he was the one at fault, when he was in fact the innocent party. "But, yes, if she was pregnant, I would be duty-bound to marry her, regardless of her birth status."

"But many men keep a mistress along with any illegitimate children they have," his aunt replied. "Why would it be any different for you if she were pregnant?"

"Because I wouldn't let any child of mine suffer a lifetime of being labelled illegitimate."

"Your father wouldn't have approved."

Alex scoffed. "All the more reason to face a scandal in doing so then."

"Oh, she's not actually illegitimate," his aunt said. "So, if you did marry her, you would face no scandal."

"What are you talking about? She said she was. I don't think one gets that sort of information wrong." Though she had lied to him about who she was, so perhaps she'd also lied about her parentage? "Unless she was lying about that, too."

"She wasn't lying. She just doesn't have all the facts."

"And you do?"

"I should. Her mother was my lady's maid, and she ran off with Thomas's brother, Peter, who was staying with my husband and I at the time. Caused quite a scandal in America, I'm told, as I believe

Peter's father had arranged for him to marry a New York heiress to merge her father's company with his. But when Peter didn't do that and instead ran off with my maid Odette, it put a halt to those plans."

"I don't understand how that makes Evie not illegitimate?"

"I received a letter a few months later from Odette after she and Peter fled together, and she was apologizing for running off and leaving me in the lurch without a maid. She said she and Peter had fallen so in love with each other they hadn't been able to help themselves. She also sent me a photo of her and Peter getting married at a small church in Paris."

"Did you tell Evie this?"

"No," his aunt said with a shake of her head. "I didn't even know she was Odette's daughter until last week. I didn't know Odette and Peter had had a daughter, in fact. About a year after I got that letter, I received word from Thomas that Peter and Odette had both caught cholera and died. There was no mention of a child. In any event, after last week, I told Thomas about the photo and he sent a man over to Paris to verify the information before he mentioned anything to Evie as he didn't wish to get her hopes up if it wasn't true. But they did marry, so Yvette Jenkins is actually Yvette Thornton-Jones, and heiress to her late father's fortune, making her one of the richest Dollar Princesses ever. And given she is a true Thornton-Jones, she'll soon be inundated with men who are all eager to court her and marry her."

"Eager to steal her fortune, don't you mean?"

"Yes, but what do you care? You only ever loved an imaginary woman, not her. Isn't that what you said?"

"I know what you're trying to do, and it won't work."

She peered at him through her lashes, all innocence. "I don't know what you're talking about. I'm merely stating facts."

"Well, state facts all you like. It's not changing my mind," he told her, his voice firm. "I should have known never to trust her. Hell, I couldn't even trust my mother when she promised to come back for me. Why would I think I could trust another woman ever?"

"It wasn't your mother's fault that your father refused to let her see you again." Agatha sighed. "Goodness, even the courts wouldn't let her see you. You can't blame her for that."

"What do you mean the courts wouldn't let her see me?"

Agatha looked taken aback for a minute. "She petitioned the courts to allow her to visit you when your father kept denying her requests."

"What?" Suddenly everything Alex thought he knew seemed wrong. "She never tried to see me… I never heard from her again after she left."

"My dear nephew, you were probably too young to remember, and mostly at boarding school while all of the drama was unfolding, but she most definitely did try to see you, but my brother kept refusing her. She went as far as to petition the courts to allow her visitations with you, but up against a duke, and as a divorced woman, she was not successful. Didn't you get any of her letters?"

"What letters?" Alex felt as if everything had been turned on its head.

"Your mother wrote to me shortly before she died, telling me she'd sent you a letter every week since she'd left you and that she suspected your father wasn't allowing you to see them, let alone read them. She begged me to plead to your father to let you read them. Charles relented and promised me he would let you."

"It's the first I've heard of any letters." His mother had written to him? And every week? Alex had thought she'd forgotten about him, living her new life in America.

"I should have known Charles wouldn't keep his word about them." His aunt sighed and rubbed her temple, looking suddenly very tired. "When it came to anything related to your mother, your father could never see reason. When your mother left him, everyone thought he cared little of it except for the scandal she created in doing so. But I think the truth was that Charles was heartbroken but far too proud and stubborn to ever admit it. Just as he'd been too proud and stubborn all throughout his marriage to admit any love he might have felt for your mother. A fact which drove her into the arms of another."

"My father never loved anyone. He was a cruel man who only cared about the appearance of things, and god help anyone who couldn't live up to his standards." Alex could still feel the sting of his father's belt against his back. Lash after lash for having got an equation wrong on a test when he was eleven, or for mispronouncing a Latin phrase, or for daring to speak back.

"I suppose he must have got rid of the letters," she continued.

"Perhaps." After his father's death, Alex hadn't bothered to go through any of his things, instead ordering everything to be boxed up and stored in the attic. If he'd kept her letters, they'd be in those boxes. But did Alex want to read them? He'd spent most of his life thinking his mother wanted nothing to do with him, yet if she'd written to him that clearly hadn't been the case.

His aunt leaned over and grasped onto Alex's hand. "Don't end up on the same path as he did. Alone and too stubborn to love, pushing everyone away."

Alex gritted his teeth and gently but purposefully pushed her hand away. "I really don't know what you want of me."

"Follow your heart, not your head," she implored him. "I want you to be happy for once in your life, Alex. And I know you could be with Evie, if only you would let yourself be."

"Every memory I have of her and what we shared is false." Twisting on his heel, he stalked over to the window and pressed his forehead to the glass. "How could I ever trust her? She manipulated me and played with my emotions."

"Do you really think that's what she did?"

"What else am I to think?"

"That she's young and was living an adventure by swapping places with her wealthy cousin. Silly, but understandable."

"It's not that simple!" Alex roared, turning back to face her.

"Isn't it?" she asked, raising her eyebrow. "I rather think it is. She meant no malice in her actions. Anyone only had to look at her devastation from your rejection of her to see that. And if you thought rationally about it, rather than with emotion, you would, too."

He dragged a hand through his hair, images of Evie smiling, of her laughing, of her crying, clashing in his head like a cymbal. There wasn't a moment since he'd watched her walk away from him that he hadn't thought of her. Hadn't dreamed of her. Hadn't seen her face everywhere he looked. "I could never forgive her lying to me."

"Then you are blind, my nephew, and following exactly in your father's footsteps." She shook her head. "You have been given the gift of love, Alex, and yet you are blithely throwing it away." She walked over to him and gently reached over and patted him on the arm. "I desperately hope you don't choose your father's path. I hope instead you choose love and happiness rather than holding on to a bitter sense of righteous indignation that will only leave you empty and lonely for the rest of your life."

She stepped backward and raised her chin. "Now that I've said my piece, I will return to my residence, and hope against hope that you choose love instead of anger and loneliness, for you deserve to find happiness for once in your life." And with that, she turned and left him alone in his study.

Alone but filled with uncertainty.

All the women he'd cared about had lied to him.

He thought of his mother's letters, and suddenly he wasn't so sure, but he knew he had to find out. Five minutes later, he was in the attic sorting through box after box of his father's possessions, hunting for any letters she'd supposedly sent him. Ten minutes later, with nothing to show for his efforts, he was about to give up, when out of the corner of his eye he caught sight of an old trunk with an inch of dust on its surface and a padlock protecting its contents.

The old man probably would have locked away any letters from his mother, knowing Alex wouldn't have dared to break a lock when he was a boy. Well, he wasn't a boy anymore. Grabbing an old metal poker, he swung it hard against the lock, taking great pleasure in hearing the grating of metal against metal, until the lock broke and clattered to the floor.

He lifted the lid of the chest and paused. Inside was letter after letter, all addressed to Alex. Tentatively, he picked one up and turned it over. His mother's name and an address in Boston were scrawled on the back. She had written to him, and by the sheer volume of letters in the chest, written to him every week like she'd said.

For the rest of the day and into the night, Alex sat in the attic, reading each letter from his mother. She told him of her life in Boston, of her trying to see him, even returning to London on six occasions to petition the courts to let him visit her, but to no avail.

It was pitch black outside by the time he managed to get through all the correspondence, having only managed to eat a few bites of the sandwich and a few sips of the water his butler had brought up to him hours ago.

Alex didn't know how long he just sat there on the floor in the now-dark room with only a small lamp lit for some light, lost in his thoughts and memories, realizing his mother had never abandoned him. That she'd tried desperately to see him, but his father had forbidden it, making Alex believe she'd forgotten all about him when that couldn't have been further from the truth.

If his father had still been alive, Alex would have happily clocked the bastard in the jaw for such callous disregard. How could someone be so cruel as to deny his son from seeing his own mother? To make his son think she didn't love him just as she no longer loved his father. A cruel, lonely, and loveless shell of a man was who. And his aunt had said Alex was on a path to end up exactly like him…alone and without love.

He laughed, but there was little humor in the sound. Perhaps that was the life he was destined for. He certainly hadn't had any luck in love, had he?

Liar. You found love, but you tossed it aside.
She lied and manipulated me!

But then he sighed, the anger over her actions suddenly draining away. She might have lied, but there was never any manipulating. He could at least admit that truth, and as much as he might try to convince himself she had played him like a piano, he knew deep down to his soul that when she was with him, she hadn't been playing a role. She'd been genuine and kind and real.

Yes, perhaps she'd put on an American accent and lied about her name, but no one was that good a liar when talking of fossils and reacting to seeing them. Their talks and everything they'd shared hadn't been an illusion. Her response to him when he'd touched her hadn't been false. It had been real and whole and so all-consuming that Alex couldn't forget it. He couldn't forget her. And, suddenly, he didn't want to. He wanted her in his life. He wanted to choose love and happiness, instead of the bitter loneliness his father chose.

But glancing out at the moon, he knew it was too late to stop her leaving now. She was on a steamer back to America and back to her life. He'd said some harsh things to her, things that she might never forgive him for. Well, damn that, he wasn't going to let that stop him from trying. Hell, if he had to get down on his knees and beg her to forgive him, then get down on his knees he would.

He loved her, and he was going to win her back no matter what it took.

CHAPTER THIRTY-EIGHT

Evie stared at her reflection in the floor-to-ceiling mirror, almost as if she were an outside observer looking in.

She was dressed in one of Aimee's Worth gowns, looking resplendent with the soft cornflower blue of the material perfectly complementing her eyes and the thousands of blue crystals sewn into the bodice and skirts of the dress making her reflection sparkle. She should have felt like a million dollars, which, apparently, she was now worth after Uncle Thomas had sat her down and told her he'd recently been able to confirm that Evie's father and mother had married, making Evie legitimate and her father's heir.

The news should have shocked her, or at least made her happy, but it hadn't. Instead, she felt like the same empty shell she'd felt like ever since the night of the ball at Alex's estate. The night her heart shattered into a million pieces, never to be whole again.

She'd barely even paid attention when Uncle Thomas had apologized over and over again for the fact that he hadn't been more diligent after his brother's death. That he hadn't even known she'd existed until he'd gotten a letter from her dying aunt informing him of Evie, but even her aunt hadn't known Evie's parents had secretly eloped before Evie was born, dying only a few months later in Paris before they could tell anyone. So how was her uncle to have known let alone be sorry for the fact he hadn't?

If it hadn't been for her mother sending a letter to the countess with a picture of their wedding, no one would have ever discovered that Evie was in fact born in wedlock and not illegitimate as everyone had incorrectly assumed. A month ago, the news would have thrilled her, but now it meant very little, except for the fact that she was an extremely wealthy heiress who wouldn't have to be a secretary. One good thing, she supposed.

But what good was money if she was miserable?

Aimee had tried to cheer her up, talking of how Evie could now travel to her heart's content and visit all of the museums everywhere to see fossil after fossil, but even the thought of doing that made her think of Alex and the time they'd spent together looking at fossils. The pain was agonizing.

She didn't know how long such feelings would last, but she suspected they would never fully go away. So she tried not to think of anything that would make her remember Alex. Not that she succeeded very well. It seemed everywhere she turned something reminded her of him. A tall, dark head of hair in a crowd had her catch her breath thinking just maybe he'd changed his mind and realized he couldn't live without her and had come for her.

Such thoughts always ended in bitter disappointment.

He wasn't coming for her. He never would. He'd made that abundantly clear when she'd last seen him on that fateful day, exactly twenty-five days ago.

Twenty-five days since she'd felt his lips on hers. Twenty-five days since she'd felt the heat of his touch. Twenty-five days of abject misery.

The trip back on the steamer had taken eleven days, and they'd been back in New York now for a week. A week that had initially been spent with Aunt Edith chastising them both for swapping identities, though mostly her aunt had been furious with Aimee rather than Evie. Though, in Evie's opinion, it was more her fault than her cousin's. If she'd only said no to Aimee, they never could have swapped in the first place. But then she never would have experienced Alex's touch. She never would have even met him. Perhaps that wouldn't have been so bad? At least then she wouldn't feel so empty. So alone.

Aunt Edith must have sensed how broken Evie was inside, because as soon as the doctor had given her leg the all-clear, her aunt had ensured Evie's days were filled with a whirlwind of activity. Fittings for new gowns, shopping for gloves and hats. Visiting Society matrons to ensure everyone knew the truth of Evie's parentage.

Though Evie would normally hate such socializing and shopping, she hadn't minded it so much this past week as it had at least made her think about something else other than Alex, for a little bit of the day anyhow.

Now, they were due to attend the Astor ball, which was the social event of the season, and the first invitation the Thornton-Joneses had received from New York Society's matriarch. None of them were under any illusions about why they'd been invited. Everyone was curious to see Evie, whose escapade of being engaged to a duke and a secret heiress at that was all anyone could talk about. At least they didn't know she and Aimee had swapped places.

So here she was all dressed and ready to be paraded in front of Society as Yvette Thornton-Jones, lost heiress and legitimate daughter of the late Peter Thornton-Jones. No longer the illegitimate companion to Aimee, sitting in the shadows at society gatherings, but instead a woman people would pay attention to.

Attention she didn't want and didn't need.

But her aunt and uncle were so thrilled to be trying to make it up to her for what they thought were years denied to her of her true birthright that she didn't want to disappoint them. In truth, though, Evie just wanted to curl up under her quilt and bawl her eyes out, which of late was her favorite pastime at night when she was finally left alone and could stop pretending she was fine when she was anything but.

It was then she could cry and think of how desperately she missed Alex and how she'd ruined everything with him. How she'd hurt him. Which was the worst part of it all. Seeing the betrayal in his eyes and knowing she was responsible for that had cut her to the quick, especially given she was in love with him and knew her heart would always belong to him.

Why hadn't she heeded her own warnings not to

give him her heart? She'd known doing so would be fraught with risk. Known her heart would get broken. But she'd done it anyway, unable to resist the pull of her feelings for him. And now she was paying the ultimate price.

"Oh, you look so beautiful, my dear!" her aunt Edith exclaimed as she strolled into the room, her own ruby-red ball gown glittering stylishly, and only a slight limp still noticeable from her carriage accident the other month. "You shall be the belle of the ball tonight!"

Evie tried to smile at her but only managed a brief twist of her lips.

"Come on, then." Her aunt took her hand, and they made their way down to the carriage outside, where Aimee and Uncle Thomas were already waiting inside.

The trip to the Astor residence just further down on Fifth Avenue took ten minutes, and before Evie even realized it, she found herself being announced and escorted into the grand ballroom by her uncle, who was beaming proudly. *Yvette Thornton-Jones*. It still sounded odd, especially as she thought of herself as plain old Yvette Jenkins. But perhaps a new identity was exactly what she needed, a new persona, too. Anything to try to forget the pain over Alex.

With that thought in mind, she twisted her lips up into a smile, the action feeling uncomfortable having not smiled in several weeks, but she smiled nonetheless at everyone she passed as her uncle led her onto the dance floor for a waltz.

"It's nice to see you smile, Evie," he said as he

began twirling her about around the ballroom, several of the guests eagerly watching them. Probably trying to see if she tripped was her guess.

"Thank you for everything, Uncle." He'd been helping her practice dancing this week, and because of it she felt much more confident than she had when she first danced with Alex.

Her smile vanished with the thought of him, and her stomach clenched. She was starting to get sick and frustrated by this reaction of hers every time she thought of him. She could never seem to escape him, even from her memories.

"What's wrong, my dear?" Her uncle peered at her in concern. "You seem upset all of a sudden."

"Just bad memories, Uncle, which I am determined to overcome." She took in a deep breath and smiled over at him. It was forced, but it seemed to appease him.

"He was a fool to let you go."

She pressed her lips tightly together, even more determined not to cry right there in her uncle's arms. "I lied to him, Uncle, right from the beginning."

"You did. And I daresay he was angry at that fact and had every right to be. However, I still stand by my comment that he was a fool to let you go."

She smiled at him, genuinely this time at the absolute certainty in his words. "Perhaps he was a fool, though his actions were understandable."

"Your heart will eventually heal, my dear girl."

She squeezed his hand as he deftly swirled her about the room amongst the other dancers. "I hope you're right, Uncle. It certainly doesn't feel like it will."

"Time has a habit of healing all wounds," he replied. "Or at least making us better able to cope with the pain. When your father ran off with your mother, I was furious at him. Absolutely furious he'd thought about his heart more than his family. I refused to speak to him when he fled to France."

"We all do things we regret when we're hurt." And that's what she was telling herself Alex had done. He'd been hurt and justifiably so. It was no wonder he'd reacted as he had. A reaction Evie couldn't blame him for.

"That we do. The day before your parents died, I refused to take my brother's phone call. Did you know that?"

Evie shook her head.

"I answered the phone in my office and the operator said she had him on the line, but I refused to take the call." He was looking off into the distance and then blinked as he returned his gaze back to Evie. "I think he was calling because he was sick and he wanted to tell me about you, so I would go and get you and raise you as you should have been raised in case anything happened to him. But I didn't take his call… I never got to speak to my brother again, and I missed out on helping raise you, all because I was angry with him for following his heart instead of marrying a woman our father had chosen for him."

He took in several hasty breaths, and Evie saw the sheen of moisture in his eyes.

"I'm so sorry I robbed you of a childhood of

privilege all because of my pride. Will you ever forgive me?"

"There's nothing to forgive, Uncle." She squeezed his hand tightly for a moment. "My aunt Beth loved me so much that it made up for not having all of this wealth. It made me who I am today, and though I would have loved to grow up with you, Aunt Edith, and Aimee, I wouldn't change anything for the world."

"You are the true gem, Evie." Her uncle nodded and pulled her to a stop on the dance floor along with everyone else as the music ended. "And I'll say it again, that duke of yours was a fool to ever let you go."

"He was never my duke. Not really." She leaned up and brushed a kiss on her uncle's cheek. "I am lucky to have you as my uncle, though." Her life could have turned out so different if he'd ignored her aunt's letter informing him of Evie.

"As we are lucky to have you, my dear child." He smiled and patted her on the hand. "Now, promise me you will at least try to enjoy yourself tonight?"

Nodding, she returned his smile. "I will try."

"Good, because I already see many eager young gentlemen trying to catch your eye for the next dance."

She glanced around the edge of the dance floor, and sure enough several young men were indeed smiling at her. "I probably should dance with one of them."

"That would make your aunt happy. I think she's resigned herself to the fact that Aimee has no intention of marrying just yet and has set her sights on trying to see you settled instead."

"God help me."

Her uncle laughed. "Indeed. I also need God's help as I have agreed to allow Aimee to start to take a more active role in my businesses."

"You have?" The news made Evie happy as nothing had in weeks. "Oh, Uncle Thomas, that is wonderful news. It's all she's ever wanted."

He sighed. "Yes, it wasn't until your little swap with her that I realized how serious she was about it, and if I didn't do something about it, then goodness knows what else she'd do."

The music for the next dance began to play but then abruptly stopped, and a buzzing murmur in the crowd started to spread across the room. Evie glanced around and saw everyone starting to look over to the entrance of the ballroom.

"The Duke of Hargrave," the butler announced with a decided flourish.

Evie grabbed ahold of her uncle's hand, certain she would slip to the floor if she didn't as a kaleidoscope of shock and denial suddenly filled her. Alex couldn't be here. Could he? No. He hated her and never wanted to see her again. He wouldn't be here; the announcement had to be wrong. But the sea of bodies seemed to be parting, clearing a path directly toward her.

She gulped, every single inch of her body alert, a part of her wanting to flee out into the gardens, but instead she stood frozen to the spot as she caught sight of Alex striding across the room toward her, a determined glint in his eye the closer he got.

"Perhaps he's not such a fool after all," her uncle whispered to her a moment before Alex came to a stop in front of them.

"Mr. Thornton-Jones," Alex acknowledged her uncle with a nod of his head before swinging the full force of his attention onto Evie. "Miss Yvette Thornton-Jones." He nodded to her and picked up her hand, his eyes never leaving hers as he placed a kiss on her gloved knuckles. "It is good to see you again."

Evie felt his kiss all the way down to her toes, and she didn't know why but suddenly she felt like bawling but managed not to and instead did her best to plaster a calm expression on her face. Or at least she hoped it appeared calm. "Your Grace." She curtsied to him.

"Duke," her uncle replied, nodding his own head in acknowledgment. "I must say, I didn't expect to see you in New York so soon after our last visit together. But I'm glad you've come to your senses."

Had he come to his senses? Or had he come here to humiliate her as he might have felt she'd humiliated him? She didn't think he'd be so cruel, not the Alex she knew, but he'd been so hurt by her charade, and he'd made it clear his love had been an illusion, so who really knew what his intentions were?

"What are you doing here?" she whispered, her eyes latching onto his, unable to disguise the pain and longing that was beginning to overwhelm her.

He was but a few feet away, and she yearned to

reach out and wrap her arms around him. Hold him and never let him go. But he'd also hurt her so much she didn't think she'd survive being hurt like that again.

"I've come to…" His words trailed off, and he took in a deep breath. "I've come to apologize to you."

"You have?" Could she really believe him? What if he was simply toying with her emotions? Her heart desperately hoped not, but her head wasn't so sure. He'd been so angry the last time she'd seen him. "But why? I thought you never wanted to see me again."

"I was angry, Evie. Angry because I thought everything we'd shared had been a lie. I should have let you explain." He took in another deep breath, and Evie noticed his hands were shaking lightly. "I never should have said such harsh words to you, and I needed to apologize. It's the only way I think I'll ever be able to sleep at night."

"You're here to apologize to me so you can sleep better at night?"

"I am. I wanted you to know how sorry I am for how things ended between us."

Bitter disappointment surged through her, and Evie had to swallow away the lump in her throat. She couldn't fall to pieces in front of him. She wouldn't. She raised her chin higher and stared him straight in the eyes. "There's nothing to apologize for. I hurt you and lied to you, and that's why you said such harsh words to me. I don't blame you for that. If our roles had been reversed, I'm sure I would have said similar things to you."

"It's not just that…" He dragged a hand through his hair. "It's…"

"What? What is it?" she demanded, caring little that half of New York's elite were making no effort to pretend they weren't avidly listening to every word that was said. "If you're trying to assuage your guilt and are seeking my forgiveness, then I forgive you, Alex. You can leave New York and return to London with your mind completely at ease. There, will that help you sleep better now?"

"No. It won't," he said, his voice so low she had to strain forward to hear it.

"What do you want of me, then?" She placed her hands on her hips and glared at him. Didn't he know how difficult he was making things for her, how he was only prolonging her pain?

"I'll never sleep properly again. Not in London, not here. Nowhere," he said. "Not unless you're with me."

Her hands dropped to her side, shock replacing her anguish from a moment ago. "You won't?"

He shook his head, and a tentative smile spread across his lips. "I was a fool to ever let you leave London in the first place."

"You were?" Was this really happening?

"He was the biggest fool imaginable," her uncle Thomas chipped in, and Alex laughed.

"Your uncle is correct. I was the biggest fool imaginable to ever let you go."

Evie didn't know what to say. Was he actually being serious? "Is this some cruel joke you're playing on me?"

"The cruel joke was me ever letting you go in

the first place. It's something I will always regret, but that I'm hoping to make right tonight. Will you forgive me, Evie, for being such a jackass?"

There was such an earnest pleading in his eyes that Evie knew without a doubt he was telling her the truth. Slowly, she smiled. "I will."

A huge grin spread over his face, and then in front of everyone he dropped down onto one knee and took her hand in his. The very touch sent her pulse skittering out of control.

"Yvette Thornton-Jones," he said, "will you make me the happiest man in the world and agree to be my wife?" He pulled out a ring box from his jacket pocket and with one hand deftly flicked the top of it open, revealing a shining blue square sapphire encircled by brilliant diamonds nestled in the box. "Marry me, Evie. I can't stand the thought of being in this world without you by my side, always. I love you. I fell in love with you from the moment my eyes latched on to yours. I was just a bit slow recognizing it at first."

"You called me a title-hunting jezebel when we first met."

He cringed. "Yes, I might have done that."

Evie narrowed her eyes upon him. "You did do that."

"Well, we've already agreed I am the biggest fool imaginable, haven't we?"

"We have, Alexander Trenton. But you're my fool, and I love you so much, too."

A grin spread over his face as he jumped to his feet and pulled her into his arms and kissed her right there, in front of everyone. The Astors, the

Jacobs, the Vanderbilts. Everyone. And because he was a duke, they loved it, everyone cheering and hollering, while Evie wrapped her arms around his neck and savored the feel of him against her.

He gently pulled back and stared down at her, his eyes sparkling in joy. "I take that as a yes?"

Evie laughed and swatted him in the chest. "Yes! Yes, I will marry you!"

His lips crushed hers again before he pulled out the ring and gently placed it onto her ring finger, the crowd around them breaking into applause once again.

Before she even knew what he was about, he swung her into his arms and carried her over to the balcony doors and away from the crowd, who all gasped through their laughter and smiles.

He stepped outside, carrying her over to the balcony, before gently placing her back onto her feet. "I think your uncle will give us a couple of minutes out here alone before he marches out here to stop us from getting too carried away, don't you think?"

"I'm sure he will." Then without waiting for Alex, Evie launched herself into his arms and kissed him with all of the love she had for him. A love to last a lifetime.

"God, I've missed you," he groaned.

"I've missed you so much, too."

He pulled back from her and stared down into her eyes. "I love you, Evie," he said. "I love you so damn much, I was lost without you. A shell of a man who was a complete wreck, without purpose or direction."

"That's a bit hard to believe." She couldn't imagine Alex being so lost. He was so strong and resilient.

"It's true," he replied. "Aunt Agatha insisted on staying with me after she visited one morning and found me drunk."

"You weren't?" Evie gasped and then couldn't help the laugh from bursting out of her chest. "Oh, Alex, she must have been beside herself to see you in such a state."

"She was most unimpressed." He grinned back at her. "But, in the end, it was she who convinced me what a fool I was being to let you go. Her and my mother's letters."

"Your mother's letters?"

He quickly told her all about them. "After reading them, I realized my father had poisoned my perception of women, fostering a distrust in them, because of my mother's supposed abandonment of me. I knew I didn't want to end up like him, bitter and alone, without any love to warm him. And I knew that without you in my life that's exactly what I was becoming."

Evie leaned up and cupped his cheek with her hand. "I shall have to thank the countess when I next see her, and I will thank your mother in my prayers, too."

"And I shall have to thank your cousin Aimee."

"Aimee?"

"Yes. If she hadn't convinced you to swap places, we never would have met, and I would have grown old and lonely with just my fossils to keep me company."

"I nearly forgot all about your fossils! After we're married, I'll be able to explore all your caves to my heart's content. Why, I'll even be able to excavate my own fossils!" She clapped her hands together in excitement. "I can't wait!"

"I see it wasn't my title you were after but rather my caves and fossils," he murmured. "I should have known."

She laughed, happiness filling her entire body and making her feel so light, almost as if she were floating. "Yes. And in your case, though you didn't want to marry an American Dollar Princess, in the end, that's exactly what you're doing."

"I wouldn't have it any other way," he whispered against her mouth, his own lips mere inches from hers.

"You wouldn't?"

"Not for a minute. Not even for a second. I love you, Evie, more than I ever thought it possible to love another. And I will love you every single second for the rest of my life, my beautiful Dollar Princess."

As his lips pressed down onto hers and he wrapped his arms around her, Evie felt such contentment and happiness, living the happily ever after she never thought was possible, knowing in Alex's arms she'd finally found her home.

EPILOGUE

Watching her husband stride across the ballroom toward her always brought a smile to Evie's face. Alex cut such a dashing figure in his black tuxedo that not for the first time that night she sighed, thinking she had to be the luckiest woman in the world to be married to him.

She still had to pinch herself most days to convince herself she wasn't dreaming, and she really had married her prince, or rather her duke in this case. Her duke who made her the happiest she'd ever been, especially given all the time they spent together, exploring their caves and hunting for fossils.

Already she missed being at Hargrave Hall, but regardless of their preferences for spending as much of their free time there as they could, Alex had responsibilities in London he couldn't avoid, which meant attending balls and soirees whenever they were in town. Even hosting their own balls at times, which was what they were doing tonight, and surprisingly Evie was getting rather good at doing so.

It was an odd thought that she was now a duchess who either hosted balls or was invited to them, her presence signifying the success of whichever ball she chose to attend. What a funny world that she'd gone from a penniless orphan to an American Dollar Princess, then to a duchess, marrying into one of the oldest and most prestigious aristocratic families of English Society.

Unbelievable was a more apt word to describe the whirlwind events of the past few months.

"Is everything all right, my love?" Alex asked, coming to a halt in front of her, concern replacing the wicked grin that had been on his handsome face as he handed her the glass of water he'd fetched her.

"I'm fine," Evie replied, accepting the glass from him and taking a small sip. "Did you manage to spot Aimee in the crowd?"

He shook his head. "No, though the butler gave me this note for you." Alex pulled out a small piece of paper from his jacket and gave it to Evie, while taking back the glass so she could read the thing. "Looks like Aimee's handwriting."

Evie glanced down at the scrawl. It was Aimee's. Quickly, she read the note and then scowled. "Not again."

"She's not coming?"

"No." She blew out a breath. This was the third ball in a row Aimee hadn't attended, despite her assurances yesterday she would. "She says she's busy working on this new project for her father."

"You don't believe her?"

"Oh, I do," Evie replied, her eyes narrowing as they glanced around the room. "But I'm more certain she's not coming because of a certain gentleman being here." Her eyes landed on the man in question, Harrison Stone, Aimee's nemesis.

"Surely she's not still trying to avoid him." Alex's eyes followed Evie's across the room to where Harrison was currently talking with the Earl of Craven.

"Obviously, she is." Evie sighed. "What I wouldn't give to know what happened between the two of them when she and I were swapping places."

"She still won't tell you?"

"Not a hint," Evie replied. "Though I'm determined to find out."

"Of course you are, my love." Then Alex started to grin as the musicians began to play a new tune. "May I have this next dance, wife?" He held his hand out toward her.

Evie grimaced as she heard the first few strains of the next waltz. "Oh no, you didn't…"

"How could I not?" he replied with a wink, taking her hand in his. "You know how I love dancing Her Grace's Gallop. And you should, too, being its inventor."

"I hate it." Her Grace's Gallop, as it was now called, had quickly become *the* waltz to dance in every ballroom and assembly from England to the States, despite its dizzying tempo that everyone was still yet to properly master.

And given Evie had been the one to introduce it to English Society, someone had named it in her honor. A someone she heavily suspected was her husband, who also made certain it was played at every single ball they attended and that they danced it on each occasion.

"It's our special dance, my love," he said, leading her to the dance floor before he began to deftly twirl her across the space, regardless of the impossibly fast music. "It brings back such fond memories of our first dance."

"What? Of me stepping on your toes?" Evie tried to maintain a cranky expression, but it was almost impossible when he was grinning at her with such a devastatingly handsome smile. It was a smile that never failed to melt her heart, and the man knew it.

"You haven't done that in months, my darling," he was happy to point out. "In fact, you've gotten proficient at our waltz, making us the only couple who don't wobble around afterward, knocking into each other and others."

Evie shook her head but couldn't help a small smile from twitching at the corners of her mouth from his observation. "You had best enjoy this romp around the ballroom with me, my darling husband, for I fear it shall be the last of Her Grace's Gallop we shall dance together for months."

"You would deny me my favorite dance?" His grin was replaced with a pout, though Evie could see the twinkle of amusement in his eyes. He still enjoyed teasing her, the cad. "Surely not?"

"It shall be our last," she replied pertly. "Well, at least for the next seven months or so, as I imagine soon I won't be in any state to keep up with this whirlwind tempo. At least not without getting sick."

His grin was replaced by a frown of confusion for a moment. "Seven months?" Then the confusion gave way to an expression of shock and disbelief. "Does that mean that…that you're…"

"With child," she finished for him, and this time Evie couldn't help her own grin from spreading right across her face. "Yes, it does mean that."

Abruptly, he pulled them to a stop, and without a care for their audience, he stood in the middle of the dance floor, staring down at her. "You're having my baby?"

She nodded. "The doctor came this afternoon and confirmed it."

"Are you serious?"

"Entirely." Then suddenly she felt worried. What if because of his own terrible childhood, he was regretting trying to get her pregnant in the first place? "You are happy about the news, aren't you?"

"Happy?" he let out a breathless whisper. "Happy doesn't even come close to describing what I'm feeling... I'm beyond happy. I'm ecstatic! Breathtakingly ecstatic." And then before she knew what he was about, he leaned down and kissed her right there and then in the middle of the ballroom. A thorough, no-nonsense, to hell with Society's edicts and rules kiss as he demonstrated to everyone just how happy with the news he was. Etiquette be damned.

A few moments later, his lips gently pulled away from hers, and then with a laugh, he swung her up into his arms and swirled her around the space. "We're having a baby!" he yelled aloud to the startled onlookers, his voice echoing across the whole ballroom.

Claps and congratulations followed fast and thick as Alex gently placed Evie back on her feet and then kissed her again, caring little for their even larger audience, his attention so entirely on her that Evie felt as if they were alone in the room together.

"Definitely no more Her Grace's Gallop for you," he murmured against her lips after his own gently parted from hers.

"Thank goodness," she said, laughing aloud. "I think I shall have to fall pregnant a great many more times if that's the case."

"That, my darling wife, will be my absolute pleasure to assist with," he murmured as his head bent next to her ear. "After all, 'tis my most favorite activity that we partake in together."

"Mine too," she whispered back to him.

"More than fossil hunting?" he teased, leaning back and raising his brow.

She laughed again and wound her hands around his neck, caring little for their audience, who were by now becoming accustomed to the duke and his American Dollar Princess's frequent displays of affection. "Yes. Though I must say when we combine the two in the caves, well, that is perfection. Truly a match made in Heaven."

His rich laughter ricocheted around the room. "You, my love, are the match made in Heaven. You and you alone." His hand reached down to her stomach. "You and our baby are my everything, Evie. I love you, more than I ever thought I could ever love anyone. And I will always love you, and our children, with everything that I have, for the rest of my life."

Evie took in a deep breath, the raw emotion and love shining in his eyes making her feel like the most special woman in the world. She placed her own hand over his still resting on her belly. "I love you, too, Alex. More than I ever thought possible. You are my prince from a fairy tale I never believed possible. My fossil prince, who I'll love until my very last breath."

She leaned up and kissed him with all the love she felt for him. She was finally living her real-life fairy tale, and what a fairy tale it was, filled with a love she knew would transcend a lifetime.

A love she would hold close to her heart and never ever let go.

ACKNOWLEDGMENTS

When I first dreamed of being a writer as a child, I used to daydream about what it would feel like to have my books on the shelves in a bookstore, and now with Entangled's faith and belief in this story and series, I get to make this long-held dream of mine a reality. I get to see my books in the hands of readers, and to experience the joy and thrill as readers embrace my story—it's exciting and humbling to say the least, and I'm so very grateful to everyone who has picked up Evie and Alex's story and given it a go.

I also want to give a huge shout out to the entire team at Entangled for all the work they did on this book behind the scenes, which is nothing short of amazing! A big thanks to my editor Alethea Spiridon, who helped me get Evie and Alex's story in shape! And to my agent, Pamela Harty, thanks for always being there for me and checking in. Also, to Stacy Abrams and Jessica Turner, thank you both so much for embracing the initial concept for this book with such enthusiasm—I had such fun brainstorming with you ladies!

A big thanks to my seriously amazing husband and daughter, who support me in this craziness that is the writing and editing process. I'm so lucky to have them; they make me laugh and feel blessed every day. I of course also have to thank my beautiful mum, who is my biggest fan and always reads and loves my books (a mum has to, doesn't she?? Lol). I love that I can always rely on her to read my books and help in the proof editing stage—she's such a legend, my mum.

And finally, a massive thanks to my readers, who make this all possible. My gorgeous readers, you all absolutely ROCK! I can't thank you enough for your support and encouragement—you have no idea how much it means to me when you let me know how much you enjoyed my books!! Honestly, it makes my day, so thank you from my heart to yours.

Happy reading!
xox Maddison xox

A reluctant duke…and the
wife no one *expected.*

$Four$
$Weddings$
AND A
$Duke$

USA TODAY BESTSELLING AUTHOR
MICHELLE MCLEAN

As the middle—and least marriageable—sister in a
bevy of swans, Lavinia Wynnburn is quite content
being the odd duck out. This way, she's free to com-
mit social faux pas without anyone much noticing.
Until the Duke of Beaubrooke turns up the morning after a ball, asking for her *hand* in marriage.

Alexander Reddington doesn't particularly care
for social niceties, nor is he particularly good at
them. But now that the spare has become the heir,
he must marry…and soon. When he stumbles into
the same corner as a socially awkward wallflower,
he knows he's found the perfect wife: one who
won't bother him to attend every simpering event
of the season.

Only, Alexander's shy and pretty new wife is
finding her new position surprisingly exciting and
keeps accepting every invitation that flutters past
their door. And worse luck, he might even be *falling*
for her. Now he must hide the truth about why he
really proposed…before his unexpectedly happy
marriage is dashed to pieces.

The Heiress Swap is a fun story of how two cousins swap places to unlikely and desired outcomes. However, the story includes elements that might not be suitable for all readers. Death, near-death, divorce, abandonment by a parent, and orphans are mentioned in the novel. Readers who may be sensitive to these elements, please take note.